QUEER QUERIES

Also by the author

Improbable: Male Love Stories

Fairy Swatter: Short Stories

Accidental Parents

QUEER QUERIES

a novel

PETER MELILLO

Published by Querelle Independent, a division of Querelle Press LLC
2808 Broadway #22, New York, NY 10025
www.querellepress.com

Cover design by DesignCrowd
Typeset by Raymond Luczak

ISBN: 979-8-9901248-0-6 print edition
ISBN: 979-8-9901248-1-3 e-book edition

Distributed by Ingram Content Group: ingramcontent.com

Printed in the United States

First edition 2024

For

Huynh Luong

10/9/1965 – 10/2/2022

Thirty-one years of shared love and life.

I miss you every day.

Chapter 1.

Route 52 is the main drag in and out of my little suburb. We call it Broadway when it has buildings instead of deer saltlicks on either side of the highway. It's wider than most roads around here and goes straight through town without a traffic light to separate locals from interstaters. For example, buses from the city drive in and out of our 'burb but only stop if requested.

Fifty-two Pickup was on the northeast corner where Route 52 and Main Street intersect at an odd angle. The Pickup was a small convenience store with four working, almost worn-out gasoline pumps from another era out front. In the store was always decent fresh coffee along with eclectic cellophane packaged snack food. No shelf-space was made for nonfood. So, hardware and all sorts of other brick-a-brack were piled helter-skelter on tables against the back wall and corner walls. The store shared a well heated wall with ovens from Mario's Pizzeria next door. The best pizza and subs at a fair price in the whole tristate area.

My first job out of graduate school was as a parole officer. I'd just completed training, and Thursdays were my assigned late nights at the office in case of afterhours emergencies. It was my first week after training and trying to figure out what was what. Going home even later than expected I decided on a slice of pizza for dinner. The car in front of the pizzeria with a driver and motor running didn't get my notice until it started blowing its horn as I approached the pizzeria's front door.

Just as I entered, heralded by a blaring car horn, two gunmen wearing ski masks were apparently startled and shot Mario and his father-in-law Vinny. I had promised myself never to use the service revolver I was required to carry for my new job. Without thinking I flipped over a table, got behind it with my service weapon drawn.

As the masked men turned their smoking guns on me, my gun shot, first hitting one then the other man in the center of the chest. What happened was exactly like with paper targets during training drills at my job's gun range. Only I don't remember shooting these men or their bullets hitting the tabletop between us. I remember calling 911, checking that Mario, Vinny, and their robbers were dead. Then checked that the car outside was gone. Rushing to the convenience store, I found Mrs. Shaw and her high school helper Bud dead from apparent gunshot wounds, their cash drawer open and empty.

I went from being the green, new shy guy parole officer to rumored, "Shoot 'em first, ask questions later." The trigger-happy reputation brought me a level of respect from parolees it took my colleagues years of intention to attain. Only it felt bogus to me. I don't remember shooting, and I broke a promise to myself to always keep the gun holstered, no matter what. In the end it didn't make a difference, I hated the job once I learned to do it well and keep my head above the paperwork.

In the blink of an eye Fifty-two Pickup and Mario's Pizzeria were smashed flat into their shared basement by an out of state demolition contractor in a hurry to get on with the next job. It all happened so fast I could hardly register the loss of life and generations-old landmark. Then the space was dug-up and built-up by a fast-working construction company from somewhere up state.

Before I knew it, there was a super modern, twelve-pump, mega gasoline station out front and eight electric car charging slots on one side of a glossy plastic-coated modern convenience store facing the gasoline pumps. To add injury to the insult, the new place served terrible tasting weak coffee alongside unwrapped tasteless, overpriced greasy food. But hey, I may not be impartial I had a hand in how they got there, *and* they hadn't used any local construction labor.

I resisted sampling the new mega gas station coffee-slopshop for a while. It was in silent protest of the loss of Mario's delicious pizza and Fifty-Two Pickup's curious selection of wares you didn't know you needed until you did. Oh, and my almost being shot dead there.

But alas, Fifty-Two Pickup was close to home and more often than not on my way to one destination or another. On the plus side, I was cinching my belt tighter since Mario's demise. I eventually yielded to the weight of my geography's limitations. I hate to admit it but can get used to shiny new if it makes time management less onerous. New can begrudgingly work for me with the old unavailable.

It didn't take too long to get past my armed robbery PTSD and fall into a routine at the new gas-up place. My legitimate complaint was the new gas pumps constantly had a problem accepting any of my credit or debit cards for payment. The result was I had to trudge into the convenience store, leave a plastic card, go back out, pump gas, then walk back inside to sign for the sale, and finally traipse back to my car and go on my way. Okay. So, I'm lazy and my shoes have real leather soles.

Martha, the store manager, swore her central office was working on the pumps' card-reader problem and she was assured it would be fixed soon. Soon seemed to have variable meanings at her central office; for instance, they were still fixing the problem eight months after the grand opening pennants came down. You'd think they'd want to be more efficient getting their money immediately from debit card sales and for their customers' excess walking convenience, but obviously not.

On my way in to fork-over my plastic card that morning, I noticed a beat-up, rusted hulk of a car parked near the convenience shop's front door. To enter the store, I had to pass close to the two miserable looking guys sitting in that car stony faced, not talking or listening to music. Normally, I would not have paid attention. But the driver was checking my crotch out blatantly. At my age, forty coming too soon, a cute young guy's cruise is flattering. If nothing else it reminds me, my youth is gone, and I'm supposed to be a responsible adult who should know the score and stick to age-appropriate playmates.

To be fair to me in this situation, minding other people's business is part of how I earn a good living. I notice and remember things, make connections, and draw conclusions others can't be bothered to notice. On the other hand, it would have been hard to miss what was going on with the guy's eyes staring laser beams at the crotch of my hand tailored slacks, while otherwise looking forlorn. I'll admit it, I'm a sucker for big, sad puppy dog eyes.

Returning from the store to fuel my car I stopped at the old junker car and said, "Do I know you?"

"Not yet. I'd like to make you a business proposition."

"Sorry, pal. I'm looking at a long hard day's work and this is neither the time nor place for business talk. Perhaps another time," and I went and gassed up my top-of-the-line, big European-built SUV. Finished, intent on retrieving my credit card after signing for fuel, I moved briskly trying to ignore the rattletrap car next to the entrance.

As I walked by, the driver pleadingly said, "Mister I only need a minute of your time."

I should have known better, didn't, and stopped. But this time I took a hard look inside the car. The androgynous looking passenger appeared very young and out of it. He-she had a chalky-pale-complexion, white-blonde limp-straight hair cut around a soup bowl with bangs in front, and almost albino light blue eyes. The driver was in his early twenties, built like an athlete, military short gold colored curly hair and matching eyebrows over deep-blue intelligent eyes. "Are you two sick?"

"No. Why?"

"You both have green tinged skin tone."

The driver held up his hands for self-inspection then said, "We haven't eaten any solid food that wasn't green in a few days."

"Why's that?"

"We're on a green cleansing diet. I'm Coy Goff and this is my cousin Darrell-Wayne Goff."

"You look sick to me. Tell you what, if you come inside the convenience store, I'll buy you boys something to eat that isn't green. But only as a good Samaritan."

"Why would you want to do that?"

"It's what Jesus would want." I'm not a religious man, in fact I don't believe in any kinds of superstitions. I just figured Jesus was an easy universal for helping strangers without coming off as a total nut job, or with ulterior motives. In a worse-case scenario Jesus would protect me from Coy's apparent carnal interest in the inseam of my cut to measure slacks and crotch.

"I want to offer you a blowjob in exchange for a tank of gasoline. I give amazing head and Darrell-Wayne and I are completely out of gas."

I was expecting a hustle, but not such an overt sexual proposition first thing in the morning. "My offer to buy you some grub stands. But I'm in a hurry so I'll have to respectfully decline your outlandish offer of oral sex."

Sitting up straighter behind the steering wheel and making eye contact he said, "I'm really good. If you want, I'll give you a free sample to prove it."

Pushing the glassdoor open with my right hand I said, "Right now, I'm going inside this store, you can come with me or not, your choice. It won't be a fancy breakfast I can assure you. They don't have much of a menu though there should be something you can eat."

"I give great head, you won't be disappointed."

"If you don't follow me inside, I'm on my way out of here, nice meeting you."

"We're completely out of gas, the tank is dry. If we don't move the car the manager says she's going to have us towed to a scrap yard."

Keeping eye contact longer than I might usually I said, "When did you eat nongreen solid food last?"

"Two and a half days ago. But right now, we need gasoline not food."

I could see written on his face I'd won round one. "Follow me or wave goodbye." As I entered the convenience store the two from the junky car were right behind me. "Go sit down over there. No, wait, what do you want to eat?"

Finger on chin, he had nice looking hands, he said, "Let's see … hmm … uh, I forgot how to break the fast. What the hell, okay then, I'll have a slice of pizza and Darrell-Wayne likes hot dogs with everything on them. That's the old reliable diet we were cleansing from."

"Unless you want to upchuck that right away, I better guesstimate how to break a fast for you."

Head drooping in resignation he said, "Whatever. Your money, you get to choose. Remember this is all about we need gasoline not hot dogs and pizza."

Feeling I'd done my good deed for the day I came back to the table with one tray, it was holding two identical dishes, two cups of tea, and a coffee for me. Putting down the tray between the two strangers I said, "Bon appetite."

"Wait a minute, I said we aren't sick. This looks like sick people's food. How'd you even get this? I don't see poached eggs and toast on their menu board." He said this with his face showing his mind was on getting a tank of gas to get out of there.

"Coy, look carefully. See the breakfast special sandwich? That means they have eggs. Bread, and a toaster. That's what you see before you only in a different configuration. Eat up or it will get cold."

Clearly stalling for time to bring the conversation back to gasoline he said, "It says there's bacon on the breakfast sandwich special, where's the bacon?"

"You, my friend, are too high maintenance. So, my coffee and I are leaving. Your food is paid for, enjoy it before it gets cold."

"No wait, sir please don't go! I can give you the best BJ of your life. Without that car we are up shits creek. Please, please help us out." With that said his face looked like a sad big eyed begging puppy.

"I need to have my head examined. All right I'll buy you a tank of gasoline but pass on the slurpy sex. As tempting as your offer is, I'm probably close to your father's age."

The puppy's hackles went up and he said, "NO! We don't take charity. It's a matter of honor, I earn my way, so does Darrell-Wayne. Listen, I'm a good cocksucker, you won't be disappointed."

Going against common sense and instinct to leave my mouth said, "I know I'm going to hate myself for asking, but where do you imagine doing this deed?"

"Behind the dumpsters in the back of this store."

Reality checked in with my mouth speaking, "I think not. Why would I risk the licenses I depend on for a living, and jail for public indecency, for a quick little tickle thrill?"

Pondering my objection like a philosopher with a serious question while eating poached eggs Coy said, "I know a deserted place we can drive to and do it in your car."

"No, thank you."

"There is never anybody around, it's deserted." And now he looked like I'd won again.

"How were the eggs and toast?"

"Salt and pepper made the food go down easy; I was hungry. Did you know the human body can go three weeks without food? Imagine, we didn't even last three days on a one week fast, isn't that pathetic?" His body language indicated we'd turned a corner from strangers to something else.

Lowering my defenses slightly I asked, "How come your cousin doesn't make eye contact with me? What's he ashamed of? Or is he she?" I was awkwardly still trying to make an exit .

Puffing up defensively Coy snapped, "Darrell-Wayne is male."

Just after I thought two strangers had moved from pure transaction to something more human, my mouth blurted out, "Uh huh, that's interesting, is he a cock sucker too? Is that why he won't look straight at me?"

His body language showed him go into full defense mode. "No. Darrell-Wayne is autistic. He's high up on the spectrum, but not up to Asperger." The words were spit out at me like a challenge.

Unintendedly, I'd blown whatever chance there might have been for us to be more than strangers. "I see. Don't take this the wrong way but you two could really use a shower." That was the moment, last chance, I stood up, ready to leave, and don't know why I didn't.

The big puppy eyes were back, his face open and frank. "Giving Darrell-Wayne a bath is a big loud production. It takes some doing and a lot of time to bathe him since he doesn't like to be touched, anywhere. But I wouldn't mind washing my stink off with a quick shower. Are you offering a place for a wash?"

Caught off guard without thinking first I said, "Nothing bashful about you."

He was quick with a wink. "But isn't that what Jesus would want?"

I laughed, he was good and won that round. When I pushed, he pushed back. I seldom found that on first meeting these days. "Okay, tell me, exactly what would Jesus say? Get it right and you get a shower."

"Jesus said, 'I was naked, and you clothed me, I was hungry, and you gave me to eat … these things you do for the least of my brethren you do for me.' How about it, can I catch a quick shower and give you head in exchange for a tank of gas and this food?"

"It was a gift, not barter."

Puffing himself up again he said, "But it's important to me to earn my way."

Trying for a neutral tone I almost got it. "What do you do for a living Coy?"

All defensive again then mellowing Coy said, "Are you going to write my biography? Oh sorry … all right … uh, I just got an honorable discharge from the army. I was a training sergeant, went in on my eighteenth birthday, did five years, was given a discharge when they changed things around, and now I'm looking for work. There's nothing that pays worth a damn around here. I may have to look in the city or even go to a different state."

"What kind of work are you looking for?" The sincerity in my voice was not put on.

"I grew up in Dojos. I have the highest degree rank in several martial art disciplines. That's what I did in the army, taught hand to hand combat to recruits, and occasionally served as a bodyguard for VIPs. I'm good at both and thought I could at least get work teaching civilians basic self-defense. I wrote up a whole curriculum before I realized there is politics and nepotism in the dojo franchise business. Stupid me, should have known!"

With a conspiratorial smile I said, "And *now* you want me to take you to my home?"

He returned my smile with youthful enthusiasm, "You carry yourself with confidence, like you know fighting moves and you have a pistol strapped to your ankle. I won't ask why. But trust me, I have no reason to be a threat to you. The hand that just fed me."

Now he had my full attention. "What else can you tell me, about me?"

"You're overdue for getting laid. I'll bet you're horny as all hell and won't admit it. I can help with that in a most memorable way."

God was it that obvious? "You, my young friend, have just gained my attention. Come with me, you can use my shower if you clean it after you finish. But I'm not sure about the rest of your plan. Though I must admit yours is the best offer I've had since breakfast, but hey the day is still young."

Coy told Darrell-Wayne to go sit in the car and not let anyone tow it. He said we'll be back soon. With his head down the young autistic person went and did as told. He sat statue still and with his pale complexion a casual observer would have to do a double take, he wasn't a plaster mannequin.

***

My hidden house is a four-bedroom, three-bath bungalow blended into the foothills from underneath a four-car garage. The garage and house exterior are constructed from large multicolored river stones. They sit back a good way off the road out front. Only the semicircle driveway and parking garage are somewhat visible through the security fence and hedges from the elevated road out front.

Below the garage the house slopes into the surrounding hillside's irregular topography. From the ascending road climbing into the foothills my house is completely invisible, lying below a normal-looking garage which is behind rows of tall shrubs.

For the most part, hidden from street view is the half-circle driveway which can only be entered from either side of the hedges. Entered through intimidating electronically controlled eight-foot-tall heavy black steel gates. Stone steps on the side lead down from the oversized garage to the house underneath. My sprawling place fits so naturally into the irregular rocky hillside it's almost invisible to the hills across the way and aircraft overhead. It's a safe fortress, functional, but not fancy inside. I like the word functional because it suits my personality.

I won the side of the foothill my house sits on in a poker game. Then when I hired an architect to build a home on the land, she said due to global warming my property had become the new tornado alley around here. She had to build my house strong enough to withstand the worst tornadoes conceivable which means if the foothills all fall down my garage will stay standing. Fortunately, at the time I'd solved one then another high publicity major case with windfall rewards to cover the extra costs.

As we drove through the security gate Coy said, "Where's your house? Do you live in a garage?"

"Be patient, you'll see."

Leading him down the steps and into the house he said, "You have a sneaky house, it's hiding from the road and the hills under a garage. How can you see topside from down here?"

"Periscopes with cameras connect to security screens."

"Wow, I like that. No door-to-door salesmen or religious cults bother you."

I winked and said, "I've got work to do, so you get the grand tour of the place another time. Here is a bathroom you can use. Extra towels are in there, soap and shampoo over there, and I'll be in my office through that door down the hall. Knock on the door frame when you're ready to go back for your cousin. No rush, take as much time as you need, I've got lots of phone work to do."

"Thanks. Being clean matters to *Jesus and me*." With that said he turned and went into the bathroom leaving the door open as he disrobed.

I walked to the master bedroom turned home office wondering, *Was my inviting a stranger home to bathe symptomatic of declining mental state or was I hornier than I wanted to admit?* A home office was my accountant's idea of tax savings. I have a respectable enough office in a short, squat professional building near Broadway and Main Street, complete with abundant parking.

Most phone calls finished faster than expected, so I telephoned my other office. "Good morning, Ameli, any emergencies I need to know about?"

"No, boss. Don't forget you have a termination session at two, new client interview at three, otherwise your day is free. Unlike this poor wage slave with her nose pressed firmly to the grindstone. "

"When did we start using grindstones? We don't have a permit for one, and they are so last century passe for a modern office. Oh, also, just so you know, slavery went out in 1865, Lincoln emancipated you. "

"If not a slave, what do you call your fulltime office manager, bookkeeper, private secretary, personal assistant, bank messenger, and bodyguard in a pinch, all for just a mere pittance of renumeration? Lincoln would not approve. "

"Ameli, I pay you twice the going rate for receptionists, which is the job you were hired for. "

"My cerebral palsy support group thinks I'm underpaid for all I do running this one-woman super-efficient office."

"Anything you chose to do besides reception is on you. "

"Just because you spoke to them, doesn't mean they all will stand up and pledge allegiance to you."

"Want to bet?"

"Oh, before I forget, check in with Tony, Nancy, and the lesbians, they left messages."

"Will do, right now. See you later. Bye."

"Have a good day, slave driver."

I no sooner put the phone down than Coy walked through my open office door. He was a vision of perfectly put together male nakedness, rosy complexion, just buff dried, fragrant soap scented, straight from a shower statuesque. Seeing him standing there caused a stirring in my pants. That's when I knew my need for physical relief was overruling my commonsense. It wasn't early onset senile dementia, after all.

Swiping his tongue across his plump lips, looking eager to get started Coy said, "Shall I blow you at your desk or would a bedroom be more comfortable?"

"Bedroom. This way." My tenting erection with a mind of its own led the way.

He stripped me out of my clothes like he knew what he was doing, then pushed me back onto my bed. "Coy, I prefer fucking to receiving head."

He sincerely said, "Sorry, I'm saving that hole for my wedding night."

"When is that ceremony scheduled?"

"I must meet mister right first. Are you interested in applying?"

Now he really was moving too fast for my taste, as I glanced over his perfectly put together masculinity. "I'm not the marrying kind, been there done that not so well. Now I'm older, wiser, and know better. "

With a wink and grin, I was getting used to he said, "Let me demonstrate what you've been missing. You won't be disappointed."

It has been said all flesh is weak. That day mine was, and *he was excellent at applying his fine honed craft to it.* His technique was attentive, intuitive, and adept using unexpected well-tuned skills applied at just the right moments as if he vicariously felt what and when I was feeling his detailed ministrations.

To recap without hopefully being overly graphic, Coy tongued my nether region as an attention arousing appetizer. Next, he moved on to more developed robust titillation like a virtuoso violinist performing a well-rehearsed great master's concerto with me being turned into his Stradivarius. He was the soloist and conductor all in one and brought me close to the brink of a resounding full orchestra *forte fortissimo* climax, several times. Then he'd backed off at the last possible microsecond, changing the subject with musical bonbon distractions.

It seemed every time I was ready for another grand *credenza* into a glorious final resounding climax, he built it even bigger towards a better culmination, and then distracted my attention at the last nanosecond, just before I went over the pinnacle. Finally, when my limit for titillation had exceeded saturation, he catapulted me into an astoundingly long full body bliss, toes to head hair follicles. I came joyously long, profusely, and he swallowed it all down like a parched man finding a desert oasis.

Once my panting stopped and regular breath returned, I said, "Your turn. How do you want to get off with me, mister anonymous stranger?"

"It was transactional, the deal was I get a full tank of gasoline. Breakfast was your idea but included."

"Then consider your getting off a tip or simply a return of a favor. Whatever you want to call it, I won't be as good as you. But I've not had complaints."

Speaking with sincerity he said, "Maybe another time if there is another time. Unless you want to offer me a fulltime job, then you could have blowjobs on demand whenever. As an employee we could sperm together doing sixty-nine if you wanted."

Matching his heart-felt words I said, "I already have one fulltime employee. I'm not sure what I'd do with a second, but your offer is tempting, send me your resume."

"I will. What's your name?"

"Oliver, Oliver Kulgu, nice to meet you, Coy Goff. Let's go get you gasoline, fair is fair." With that said we dressed and left the house in my car.

All seatbelts buckled in, Coy said, "What kind of name is Kulgu?"

I don't usually give my history to strangers at first meeting, or ejaculate down their throat. "My great, great grandfather immigrated here from Finland. At that time the U.S. government offered Scandinavians free land in the upper Midwest. My gramps wasn't busy at the time and didn't believe in turning down free farmland. What's the origin of Coy?"

"My mom wanted me to be Corey and my pops wanted a Cody, they seldom agreed on anything. After three days of hard labor hatching me, my exhausted mother made a spelling mistake. I was supposed to be Cory, their compromise. Then later it became too much trouble and expense to change my birth certificate. As you noticed I'm the opposite of coy about most things. Is Oliver Finish too?"

"No. It's English from my mother's side of the family. My brother and sisters' initials, like mine spell O.K."

***

I live only ten minutes away from Route Fifty-two's Fifty-Two Pickup. As we drove in and parked next to his rusted-out tattered wreck of a car, Coy's body tensed noticeably and he loudly ejaculated, "Where's Darrell-Wayne?" We weren't gone forty minutes.

"Could he be in the restroom?"

"No. It's necessary to ask for the restroom key at the counter. He couldn't do that."

"Maybe his bladder burst and was sent to the hospital."

"It wouldn't. He'd squat and pee on the ground with the car door open to cover himself."

"How about over there? Could he be doing his business in the bushes?"

"I doubt it but let me go check."

"Wait. First help me push your car to a gas pump, then I'll go inside leave my credit card and fill it while you search the bushes." It turned out the vehicle was light enough I could have pushed it alone. As I expected, his car only took twelve gallons and of the cheapest grade gasoline. My big expensive car only drank the highest grade and priced fuel at double his car's capacity. But I wasn't of a mind to offer to trade vehicles, that generous I'm not.

Looking panicky, Coy rushed back to me replacing his car's rag as gas cap. "He's nowhere to be found. Darrell-Wayne can't survive on his own. My aunt and uncle are going to kill me if I've lost him."

"Don't panic, I'm a finder."

"But where else can we look?"

"See if your car starts first."

"No. I need to find my cousin before something bad happens to him."

"Start your car and I'll go ask the store manager, maybe someone saw something."

Nobody inside the store noticed anything unusual. The manager's name tag read Martha Matatus. I asked to see the store's security-camera tapes. She said no, and pled ignorance of its operation.

Just then Coy joined us and picked up on the impasse and said, "Then call the police. We'll need them to put out an Amber Alert, my cousin is missing."

I pulled out my wallet and showed Martha my license and said, "I know how to operate security systems, we need see the last hour's tape for your front door parking." She looked doubtful till I said, "Or, do you want a whole gang of police officers in here all day repeatedly asking you and your customers the same questions over and over?" She didn't say anything but turned and led the way back to her office.

The gas station's whole security setup was little more than a joke. On the other hand, they were open for business twenty-four seven, 365 days. So, staff were always there. We lucked out, one camera on the cashier and cash drawer also partially showed through the store's front window, Coy's car and parking on either side.

We watched the grainy black and white tape show a restored-customized older American-made low-rider muscle car, painted a flat dark color, with bright colored high gloss flames decorated on each side, roll in. The car park to the right of Coy's old jalopy. Immediately, out of nowhere someone walked up and transacted what appeared to be a drug sale through the passenger's car window. The transaction completed the buyer disappeared as quickly as he materialized.

Their business done the drug home-delivery car started to pull out. Then they must have noticed Darrell-Wayne sitting statute still in the next car. Swiftly the passenger stormed over to Coy's car and yanked Darrell-Wayne out of it through the open window. The startled boy was kicking and looked to be screaming as he was roughly manhandled then unceremoniously dumped into the muscle car trunk, after the lid was slammed shut the car sped off, burning tire rubber.

I turned to manager Martha Matatus and said, "Do you know those guys?"

"Not by name, they are from the Pachucos-88 gang. The guys on the tape are street soldiers. This business is in the gang's territory. Just after we opened, I reported them selling drugs behind the store to the police precinct. A detective named Reynolds, head of the local drug taskforce, sends undercover cops around from time to time. Now the gang sells drugs in front of the store to show their contempt for me when the cops aren't here."

"Did you tell the police?"

"I did, but like I said the gang only comes around when the unmarked cop's car isn't. Lately, the police are coming less often claiming there's nothing to see. So, now the drugs are being sold by my front door to let me know who's dominant and what's what."

Coy looked like his poached eggs on toast or my fresh cum wasn't agreeing with his digestion. Morosely he moaned low, "Do you think they will kill Darrell-Wayne?"

I put a reassuring hand on his back and said, "Not if we act fast." That said I whipped out my cellphone. My first call was to Willis Washington, a fulltime police detective who also works part-time per diem for me. He copied down what information we had and said he'd talk to detective Reynolds.

Then I called Ameli and asked her to find current Pachucos-88 addresses post haste and call me right back. Next, I phoned Tony, Nancy, and then the lesbian couple to check in on their current assignments and said, "I've got a pro bono pot boiling are you up for some gunplay if it comes to it?" They were ready and didn't react when I said they might need shotguns.

Coy was agitated and said, "Shouldn't we call the police? You wrote down that car's license number off the tape."

Martha Matatus cut Coy off and said, "I have Detective Reynolds' private cellphone number. He knows me and might have an idea where they took the boy."

"Both of you chillout, my first call was to the cops and gave them the plate-number. I suggest we sit down, order coffee and wait for call backs. More calls from us will only gum up the works and slow down what I started."

Martha had been paying attention and noticed when I made a face mentioning her coffee. She spoke right up, "We have a weekly special on donuts; buy one get one free. They make the coffee go down smoother." Then in a rush she said, "But you don't have to order anything to wait for the police."

Coy turned to Martha and said, "I need to do something. I can't just sit here when my cousin is in danger."

As he was speaking my pocket phone beeped, and Ameli said, "The current main Pachucos-88 headquarters is a house at 119 President Street. It's one of several houses, but 119 has heavy weapons and lots of activity. Or so my sources say."

I no sooner rang off with Ameli than the phone beeped again. I put it on the speaker phone to settle Coy's nerves. "Hey, Willis. What you got?"

"I put together a team on the fly between Reynolds' task force and the people trafficking crew was just standing around. I also gave the child welfare abduction's team a heads up. We're ready to move, just need a location."

"119 President Street, they're armed to the teeth. I've got four gunsels who can be there in a hurry. You want outside help?"

"No, we got this. We're rolling. I'll keep you posted," and the line went dead.

"What kind of donuts?"

"I'd like to say too numerous to name, but I ate the last French cruller on my break. Just go up to the counter and see what's left. Pick four when you order coffee and Tell Hank I said it's on the house."

"Martha, how about I buy you coffee and donuts? As a thank you for your help."

"Thanks, but no thanks, I've got inventory and several deliveries coming any minute." That said, Martha walked to a storage area, and we walked to the counter to order coffee and leftovers.

Seated in a booth with our caffeine fix, Coy looked me up and down and said, "You seem awfully calm. Don't you realize Darrell-Wayne may be dead already? And who were those people you told to bring shotguns, and why did the cops act so fast? In my experience it takes the police forever to get moving."

I explained we were in the middle of the action. It's the results of the end that the waiting is for. Reaching over and taking his hand I instructed chill out,pray if that helps, it's what Jesus would advise. Also did Jesus get his car started? He wanted to know if I was a Jesus freak. I told him by invoking his name I had hoped to avoid Coy's Bible thumping if he was.

Disentangling our clasped hands Coy said, "What did you show Martha to change her mind about us seeing the security tapes?"

With my hand dropped back in my lap I said, "I run a private detective agency, Queer Queries. I showed Martha my private investigator's license and state electronic security system certification card."

"So, that's why you wear an ankle gun. I thought private dicks always worked alone like in the movies. You seem to have people answering when you call."

"I use per diem workers. Retired and employed police offices workout best. It's all legal, doesn't affect their pensions and employed cops are allowed to moonlight part-time. I supervise all my cases, so they're used to taking my phone calls."

"Is it like, a community college major or something? I mean how does anyone start a private detective business."

"It's a long story, I'm sure you'd be bored."

"I've got nothing better to do than worry if Darrell-Wayne is dead or alive."

"Stop me when you've heard enough."

"I wouldn't."

I explained my roommate killed himself in college. "I was upset after the suicide and going to quit college. When I told my favorite professor I was quitting he said there was a critical shortage of mental health workers."

"He was more than just a roommate, right?"

"You are very perceptive, Coy. We were never officially in love, only dear friends with benefits. He'd been fighting bouts of depression since puberty. The stress of college, his not wanting to be gay while loving gay sex with me *the roommate*. It all became too much for him."

"Duh, what does social work have to do with being a private cop?"

"I graduated with a MSW and student debt. A scholarship and part-time work didn't pay all the school bills. The most lucrative MSW job I could find after graduation was as a parole officer."

"That doesn't sound like a master's in social work kind of job."

"People helping people work that interested me in the first place wouldn't pay my rent or buy food beyond Ramen noodles. As a parole officer I was required to carry a pistol and use the shooting range at least once every three months. The impossible job had a high worker turnover rate. Which was why they had a big sign on bonus, highest pay scale for the required graduate degree, and forgave all student debt after three years on the job."

"Sounds hopeless, what did you do?"

"Over the three years, I grew to hate the futility of my job, and the parolees who through no intentional fault of their own were damaging my mental equilibrium."

"You didn't answer my question."

"That was just background I needed you to know and me to get off my chest."

"Feel better?"

"To answer your original question, I was invited to a cop's retirement party. After retirement he became a part-time security consultant and needed a private investigator (PI) license to do it legally. But when PI work started interfering with his fishing and beer drinking, the retired guy, Miles Griffin invited me to become his partner. The retired guy was an idealist. He said he took me on for my social work divorce mediating training and license, but then shoveled all the PI work he didn't want to be bothered with to me. I got busy and left the parole department with no regrets."

"How'd you end up with the business?"

"Miles died in a car accident driving too fast on ice. Ice fishing was one of his hobbies. His divorced wife didn't want anything to do with anything that couldn't immediately be turned into cash."

"True love to the end."

"When it came to Miles' private detective hobby, his ex-wife said, 'Close it down or take it with my compliments. When we were married, that fatherless twerp beat me when he drank, and he drank all the time.'"

"Didn't that leave you high and dry?"

"No. In three months, I turned his iffy business into lucrative Queer Queries, a solo PI agency."

"This is probably a silly question, but are all your per diem workers gay? I only ask because you were so overdue horny when I blew you, you could have been a straight guy."

"Things didn't work out like I expected. My intention was the name Queer Queries would self-select clients so I could run a small one-man gay operation dealing with gay people and their gay problems. It didn't work out that way. Most of my clients are straight, and there are many more of them than I can manage alone. As a result, most of my per diem are straight and don't seem to mind the business name or having an out gay boss sign their checks."

"Are you disappointed?"

"Not really, the business is successful, a lot of people I like get money for life's extras, and we solve big and small problems. My social work skills smooth over many of the private detective's necessary hard edges."

"What do you do beside make telephone calls?"

"I'll humor you because you're worried about your cousin."

"Then answer my question."

"I screen all QQ cases with an initial social work type intake interview. Then it's my job to supervise part-time professionals on cases I accepted. I do that mostly by phone. When the job is completed, I do an exit interview with the client and get feedback on how we can improve. My receptionist collects the money, and a part-time accountant keeps track of it and pays the bills, per diem, and taxes."

"If your receptionist has cerebral palsy and collects the money, isn't she a sitting duck for robbery?"

"Her tremors are medically controlled with pharmaceuticals, and she has a 410-gauge revolver. An accurate aim isn't important if you're shooting buckshot at close range."

"Is that a good idea?"

" She insisted on having a weapon, so far, she hasn't had to use it. I take her to the gun range when I go every three months or so. I taught her standard handgun safety."

"If the majority of your work is for heterosexual divorce, which must be boring for an out gay man."

"From what I've said you'd think so, right? QQ also provides bodyguards for celebrities, sport stars, and politicians when they are in the area. I usually use off the clock police officers for that work. Our big money comes from evaluating and regular upgrades to electronic state-of-the-art security systems. It's very, very profitable work with little competition. To guild the lily, QQ is the only PI agency in the tristate area that provides aerial surveillance. Yes, I have a pilot's license and an aircraft."

"Wow, I thought divorce was how PI's put food on the table. You are really diversified."

"I work with a married lesbian couple who take most of my divorce cases. They're retired police officers who handle straight and gay divorce with a high degree of empathy and know how to get rough when necessary. "

"Huh, and you do all that by yourself? I'm a loyal hard worker with recent army combat skills. You could use me to improve your business."

"Like I said before, send me your resume. I'll give it a serious review."

"Really?"

"Really."

"I'm impressed! You seem for real … all right! Let's see, I could easily be a bodyguard; I did that in the service."

"In the meantime, let's find your cousin and then maybe I can salvage the rest of this workday."

"If I'm not being too forward, I'm beginning to like you more than just as a pretty dick to suck on."

"I'm close to twenty years older than you?"

"I find guys my age mindless nincompoops, that's who I trained in the service. I prefer a well-seasoned man whose had a few adventures."

"Interesting, I guess I fit that description." Then, my cellphone beeped. "Hey Willis, what's up … damn … that's major. You'll be remembered BIG TIME with this year's Christmas bonus. We'll meet you at the precinct. Thanks a lot."

"Did he find Darrell-Wayne?"

"And a lot more. Your cousin is being taken to the tenth precinct as we speak. He gave everyone a hard time, the bad guys, the cops, and now child welfare won't take him without a muzzle. Follow me in your car."

"Wait, this village has ten police precincts, are you kidding me?"

"No. Just one, the tenth. Village founding fathers had unrealized expectations. The first nine precincts were supposed to be scattered around the tenth in a circle of the yet to be developed, megalopolis, which hasn't happened nor likely will. But the tenth is centrally located."

****

The Tenth Precinct was a redbrick structure more than 100-years old, only slightly younger than the suburb. It had been renovated so many times over the many years, different layers of paint could be counted where the door frames were chipped. The deep scratches show a rainbow of institutional shades of green or gray colors, and one pink. I'd rather not know the reason a long-ago village counsel thought the inside of the tenth police precinct should be pink. I doubt it deterred any crime, or improved mood.

We parked in spaces marked visitors and hurried inside. I knew the desk sergeant from years before. He'd been a hell of a good street cop then got stabbed and now sits behind a desk pushing papers waiting to retire with a full pension. "Hey, Conrad, how's it hanging?"

Oliver. That bust is quite a feather in your cap. It looks like promotions for Washington, and Reynolds if openings ever occur around here, and commendations from the governor for the rest on the bust. Thank you, and oh let's not forget a nice cash reward for yourself, okay, private eye."

"Please, don't break out the bagpipes just yet."

"If you are going to be like that, you and your young friend can sit over there. Detectives and kids should arrive any minute, your highness."

Without another word spoken Coy and I sat as directed by the sergeant. The old-fashioned, worn, and abused oakwood armchairs were surprisingly comfortable.

"Oliver, what was he talking about?"

"You familiar with the word *cascade*?"

"Yeah! What's it got to do with what happened to Darrell-Wayne?"

"If I tell you now, it will have to be revised later. I didn't get the details. Wait and get the best information in a few minutes."

"TELL ME!"

"Take notes. I won't repeat myself doing revisions."

"Got a pen? ... thanks."

Willis Washington his partner, two guys from the people trafficking crew, and

Reynolds and three other narcotic officers arrived at 119 President Street just before a sixteen-wheel tractor-trailer pulled up. They laid back, called for backup, and waited and watched. Then they witnessed young teenage girls being loaded into the truck's cargo trailer. Darrell-Wayne, fighting, with two black eyes, and limping was brought out and put in the freight trailer last. "How'd they know it was Darrell-Wayne?"

"Remember, you gave me his ID card with a photo. I sent it to Willis using my cellphone."

"Then what happened?"

"Concerned backup wouldn't arrive in time, the cops on hand surrounded the tractor-trailer with their unmarked cars, front and back. Luckily, just then regular patrol cars started arriving from the call for backup. Washington and his crew saw an opportunity, the house front door was standing open from transferring the kids, and then the commotion outside. It was the element of surprise, and then overwhelming numbers of police. Cops' cars kept coming from nearby villages, the whole thing went down fast, furious, and without a shot fired."

"So, they saved Darrell-Wayne with lots of police, is that the cascade?"

"In addition to ten kidnapped underage girls along with your cousin being trafficked, they found a large quantity of uncut heroin, fentanyl pills, and assault rifles, handguns, and an assortment of explosives in the house. They hit a trifecta."

"What aren't you telling me?"

"What doesn't concern you."

"Overhearing your phone conversation and again just now with that desk sergeant, you made money off this. Didn't you?"

"If it happens. After arrests are made, courts convict, prison sentences handed down, and who knows what other formalities satisfied, there should be reward money enough to share in the distant future with my per diems."

"FOR ME TOO? How much?"

"I just told you, there are a lot of moving parts. I'd be surprised if we know the final tally much before next Christmas and see any money before that Fourth of July."

"Come on, throw a financially drowning man a small lifesaver of hope."

"I don't have a clue to the numbers. Ask Ameli in a week or so. She's good with figures and untangling bureaucratic knots."

"Just a rough idea, hundreds, thousands, what?"

"So, you can spend it before it arrives. No, I don't think so."

"But I helped."

"I refuse to enable unsound economics. I was trained to be a social worker. You'll wait."

"You know the last few hours have been the most exciting since I left the army. That includes blowing you which I want to do again soon as a thank you. You are a man who requires regular service, by me. I'm ready to make a long-term commitment."

"Not so loud, don't give away QQ trade secrets in public places."

"Oh look, here comes Darrell-Wayne. Coy stood and rushed over to his cousin. "Officer, why is he in handcuffs?"

"He attacked two child welfare workers. Don't worry, the cuffs come off when he learns to behave himself." Speaking to Darrell-Wayne the officer said, "We have leg irons too if you can't behave."

"He's autistic and can't stand to be touched. Let me help you, I'm his cousin, he knows me. Here I have his ID, and this is mine, you can release him to me. I'm family see we have the same last name."

"We follow procedure around here, Bubba. He bit two people. That must be sorted with rabies control, it's the law."

"He's not a child, only looks like one. Child welfare shouldn't have put their hands on him."

"Doesn't matter, fella, all these kids need to be processed before they can go home. If he throws fits, kicks, bites, and screams some more instead of talking, I'll book him, and he won't be going home until he learns to behave."

"Officer, please, it freaks him out to be touched."

It looked to me Coy was about to bug out. His deep feelings of fear appeared to have bubbled to the surface of his frayed nerves. So, I put a hand on his shoulder and gave it a reassuring squeeze. It was a way to let him know he wasn't alone in a situation that could go horribly bad. My hand seemed to bring him back from the edge of an explosion that would have gotten him locked up.

The cop reading what was going on said, "I'm sure child welfare will be happy to turn him over to you once we finish. Now you go sit down and let me do my job or I have a holding cell for you to wait in with some not very nice bad hombres."

Detective Washington arrived and waved me over to his work area in back. Coy followed me like a shadow. Willis is a large, impressive man with a big heart, and bigger brain. I've known him for years and was best man at his second wedding. He's the first one I call when we need a bodyguard for important clients. Unfortunately, as he moves up the police command ladder, he has less free time for moonlighting. I like him, and his wife, it's mutual.

"Okay, Oliver, the way I see it there is a large cash reward for recovering the girls about to be trafficked out of the country."

"I wasn't expecting more than the teenage boy for his cousin."

"Get Ameli started on the DEA's cash reward. It will be based on the weight of the drugs confiscated from your tip. It looked heavy to me, and you will get fifty dollars for each firearm we took off the street during the raid. I didn't count the guns, but it looked like a lot of nasty weapons. The money from the drugs and guns will take a while if there are no complications, otherwise longer. Overall, not a bad day's haul for one telephone call."

"It was excellent work on your part. You pulled it together in a hurry and without injury. I won't forget your commitment at bonus time."

Mr. and Mrs. Goff arrived to take possession of their son Darrell-Wayne. While waiting they demanded to know from Coy how their son ended up looking frightened, with two raccoon black eyes, and shackled in police custody. They accepted the partially true sequence of events. They seemed like nice, concerned people. When their son was brought out and handed over, he looked miserable, roughed-up, and relieved to be with his parents and cousin. I nodded hello and was ignored.

Chapter 2.

Six months went by fast; I kept busy as business continued to grow. Coy's relations with his aunt and uncle cooled quickly after temporarily losing Darrell-Wayne. We dated briefly until he gave up job hunting in town when he found a job online. It was in the nearby city as assistant manager for a recently opened independent dojo. He moved to the city, and we mostly kept in touch by telephone.

It didn't take Coy long to get his new job running smoothly. To build clientele he gave free introductory self-defense classes at the gay community center on Tuesdays, his one day off. I surprised myself, it didn't make me jealous he was giving free lessons to gay men and lesbians. Dating him I had to come to grips with my issues about our different ages. With physical distance between us and regular phone contact, the guy was growing on me despite my ageism.

While he was working hard to increase the dojo's clientele, it went bust. Coy went to work on a Monday expecting to clean up the place, paint trim, and found the door padlocked and an eviction notice pasted to the front window. The owner had underfunded and over leveraged the new business, got behind paying his debts, and the bank called in his loans.

Through his work at the Gay Center, Coy found a series of per diem gigs leading exercise groups at affluent senior centers. That soon led to a lucrative personal trainer practice in clients' homes. He had the personality to make exercise fun and the army discipline for the seniors and other private clients to see and feel results. But his connection to our burb and me was strong. For special occasions like birthdays or if Darrell-Wayne was much more difficult to handle than usual, Coy came to town and then slept at my house.

For the first time in his life Coy was making enough money to start saving for a dream, his own brick and mortar dojo. I offered to match his savings, as a silent business partner to help his plan come to fruition. It was the least I could do in return for the extraordinary personal service he provided and getting me back in touch with long dormant feelings.

When I needed to stay over in the city on business, I slept with Coy in his tiny one-bedroom apartment. Somehow, I was having a lot more business in the city than before I met him. After all the city was where the tall buildings in need of expensive electronic security were located, right?

Coy casually called us friends with benefits. I knew it was more but was still too much an ageist to give it a proper name. So, I called what was going on between us a long-distant, short-term affair with no possible future due to age difference. Naturally I didn't mention that to him. I think on some unconscious level I knew I was being self-delusional. It was self-protective for me not to expect any relationship to last longer than my previous short-lived affairs of the heart. They all ended badly, and I was preparing myself for more of the same.

While dwelling on our almost twenty-year difference in ages as a major deficit, it occurred to me I'd built an emotional wall around myself after my college roommate's suicide. He and I had shared deep feelings, a first time for both of us. It was in between his crushing bouts of depression I was too busy to notice. We'd even mixed our future hopes and dreams in with spectacular sex. To foster those dreams, I'd learned to tickle or joke him out of his bleakest depressed moods without naming them. My efforts most often paid off. Then he died and I blamed myself, not the other contributory's out of my control in the context of our lives.

At the time I wasn't mature enough to know his mental illnesses could not get better solely from my good intentions. Suddenly, his depression got worse at the end of term. He was hospitalized while I was cramming hard for final exams with all-nighters at the library and then going to my part-time job semiconscious. Never can I forgive myself for not being available when he needed me. I let final exams screw up my priorities and promised never to be in that situation again. So, I kept emotional attachments at arm's length before Coy came along.

It had been circumstance that allowed Coy to get into my deep, obsessively locked feelings. Plus, when Coy was in a bad or down mood, he increased his physical workout. He kept his mental health balance by adding extra weight to his bench-press bar or doing extra pullups. That allowed me to let him get closer than my usual short-term limit.

***

Residual dread from when I was a parole officer washes over me when the phone rings in the middle of the night. *Which of my parolees hurt who, and wasn't it my job to prevent it?* I know it's a leftover that needs to be exorcised with therapy or voodoo. Somehow, exorcising my demons is always a low priority on my to do list, and I don't know why I don't take better care of myself. It could be residual self-hate from being a fag having a good life.

"Hello ... slow down ... Coy what happened ... where are you?"

"The police have me locked up. Please, find Darrell-Wayne. He's missing again."

Coy relayed he was held at the police precinct, no charges filed yet. Darrell-Wayne had phoned him bugging out. The boy screamed something bad was happening, then babbled incoherently and the line went dead. Coy drove here breaking speed records and found his aunt and uncle murdered and his cousin gone. He dialed 911, had a misunderstanding with the first uniformed officers to arrive, and was now in county lockup pending assault and resisting arrest charges.

"Don't say anything to anybody. I'm calling my lawyer as soon as we ring off. After she gets you out, go to my place. I'll talk to the police at the crime scene and see what they're doing to find your cousin."

I got dressed going through the door and broke my own speed records getting to the murderer's house. I knew one of the homicide detectives at the incident from my old days as a parole officer. He was barfing in the bushes. "Hi Jack Warren. Here, takes my handkerchief, it's clean."

"Thanks."

"This one is personal; my extended family lives here. Know what happened?"

"Long time no see Oliver, and how are you?"

"I'm upset and not just because my sleep was interrupted. In addition to regurgitating your guts at what you saw, what else can you tell me?"

"How are you related to this gory mess?"

"They are my boyfriend's aunt, uncle, and their child. His cousin is in the wind, and we are worried if he is all right."

"Since it's family, I'll tell you off the record. This couple was tortured then hacked to death. It's a disgusting grisly mess inside there, looks like a machete or ax might have been used for the chopping. The couple's' nephew found the bodies and had an altercation with the arriving officers he called. It took four cops to subdue him. *You got yourself a fighter.*"

"Tell me about it. "

"My partner and I just began processing the crime scene. It looks like nothing was taken which rules out home invasion gone bizarro. But a bunch of framed photos were disturbed, it's possible some are missing. Your boyfriend was too busy punching to do much talking. Now you know what I know. You have anything for me?"

"Remember that big bust about seven months ago, on the westside, people trafficking, drugs, and guns? The missing boy had been snatched by Pachucos-88 and recovered by the police during the bust. I don't know if it's related but if it were me, I'd look there first."

"Ugh, that doesn't make any sense. If he saw something, why not kill the kid and leave the parents?"

"You got there before me."

"Or take the kid, demand and get a ransom, and then kill the kid."

"You got questions. I don't have answers."

"You're right, these criminals get more stupid the older I get. Do you know what, when I retire, I'm writing a how to book for doing serious crime without serving time. These guys need a handbook."

"My former colleagues at parole would call that a community service to reduce their workload."

"I'm always happy to support a good cause."

"Did you know the boy is autistic? He'd be no good in court as a witness. A half-assed defense attorney would eat him up on the witness stand."

"This case gets stranger by the minute."

"I wonder, maybe the bad guys don't know he's autistic."

"Does he look and act normal?"

"As normal as any teenager ever does these days. Whoops, I'm dating us detective Warren."

"Yes, you are. Thanks for dropping by, Oliver. Keep me posted and I'll share what I can. Now that I upchucked my goulash dinner, let me get back in there and solve this murder."

"See ya, Jack."

***

When I returned home, Coy was pacing in the living room, his face a fright mask. "When you were at your aunt and uncles did you check Darrell-Wayne's room for his things?"

"Of course, his bed clothes were rumpled like they had been slept in. His pajamas were on the floor. Usually, he's meticulous about folding his clothes a certain way after he removes them. His everyday shoes were missing. I checked the garage, the bicycle I bought him for Christmas was there along with his old bike."

"From the grapevine I heard Pachuco-88 is finished around these parts after the big bust we instigated. At least they're gone for now, otherwise, that would be where I'd look."

"Me too."

"Does your cousin have a cell phone?"

"That's how he called me."

"Is he answering it now?"

"No. I found it on the floor in his room near his PJs."

"Any idea where to start a search?"

"My cousin could have gone out his bedroom window. It was open wide, it's usually not *that open*. He's afraid of the boogeyman but likes fresh air."

"Focus. Where's a good place to start looking?"

"I know the parks he likes near his house. Let's go check them out."

We were still cruising neighborhood parks looking for Darrell-Wayne when dawn broke. All we'd found were stoned junkies nodding, winos sleeping alcohol-fueled dreams, all in the open laying prone on park benches. Going further afield we found scuff marks, cigarette butts, and recently used condoms behind bushes.

With daylight more joggers appeared to do stretching exercises, none had seen a teenager who looked twelve. Once they were running the runners refused to stop or talk. I couldn't tell whether it was dedication or bad manners. We had to run next to the runners to ask questions, their rude lack of cooperation pissed me off. I resisted an urge to shove them over.

"Let's get breakfast, before I punch one of these flat of foot yahoos in the nose. After we eat, I'll make cop calls."

"I have no appetite."

"You'll feel better with food in your belly, that's how we met, remember?"

"Don't remind me of how this all got started half a year ago."

"Yeah, at your insisting it wasn't going to be romantic, either."

"Hey, don't joke about it. You've been good fortune for me, up to this happening."

"I don't know why I said that. Maybe, I'm voicing my fear of commitment."

"I'm so wired. What I really need is sleep, even just for an hour or two."

"Not to worry, I have Ambient pills at home. Let's go put you to bed and I'll clear my desk to find Darrell-Wayne."

"Will you cuddle with me until I fall asleep?"

"Sure, even hum a lullaby."

***

As usual Willis Washington had the best intel in a hurry. The Federal Bureau of Investigation had grabbed the local Pachuco-88 gang ringleaders on federal warrants for people trafficking back and forth, gun export, and for drug import. The perps were transported to Washington D.C. for protracted interview sessions. Meanwhile, Homeland Security's Drug Enforcement Agency, and Alcohol, Tobacco, and Firearms took the lower echelon gang members to their out of state facilities for lengthy interrogations, while locked up awaiting changing court dates. The feds believed they had the most important gang members not already in the wind and would have them all in custody before any court dates were permanently set.

Willis said if we report Darrell-Wayne as kidnapped, the FBI was mandated to investigate and might coordinate with the law enforcement agencies working the aunt and uncle murders. The feds had manpower and resources beyond the local cops. Technically we were supposed to wait forty-eight hours to report a missing person over eighteen. But an exception could be made for the handicapped or a potential witness to a double murder.

Washington mentioned something else I didn't know, Pachuco-88 is an international criminal consortium. It is based in the Central American triangle of El Salvador, Guatemala, and Nicaragua. They were a leaderless consensus criminal syndicate run by equals with divisions headquartered primarily in each country. Searching the dark-web, Washington found Pachuco-88 was involved in thirty-five percent of all international illegal drug distribution and twenty-five percent of nongovernment gun sales, worldwide. He verified his findings with Interpol, and that information was more than all my other professional friends or contacts knowledge together.

When Coy woke-up mid-afternoon, he wanted to do sixty-nine. Like most people I guess he coped with death using sex. Since I too was in the mood seeing him freshly scrubbed straight from a shower, naked and ready. We dealt with his loss and my physical urge cooperatively. After sex, we cuddled in afterglow to get our respiration and cardiology back in normal range. It was a joint venture we were cultivating without a lot of verbiage about it. Like most folks, I'd rather have sex than talk about it.

Stirring from the serenity after exhilaration Coy asked, "Anything new?" I told him what I'd just learned.

After chewing over the international nature of Willis Washington's new information, Coy remembered a Brigadier-General whose son he'd taught martial-arts. When Coy refused payment for the afterhours favor, begging off with, he was already paid by the army and no double dipper. The general said, "If you ever need a favor back, don't be afraid to ask."

Using first my home-office computer and then his cellphone, after an hour and a half, Coy tracked the General down. It took another hour to actually get the general on the phone and call in the favor.

Brigadier-General Ivan Navarro remembered Coy, listened to his request. Then probably buying time thinking over the request for help remarked, "The fundamentals you taught my boy were highly praised when he applied to a distinguished dojo here in Djakarta." There was a phone pause then the general said, "I don't know what *I* can do from here in Indonesia, but now your missing autistic cousin has my full attention. I have subordinates back in the States who will find out everything they can and help you get your cousin back, safe. Just give me a little time to shake the trees. Is this a good number to reach you at?"

"Yes. Thank you, sir." Coy looked satisfied with the phone call, like a man who did everything he could think of in an emergency.

I phoned Ameli to send out her minions to search higher and *lower* for Darrell-Wayne in unlikely places. Members of her handicapped young adult group fancied themselves highly talented amateur sleuths. She said they loved a challenge to prove they had unrealized capabilities. When I telephoned Warren, the lead homicide detective on the case, he had uniformed cops knocking on neighbors' doors trying to find Darrell-Wayne or information. Nothing had turned up so far, I could hear frustration in his voice.

After spending an hour on the phone Coy and I revisited the crime scene. Darrell-Wayne's bikes were there but his electric scooter wasn't. Coy said, "It's fast, and he manages crossing intersections with more caution than I'd expected." We knocked on doors in a nearby area the cops might miss. It was where Darrell-Wayne tricked or treated for Halloween. The locals considered it a safe area. His distinctive costume was remembered but nobody had seen him in the last twenty-four hours.

We went back to the parks we'd checked the night before. We had nothing to go on, nobody we asked so far had seen the missing teenager. Grasping at straws, I sat down next to a homeless guy and showed him a photo of Darrell-Wayne. "Have you seen this boy around here recently?"

"What's in it if I had?"

"Five bucks, if you tell the truth."

"I saw him here, two days before yesterday, or it was last week. I won't lie to you for five dollars, but he's never alone. He usually has an adult with him." Then pointing at Coy standing just off to the side the vagrant said, "Him or an older man or woman always accompany that kid. What's he done?"

"Are you here a lot?"

"Much of the time. This park is my home. I don't go out much anymore."

"I didn't see you here last night."

"I saw you and your friend over there. I like to watch the fairies fuck in the bushes. It reminds me of when my cock used to get hard. Now it's just a decoration to pee out of. It's been said that cheap wine takes the lead out of your pencil. I guess it's a small price to pay. I was never that much into breeding back when I could, know what I mean?"

"I guess your home has many visitors."

"Nobody ever called me a stud. I'd knock them down if they did."

"Visitors."

"Visitors, yes, I do, they come in shifts. Early in the morning the exercise nuts come running, jogging, walking funny, skipping rope, shadow boxing, and when they go, old people show-up as a mob to do slow motion pretend fighting. I watch the visitors do funny shenanigans." The speaker paused a moment probably to reflect on my five-dollar question.

"I think what the old people do is called tai chi."

"Oh, that's nice it has a name like that. Midmorning the nannies and poor mothers come out with little kids in strollers. At lunch time in mild weather, workers clog-up my benches but sometimes share their food with me. I get the fiber in my diet from their leftover apples, bananas, peaches, or pears in season. They're stingy with grapes, cherries and apricots, my favorites of course. Occasionally, I even get a sandwich on whole wheat bread. Now that's healthy fiber, but I don't like mayonnaise or cheap ballpark mustard."

"Do you ever see teenagers hiding out here?"

"No, I don't think so. Afternoons its after school small children and their minders first, then the bigger kids come to play music and smoke dope. Sometimes the little ones play hide and seek is that what you mean?"

"No, like runaways hiding from the cops?"

"I don't allow police officers in my home when I can help it, I'm a staunch Christian. They shoot Black people just for no reason. I was Black in a previous life, that's how I know. I was shot by unruly cops in a former life."

"Well, thank you for your time. But that wasn't worth five bucks."

"By evening you could use a big bully policeman around here. This place has hard-core drugs for sale and hetero lovers with no better place to breed other than to gum up my place. I can't stop them, I've tried, but they get all threatening like they think they can scare me. I was a veteran for a brief time. I almost saw war up close. After midnight, the fairies come out to play, like I said before. But they never threatened me. Oh, wait a second, if you think about it what I told you just now is worth more than five dollars."

"You're right, it almost is. So, to prove my word is good, here's two dollars."

"Thank you very much. You are a gentleman and a scholar. But five would have been better. Ugh, I don't suppose I could talk you out of the other three if I know something you didn't ask?"

"Depends, what do you know?"

"You aren't the first looking for that kid. Before you came here last night, desperado looking outlaw dudes were shaking the bushes looking for him too. It probably was the same kid you want. I don't know why he's gotten so popular suddenly. He looks ordinary, maybe he can sing and dance. But I never saw him do those things. Believe me, those outlaws didn't look friendly and weren't handing out dollars either."

"Can you describe them?"

"Like how?"

"How many, what did they look like?"

"You got a fin for it … oh yes, I see you do. Good man. Okay, what do I remember? You know that cheap wine plays tricks with my memory occasionally. Normally I only drink Night Train, when they don't have it, I'll make do with Midnight Special, but on rare occasions like my birthday I'll indulge with a pint of Tropical Jungle Juice. It costs more because it's flavored like real fruit punch, very tasty."

"You were going to tell me what desperados or outlaws look like."

"Calm down … I will … don't rush me … um … let me think! Oh yeah, there were four. One was fiftyish, with gray hair and beard gray around the edges, two thirty somethings, black mustaches with long sideburns, and one had no face hair, young twenties or close."

"How would I know them if I saw them?"

"They spoke Spanish to each other but the young one talked to me in the King's English with a Queens' accent, know what I mean."

"No. Not at all."

"Not as smart as you look, eh? That guy must have been their interpreter born and bred in Queens, New York. Okay, that's enough, I told you they all had facial hair except one. They were not too tall or fat and dressed like they were not from around here. Oh, eh, I know what you want to know. They all wore cowboy boots with silver tipped toes. To tell it accurate they looked like expensively dressed uptown thug cowboys from way down south of here, and you'd be smart to avoid them … if you want to know … nope you don't … then just be careful and always bring me cash."

"Is that all you got?"

"The kid you want wasn't here to find yesterday. Those other guys weren't happy about not finding him either. I don't know their story, but I hope the kid stays clear of those rift-rath hoodlums. Their eyes are dead … know what I mean? … You do too. Now give me my money or I'll make a stink. This is a respectable park."

Handing over the cash I resisted saying he *was* stinking up the park. He was well beyond unwashed body, dirty clothes, alcohol breath, and tooth decay odor. It wasn't his fault the richest country on earth didn't provide places to wash or otherwise live half decently within functional homeless limitations it created for social control.

Nevertheless, there was no shortage of cheap fortified wine sold in hip pocket size bottles to console the destitute society discarded for its purpose. In the good old U.S.A., it's all about the few extremely wealthy at the expense of downtrodden masses to be at bay with threats of stinky homelessness or worse.

As we walked away, I asked Coy if he had heard all the homeless man's recollections. He had, and suggested we go to the other park we'd visited last night to back up the story. Doing so, we found out from a homeless hetero couple with three small children and ten more of my dollars, Darrell-Wayne hadn't been there in a week. They also conveyed four Spanish speaking, evil looking cowboys with silver tipped boot were ahead of us in our search. They were adamant we should avoid the cowboys at all costs so we could visit their homeless family again.

By then it was dinner time, and I knew a decent Greek diner nearby. After ordering a daily special we went over what we knew versus needed to know. We had hints of who and from where. We needed why and who else was involved. Just after our food arrived, it looked good and smelled delicious, my cellphone beeped. "Hey, Ameli, you working afterhours? You never do that. It's one of your rules *that I support*."

"It's my rule because you're a cheapskate and don't pay time and a half overtime. Anyway, I make exceptions for missing children *and the disabled*."

"You're interrupting my dinner."

"Bon appetite. I don't have much, but it may help you to sleep better to know Darrell-Wayne was seen in transit and appears protected."

"Details please."

"There is apparently an under the radar network of safe houses loosely run by unpaid do-gooders for autistic people in trouble. Two Asperger young women from my support group claim to have seen *the subject of your investigation* with an older blind woman. Apparently, she's a kind of Dorthey Day for the autistic in trouble and may or may not be an entry point for a network of safe houses. Don't ask, but I heard they communicate by anonymous telephone calls. My source is dependable. Getting what I got was not easy and so you should give me a raise."

"You do know your words sound preposterous, like a comic book adventure story, right? A blind woman with superpowers to the rescue autistic people in trouble and nobody knows anything about it. You want a raise, for a fantasy, I think not. One might say you are already over paid."

"Preposterous or not, your subject was seen for sure, being put on a train going somewhere upstate on the Metro North Line. Then the blind woman returned alone the way she came. The boy looked okay but extremely sad. Anyway, that's what I was told from reliable sources."

"Subject of my investigation? Ameli, are you adding journalism to your many talents? What happened to person of interest?"

"At the moment I'm working on locating your missing person. It has been suggested by *unreliable sources* he is being moved around for his protection. So far, I can't verify that. Do I get extra pay for fencing with you over colloquial phrases indicating lost person while working unpaid overtime?"

"You do realize what you just told me is hearsay, right? Secret underground network of homes for autistic people in trouble. Where could the financial sponsorship for such bureaucratic arrangements come from? Whose turf or worse, cash cows would be trampled for the good of such a select few? It all sounds highly unlikely, especially reported from unreliable witnesses sighting blind sources. It won't stand up in court."

"What do I always tell you, 'You are too social work orthodox to be a respectable gum chewing PI.'"

"You do get points for *trying* and a little extra regular pay for writing up your after-hours account, on your own time. Hey, Coy and I say thanks for the effort, but go for provable facts we could use in court if it comes to that."

"Listen, smarty pants, my support group says there are no foster homes for bashed, battered, burned, or sexually abused autistic children or adults."

"And so?"

"Okay, just you imagine how much work would get done in city offices with screaming hyper children and adults running around freaking out needing non-available foster care. For how long? Of course, boss man, it has to be underground hearsay to survive. That's what's possible in the comic book world I and my support group live in."

"Got it, I've formed a graphic image of domestic violence from your words. Thank you for that, it'll be hard to forget. Now please find us where to look next."

"No, you don't get it. I'm betting there are unofficial unfunded support groups for parents and relatives of the autistic, and they pieced together what's needed when and where it isn't a phone tree. Is the picture getting better in focus?"

"New information for you, Ameli, it appears thugs are looking for Darrell-Wayne, and have been one step ahead of us."

"Why do they want him?"

"Good question. Maybe to finish what they started with his parents. I'll tell you everything I find out at the office tomorrow. Right now, my food is getting cold. Goodbye."

"Thugs, huh! I better clean and oil my weapon, may have to use it soon."

"Ameli don't shoot anyone I know, especially me."

"Relax, boss, your cold food will be hard to digest, don't eat it, order fresh. Good appetite, bye now."

Chapter 3.

I glanced over at Coy who looked guilty. My dinner hadn't gotten cold, he'd eaten it probably while still warm. I motioned the server over, ordered another dinner for myself and whimsically suggested Coy order dessert while the order taker was at hand. To my astonishment he ordered slices of pie.

We all deal with stress in our own unique way, Coy eats his. I get stony calm, cold, objective, and Ameli goes into hyperactivity sleuth mode leading her sleuthing handicap support group. I have no doubt she will pass the private detectives test she is studying for, with high marks. It's her in hot pursuit of an armed villain in her wheelchair I worry about.

Normally, I can easily skip a meal or four without notice when brain chewing on a difficult case. But at that moment the house dressed tossed-salad, lemon-garlic-butter red snapper filet daily special, fresh green beans with slivered almonds in thyme sauce, and rice pilaf were delicious, hot from the kitchen.

Sitting back satisfied, I temporarily forgot we were on a mission searching for Darrell-Wayne Goff and was tempted by one or more of the desserts the server had arranged in front of Coy. A slice of each kind of pie the diner sold formed a crescent in front of him. Each one looked better than the next, and mile-high lemon meringue pie was loudly calling my name as his fork attacked. His aunt and uncle's murder and missing cousin was having a deleterious effect on his appetite.

It also occurred to me Coy was having a bad influence on my recently improving waistline, so, instead of eating pie, I called Warren. "I want to give you a heads up, there are four unsavory looking characters after Darrell-Wayne, along with the rest of us. They are Spanish speakers and wear cowboy boots with silver in front. They are one step ahead of us in the search."

"A gray tinged beard, two heavies, and a young punk?"

"Yeah. How'd you know?

"One of the victim's neighbors is paranoid. He has closed circuit cameras all over his property. We have the guys you mentioned on tape coming and going from the crime scene. Hold onto your hat, there may be a second group after the boy as well. The uniform cops doing house-to-house interviews spotted a suspicious car watching the murder house. They drove off in a hurry when officers approached them."

"This case gets screwier by the minute."

"The tape images we have aren't clear, it's an old-fashioned security system. Nothing like the fancy gear you sell, okay?"

"Who else is clogging up recovering the teen?"

"This second group looks like foreigners too, Russians or Albanians maybe. They were in a recently stolen car. The cowboy boots you described are from way down south of Mexico."

"Any idea which bunch did the murders?"

"Two south of the border types went in and came out of the house with machetes. There appears to be what looked like blood all over those perps and their blades leaving the house. But at this stage who knows, I've been wrong before, just not often."

"Wrong? You have an impeccable record."

"Do you know what the missing kid and his family were into?"

"Don't have a clue. They were straight arrows as far as I see."

"Me too, you find anything else?"

"Ever heard of an underground network to protect abused autistic people?"

"Never, got names and addresses?"

"We're working on it."

"The reason I haven't called you is, I think this case has gone beyond a local police matter. It's feels out of our league."

"Why say that?"

"Okay, you know I've been doing this work a long time and can tell when we're boxing too far above our weight. Due to its various international dimensions, I'm getting ready to write it up for a hand off to the feds. They have many more people and resources to figure out all the pieces, and to do it right."

"Warren you are good at what you do, don't quit on me."

"Sorry. Okay, Oliver, this case is not just a double homicide with a missing disabled child. It's international on at least two fronts. It could be competing foreign perpetrators. Interpol should be on this case, not us, and the Feds would bring them in."

"It's a family matter for me."

"My advice is back off before bullets start flying. There are too many unknowns, no clue makes sense, and I've carefully dotted my I's and crossed my T's and got nothing to show for the extra work."

"Please give me a little more time, I might find something soon. I'll owe you."

"Let me tie up a lose end or two. I've still got a few phantom leads to chase. I'll give you a definitive answer when I run out of ghosts to hunt."

"How much time?"

"At this point I'd say you have a max of forty-eight hours."

"That's it?"

"Yes, if I decide to throw in the towel and that's the way I'm leaning right now."

"I appreciated your help but will hold you to two days."

Coy and I left the diner stuffed and too keyed up to go home. We had forty-eight hours, and nothing happened. We drove around and checked out parks not visited before. It was a waste of time but at least we were doing something. Finally, fatigue taking over, we accepted the futility of our effort and drove back to my place, in silence. After showering together, we had slow, nonverbal fulfilling sex.

Unlike my previous relationships, not having expectations or even naming it, made tactile wordless expression uncomplicated. I let whatever was happening with us just be. It was so much freer than my usual weighty over analysis of age difference and everything else imaginable. It freed my mind to focus on finding the missing boy.

***

My cellphone woke me early, with dread as usual. I swiftly muted the ringer. Coy was in a deep sleep he'd earned exercising his suction techniques twice the day before. A quick glance showed Willis Washington was calling. I rolled out of bed nude and padded to the kitchen to start the coffee. "Hey, Willis, what's going-on?"

"Weird shit."

"I'm all ears." Water went in the tea kettle, then set it onto the fire. I primed my French-press with freshly ground smoky Italian roast espresso coffee and a pinch of salt.

"I've found some disconnected pieces that may be connected to the case you alerted me to. Did you get details on that grisly torture double murder?"

"I did. They were Coy's aunt and uncle. Jack Warren is the lead in it. Do you know him?"

"Not really. I've seen him around. He's one of the few old timers I never worked with. The word is he's a strictly by the book kind of guy."

"That's him. What's you got?"

"Since my promotion I've been trying to align work between the district attorney's office and the police department to minimize redundancy. I told you the feds swooped in and took everything with a promise our district attorney gets it all back after the feds prosecute, right?"

"Right. Now Jack Warren says he wants to handoff the murder and missing teen case to the feds too."

"Why so?"

"Warren's not getting any traction on the case. Reading between the lines, he's taking heat from on high to solve the case or pass it on. Elections are coming soon, and negative publicity about slaughtered citizens and their missing children makes incumbents nervous."

"Tell him at present my perps are scattered in federal alphabet soup. The FBI,

DEA, ATF. Now DHS, the Department of Homelands Security's immigration division wants to be ringmaster of the show. "

"Sounds like standard operating procedure to me, pass the hot potato around. What's on your mind beside a need to vent?"

"As near as I can tell, we eliminated Pachuco-88 in this state with the bust you called in. So, why does a double murder look suspiciously like their work? Then to make it more complicated the missing child is being pursued by Eastern European heavy hitters, according to my confidential informant."

"Tell me what I don't know."

"Then add this to your grist mill, two guys in suits with ID from army intelligence came to my office last evening at quitting time. They asked questions they shouldn't have known to ask about our big bust and the missing teenager in the middle of a double murder. In all my years on the job I've never officially talked to a national security operative. I thought they were only a myth."

"I don't know anything you don't, except the army guys in suits came from the missing kids' cousin who called in a favor from an Army General."

"Ah, that explains how they knew what questions to ask."

"Always glad to solve a mystery, I'm a PI."

"I'm calling with a heads up, you should expect to hear from the Army suits, they mentioned your name. Do you know what the hell is going on with this case?"

"Usually, in a missing person's case I look for simple answers, I've run out of those this time. Willis, ever heard of a secret underground transit system to protect autistic people in trouble?"

"Yeah, over the years, I've heard rumors. It's not only for autistics. Vulnerable folks of all stripes get abused and then ignored in places to help."

"I thought the handicapped had full citizenship rights."

"Don't be a wiseacre, the truth is without reliable witnesses and accurate information to build cases, there's not much the police can do for most disabled people."

"I'm not judging."

"Even when we get involved, if it isn't murder, everything else requires resources we don't have. That's why most special needs end up unsolved on the bottom of cold case files. You know the bosses only want numbers of solved cases, in a hurry."

"I do remember that."

"So now, Oliver, that explains why there is a secret underground network to protect the most vulnerable in society and officially we don't know anything about it. This is America if the right way doesn't work the public finds another."

"The mother of invention and all that, right?"

"What can I do to help you with this case? Where's *your* blockage old friend?"

"Too much alphabet soup from Federal policing agencies and now the Army's butting in, I get it. They are not helping."

"No. At this point I need a score card to keep track of what's where and coordinate all the outside helpers not to get in the way. I doubt the Army will just go away now they've introduced themselves."

"My current concern is I may have overlook something important with two sets of antagonists."

"Then you don't have concrete information that can help my people find the teenager."

"I'll keep you posted if we have reason to believe Darrell-Wayne is safe in the fore mentioned underground network. By the way homicide detective Jack Warren gave me forty-eight hours before he bails."

"Oliver, how are you holding up?"

"If it just weren't personal. I do my best work when I'm objective."

"Wait, how, is this case personal?"

"I'm sleeping with the missing boy's cousin. He's a nephew of the murdered couple. You met Coy after the big bust."

"Oh yeah, he qualifies. And by the way, he looks like a keeper."

"What we started has grown to more than short term casual for me. I agree with you, he's a keeper, and, Willis, you know me, I have trepidations about it."

"Well, I say good for you both. It's past time for you to settle down with somebody."

"Thanks for saying that. Your reassurance matters to me."

"Since the feds are gumming up the work around here, I've got a minute to shake the trees for information before Jack cuts down the forest, and the DA finds new busy work for me to delegate. I'll be in touch. Bye."

"See ya."

Sitting at the kitchen table, staring into a big mug of steaming black coffee, I tried to organize what I knew, the cops knew, and what help from the Army could be. Darrell-Wayne's parents were not into anything criminal, Coy says he would have known if they were. The missing eighteen-year old's dad was a librarian and his mom drove a brown package delivery truck. It was impossible to imagine how any of them could rouse the attention of Spanish speaking gangsters or Eastern European mobsters.

I felt his presence, then looked up from my coffee to see Coy standing in the kitchen doorway. His hair tousled, bare foot, wearing only his almost transparent tangerine-colored bikini briefs, leaving little to my imagination. His face still looked groggy as the tangerine briefs were coming awake.

After a toothpaste flavored kiss, I indicated he sat across from me and fetched him a mug of coffee. A soundless musing passed back and forth between us. Done with sitting in silence, I pushed bread down the toaster, put fire under the frying pan, and put precooked breakfast sausages in it to warm. While he watched me, I beat eggs together with Worcestershire sauce, salt, pepper, and a little shredded sharp cheddar cheese. Moved the sausages from the pan to the oven to keep warm and dropped liquefied eggs in the sausage pan.

Minutes later we were eating, and Coy said, "You were talking on the phone, but I couldn't hear what was said. Any news?"

"Two military intelligence guys asked my friend Willis about Darrell-Wayne's recent history. Your general is as good as his word. Otherwise, it looks the same as when we went to sleep. Nothing makes any sense to me. For instance, how are the Central Americans involved, and why commit murder? What's Darrell-Wayne got to do with this? Are the Eastern Europeans working with or against the Central Americans and what's it all about?"

"Lying in bed I remembered something. One of the missing photos from my aunt and uncle's home array showed a street sign near the first park we went to."

"Good, that's one mystery solved. At that park they probably learned about the other parks they beat us to."

"Darrell-Wayne must be scared half to death. He doesn't handle stress well. What's today's plan?"

"I'm waiting to call Ameli; she may have something new about the underground network. If not, I'll go over all the police calls from last night, I have a scanner that records them at the office."

"What can I do?"

"You might want to talk to a mortician about arrangements for your aunt and uncle for after the police release their bodies."

"This nightmare feels bottomless. They were good, honest, hardworking people. Who'd want to hurt them like that?"

"Was your spending time with Darrell-Wayne just from lack of something better to do or were you his bodyguard?"

"Why would he need a bodyguard? My aunt and uncle lived regular middle-class lives. Darrell-Wayne can be a handful when it's a full moon, he's not in the mood for his favorite breakfast cereal or needs to be washed thoroughly. He can be a lot to deal with after a hard day at work. I was always happy to help them out. He responded to me differently than to his parents."

"How did you first become part of your cousin's support system?"

"I was friends with his older brother and learned from watching Eddie. Then after military service, I didn't have a place and my aunt and uncle offered their other son's room. It was supposed to be temporary. I stayed longer than intended after seeing the relief they enjoyed having live-in help with Darrell-Wayne. But a man needs a job to respect himself. That's the only reason I left town. It was nice being part of a family again until I pissed them off losing Darrell-Wayne. "

"I didn't know Darrell-Wayne had a brother. Could this be about him?"

"Eddie was two years older than me and died from an IED in Afghanistan three-years before I got there. Sometimes it looks like Darrell-Wayne thinks I'm Eddie.

That's one reason I think I can manage him when his parents lose patience. He's really a sweet kid who just requires special handling and a lot of energy."

"He sounds like a lot to deal with."

"I can't imagine how he's coping on his own. He never had to."

"Don't shoot me, could this be about something in your past?"

"ME? You know me. I taught green army recruits for four years after almost a year as a private first-class dog-faced infantry grunt in a war zone. Except for the war, my life has been as boring as my aunt and uncle. You've met and fed me. Did me or my cousin impress you as criminal masterminds?"

"No. Neither. Not that I'd know a criminal mastermind if I met one. Let's go to my office, you're going to want to meet Ameli."

"Does she bite?"

"Just be aware she forgets she has a sharp tongue and don't take everything she says personal. *She* will let you know if she thinks you're out of line."

***

I like to think of my downtown office as nondescript, it certainly isn't fancy. It occupies the third floor over an orthodontist, and he's above the biggest-best hardware store in the area. The building has one huge passenger elevator because it was once six stories. Years before I took occupancy, they say, a tornado irreparably damaged floor four through six.

Since the hardware store owned the building, demolishing and rebuilding was not an option. After structurally unsound floors were removed and a new insulated metal roof put in place, it proved cheaper to keep the oversize elevator than downsize it. The elevator's important guts are in the basement as was the elevator car when the tornado took the top off the building. I must admit now it's a funny-looking building. I wouldn't have taken the office if it were a walkup. Many of my clients have mobility issues one way or another. But that's a long story for another day.

I negotiated a long-term cheap lease because popular parlance believed the building was unlucky and unsafe in tornado season. The way I figured it at the time QQ got started, people who hire queer private detectives often consider themselves unlucky and are unsafe. Of course, that was back when I expected to be doing mostly gay divorce work.

At present I should move, except we have a lot of room cheap, plenty of heat in winter, and the elevator is strong. If I were more of a go getter, I'd open an annex for my security business in a fancy high-rise-tech building, another one for my personal protection services over a boxing gym and keep the original for missing persons, divorce, or whatever. But alas, annexes won't happen cause I'm a control freak who needs to keep a finger in every job I take. If I accept a case, it's mine or at least supervised by me from intake to exit interview and all from one central tornado prone location.

As soon as we entered the frosted glass door of my offices, I said, "Ameli Tsai, this is Coy Goff. Coy this is Ameli."

"Hi."

"Nice to meet you."

"Coy is worried about his cousin's safety. Do you have any news?"

"Yes, but first I need him to finish his cousin's intake form. I am a professional. In other words, this form is blank. Also, is he gay like you?"

"What gave me away?"

"The way you and my boss look at each other. You did read the gold lettered name on the door, correct? This is the office of Queer Queries. I'm usually the only real queen in these parts. That's queen as in the female in charge."

"Darrell-Wayne's parents liked to say he showed signs of being bisexual. We never discussed his sexuality because I was out since age-eleven, and he didn't seem to be interested in sex."

To show my ignorance or not to be completely ignored in my own office, I said, "I don't think autistic folks liked sex since they are antithetical to body contact."

Never one to lose an opportunity to be in charge, Ameli said, "I dated an Asperger guy once, he was insatiable in the bedroom."

"I've heard this story."

"Well, I still require a filled-out form to make a case record. What is your cousin's sexuality?"

"Write indeterminant."

"Huh, poor boy."

"Let's ask him when we find him."

Like a frustrated old-time schoolteacher, Ameli threw her hands in the air and said, "Coy just fill in missing information on Darrell-Wayne's intake form. Then if you behave yourself, I'll tell you what I know that's new."

He took her clipboard and rapidly scribbled on it. Then handed it back, Ameli checked it, then returned it for his signature. Finally finished, sitting back with authority she said, "Breaking news! The secret network on one hand seems chaotic and yet highly effective. The latest I heard was Darrell-Wayne was moved upstate, destination unknown."

"You told me that yesterday, Roscoe, right?"

"No. Now farther north. He's in transit to the Buffalo area, and reportedly phony papers are being prepared there to take him to Canada. Soon."

"Why?"

"It seems something happened after Darrell-Wayne was moved to Roscoe, New York."

"What?"

"South of the Boarder Cowboys showed up looking for him. A Roscoe resident told her next-door neighbor, an off duty parttime deputy sheriff, that strangers pushed into her home asking a lot of questions she didn't have answers for. Then they showed her a picture with a young boy in it and asked where the Blue Moon Cabins were located. Because she didn't know the boy, or the cabins, they slapped her around then left with a threat to return if she called the police. She ran next-door."

Coy's face lit up with a question. "How could they know about the Blue Moon Cabins?"

"According to my source a photo showed a family group of four adults and two young boys standing in front of a large sign for Blue Moon Cabins."

"That must have been one of the pictures they stole from the murder scene. My aunt and uncle vacationed there until it went out of business. They were friends with the owners who retired to Arizona, or some other Gods forsaken place."

"My source checked historical records and says the Blue Moon Cabins were sold and new owners changed its name to Trout Heaven Mini bungalows for Fishermen."

"Now, something makes sense. Let's go to Roscoe."

My impatience was showing, so I said, "Ameli, finish your story. What happened after the push in?"

"The off duty parttime deputy calls in the license plate number his neighbor wrote down and warned, 'proceed with caution.' When an on-duty county sheriff deputy spots *the* license plate speeding, he pulls the car over and calls for back up. Two state trooper cars were in the area and responded to the call."

"Ameli did you make coffee?"

"Yes, Oliver. Don't interrupt me just when the story you asked to hear gets exciting."

"Sorry. Please continue while I fix Coy and myself a mug of your bitter brew."

"Four Central Americans exit their vehicle shooting. While the two troopers and deputy sheriff were diving for cover another parttime deputy sheriff responding for backup arrived, from a different direction. Since they patrol alone most upstate cops have an assault rifle and shotgun in their car."

"Ameli, please stick to the facts."

"Those are facts. *Allow me to finish please.*"

"Then continue ... go ahead." The look she gave me would have quaked strong boots.

"The second deputy sheriff grabs his rifle, sets it on automatic, and empties an extended ammo clip at the Central Americans who are all busy shooting at the first police to arrive. All the bad guys were clustered behind their open car doors facing the wrong direction and died from multiple high velocity rifle-bullets in the back, from the late arriving deputy. The other cops, uninjured, never got a shot off but had many bullet holes in their cars to prove they were in a big shootout. The late arrival deputy sheriff was hailed a hero, those desperados are no more, and that's the end of their story in Roscoe, New York."

I said to no one in particular, "Damn it! Now how will we to know what this is about."

Addressing me Coy said, "Where was Darrell-Wayne during this action adventure? Do you think he was unhurt or retraumatized?"

All I could do was shake my head side to side, I didn't know.

Coy bemoaned, "Poor kid. He's not over grieving his brother Eddie's death, his parents are murdered, he's chased by gunmen, and now in a shootout."

Ameli's tone of voice shifted to mollifying. "He probably wasn't there. Most likely he was on the move one or two steps ahead of the gangsters."

"Why do you say that?"

She calmly placed folded hands across her stomach and said, "His name never came up in the upstate police reports. So far nobody up there has connected the Central Americans to the double homicide down here, or the federal agencies having a jamboree with local police's work."

"With no knowledge of what this is about, the best thing for Darrell-Wayne and Coy is to comfort each other. What do you think, Ameli?"

"I agree. Except, you said there may be other men after Coy's missing cousin. It appears there is competition in this line of work."

"Right, so it seems! We must put muscle around the boy."

"Let's get him back first."

"Right again. Locally, I can get as many armed men as needed. Ameli, exactly where is Darrell-Wayne now?"

"I can only find out after he's been moved. It's all hush hush off the grid secret network. The people working the underground transport system don't even always know each other. I haven't figured out how it works yet. But it certainly does."

"Damnit, this is not how I operate, constantly running from behind. I don't like this."

"You know boss, after last night's shootout I'm not so sure we have enough people power to keep the teenager safe. Most of our gunslingers are part timers."

"I should go to Canada if that's where my cousin is headed? Maybe I can intercept him."

"Do you know anyone up there?"

"No."

"We do, don't we, boss?

"Coy, you just started a business in the city. I know from experience if you don't nurture a business, it will die. Go grow your personal trainer enterprise and let Ameli and me find your cousin. We've done it once already."

"That was different. I want to help this time. I've got muscles, and the army taught me to shoot straight."

Ameli had experience with temper tantrums from her support groups. She could see one brewing. "Listen Coy, if they won't tell me where your cousin is, why would they tell you? My handicapped support groups are closed to the able-bodied. We have unobserved ears and eyes everywhere."

"They trust you. Why not me?"

"Because we are safe. Nobody ever sees us or at least pay attention."

"Coy you are out voted. Go back to the city and run your one-man enterprise. I'll go listen to the police scanner tapes, it's a long shot, but it sometimes pays off."

"Okay, if you promise to call me as soon as you have anything."

"Promise."

"Ameli, who was that guy we used in Canada a few years back?"

"At your service, master … here it is. Brian Mahoney of the Royal Canadian Mounted Police. I think that means he wears a red coat, funny hat, and rides a horse. He operates around Toronto."

"Thanks. Get him on the phone please." I walked Coy to the door and said, "We'll talk tonight, safe travel." Then I gave him a kiss to send him on his way.

He turned making eye contact with Ameli. "Nice meeting you. Goodbye."

"Ciao."

Chapter 4.

Brian Mahoney was a typical no-nonsense, straightlaced, brainy, slow talking Canadian police officer who'd forgotten how to smile from witnessing too much human tragedy. I'd not remembered, last time we worked together he took offense at my probing queries into his methods, which I was paying him to do. I wasn't questioning the quality of his work, just covering all the bases for QQ records. He didn't do anything wrong, just proved to be thin skinned. As sometimes happened, information my per diem worker hadn't considered important became crucial to resolving the case. It is my belief as the boss, we all do our best work when closely supervised.

My telephone conversation with Brian Mahoney was short and to the point. I could tell on the phone he held no grudge from the last time we worked together. Then after only one day, he reported back. Brian was confident Darrell-Wayne Goff was not in his part of Canada, Toronto to Nova Scotia and refused to be compensated for his labor to find that out. He suggested I contact his colleague Charles Cox, who also had a stellar reputation for finding missing persons in Canada. Cox's territory covered Vancouver up to Mahoney's turf.

Normally I'd question any worker's speed at reaching a high confidence decision in such a brief time. At least I'd require to know their methodology. *But* I was not in the mood for Mahoney's brittle ego while keeping in mind his outstanding networks reputation for finding lost people. I gave him a pass for turning down easy money. Trust never came easy for me, still more than likely Brian knew what he was talking about, and *I* was being overly rigid. I've been accused of that on more occasions than I choose to remember.

I phoned officer Cox in Vancouver and he said, "Brian Mahoney is a good man, and I appreciate his recommending me. But I'm on the job full-time and writing a memoir about lost and found people cases I've worked to successful outcomes. Trying to do both has me seriously sleep deprive as it is."

"Brian said you were the best. This case is personal to me."

"I can give you the name of a protégé who has a natural flair for finding the missing. His moonlighting fee is going to be much less than mine."

"I can't risk a newbie on this. We already have six dead and don't have a motive.

To add complexity the missing boy is high on the autism spectrum."

"Now you've got my attention. I have an autistic niece, but she can make it hard. Let me think about it. But I'm really snowed under here at work. Who died?"

"The boy may have seen his parents' torture and murder. Four dead killers who were after him for reasons unknown other than maybe he witnessed the murder of his parents."

"Eh, interesting, we love a good mystery to occupy us on cold Canadian winter nights."

"Ever heard of an unofficial underground safe-house-network for vulnerable people?"

"No. But what you have already sounds like my kind of case and it would spice up my book."

"Then you'll take it?"

"Tell you what, it will take me a day or two to find the bottom of this pile of work on my desk. What do you say I put my protégé Arthur Dewberry on what information you have? If it gets too heavy too fast, I'll make it official business and bring a full contingent of Mounties."

"Charles, you come with the highest recommendations, but I'll still need numbers for my end. How much?"

"If you pay in American dollars, give Arthur $100 a day, plus expenses. If it gets too hefty for him, I'll pitch in pro bono. Eh neighbor, cheap enough?"

"How about I make it $300 a day plus expenses for the first five-day week. You divide it as you decide. The per diem contracts, what I know so far on this case and photos of the teenager are in an email attachment I'm sending you as we speak … okay, now it's in cyber space on its way to you … in your email inbox yet?"

"Waiting, waiting … here it comes."

"Fill out the contracts with bank account and routing numbers and I'll deposit a retainer of $1,500 in your account. We'll settle expenses when the job is over, keep receipts."

"I don't get you Yanks. I offered to do it for free and you insist on paying."

"No argument here. My insurance doesn't cover pro bono workers. If you can get the teen back in good shape, fast, there is a bonus. Any questions?"

"Yes. Looking over what you sent, this case would fit in my book nicely? May I include it?"

"I'll ask the boy's uncle for permission. Email me updates and any questions as you go. Let's talk on the phone when you have something. It was good talking with you. Bye neighbor."

"I'll put Arthur right on this. We'll be in touch."

***

During this time Coy had to make regular trips to our burb to clear up charges of resisting arrest and assaulting four police officers. My lawyer MT helped him with that. She also suggested Coy see if his aunt and uncle had their own lawyer. Rummaging through the murder scene's upstairs bedrooms, sure enough, his aunt's trucker's union supplied members legal services as a fringe benefit. He also found a bank safe deposit box key among personal papers. The union lawyer showed Coy a copy of his aunt and uncle's last will and testament. Coy was named executor and legal guardian for Darrell-Wayne. When he produced death certificates, the union lawyer would settle probate and other legal formalities to conclude the estate.

I insisted on tagging along to open the bank's safe deposit box. But as it turned out there were no surprises connected to international gangsters, anything untoward, or even all that interesting. The box held what you'd expect, life insurance policies on family members, birth certificates, earlier last wills, titles to their cars, house deed with a bank lien of $16,567, and wedding photos. As executor Coy planned to pay off the mortgage with life insurance money. Darrell-Wayne would then be worth several hundred thousand dollars, without selling the house currently valued at $350,000. That was not enough money to warrant the criminal attention the family had attracted.

Coy and I had grown close fast, first out of necessity and then more warily on my part after acknowledging deepening mutual attraction overruling my ageism. Normally I'd think I was crazy to even consider a relationship the way ours started, bartering over an impromptu blowjob. Bartering for anonymous sex was never my style. It was unthinkable. I mean, *How crazy was that?* The uniqueness of the situation made me say to myself, *Fuck it. Let the adventure begin, it's not going to amount to anything anyway. What a bizarre way to start the workday.*

Without the burden of expectations whatever developed between Coy and me appeared to take on a short life of its own. I didn't have time or interest to contemplate why I was allowing Coy into my world, beyond enjoying frivolous moments of pleasure.

He needed to find his cousin, I wanted to help, and had an agency that found lost persons. While common sense warned against trifling with gangsters, no matter what their involvement in getting Darrell-Wayne back alive superseded my parole department universal aversion to organized crime.

Coy was kept busy with activities such as buying burial plots, planning a funeral, and favorite hymns. If that didn't keep him busy enough, out of the blue, the bank in the city offered Coy the bankrupt dojo he had worked in. To sweeten the deal even more the bank would give a deep discount for ongoing banking services if Coy paid cash.

"Coy, what's up with that bank?"

Scratching his head he said, "The only thing that makes sense is they're desperate to sell and willing to accept a lower interest rate rather than take a total loss."

Naturally, Coy buying the dojo for cash meant taking me up on my silent partner offer. That meant me committing to our affiliation of hearts with hard cash. It was the first reality check on my affection. After some thought, I matched his savings and more from my rainy-day fund. Suddenly our relationship was money cash serious in a grownup way, it had been my last chance to exit the comfy closeness. I chose to stay.

Coy was glad to switch from half completed family end-of-life arrangements to start making his new dojo a success. He was more than willing to let the funeral home director finish what he started for his dead aunt and uncle. Then out of the goodness of her heart, Ameli volunteered to take on Coy's role transition tasks.

Free from the responsibilities to the dead and society, Coy signed up many of his private personal trainer clients with free one month trial dojo memberships. They spread the word. Next, he handed out flyers on street corners offering grand reopening special trial memberships. Finally, he offered a free lecture with demonstrations on self-defense at community activities in the dojo's neighborhood. The demos were well attended, and fifty new paying members signed up, the number he needed to start to show a profit over expenses.

As it happened, his opportunity came when my business hit a spike in new cases. Up to that point the time and money I was laying out to find Darrell-Wayne came from my expected chunk of reward money from rescuing the trafficked teens. That anticipated money was dwindling the longer Darrell-Wayne was missing.

With small enterprises like mine, it's often feast or famine or out of desperation attachment to a big law firm that has no relevance to QQ's original mission. When I started Queer Queries, respected advisors suggested if I want to serve an interesting gay client base, not to grow too fast and have a plan ready to downsize on a dime. So far, the advice has served me well.

You'd think both Coy and I being busy making money would interfere with expressing our affections. The opposite proved true. Setting up *his* dojo with both our different life experiences became one more thing to share and learn from and about each other.

Meanwhile, three days after my original contact Charles Cox sent an email. Arthur Dewberry has located Darrell-Wayne. The teenager was safe, seemed physically well, but we couldn't tell much more than that at present. Getting him back from the Arctic was a delicate matter, quite tricky indeed. If extracting him isn't carefully handled, we could lose him permanently to Greenland. A more detailed report would follow with particulars. By the way, what did his uncle say about inclusion in my book?

I forwarded Coy a copy of Charles Cox's email. Coy telephoned as soon as he read it and said, "How did Greenland get involved? How is he defining tricky?"

"Don't know."

"Oliver, what's going on?"

"Beats me. What do you want to do about being in his book?"

"Ugh! Let me think ... you can say Darrell-Wayne's cousin-legal-guardian says okay to be included in his book, only after my cousin is returned unharmed. But he can't use our names."

I took time to study an atlas before emailing Charles Cox what Coy had said. Cox emailed back right away, "Several irons in the fire, we'll let you know exactly what your options are and full definition of tricky when we talk. Tell the cousin thanks."

The next morning Jack Warren telephoned and said, "Sorry. Okay, Oliver. I worked this case as far into the ground it would go. We got nothing from too much trying for something. The bosses are deciding whether to let it steep until something miraculous brews or request the feds take it off our hands. You hear anything new?"

"I've nothing definite but aren't ready to quit. Thanks for the heads up, I know you didn't have to tell me."

Three hours later Willis phoned to say the fuzzy tape images of guys surveilling the crime scene were identified through facial recognition software. They are Albanians, most recently from the Bronx. Interpol has a file and open warrants for each of them from before they became U.S. citizens using different names. At the moment they are in the wind, who knows where, definitely not in the Bronx at the moment. Pleased with himself, Willis promised to let me know if anything new materialized. I told him Jack Warren had bailed on the case.

***

As much as possible Coy was sleeping at my place or I in his small studio apartment over the dojo in the city. At one sleep over at my home we cuddled after excellent sex procrastinating dinner. We were jointly contemplating preparing a healthy supper put together with odds and ends on hand or alternatively going shopping for fresh ingredients to make a well-balanced healthy meal.

Hunger overruling afterglow Coy said, "After that most satisfying mutual discharge, it's a downer to get dressed and go out shopping. Then come back and prepare food. I want to just luxuriate in your arms until the sun goes down good and proper."

"I have an idea, let's order in. My treat."

"Oliver, it isn't okay. If we are going to have an equal fifty-fifty marriage, it can't always be your treat. If concocting a somewhat nutritious dinner from your fridge and cupboard isn't possible, then takeout must be my treat. Or I know you hate the idea; but we could go Dutch."

Waving jazz-hands in the air I said, "Oh gosh, it makes me all tingly when you are so assertive and overrule me."

"That's good for me to know."

"But we can never be equals, I'm twenty-years older than you and beginning to show gray in out of the way places."

"If it bothers you, shave your pubic hair."

"That's an idea."

"I plan to still love you just as much when you're eighty and gray all over. Can you say the same for me?"

Yes, I can. I'll admit it, against my better judgment, I'm planning for the long haul with you, wrinkles and all."

"Wow, a confession of love after sex and before dinner. That's out of character for you."

"Coy, did that make you uncomfortable, sorry, choose a different topic."

"You think playing the age card is cute, but it's only sometimes."

"Mmm, checkmate?"

"You're not old just ripe, so spit a memory out." Saying that with a dismissive hand gesture, Coy phoned our favorite French restaurant. He ordered the day's house special for two and a large, green-tossed salad to share as a side.

"My meeting Ameli is a boring tale, shall I bore you."

"The restaurant says thirty-five minutes till the order is delivered. Tell me your story and out of the goodness of my heart I'll let you give the delivery person a tip."

"After a year running Queer Queries on my own, I'd resisted hiring a receptionist for as long as possible. There was something comic book heroic being my own sole employee. Also, I grew to dislike being in the office alone any more than necessary. On the other hand, the idea of my supervising someone sounded like work and that took the fun out of what I was doing."

"God forbid your fun should be diminished by doing business."

"Then I hit a wall, without a fulltime receptionist to answer the phone and take walk-ins I was losing work. It was rudely pointed out I was losing a lot of work, money, and at the expense of developing a trustworthy reputation. To make it even worse, jobs I had were getting screwed up from communications failures because I couldn't be two places at the same time."

"Help me understand how bad it got."

"By the time I got around to answer recorded telephone messages the callers had found another PI, probably with receptionists."

"Hmm, I see."

Finally, tired of filing IRS tax extensions for me because of incomplete paperwork, my part-time accountant got adamant. 'Either get office help or find another accountant.'"

"My heart, who was the boss?"

"So, begrudgingly I put the word out I'd be interviewing for a minimum wage, no benefits, fulltime receptionist in a ho hum office, situated in an unlucky tornado prone building."

"That was very brave of you to go against your own wishes and wants for the sake of your parttime accountant, and future of your business."

"I know. I'd rather face a shootout any time."

"Did all your acquaintances send their gum chomping teenage daughters and rickety old grandmothers desperate to detox from daytime soap opera addictions?"

"Who told you?"

"That's what happens when you put out a cattle-call for a minimum wage sit down job."

"You sure you want the rest of this tale? You seem to know it already."

"Most assuredly, I've not heard all of it yet. More please lover man."

"As I'm wrapping up the job interviews, none were suitable. Then in rolls Ameli. According to her, she was in the hardware store downstairs talking to a salesclerk about needing eye-woodscrews, a wallboard-hook, and wire to hang her recent college diploma. While listening to the salesperson pontificate on the importance of the right picture wire gauge for the weight of frame, she noticed a stream of either young or old women getting off the elevator. At ground floor the elevator door opens in both the hardware store and street.

"Ameli makes her hardware purchases and rolls out by the curb in front of the building. The next woman who walks out Ameli waylays. She finds out I'm interviewing for a no benefits minimum wage receptionist. Ameli is looking for work and has had too many condescending job interviews. So, she decides I'm like the others and must be a complete asshole male chauvinist pig like her previous experience seeking work. She comes up to my office intending to break my balls, and the rest is history."

"Earlier I licked your balls, they were not broken. In fact, I'd testify they are in good working order."

"From the get-go it was clear Ameli's purpose was to give me a hard time. When I did try to brush her off, she threatened to report me as a misogynist."

"You are not a misogynist. How did you settle her gripe?"

"She demanded the same interview I gave the others, or else. I'm ashamed to say I took the course of least resistance."

"Which was?"

"The other job seekers were terrible doing role plays and Ameli was better than good. But I still didn't want to hire her. I mean what kind of confidence does a receptionist with Cerebral Palsy project for a two-fisted queer private detective agency."

"I see the problem using queer in the name."

"She instantly picked up both her handicap and not being queer blocking, her being hired."

"Poor Oliver, trapped between bread and butter and political correctness. My poor baby, what did you do? Don't tell me you went all campy. That's not you."

"She said since the job was open, she was entitled to a probationary trial work period based on federal antidiscrimination laws to protect straight people from bigoted gay employers. I'm sure she made that up, but I was surprised by her ingenuity."

"I concur."

"I was trying to say no in as many *soft* ways as I could just short of pushing her wheelchair into the elevator."

"I feel the tension raising just in your telling it."

"Then a potential new client walked in off the street. Before I could get control of the situation, Ameli managed the client like a well-trained receptionist, including asking relevant prescreening questions. Don't ask me how she knew I have no idea. It was the kind of endlessly messy case I wouldn't take no matter how desperate for money."

"Wow!"

"Ameli firmly suggested the case was best suited for the police. Before there could be any talkback, she quickly scribbled the address of our tenth precinct house and gave it to the walk-in. Instead of the usual argument and hurt feelings when I decline work, the not for us client said, "Thank you so much." He left clutching the address like it was something precious. What she did was so simple the man came in for help and she gave him something tangible on that paper to leave with."

"A piece of paper *and* reason for hope."

"I hired her on the spot."

"How's that working out?"

"Okay, it's when I have to tell a client, who may have paid QQ a lot of money, final results they don't want to hear."

"Such as?"

"Humpy-dumpty can never be put back together again no matter how much love there was before he fell."

"I see the problem."

"In one scenario the client cries inconsolable rivers of tears for what seems like hours. In another the client gets so angry they need to punch whoever is in front of them. That's usually me."

"That part of your business never makes it into the noir movies."

"I know, fortunately social work school prepared us to take verbal abuse and threats for being alive. Now, these days disappointed clients go out and repeat to Ameli what I told them. Only she made up a list of therapists in this area and hands it out to our irate inconsolable clients after she lets them spill their venom and tears all over her. Her tolerance for dramatics is higher than mine."

"Goodness! You guys suffer a lot of people's pain, insults, and threats. How is Ameli still so empathetic?"

"Beats me, but that's how Ameli joined QQ, in a nutshell, and now how my work world turns."

"Given what you said, I see Ameli needing a pistol, even with her C.P. It's only the image of her brandishing that big revolver that gets stuck in my head."

"Like I said before, carrying a weapon was her idea, and so far, she isn't trigger happy."

"Do you two have office rules?"

"You mean the three cardinal P.I. questions, motive, means, and opportunity."

"No. I wouldn't presume to go there. But armed disabled citizens go against their public image and other gun owners' sense of dominance."

"The first thing I did to be sure she wouldn't hurt herself or innocent bystanders, was to take her to the gun range. By target shooting, she discovered her 410-gauge revolver is a joke at sixty feet and beyond, but very lethal at thirty or less."

"Good man, the public's safety is important."

"As is keeping my PI license."

"The doorbell means dinner has arrived. Want to open a bottle of wine while I get the door?"

Fetching a bottle of red wine and corkscrew I said, "Just to finish what I was saying, in my line of work when business is slow the old timers snoozed, solved crossword puzzles or read trashy crime novels."

"Or go ice fishing."

"Right. Now a days the newbies play video games and watch daytime T.V. soaps. That is until I hired Ameli. When business is slow now, she sets up presentations for me to give. It's her way to drum up new business to pay for the fancy benefits package she talked me into providing."

"Damn, I didn't want to mention it before, she acts like your boss."

"You got that, did you? Sometimes it does feel like I'm in a duel."

"Why was that? "

"Just because."

"I think you look so cute, all flustered."

"Public speaking was never my thing in school *where it was a required undergraduate class.* Anyway, what do I have to say to a group of strangers."

"Motive, means, and opportunity, and you walk around all self-assured like living a rich man's life. Meanwhile your house hides under a garage."

"The first of these presentations was for one of her handicapped young adult support groups. She wrote a short script on private detective process and knowing the group suggested I leave plenty of time for Q&A."

"How did it go?"

"What I was dreading turned into fun. At the end of that first presentation, I had enough crowd tested material from their questions for interesting future presentations. Even stuff enough for a standup comic routine if I want to change careers."

"Another success story. You are full of them today. Let me get the door before the doorbell gets broken."

"As you suggested I've gotten comfortable standing in front of strangers."

"Let's eat. Tomorrow, I'll contact Rome and put your names in for sainthood."

"Speaking of sainthood and such. Except for what they taught us in social work school, I don't know much about autism. If you and Darrell-Wayne come as a package deal, what further education do I need in that department?"

"My cousin Eddie, Darrell-Wayne's older brother was kind, generous, and supportive when I was growing up, especially after my parents died in a car wreck. In my bumbling way I've returned his kindness to his younger brother. Eddie had figured out how to minimize his little brother's long loud frustrated outburst. I learned from watching Eddie. He short-circuited Darrell-Wayne's rage or terror or extreme exasperation which leads to out-of-control outbursts. I use loving kindness. Unfortunately, that same approach doesn't work every time. What helps me in those times when Darrell-Wayne is out of control and nothing is working, I let him imagine I'm his big brother Eddie. I know I shouldn't facilitate a false reality, but it works when everything else failed."

"What are you telling me?"

"For me it was all on the job training. You and Darrell-Wayne will figure out how to get along between yourselves, and you'll surprise yourself when it gets loud and long."

"Didn't I read someplace there is a special therapy for autistic folks? How, about recommending a book or two for me to get a handle on autism?"

"Sorry. The family found BCB therapy too punitive for Darrell-Wayne. We feel he's already gone through too much unnecessary suffering due to his condition at the hands of money-grubbing lying sons of bitches, ass hole quacks."

"Wow, I only wanted a guidebook."

"What I've read is either crackpots' wild notions calling autism demonic possession, or at the other end of misinformation spectrum, academic research based on such small samples my cousin and most autistic people don't fit their conclusions."

"You're making my wish to help seem grim."

"You'll see, most experts are just drips under pressure." Coy's frustration showed on his face as he spoke out against malignant ignorance masquerading as promise.

Apparently, I'd hit a nerve. That seldom happens unintentionally with me. "I hear you, it's between your cousin and me to build a relationship. My intention was not to get you upset."

"No. I rarely get a chance to vent about autism. I want us to be a couple and my cousin is now my responsibility."

"I'll figure it out."

"Start by watching what I do to prevent or during outbursts."

"I should know by now there are never easy answers, or why I keep looking for them."

"I switch it around. What works for me is remembering my cousin's realities, and my generally accepted reality are different. Sometimes it feels to me like they are mutually exclusive existing in different universes, and then they're not. It's crazy making."

"I'm impressed, you know a lot more about autism than I learned in school. To be fair, working my way through, I missed a lot."

"Just remember, we all have good and bad days, so does Darrell-Wayne. Most of us occasionally wonder what we are doing here. My cousin has those days too, but without a socially acceptable way to communicate them."

"To be simplistic, in my travels people either live close to the surface of their lives, often with what is inside showing on the outside, or live mysteriously deep and only begrudgingly show small details of themselves to a few they trust. Does the later describe Darrell-Wayne?"

"I know of what you speak, the first group wants to be your best friend upon meeting you, and the second needs a lot of time to decide if friendship is even an option. If you watch closely, I think my cousin can be both depending on his mood. I want to cop out and say he's just different, but he's not if you get to know him."

"Sorry to be so dense, what do you mean?"

"So far, from time to time I get glimpses inside his head watching different situations."

"That's different, could you maybe give me an example?"

"I'll try. If I tell you, I've had a bad day. My hope is at the least you'll give me a hug and sympathetic ear to hear about it. If I saw my cousin was having a bad day and tried to give him a hug, he'd more than likely go ballistic. Riled up his brain circuits don't distinguish between being comforted and attempted murder. And yet when his friend Greggory was alive, they would instinctively know how to comfort each other. I haven't found that wavelength yet."

"Damn."

"Darrell-Wayne can't usually connect physical action and emotion, so he gets easily into frightened mental overload without probable cause."

"You lost me … why is that?"

"He can't read facial or body language."

"Yeah, but neither can blind folks. They seem to manage all right."

"Blind people intuitively know good touch from bad, most often before the touch happens. Not so with my cousin."

"Then he *is* developmentally delayed, what was called retarded back in the unenlightened backward dark ages days of my youth. Is that what *you're* saying?"

"No, *I don't think so*. Darrell-Wayne and most-higher on the autism spectrum can spell, and some like most with Asperger graduate college with high marks."

"What? Wait, you just said he doesn't have language to express himself."

"Let me explain, if I hold up an alphabet chart, my cousin can point to letters that spell words. Some of his words are complicated beyond my average high school vocabulary. But if I don't put spaces between his words it looks like gobbledygook."

"Does what he spells make sense?"

"He can accurately spell words describing what he sees and occasionally even thinks. Or feelings like he's cold, thirsty, hungry, or tired. I doubt he has a clue what empathy means but will spell *friends are supposed to be nice and not fight.* Or *it's too bad Mary lost her little lamb.*"

"So, he can read and write?"

"Thanks to the infinite patience of his special education teachers my cousin can read and write when he wants to. He isn't always in the mood. Keep in mind not all kids on the autism scale are at the same cognitive level."

"You're right, he doesn't fit what I was taught about developmental delay. Even if his communication skills are emotionally stripped-down. I'm beginning to see how every case maybe unique."

"The older Darrell-Wayne gets, the more my hope he'll have a normal life dim. Yet, I see the progress he's made interpreting a world foreign to him, using his own homegrown tools. I'd understand if a relationship with me and Darrell-Wayne seemed too much to consider. But know I'm having feelings for you Oliver Kulgu, and at the moment I'm all Darrell-Wayne has to explain his alien world to mine."

"I wonder if the Church gives a group rate for sainthood."

"Reality check, Oliver, his parents wouldn't allow him to be institutionalized. So, I won't do that no matter how hard he becomes to manage or old and feeble I get managing him."

"Hey, we both come with baggage. Let's get your cousin back and see how he adjusts to me and us together. If he's in the mood for remembering, he liked poached eggs on toast."

"He'll remember that."

"Huh, he and I did all right over that impromptu gas station breakfast, didn't we?"

"Right. He doesn't usually take to strangers. But then again, he was hungry, and you gave him hot food. Mm, he would never have eaten poached eggs if I or his mom made them, or at least not without a big fight."

"Had he agreed to that green fast?"

"Well, kind of he did. Anyway, that cleansing diet only looked good online. It never worked for us and that's why I usually avoid fads. You saved the day in more than one way."

"For the record, I didn't dislike my limited contact with Darrell-Wayne, such as it was while trying to fend off the best blow job I've ever had."

"I can be persuasive, can't I? You should hire me to work for your firm."

"One step at a time buck-ho. I look forward to more interaction with your cousin and learning to negotiate his reality. I'm not always pleased with mine."

"And the but is?"

"If you can tolerate Ameli's blunt in your face manner and your cousin can tolerate me, we might have something solid to build on."

"How do you feel about gay weddings?"

"Is that a lefthanded proposal, Coy?"

"Nothing gets past you no matter how obtuse. Yes, it's a proposal. The ring comes later."

"Sure, yes, I guess. How about a nonwhite wedding?"

"No. Wait. It seems wrong to talk about our wedding right after my aunt and uncle were murdered, and my cousin is missing. Weddings are supposed to be celebrations, and my head is not in a happy place."

"Like I said, I can be flexible."

"Being gay I never expected to have a wedding. Oliver after Eddie died and before I met you, I thought of myself as a loser loner with exceptional BJ skills. A select few who showed an interest in me I gave head, one time and then never again. It was my strict rule to avoid muddles."

"Since my college roommate died, I've not allowed myself to get close enough for anything to develop close to what we have grown. Which means I can wait till you grieve your bereavement before we talk dark-chocolate wedding cake with white piping and two grooms on top."

"Huh, could it be the stars are aligned just right for real change in our future."

"I don't know anything about star alignment, or wedding planning when the time comes."

"Once again protecting me, a lowly Army combat veteran adept at self-protection by hand-to-hand combat skills."

"If I heard you correctly, Darrell-Wayne understands our level of existence concretely by spelling words. But his emotions outside the extreme of hot or cold are beyond his grasp. Yes, or no?"

"Yes. I was told his brain works visually, where ours is by association. Anyway, that's what some doctors say. I'm not sure it's that black and white."

"Let me try to understand, I think you just said, most people experience emotions firsthand. Like me right now. While Autistic people observe emotions without feeling them. Correct?"

"Yes. But I left something out, he can draw what he observes. When he wants, he can draw accurately but without sentiment to embellish, and yet he is very possessive of his drawings."

"Does sentiment mean color instead of black and white?"

"No. He draws what he sees like a camera. Only sometimes his images look cockeyed to me, you'll see."

"So, if an object had letters, numbers, or symbols, he would accurately draw what he saw?"

"Most likely. The only issue with his drawing is if he runs out of paper and is impatient to keep drawing. Then it can be a big, long, loud problem for even distant neighbors to complain about. Darrell-Wayne was never good at postponing needs or wants."

"I too have a low frustration tolerance at not getting what I want when I want it."

"You know Oliver, I've noticed that. I think it's a good thing I submit to your every whim, *most of the time.*"

"Stop fooling around, is it remotely possible your cousin saw something while being imprisoned and drew it."

"Don't be mad. I suppose anything is possible with Darrell-Wayne. Most people don't see my cousin as autistic unless he's drawing attention to himself having a meltdown."

"I wonder if Darrell-Wayne and Ameli could forge a mutually meaningful friendship … if we encouraged it?"

"If it developed naturally, without pushing, it might be interesting to watch."

"You're right."

"I'm always right!"

"I was just fantasying Ameli taking your cousin to her young adult handicapped support group. Yes, it's true, I do have a rich fantasy life despite claims to the contrary."

"Then don't leave out their getting married, raising children, and being out of our hair except for holidays."

"Coy, you are much too young to be a grandparent."

<h1>Chapter 5.</h1>

When Charlie Cox's emailed report arrived, I didn't automatically send it to, Coy. It was longer and more complex than expected, and I needed to get my head around the information before passing it on.

Cox's conclusion gave me pause. "In the best immediate interest of the teen Darrell-Wayne Sanderson-Goff, our recommendation is to leave him in place until circumstances are more favorable for a swift clean extraction."

After rereading the report three times I telephoned Coy. "Hi, good morning. My operatives in western Canada recommend we leave your cousin with the Inuit for now. I want to set up a conference call with them after you read their report. What's your schedule look like today?"

"Wait. I don't understand, who or what are Innuits and why won't they give back my cousin?"

"Read the email I just sent you."

"I will, but who or what's an Inuit? Why do they get to decide when Darrell-Wayne comes home?"

"In Canada they are Inuit in Alaska they are Eskimos same people different geography. The reason that is, I honestly don't know. Now, please read the email."

"Oliver, this telephone call feels surreal. Especially first thing in the morning, are you feeling all right?"

"Perturbed is how I'm feeling. The guys I'm paying for fast direct action are suggesting the opposite is the best way to go."

"Whoa, coffee's ready, I'm about to wake up. Now let's go back one step. How come some people in Alaska have a different name in Canada? Oh, different geography, is that what you said? Do they speak the same language?"

"According to the email the First People in Canada includes Eskimos who aren't Inuit, and they have a different language. Why do you care?"

"English isn't a universal language."

"See there something to agree on."

"This is a long-complicated email. Look, they even included maps. You usually don't send me maps. Does that mean my allure is fading?"

"The Canadian Eskimos claimed the name first and are counted among the First People of Canada. They're more numerous and influential than the Canadian Inuit who have a different ranking as Eskimos in Alaska. If you want, during the conference call you can ask for more specifics about the Inuit.?"

"So far today, none of what you're saying is making any sense, and that's how I'm dealing with you. I don't know why we can't just go to Canada and bring Darrell-Wayne home? Like right now yesterday?"

"If you read the email, you'll find the Inuit don't like unannounced visitors. According to Charlie Cox if we or his crew come calling, announced or otherwise, more than likely your cousin will have been spirited away across the North Pole to regions known to be unfriendly to our side of the pole."

"We're already chasing, what's a little more ice and snow? We've both dealt with unfriendliness before."

"Inuit territory includes Alaska, Greenland, and Russian Siberia, not to mention the rest of northern Canada, its huge, with many hungry Polar Bears. The Inuit don't recognize boarders, for all we know they are different at each location."

"So what?"

"As far as we know Darrell-Wayne is undocumented in Canada. Are you seeing a problem?"

"Shit! You're right, it's complicated."

"My investigators say if your cousin is moved again, he could be lost to us permanently. That's the reason they want to wait."

"I don't understand, he's only a goofy eighteen-year-old whose idea of fun is his cellphone. He doesn't know Eskimo games."

"Reading between the lines of the report the underground railroad for special needs people is international with many branches. As in the past, when their government fails them, ordinary citizens find a way to meet needs."

"Ugh, the more we find out the more confusing this gets. I wish I had a clue to what was going on *and why*."

"Me too! Charlie and Arthur have little more than GPS coordinates to where your cousin is, along with word-of-mouth observations from an Inuit confidential informant."

"That's not much."

"Right, so we need to talk with them about a plan. Duh, that's the purpose of a conference call … your schedule today."

***

The conference call was not a complete waste of time. We were given the coordinates to Darrell-Wayne's latest location nearer the north pole. It was until caribou hunting season, then they followed the herd to replenish meat supplies. According to Charlie and Arthur's new sources the last living Sanderson-Goff was being well cared for. He was also as safe as possible with polar bears roaming homeless, evicted by global warming melting their ice along with disappearing food source.

Most troubling was a sincere warning from our Canadian Mounty colleagues, if we botched retrieving the teenager, we'd never see him again. They felt sure he'd be moved to Greenland or Siberia rather than kept on our side of the world's top.

Coy didn't get what he wanted from the conference call. When we ended it, he shouted in exasperation, "I WANT MY COUSIN BACK TO PROTECT HIM RIGHT NOW! I'M READY TO PACK FOR THE TRIP THIS MINUTE."

Usually, I could calm Coy down physically with a good outcome for both of us. But in this case at this time, I needed alone time to think. He knew me well enough not to interpret my silence as disinterest. Maybe I was wrong. So, I postponed my need and took a minute to calm Coy down a tad by saying, "What was your impression of Charlie Cox and Arthur Dewberry based solely on their disembodied voices?"

"Is this a test or are you changing the subject, so I'll release steam before exploding?"

"Which gets you naked in my bed fastest?"

"I'll play along, only because I love you. Just remember, I still want my cousin back post haste, and I'm ordering snowshoes in my size online soon as this jackoff call ends."

"I hear that loud and clear, mostly loud. If you want to play, answer my question."

"I'll humor you … Charles was assertive. He's probably an in your face, take charge kind of guy at work and likes bossing people around. Arthur sounded reticent. Reticent is one of your fancy words for a quiet type."

"You get any more than that?"

"Whenever possible, Arthur deferred to Charles, but he wasn't a wimp about it. He played the perfect sidekick. Those Canadians are so well mannered they make us appear the opposite."

"We could be kinder and gentler with each other down here."

"Whatever you say my league. Did I pass your test?"

"Reading between the lines do you think they might have an intimate relationship outside work?"

"Huh, recalling our part of that conversation … hm mm … yes, I can see how our closeness shows clues here and there to anyone looking for them. I mean like butch private detectives or cops acting domestic with each other for instance."

"You're good Coy. What else could you tell from just the tone of their voices?"

"Sorry, I'm not prepared for this level of queer query. My missing cousin has me ossified or at least preoccupied. What did you learn besides, I'm building my vocabulary to impress my future husband?"

"Arthur may be a good cop on his own but is subservient to Charlie in not-so-subtle ways. It fitted their hand in glove interacting."

"So?"

"I got the vibe they are a romantic couple, like us."

"Really? I missed that. What I do know is, I want my cousin back unharmed at home with me, and right now."

"We all heard you."

"Talk is cheap, I'm going to book a flight to Canada and bring Darrell-Wayne home, on my own if, I have to."

"How do you propose we do that?"

"On the computer using a credit card, now I've got the most recent GPS coordinates."

"Elucidate me, what's your plan beyond booking a flight?"

"I'll fly as close to the artic circle as possible then hire a guide, *an Inuit guide*, and just show up and grab him."

"Spouse to be consider this first, our sources say your cousin is safe, well looked after, and could disappear in an instant with little provocation. Also, he's probably without legal documentation and we don't know what will happen if the Canadian authorities grab him."

"Blah, blah, I want my cousin back home!"

"At the expense of being annoying, back to which home? The crime scene is yet to be cleaned, repaired, not to mention needing partial restoration. Your small studio apartment over the dojo is too small for two adults to live fulltime."

"Okay, okay, you've got me unstuck, what do you propose?"

"How about I offer my guest room for Darrell-Wayne to use until other arrangements are made?"

"Oliver Kulgu to my rescue once again."

"Did I mention the most pressing issue?

"What?"

"In order to keep your cousin safe, we need to know why the murders happened and unsavory men are after him."

"Don't start with that. I already have too much to think about."

"Let's coordinate our schedules for a face-to-face lie down."

"Naked?"

"Of course. But first tell me what you want done with the crime scene and let me get that started for you. That'll make the lying down part less stress soaked."

"You're right. I can't expect Darrell-Wayne to live in the house where his parents were murdered, whether he saw it happen or not. Do you think I could get away with burning down my aunt and uncle's house? That would be a quick easy fix to my problem."

"Don't think like that! I suggest selling it, but not as is, nobody would buy it with all that blood spatter, and the ghosts might object too."

"What *do* you suggest?"

"I know a company that does crime scene cleanups. Prepare yourself, they are not cheap but they're good."

"That kills it, I'm cash strapped after buying the dojo. Back to marinating rags to facilitate a spontaneous house fire."

"If you let me pay for the cleanup, I can get a big professional discount."

"Dear God, it would be so easy to let you take over everything and just concentrate on making the dojo financially sustainable."

"Sounds like a choice during difficult times."

"Except, that wouldn't be fair to you, and I'd be a wilting pansy for letting you do it. You wouldn't like me as a wilting pansy."

"I don't know. It's shrinking violets that turn me off. But my inner social worker was taught in the end you'd hate me for facilitating a dependence on me."

"That sounds about right, so what's the next plan, man?"

"We work together, I'll front the money, you can pay me back whenever. In the meantime, we continue to gather Darrell-Wayne information and keep both our businesses viable. When the signs are favorable, we retrieve your cousin with as little international muss and fuss as possible."

"Interesting, you want to share my troubles but not take over my life."

"Guilty as charged, I want to fully participate with you in your life, but not rule it."

"Oh, I see, I think. Good!"

"Then if you have no objections, I'll let Ameli manage the finer points of getting the house ready for sale. She is excellent at cold as ice, glacier like solid objectivity."

"Why are you telling me this?"

"It seems to me you are emotionally close to your full limit."

"So, you are suggesting I give up my adult responsibilities, but not facilitated firsthand by you, done by Ameli."

"No. Any action Ameli takes will be after your approval, or not at all. How's that for a level of control?"

"My hero … what's first?"

"To get the best price for the house, we'll need to empty it out. Then paint the whole place after the crime scene cleaners finish their restorations. Do you have relatives who'd want mementos from the place?"

"My minds a blank. I can't think about that right now."

"Then how about a lawn and garage sale to begin with. A worthy charity can pick up the leftovers if that's an option, or the sanitation department can carte them away to a landfill."

"I'd rather burn down the place. It would be so much simpler, faster, and give satisfaction."

"The fire department wouldn't approve. One thing you could do after the crime scene cleanup is done, sell the place as is. Call it in move in condition."

"What, an alternative to arson?"

"It would mean everything except personal items go with the house. Of course, you'll get much less money from people in a hurry to move in without furniture. They won't pay premium prices."

"I'm not looking to make money from tragedy, just close a chapter and move on. But you are so right, I couldn't ask Darrell-Wayne to live in that house of horrors or my cramped room over the dojo."

"So, we can agree on that. Now, think of relinquishing the task of fixing and selling the house to Ameli. Sometimes she is so organized it's scary."

"I don't need to sleep on it, tell her sell, sell, sell, and I'll protect you from your scary receptionist."

"If that's what you want, that's what I want."

"Phew, that wasn't so hard after all."

"I'll still need to arrange for a charity store to take personal effects, like clothes and such. You should remove family mementos like photos and trinkets before I start."

"My aunt would call them nick knacks. I'll tell you what I'll do it, if when we are together next, I don't have to think about any more of this mess. That is if you don't mind taking a vow of silence regarding that horror house?"

"In that spirit, how about while we're on the phone I have Darrell-Wayne's room recreated as best it can in my guest room? Then we won't have to speak of it again."

"Did I tell you I love you today?"

"No. But I feel your love and return it ten-times."

"You can't know how comforting your caring is during my chaos and unresolved grief."

"Focus on building your dojo and get here when you can. In the meantime, I'll clear out my guest room and have it painted. We'll have the place ready for your cousin when he comes home. Whoops, I think I said too much. Bye."

"I know you did that on purpose. Bye!"

***

At work, Ameli asked after Coy and his cousin. She had done periphery work on the missing person case even before meeting Coy. Out of habit with ongoing cases, I filled her in on developments she didn't know. Hearing myself explain a case out loud often helped me see different perspectives.

I was surprised Ameli insisted on seeing the crime scene, house, and contents before committing to help with the sale. In the past she would have been all unseen insight. I guess I should have seen that coming. I'm distracted with Coy in my world. She is not up in my face as much as before because she is busy studying to take the Private Detective licensing exam.

I also had culpability, I'd already broken my own rule allowing my personal life to come to the office and detract from professional detachment. Consequently, before Ameli could have a look see, I removed all items Coy, or Darrell-Wayne might find memorable in the future.

Ameli and I took her old, beat-up van to the crime house for an inspection. The van was on its last legs, but she paid to keep it running because of the working hydraulic wheelchair lift in back. After a roll through the house, she offered to dispose of its contents without the bother of a garage sale or snooty pick and choose attitude from second-hand stores. She believed her handicapped young adult support groups, their families, and friends, could use anything she couldn't sell online to finance selling the house in pristine condition.

While Ameli appraised the house for valuables, I boxed up all Darrell-Wayne's things I'd put aside, made notes, took paint samples, and had already clicked cellphone photos to recreate the room at my place. With my tasks out of the way, I asked Ameli if I'd created a conflict of interest at work by getting her involved in my personal life. First, she punched my hipbone *hard,* then pointed to an expensive set of kitchen knives in a big teak-wood knife-block resting on her lap. She explained they were appropriated as her fee for helping me after hours since I was a cheapskate and never paid for overtime. Once again, she proved to be a smart mouth, but worth the trouble.

She also mentions free labor, and van use would be in partial exchange for the used clothing, furniture and other household items needed by members of her support group. Since many in her group drove vans, transporting large items, like furniture, air conditioners, and other large appliances was not a problem. Able bodied family and friends of the support group were happy to lend muscle and strong backs where needed to clear out the house.

As it worked out, just from the antique furniture pieces sold to dealers and aunt's jewelry sold to jewelers, enough money was raised to pay for the crime scene cleaners discount price and a whole house interior painting by professionals.

By the time Coy could take a break from building his business and visit, his family's house had been painted inside, the outside spruced up by a landscaper, and we had appointments to meet realtors for after his approval of work so far. A medium-sized real estate company with a sales representative we both felt comfortable with was picked to sell the house. So, we went to my place for a home cooked meal to celebrate accomplishments to that point.

"Coy, before we jump in the shower, I want to show you something."

"Haven't you done enough. As it is I can't thank you adequately for taking the load of that house of terrors off my shoulders. Selling it got mixed up in with my grieving process' stupor. You helped me skip an unpleasant step. Thank you."

"Come here and look at this."

"Oh my God! How'd you put everything exactly in its right place? Darrell-Wayne is so picky where his things get placed."

"I took photos with my cellphone and the Home Center's computer matched the paint."

"Amazing! Darrell-Wayne and I mixed all the leftover flat wall paint we found in the garage to get that off-beat color. And then we only had enough for three walls. We had to go out and buy a quart of that hybrid electric blue-green color with sparkles. You saw, we used it on the short wall."

"They are all odd colors but work well together."

"What can I say, my cousin and I have weird taste?"

"I brought them colors chipped from both walls. I put his bicycles and other big sports gear in my garage, he can stow them as he likes. Having the familiar around may help him adjust after his Canadian adventure."

"What you've done is so thoughtful. Let's grab a shower so I can repay you and then let's cook. I'm horny and starved in equal measure."

"Do you know what these are?"

"Sure, the spiralbound notebooks are Darrell-Wayne's journals and that pile of loose paper sheets are his drawings. Did you look at them?"

"I did, can't make sense of the journals but some drawings are intriguing, as if from a science fiction fantasy world. Do these three have special meaning? I found them tucked under his mattress. They have a different look and leave me with a different impression than all those other drawings. Do you know what they are?"

"Looks like specialized howitzer artillery shells. I'm not sure about the marking, but if I'm right these are bad. The question is how does my cousin have the knowledge to draw them? Where could he have seen these?"

"You never mentioned being in the artillery."

"I wasn't. After basic training I thought a career in the service might be a good choice. So, I studied every manual I could find to explore assignment possibilities. Some of what I got my hands on was marked TOP SECRET, but they were left lying around just for the taking."

"Any idea what's up with the four shells Darrell-Wayne drew from different perspective angles?"

"I don't know that specific color code and numbers, but I think it might be for chemical weaponry."

"I thought chemical weapons of war were banned."

"They are, but both Iraq and Iran used them against each other in their seven-year war. The Bosnians used them against Muslims, and the Syrian government using Russia's nerve gas used it on their own citizens. So, they're banned, but used. The United Nations complains but can't do anything." Shrugging his shoulders Coy said, "I think."

"What are we doing with them?"

"The Army told us we have them for deterrence. If someone tried them on us, we'd retaliate in kind. I'm not sure what the meaning of banned is anymore. It may be all mixed up with alternative facts that seem so popular with one political party."

"Suddenly there is now a new dynamic. Could it be these shells are why people are after your cousin?"

"I don't know. Who can we ask? This is not something to keep to ourselves."

Chapter 6.

After one day rest and relaxation sex Coy was ready to return to his fledgling dojo back in the city. Some of our too short time together was spent settling details for his aunt and uncle's estate. Helping him get ready to leave I asked, "Did you think of anyone to tell about those cannon shells?"

"Not really. But what I realized is most folks don't own howitzers. So, why worry about it?"

"Don't be too sure about that?"

"What, you own a howitzer?"

"No, but when our country invaded Iraq the next thing we did after disbanding their military was to liberate their armories. Then the Pentagon ordered our military to leave the Iraq armories open and unguarded since we weren't planning to stay in country more than a minute."

"Was that so the Shiites and Sunnis would kill each other off after we left?"

"That's the rumor I heard. But hey, I have no insights into superstitions that encourage killing in the name of God, Shiite, Sunni, or otherwise."

"Was there a plan?"

"Not that I know about. It looks to me *there was not* a lot of deep thinking done, if any, to arrive at our failures over there."

"I get that from history. When politicians want to cover up their mistakes, they start a war."

"That sounds about right. Our government told the people lies to invade Iraq and then more lies to keep us busy over there. We fought for years in the name of 9/11, when the Iraqi had nothing to do with 9/11."

"But why continue to do stupid stuff after the war started? I don't get it why *does* our government have to lie so much? Oh, wait, maybe those aren't lies they're alternate facts. I guess I can't tell the difference."

"I think lying to the American people is part of a strategy, for eliminating all social programs, and giving the proceeds to rich donors to maintain power."

"Most guys I serviced with in the army were conservative, like me. They only lied about their sexual conquests or not being drunk."

"You want proof of lying conservatives. Let me list some culprits, Herbert

Hoover, Richard Nixon, Ronald Regan, father, and son Bush. Oh, and let's not forget the conservative-populist Reginald Chump, the biggest bold-faced liar, misogynist, racist, homophobe, and destroyer of intact families and democracy for all."

"Let's change the subject Oliver, you are getting too riled. Has it occurred to you we may be making more out of these artillery shells than they're worth. To my point earlier."

"How can we put a value on something banned without knowing more about their intended purpose."

"Is that why you retreated into ex-presidents?"

"Damn, Coy, you do hold me to account."

"That was a yes or no question."

"My guess is these shells are not about deterrence anymore."

"Yes or no."

"No, if they are in the underground economy, they are meant to do more than scare people. Then it would follow they are worth a lot of terrorists' money. Which could explain the attempts on Darrell-Wayne's life. But how does he know about them."

"Now, you are getting all scary to me. What do we know?"

"Coy, when it became apparent, we weren't leaving Iraq quickly, our military command, on their own, went back to secure the Iraqi armories we had liberated. Guess what?"

"What?"

"All the weapons and explosives had mysteriously disappeared between our disbanding the Iraqi military and deciding their munitions didn't need protecting. There were no witnesses, and nobody knew anything."

"Oh wait, you know I did hear something about that from the liberal media, back from when I was a kid. What's your point?"

"IED stands for improvised explosive device. Many roadside bombs started out life as *artillery shells*. Then were repurposed to explode to wreck Humvees with human beings inside!"

"I told you my cousin Eddie died from an IED, over there. After all my grieving I don't think I'm over his death and now must mourn his parents on top of it."

"I'll email my per diems working on this for an emergency eight AM Zoom virtual meeting. Do you want to invite your general?"

"He really hasn't been that helpful … but okay … why not?"

"I want. He might know what those colored stripes, letters and numbers mean and if we need be worried about them. Plus, he gives our meeting a high level of legitimacy."

***

Attending my Zoom meeting were detectives Willis Washington, George Reynolds, and Owen Branford, head of our local police antiterrorism unit. I'd never worked with Branford but both Washington and Reynolds thought it best to bring him in since we might be trampling his turf, and he had expertise we needed. I also included Canadian Mounties, Brian Mahoney, and Charlie Cox. Then to round off the zoom meeting was Brigadier General Ivan Navarro, and in my office Ameli, Coy, and me. Except for me, a more conservative group would be hard to find.

I put together a short agenda. First, greetings with a very brief pedigree for each attendee and their role to get Darrell-Wayne home. I ended each introduction asking if my information was correct and asked for opening statements if any. I anticipated some would keep their computer cameras turned off for vanity or messy office privacy.

Second, our mission to get Coy's cousin home had two new pieces of information, Inuit country, and artillery shells. So, I asked Charlie Cox to bring us up to speed as to where Darrel-Wayne was and prospects for when and how to get him home. Then I asked the General to tell us what he could about the artillery shells mixed up with the case and what precautions we should take if we encountered them. General Navarro refused to believe four of our military's top secret artillery shells were on the loose. Coy scanned Darrell-Wayne's drawings of the shells into the computer and sent digital images to the General and other attendees.

Seeing the images, General Navarro changed his mind and posture. Then said he'd expand his investigation to include sources of decommissioned poison-gas-filled shells at large. He also said, "You didn't hear this from me, but those top-secret nerve gas shells are only for a specific howitzer that flies around in the belly of a C-130 aircraft with the most sophisticated targeting capabilities." He paused to make some unflattering faces then also growled, "High up the chain of command heads will roll over a breach of protocol that loses any artillery shells." Composing himself again he said, "It is imperative we get those shells back quickly and safely."

Once again, the general's tone of voice shifted to less officious and more respectful as he digested the new information. He started speaking to us as colleagues not underlings and said, "Because of biological components in these specialized rounds they have a short shelf-life. As per military procedure, the outdated ordinance had to be returned to the manufacturer for proper disposal, followed by a long-complicated paper trail at every step of the way."

Disgust in his voice the general said, "We only know of this theft because of a child's drawings. Nevertheless, the FBI, military intelligence services, and the manufacturer will now conduct investigations with public safety first in mind, and prison for those responsible. These war heads contain very lethal heavier than air gas. If in your investigations, if any of you find them, let me know and stand clear." After awkward moments of silence, his tone softened considerably again and said, "Does anyone at this meeting know who would want such hazardous material and why?"

There was no response to his question. But Brian Mahoney broke the silent interval. "My country, Canada, doesn't use or stockpile nuclear, chemical, or biological weapons. By international law they are not allowed and illegal. Your country shouldn't have them flying around. It's a violation the whole world over. I'm speaking as a police officer who finds such munitions morally repugnant. Consequently, I cannot participate further in this missing person investigation. I am leaving this meeting at once," and he disconnected with a click followed by a blank space on his previous zoom screen.

Charlie Cox broke the silence and spoke, "I agree with Brian, except it is important to me to finish what I started, see the teenager returned safely home, and maintain my perfect return record. Especially now that he is a chapter in my hopefully soon to be published book. With that said, my involvement going forward will only be the safe return of autistic Darrell-Wayne Sanderson-Goff and like it or not I'm adding the nerve gas dilemma to spice up my book."

The General didn't look happy. In fact, he looked like a poster boy for over the counter upset stomach remedies. Nevertheless, he only said, "Everything will be denied."

To fill the void and head off a confrontation, I asked the three local detectives to tell us if anything in their notes connect Darrell-Wayne to the Inuit or apparent munition terrorists. Nothing had.

Owen Branford's contribution was to tell us he would put out a red flag terrorist alert locally, send one to DHS nationally, and started his people pounding the pavement and computer keyboards looking for nerve gas on the loose intelligence. Willis Washington and George Reynolds agreed to go over their notes and interview officers involved, and review surveillance tapes from the people trafficking, drugs, and guns bust. They would be looking for possible clues to a nerve gas connection in the mélange of solved crimes.

As the meeting ended, we had more questions than answers, nothing new there. The mood felt unsettling precarious, if not downright dangerous for unknown innocents in some evil master plan. The meeting partially accomplished one of my goals. Now we at least had a clue to the gravity of what we were up against trying to bring home a missing teen. I'd anticipated the virtual meeting to take less than an hour, it took more than two. Everyone had something to say without any real new information to give except now we knew what was in those artillery shells.

***

Twenty-seven hours after the meeting, Willis telephoned with news. He and George had done an all-nighter with neighbor's surveillance tapes, and area traffic cameras images. They put together a rough timeline possibly connecting the Pachuco-88 gang's house with the transport of the artillery shells. Coy and I had concluded the only place Darrell-Wayne was unsupervised enough to see dangerous artillery shells was while the gang held him. Although not concrete proof now we had something to work with.

Timeline: day of the bust, at 9:30 AM, a newer white Dodge cargo van pulled up to the Pachuco-88's house. A Latinx looking man got out of the passenger side of the van and physically knocked on the attached garage door. It opened electronically and the van drove inside. Then a second Latinx looking man came out of the garage and he and his passenger entered the house through the front door. About an hour later an Uber-car arrived at 10:36 AM and took the two Latinx men away to points unknown.

A check of the van license plate, from the tapes, showed it was issued to a Mazda sedan reported stolen in South Carolina, the night before. That information was not known before or during the big bust because the van wasn't there. If the stolen license plate had been reported a few hours earlier, it would have been red flagged for an interstate alert. Then there was a good chance the van could have been stopped by highway patrol and the suspected forbidden munitions detected.

At eleven AM the raid day the same Uber car returned and dropped off two men dressed as Arabs. They had a medium-size brown leather suitcase with them. After a half hour inside the gang house, the two Arab attired men left in the garage van with stolen license plates, without their suitcase. Except the van was then wearing different license plates, reported stolen from a Pennsylvania Toyota Camry. A middle-aged Latinx female was the driver with a young looking Latinx male was in the front passenger seat.

At one thirty PM, two and a half hours later, a sixteen-wheel tractor trailer pulled up and tried to load teenagers into the truck's cargo container. The surveilling police acted on the fly and rescued the kidnaped children just as their backup arrived.

The Uber car's license plate number was obtained from police stakeout dash-cam video and filed. After my Zoom meeting the Uber driver Victor Romero was brought in for questioning. George Reynolds did the preliminary interrogation in Spanish. Even though Romero didn't want to talk, his driver's logbook supplied Willis Washington with immediate answers to unasked questions. For example, the names given for the driver's pickup at the crime scene house, Renaldo Garcia, and Pedro Sanchez. The log also indicated he took his fares to the passenger train depot in Scotch Plains, New Jersey. Driver Romero made a side note, the passengers were friendly and moderate tippers.

When Willis told the driver he was about to be sent to Washington D.C. and deported as an undesirable green card holder. Unless he started cooperating with local law enforcement. Victor Romero, the Uber driver suddenly remembered he spoke English, well, and became talkative. He claimed not to be a member of Pachuco-88 but often made pickups and deliveries to and from their house because his brother-in-law Rodolfo Vasquez was a gang member. At that moment Rodolfo was in custody because he was in the house when the big bust went down.

From overhearing the frank conversation in his car, Romero surmised Garcia and Sanchez were also not gang members. He concluded they were family men with minimum wage janitor jobs working for a defense sub-contractor. A friend of a friend of a friend hired them to drive a van from Virginia to our suburb, no questions asked. They were paid in cash more money for the trip on their day off than they earned in a month working. They couldn't say no, both had children in need of extensive orthodontic work.

The Uber driver said his passengers bantered in Spanish about a half albino boy they saw brought to the house, while they were waiting for a ride to the train home. The child was flailing his arms, kicking his feet, and screaming at the top of his lungs. Seeing it was upsetting and made them want to leave, except they hadn't been paid or given their train tickets to get back home. They had no allusion who they were dealing with. If they abruptly left, they'd be found, dismembered, and killed.

Romero heard his passengers say a gang house boss told one goon to throw the screaming kid in the back of the van before his yelling upset the other drugged children. Then the boss said to no-one in particular, "If that boy doesn't shut up by the time the van leaves, someone please strangle him and bury him in back with the others."

Victor Romero said he stopped paying close attention to what his passengers were talking about when he heard they lived in Virginia not Maryland as he supposed. He knew Maryland was known for making scrumptious crab cakes, and he liked crab cakes. The rotund man claimed he could eat a dozen at one sitting. While all he knew about Virginia was from Spanish television news saying it took away the right to vote from its Black citizens.

Then Romero shut down completely when it dawned on him just knowing about plans to kill children had to be very bad for his future in this country. When grilled hard by the police, what stood out most to Romero from his passengers' conversation was the idea of strangling a child. He told them a cold sweat broke out everywhere and sent shivers down his spine. He had a son, Victor junior aka Gordo. He loved his pride and joy Gordo. As disturbed as the passengers' conversation was, was how their disgust vicariously affected him. He hadn't seen the boy but knew he was in over his head with some evil hombres, brother-in-law augmented work or not.

Mr. Romero had less to say about his passengers going *to* the gang house rather than those leaving to go to the train. He never understood the new fares names, but they wrote in his Uber logbook Salam Salami, and Ali Abdullahi. They were a prearranged pick-up from the day before, booked by his Pachuco-88 brother-in-law. The pickup was at the international airport's private aviation terminal.

While waiting for his passengers to arrive Romero inquired at the customer service counter about their origination. He was told his passengers were coming on a direct charter flight from Saudi Arabia. They finally arrived, later than expected, and were all indifferent business brusque. The two men carried one medium-sized leather suitcase between them as if it contained diamonds. Romero claimed that was all he knew other than they spoke a language he didn't understand, and they were cold bordering on rude to him.

When pushed, as only the police can prod. Victor said when he tried to chat up the Middle Eastern men in English for a bigger tip, they became even more arrogant aloof. When he asked if they were Muslim the smaller one said, "We are Sunnis, and you should mind your own God damn business, if you know what's good for you and your family."

Pretending ignorance still in pursuit of a better tip, Romero asked if there were the same number of Muslim creeds as Christian sects. His passengers sternly warned him to stay away from Shiites if he hoped for a long life. When they told him to shut up again, he knew not to expect much in the way of a tip and the cheapskates didn't disappoint him.

Victor Romero said he was glad to see the backs of his passengers from Saudi Arabia as their condescension made him feel a sense of inferiority. When they arrived at the gang house, he asked his brother-in-law if the half-albino boy had been murdered. He was again told to mind his own business, and then it was whispered, the boy settled down drawing pictures when locked in the solitary confinement of the van. Apparently, the kid didn't like to be around people.

At that point Owen Branford from antiterrorism replaced George Reynolds in the interrogation room. Washington and Reynolds had passed along what they found out from Victor Romero. Owen's team had already been told, "Hands off" by the feds. They seldom responded to federal bullying without some passive aggressive push back.

Despite diminished status in the eyes of the feds, Branford put out an *all-state alert for the van* and sent cadaver sniffing dogs to the crime scene backyard. He identified both as local police jurisdictional issues, not directly related to missing person Darrell-Wayne. Feds are not supposed to interfere with local policing.

The dogs with their handlers uncovered multiple intact human remains along with orphaned dismembered body parts. The bodies and parts were of different ages, genders, and from over a wide time-period. Once the tedious task of dating the finds and comparing them to missing persons' DNA, the cases would be turned over to the local cold case section for identification and further action. At the time of the big bust everyone was so busy and then the feds took over and no one thought to look in the backyard.

***

"Hey, Oliver, guess what? I took your advice and gave my dojo one hundred and twenty-five percent of my energy and my efforts been rewarded, big time."

"I'm all ears and ready for a break from the tedium of how I earn *my* daily bread."

"Are you coming to next Wednesday's celebration?"

"What's being celebrated?"

"Oh no big deal, just the mayor is giving my dojo a community improvement commendation. It's a proclamation on parchment paper with a gold seal, suitable for framing or laminating."

"Uh-oh! Now what did you do?"

"Oliver, you said throw myself into building the dojo business to keep my mind off Darrell-Wayne at the North Pole with Santa's little helpers. I took your advice."

"And the mayor noticed?"

"It was the local police precinct community liaison officers who noticed first and told their bosses who redeployed some of our neighborhood beat cops and anti-crime plainclothes to higher crime areas. I think they recommended the dojo to cover their asses if the reassignment didn't work out for the neighborhood."

'Uh, sweetheart, maybe you should tell me this story from the beginning. Old age may have eaten my memory bank."

"Like most dojos I let in a few local kids to do what we call work study. They keep the place clean and presentable in lieu of paying the monthly tuition which they can't afford. When the number of locals without money wanting to study martial arts grew larger than my cleaning needs, I dedicated free Monday night for the overflow. In exchange for the one-day free training, they are expected to keep the dojo's neighborhood clean of litter. As you have remarked in the past, the dojo *is* teetering on the edge of a blighted urban area."

"You're headed towards getting to a point, right, or should I take my shoes off and put my feet up?"

"Instead of just picking up litter and clearing vacant lots. The local kids and young adults, on their own started escorting senior citizens to buy groceries or to the check cashing place. Now, street crime has gone way down, and break ins practically stopped. The seniors my students escort have started watching out for them, from their windows. Crime is difficult to impossible on streets under neighbors' close surveillance."

"You got senior citizens looking out their windows twenty-four seven?"

"No dummy, it's a community effort. Moms watch out the window for their kids. Grandmoms watch in between until pops comes home from work and hangs on the stoop chatting with neighbors and a beer until suppertime."

"What a great story, residents fight to save their neighborhood, and to think you only trained them to collect litter. Congratulations, you are my hero and so I'll give you something you'll appreciate more than a plaque."

"It wasn't me, the entire community pulled together to save itself. Since the trash filled empty lots got gone, community inhabitants of different ages began planting gardens. Now they keep an eye on their greenspaces from their apartment windows and cellphone photograph undesirable looking types lurking around."

"Damn. I'm impressed. You should become a cop you have an instinct for crime reduction."

"So says the founder of Queer Queries, with mostly straight workers and straight clients."

"Point taken. "

"I saved the best news for last."

"I'm all ears. "

"A national corporate karate franchise has been scoping out our city to expand its East Coast locations. They decided to open a dojo franchise here in the city. With all the free attention I've been getting lately, I'm working close to capacity due to space limitations. The long and short of it is the franchise has made me an offer for my dojo. It's hard to turn down with me preoccupied with Darrell-Wayne missing."

"But it's your dream dojo."

"I know. My guess is they'd rather buy me out than fight me for students. They're so big and rich I'd lose the fight eventually, even though I was here first. Anyway, I want to get Darrell-Wayne back, and I'm still having good and bad days grieving for my aunt and uncle."

"How much?"

"Enough to pay you back with interest and show a nice profit on my investment. I realized a dream and now it's time for me to try something else. I've grown a lot since I met you, thanks to you."

"My loan was interest free. How will you use your time after you sell?"

"I don't know yet … I could work for you. We work well together in and out of bed."

"You'd have to fight Ameli for her job. I love you both but I'm working as hard as I can to keep my business solvent at the status quo level with everything going on."

"How about you take me on to drum up new business and only pay me a percentage of what work I bring in?"

"Um. Interesting offer."

"Had a better one today?"

"No. Mm um, my counteroffer would be for you to join the next cadet class at the police academy."

"For the God's sake, why?"

"To learn how the police do their work with procedures. After being a cop, it will be easy to pass the private investigator exam and get a concealed carry permit without paying an arm and a leg for it. You do realize your goal of us working and living together puts our romance in danger of too much familiarity, right?"

"Oh, I see method in your madness. You've finally accepted our age difference since I let you into my heart. For your information, I can't conceive of ever letting you go, and you the love of my life are afraid of commitment to me, *not too much familiarity.*"

"If you are going to offer the public an alternative to the government's police, that their taxes pay for. You better know from where and how to keep your private detective license and still give the public what they are willing to pay extra for within allowed boundaries."

"How hard will it be for me to get started with the police? I don't want to invent the wheel."

"Your military record will get you extra points for the online police civil service exam. I'll help you study the test manual and give you a letter of reference. If you want help with what to expect for the in-person interview portion, I can ask my friend Willis to coach you. You've met him he's a good guy."

From inventing the wheel Coy's mood shifted as he asked seriously, "I'm just learning my way being with you. Are you planning to make it difficult for us to work together for the sake of your Lone Ranger complex?"

"No, but I don't want to have to tell you what to do either. On the other hand, I do think you should finish up with your dojo business before joining the police force."

"Back around full circle, you coming to the Mayor's Proclamation ceremony Wednesday, or what?"

" I wouldn't miss it."

"Can I live in your house with you after I sell the dojo?"

"I'd love that and will even carry boxes to help you move."

<h1 style="text-align:center">Chapter 7.</h1>

Soon my busy existence added a new dimension. Coy's involvement morphed into *my* home routine, and it became *our* domestic life. I surprised myself, not resenting at least a little, freeing drawers, shelves, and closet space for him to use. It could be said the time was right for me to give up being single to become half a couple.

My social work training encouraged a higher probability of success as a couple if we got a new place to live as a pair. But we were too busy, and I'd already duplicated Darrell-Wayne's room in my house. When we got to a normal life, then house hunting could go on the to do list.

When not together I thought about him and caught myself doing silly things I knew he'd like and put a smile on his face. Despite the most spectacular sex I never expected to have with someone who clearly cared for me beyond just the sex, the depth of the love was mutual. Even with my life happily augmented, there was a shadow of lingering doubts.

One sure way for me to short-circuit relationship doubt was by focusing on missing Darrell-Wayne living with Innuits in the Artic. How and why was still mostly a mystery. So, when that wasn't enough to keep me distracted, there was the rather enormous potential doom and gloom from absent nerve-gas artillery shells. Which at that point only the gods knew what catastrophe they portended?

To pile on the stress, there was the matter of Ameli and Coy, each wanting to split my one-person detective agency into three semi-independent pieces. I came to think of their wishes and wants as my future *holy trinity detective agency.* Coy was almost young enough to be my son, and God help us all Ameli could be a holy ghost if she half tried, but not without objection. QQ was my progeny, and gay fathers need to be responsible too. Hey, it was my imagination for distraction, I could clutter it with what I chose.

I never mentioned the trinity to my compatriots for fear they'd make the sign of the cross and genuflect every time they saw me at the office. Although, come to think about it, if I taught them a little soft-shoe two step dance before making the sign of the cross, that could be funny for our waiting clients. No, if a client saw that little show, it would confuse them about camp, *queer,* and reason to genuflect. Nah, that would not be good for my detective business.

To keep a little balance in my madness, I started giving myself timeouts to do nothing other than clear my mind of campy thoughts by staring blankly into space, after a self-inflicted dope slap or two. The question I never got around to answering in my head was, *what do I want, versus all the needs and wants of the people I care most about. I was taught in social work graduate school to take care of myself first to then be able to help others.*

The number one reason I went to graduate school was to help people. What I discovered after graduating to the world of work was, most often a social work job is to say 'no' to clients who desperately want a 'yes.' That's the way it's structured, they don't teach you that in school. The life I'd built myself with QQ, so far anyway, had a much higher percentage of 'yeses' compared to the constant 'no, no, no,' I had to officially say at the parole office. A little autonomy for my parolees would have done them good, but alas we both had to answer to THE MAN only from opposite ends.

Several events coalesced while I was procrastinating with my reflective timeouts about risk aversion versus risk-reward. Coy sold his Dojo. Then through a light in the loafer's, attractive, gung-ho real estate agent, buyers were found for Coy's aunt, and uncle's house at a better than fair price. Then just when decks were cleared for action, the next class started at the police academy and Coy was accepted with high scores on the entrance exam, physical, psychological, and interviews coached by my friend Willis Washington.

When training was finally completed a few very young-looking cadets were offered expedited probation if they took undercover assignments that required youthful appearance. Coy was a perfect candidate with his martial arts skills better than the trainers, and boyish good looks. He said yes before I could suggest that wasn't a good idea if he was still planning to leave the police job soon after probation ended. Undercover work takes time to establish relationships and it's possible to get lost in a nefarious world.

Around this same time Ameli passed her private detective licensing exam and wrote out a detailed business plan for expanding QQ. She wanted me to give her a full partnership at a small insider's price since she was already working for QQ. She'd pay the partner fee, she set, from future work she hoped to bring into our business.

I finally faced the situation, got organized and called a two PM lunch meeting with Ameli and Coy at our favorite neighborhood greasy spoon conveniently located across the street from QQ's office. Over leftover lunch specials, my treat, I proposed naming a future joint three-way venture, Deviant Detective Associates AKA DDA.

I would keep Queer Queries for my own solo detective practice keeping to my old established ways and contacts, but as a side venue. Or Ameli could choose a name for her agency if she rather. But only when she was ready to pay her own salary. After Coy finished working with the police department, he could have the same deal as Ameli. I didn't mention under any circumstances the joint venture be called the Holy Trinity Private Investigations. However, the mental image of the two crossing themselves and genuflecting to me brought a smile to my lips.

In the meantime, we'd share my office space, and a new part-time receptionist would be engaged and trained and supervised by Ameli, when we all agreed there was a need for one. After a little haggling it was decided I'd cover all expenses until my partners could pay their fair share of ongoing operating costs. Back money owed on account would be settle when they were flushed with cash, no rush.

With an attitude a mile wide Ameli said, "You are turning Coy and me into sharecroppers, you know that, right?"

"Gosh, then I should open a company store."

"What is next for us, Oliver, indentured servitude?"

Enjoying the olive oil dressed spinach that came as a side dish with the cook's blue-ribbon special cod filet I said, "If you insist, we could put all that in the business contract and not wave the thirty-three and a third percent origination fee each that I mentioned waving."

Ameli glared at me and Coy chuckled. Then back and forth talking in a circle we again agreed Ameli could work cases she generated after hours at the office, and keep her receptionist *paid* position. That is until a conflict of interest, if any developed phasing her out of QQ in its current manifestation. We'd hire more office help and Ameli could relinquish her dual titles as sharecropper, and indentured servant to have the mantle one third partner.

Indentured servitude was not brought up again. Which is good because generally speaking social workers are by education against all forms of slavery, except their own self-imposed to care for the underserved. Coy looked relieved at not having to immediately join DDA, he enjoyed the regimentation at the police and thought he might like being a police officer for longer than we planned. Following strict structure got his mind off missing Darrell-Wayne and grieving his aunt and uncle.

I was just counting the lunch meeting a success when Ameli said, "Guess what? I almost forgot; I have inside news about those nasty runaway cannon shells you guys expressed an interest in."

She went on to tell us about Chucho Nascence a new member of one of her disabled young adult support groups. She said new members tend to talk too much at their first few meetings. They are so overjoyed to find welcoming ears that can relate to a handicapped person's point of view, they forget to give others a chance to talk.

Chucho, nineteen, originally from El Salvador, paralyzed from the waist down due to a no-fault motorcycle accident. He lives with his aunt who is also undocumented but came to the States many years before him because of her jungle fighting in Nicaragua. Now she ekes out a living in the underground economy and expects Chucho in his wheelchair to earn his keep sleeping on her sofa. Together, they do off-the-book house-cleaning along with any odd jobs they find. As it turned out, one of the houses they regularly cleaned, Monday, Wednesday, and Saturday, was the main Pachuco-88 gang residence.

When the gang's house was being raided by the police, Ms. Nascence was driving a white-cargo van, her nephew, and two middle eastern looking gentlemen out of town. They went up I-95 to an address in Boston, Massachusetts. The foreign visitors didn't possess U.S. driver licenses or read maps. Unknown to her employer, neither did Ms. Nascence, but she did possess a particularly good facsimile of a license and knew how to operate the van's GPS. Chucho did have a legal license to drive a motorcycle, but the van was not equipped to accommodate his handicap.

Once in Boston the van picked up a second driver, also a middle eastern type with bad acne scars and attitude to match them, but he spoke English. He drove them to a warehouse where their passengers were met by other men who looked like them and spoke their foreign language. Ameli explained the transport tale of mysterious goods, was told in answer to a support group member's snide question, what did Chucho do besides clean toilets.

She said Chucho in response to the group members mean comment, he hung his head and said, "I do what's necessary to survive." To make his point, he told the group he asked the middle eastern looking guy in charge, "Do you need any extra help? I can be useful and I'm willing to move to Boston."

"Don't be a stupid boy in a wheelchair, know your place and stay in it while you still can, you are nothing more than an infidel not dead yet. Don't worry, you will be soon."

"Fuck you!"

"Don't get angry gimpy-boy, I am doing you a favor."

"What favor is that?"

"Soon Boston won't be a healthy place for cockroaches like you. Go home while you still have one. Ha, ha, ha, what a stupid boy ."

Chucho told this to the support group to show he'd experienced discrimination while trying to earn his way in the world sitting in a wheelchair. He expected others with disabilities to relate. But the group's interest was mainly about being invisible and lack of access. They considered discrimination how individuals grew emotional callouses unless it was about access.

Not knowing when to stop talking Chucho went on to say, his aunt Esmeralda heard him take verbal abuse, gunned the van's engine, and shouted, "*Vamanos,*" then drove them out of the warehouse peeling rubber for half a block. She located Interstate ninety-five going south and said, "Those were bad men back there. "

"Why do you say they are bad? Maybe they're just uneducated ignorant oafs who hate me for being crippled."

"I got my intuition. Trust me, they are evil."

"EVIL?"

"I overheard them talking. It sounds like they plan to ask for a ransom in bit coins for whatever we carried. Then take the funny money and turn Boston into rubble using something called heat and pressure bombs."

"Do you understand their language?"

"No. But some English words stuck out from their language."

"Like what?"

"Thermo-baric bombs, nerve gas, ransom, and Bitcoin, maybe they're the same words in every language."

"What's a thermos-baric bomb?"

"I think it's what we used to call vacuum bombs. A large area is covered with aerosolized flammables then bombs are exploded. Heat and pressure create a vacuum that sucks oxygen out of lungs and makes building's walls collapse in on themselves."

"Geeze. Then were does the nerve gas fit in?"

"If I heard them right, they'll wait for first responders to arrive then explode nerve gas. It sounds like the plan is a one two punch to eliminate Boston. I don't know, maybe it is a plan for the rest of the country to surrender ransom out of fear."

"Damn, that does sound evil. You got all that eavesdropping a language you don't understand, damn?"

"Body language, intuition, and their mothers never taught them *not* to talk with their hands. Like I tell you."

"Uh ha, and words like Boston, thermos-baric, nerve gas, ransom, and bitcoin are universal in every mother's language, right? Sure, they are."

"Ameli, if reading between the lines your friend is telling us a plot to sacrifice a city, it sounds like overkill vindictive if only about extorting money. What's your read on what you told us?"

"Yeah, okay boss, but what else could it be? Your right, overkill vindictive to gross excess doesn't fit a shakedown."

"Absolutely, either you like Boston baked beans or you don't, neither are grounds to wipe a city off the map."

In her usual bossy way Ameli said, "Now don't go and mix everything up in your usual way of solving problems. Nobody wants to hear all that about Boston. We are Americans and want easily digestible simple small solutions closed to questions."

"I *was* going to say Boston baked beans are good with molasses brown bread slathered with cream cheese. The British eat a bland version on toast."

"Don't start with politics. It never ends well for you against me."

"Who me? Go against you?"

"Yes, you who says millions of duffuses think U.S. won the First World War, which ended in an armistice. That means after millions died, nobody won. You forget nobody cares anymore."

"Remember this, my sweet Chinese American receptionist, in this country only winners count, it's called a winner take all system. Losers get nothing and draws seldom count. We aren't playing chess."

"Oh boy, here we go again. Maybe it's thermos-baric bombs that brings that old saw out in you."

Coy had sat quietly watching us fall into our regular polarized political fencing routine. When enough quibbling had filled the room, he said, "Ameli, please stop. I don't want to hear about January 6, 2021, insurrection over another government lie. If our fellow citizens want to believe it was only an exercise in free speech, let them eat our democracy."

"But I was just getting started. Don't you want to see what you are getting into with my boss?"

"Speaking of your recitation, are you finished telling us about Chucho, his aunt, and thermo-baric weapons with a nerve gas chaser? You seemed to drift into other things, and I'd like to get my cousin back soon. Who knows how Daral-Wayne is living."

"I'm not finished yet. But don't worry, I'll end the tale right now."

With that said she patted Coy's hand and continued talking. Chucho, and his aunt returned the van to the gang-house, there were police in it and all around the area. So, they took the van to their neighborhood in the South Bronx and moved it from place to place in accordance with alternate side, street cleaning parking rules.

After a week of changing sides of streets, every other day, they got tired of the futility of driving around looking for parking big enough to accommodate a van in a congested area full of small autos. The van got poor gas milage. After another week of wasting gasoline looking for scarce parking and waiting to be contacted, they decided Pachuco-88 went out of business and was not going to give instructions or pay them what was owed. So, Chucho's aunt left the van behind a busy truck stop restaurant in Patterson, New Jersey and then hitched a ride to the bus back to New York City's public transportation.

Rethinking who she was dealing with, Esmeralda Nascence telephoned a retired gang coyote she'd used decades earlier. She only got his voice mail and left a brief message. Later that day, an ominous unknown voice telephoned her from an unidentified country and said, "If you want to stay alive go get the van you left in New Jersey. Drive it to this isolated abandoned address in Westchester County, New York and burn it. Then telephone and leave a message."

When they did as instructed, their payment for services rendered was wired to a Western Union check cashing store near their South Bronx home. The payment was twice what was originally agreed and arrived just hours after they left the voice mail. How the gang knew where they lived was troubling, since being undocumented they never gave out their location. So, for their safety they moved to Newark, New Jersey to share a basement illegal conversion with undocumented people they hadn't previously known.

Amelia's information was chilling, no matter how one felt about the Boston Red Socks and Babe Ruth becoming a New York Yankee. If true, it did fill in missing information gaps in the disappearance of Darrell-Wayne. But was no help with *why* he was to be killed. Or for that matter, *who, when, where,* and how to get the target off is back.

I asked Coy to let his General know the latest hear say. Naturally, he and his people wanted to talk to Chucho and his aunt, but we didn't know where they were located. Newark, New Jersey, is a big city, and we had reason to believe they weren't using their own names.

***

An uneventful week went by. Coy was on an undercover assignment that sounded relatively safe for a newbie cop, counterfeit video games and comic books sold after school on high school grounds by tough looking specifically high schoolers. So far, all his arrests were unarmed, he barely broke a sweat taking them in.

I gave Ameli a deadbeat dad child support case. It was more for me to have something specifically to write about her detective skills in my letter recommending her. At the satisfactory end to the case, I wrote a glowing letter for her to the licensing board. What I wrote in general was all true. She was conscientious, well organized, and a diligent hard worker. I didn't mention she had a tongue that cut deeper than most knives.

I dislike collection work, but it kept the lights on when business was slow. Without resorting to threats of jail for nonpayment of child support, my usual default. Ameli got the guy to pay what he could regularly afford, along with a payment plan for back child support in exchange for slightly longer supervised visitations with his toddler son. The ex-wife's mother paid QQ's fee promptly without a long sad story.

To celebrate completing her first QQ case successfully. I treated Ameli and Coy who had time on his hands these days, since his current undercover work shift was three PM to eleven PM. The celebration was an elaborate Thai taste sampler lunch. I had acquired a discount coupon from the orthodontist downstairs who owed me favors for collecting from deadbeat patients.

***

When I hired Ameli, she found ways to boost my business to pay for her benefits package. With her new private eye license, she found special needs cases, not in competition with my regular business, but in numbers high enough to interfere with her usual receptionist all around office helper, my sidekick job.

Her complaints needing office help grew in volume along with her budding practice. I figured she'd hit a dry spell soon we all did from time to time, and she could catch up with her filing backlog, and other office tasks left undone. Instead of a lull in work, she got a contract to supply handicapped security guards to a large-sheltered workshop. She used pages from the training manual I'd developed for *my* per diem workers to train and supervise her new unarmed security guards.

I'd been either in the field or working from home for weeks when it became unavoidable for me to go to the office. Ameli wasn't there when I arrived, and someone I'd never seen before was sitting at her reception desk.

"Who are you, and where is Ameli?"

Showing me a full set of pearly white teeth in a big welcoming smile he said, "Welcome to Queer Queries. *How may I help you?*"

"I don't know you and yet I'm the founder, and owner of QQ. Why do you suppose that is stranger?"

"I'm Chucho. Ameli is on a steak-out and will return later today. Ameli hired me Mr. Oliver Kulgu. If I may say so, it's nice to finally get to meet you, sir."

Chucho Nascence looked nineteen, with a slight spattering of acne across both cheeks and chin to drive that point home. From the waist up he looked vibrant and strong. Ameli's desk and his dark-blue electric wheelchair under it obscured his lower body. The shape of his head on gym built muscular shoulders, along with potential movie star handsome face suggested conquistador ancestors. He had big, bright, warm, light brown eyes and pushed out a hand for me to shake. His grip was manly firm but not overly macho. That scored points with me, I didn't need to crush his hand.

"Do you know why I'm here today?"

"Let me check. You are early for a 3:30 exit interview with Mr. Greenblatt, you have a mediation with Ms. Shubets and Ace refabrication at 5:00 PM, and an intake interview at 6:30 with Ms. Gilhooley."

"Please pull the first two case records and bring them to my office."

"I already placed them on top of your full in-basket and prepared a new case folder for your 6:30."

"That's impressive, what have you been up to since?"

"I dusted and vacuumed your office, the conference room, waiting area, and put bowls of fresh fruit out here and in the conference room. Amelia said you like the office to look welcoming. The fruit was my idea, candy lasts longer but is not healthy."

"Chucho, what do you do if someone comes in here looking for trouble?"

"Dial 911 and duck. Oh, you mean … there is this panic button here, it rings a deafening alarm and people come up from the hardware store and dentist."

"You seem well trained how much is Ameli paying you?"

"Minimum wage no benefits, Monday, and Wednesday, nine to five, extra shifts when needed. Are you going to fire me now?"

I was experiencing a slow burn, had an urge to fire Ameli and keep Chucho, or better still fire them both and return to simpler operations. Downsizing appeared attractive or to start over with office robots. Instead, after a quick think said, "No. Are you doing a full week of work in two days? The pile for filing used to be up to here, now it's gone. Where did it go?"

"In the filing cabinets, filed. I do everything I can to earn my wages."

"Can you work a full week Monday through Friday?"

"Yes, I'd love that. Ameli said you'd probably fire me on the spot. I prepared myself to be axed. But I'm not disappointed, honest."

"She told me you are undocumented. For my business to be compliant with the law, I'll need you to see my lawyer about immigration status. She's a fixer. I suspect at the least we can get you a temporary work visa."

"Would you sponsor me?"

"Maybe later, let's first see how this arrangement works out without me having to fire you. I may still fire Ameli."

"Be careful, she carries a gun."

"I carry two."

"Can I have one too?"

"Absolutely not until I know you better. Shoot outs at the office are frowned upon by the better business bureau, private investigator licensing board, and my neighbors unless they're shooting too."

***

It had been too long since I'd sat at my desk doing office work, but the dust bunnies and grit I expected were missing. Most of what was *in* my overflowing basket was junk mail, and what wasn't, I dispatched quickly with a signature going in a self-addressed return envelope. If Ameli was working in the office, she'd have screened my voice mail and forwarded the important messages. But she was out on a stakeout. Clearly Chucho hadn't been trained to check my voice mail.

Since I had no previous business with Owen Branford, or his antiterrorism task force, I was surprised when he gave my voice mail an update courtesy call. It seems the third-hand information I passed along to him through my friend Willis, about Boston being leveled by vacuum bombs, netted Branford points with Department of Homeland Security higher ups.

In return for the information, DHS gave him what he needed to raid a Jihadist suicide vest making apartment in my town. He'd just concluded the raid, no bombs exploded, none of his people were hurt, and the bad guys were either shot dead or in custody. Owen Branford thanked me and said if I ever need a favor just ask. I made a note. That's how my business runs.

Chapter 8.

My cellphone woke me at 6:30 AM, and my free arm shot out to mute the ringer. Coy curled up spooning my back had the other arm captured by his arm across my chest. His deep breathing indicated he was deep in dreamland. He'd stayed after his regular three to eleven shift to book a comic book forgery suspect. It was his first arrest and booking with multiple warrants from other agencies. He could have let others oversee the formalities but wanted to learn the complex time-consuming process. Coy didn't get home, ate the snack I left him, shower and get into bed until 4:00 AM.

I gingerly took the phone out to the kitchen and began the process, put fire under water to boil, grind coffee beans, and added a pinch of salt to complete the preparatory ritual. Nobody calls me at 7:30 AM or should know better.

Sounding altogether too bright and bushy tailed for that hour of the day, Charlie Cox on the other end of the phone line said, "I'm about to grab Darrell-Wayne from the Inuit. If you can move fast, we'll turn him over to you at 10:30 AM our time, that's 11:30 AM yours. Meet me on the Canadian side of the Ambassador Bridge. Do you know it?"

"No."

"It spans Windsor, Canada and Detroit, U.S.A. Don't be late, otherwise Canada takes the boy into protective custody for whoever knows how long. Handing him off to you makes for a more exciting story for my book. If his uncle signs a predated missing person form, I get to keep my job without a big formal inquiry."

"Do you two think you can get here on time?"

"Yes. It'll be tight."

I woke Coy, bleary eyed from two and a half hours' sleep and told him to dress fast in his police uniform. Having gone directly undercover he only used it for funerals, parades, and fancy dress up formal ceremonies. While he dressed, I phoned Westchester airfield where I keep my plane and had them ready it for immediate takeoff. Next, I fired up the computer and filed a flight plan to Detroit, Michigan, and then phoned for an Uber ride. It was going to be tight time wise, but if we could make the Metro north train to my plane and get the promised tail wind, it would be doable.

Still looking groggy, Coy stuck his head in my home office wanting to know if he should take his sidearm. I said, "Yes. I'm taking two forty calibers. We don't know who's trying to kill Darrell-Wayne or their reach once we have him back. Give me a kiss and then let's go amigo."

"You mean mi amore."

"I do, and this is happening if we hurry."

In the Uber to the train, I filled Cory in on recent Canadian events. A sleep deprived Canadian border control agent in Toronto, working her third double shift in a row due to a new covid virus variant sweeping that country, made an on-the-job mistake. Instead of a computer verifying no outstanding warrens *by passport number* for an arriving passenger, she put in the passenger's name as it appeared on the document. The computer search indicated the passenger Surinam-Jones-Obscura didn't have a valid passport, but its number would have gone through without a problem. When the border agent's supervisor ran facial recognition software, she found multiple outstanding Interpol murder warrants for Otto Uwe, a high-priced international hitman associated with the Boynton Assassin's Organization. Canadian Immigration immediately took Mr. Uwe into custody. They searched his luggage and found an envelope with Darrell-Wayne's photographs, particulars, and GPS coordinates to his location in the upper Arctic.

When Brian Mahoney saw the police alert with Darrell-Wayne's photo he phoned Charlie Cox and told him the local alert would go nationwide in a matter of hours. For us to get Darrell-Wayne back post haste, Coy needed to sign a preexisted Canadian missing person's report in Windsor, Canada. Then we needed Darrell-Wayne out of Canada before the Canadian alert for protective custody got there.

We got to my Cessna 208 Caravan in record time, and were air born slightly ahead of schedule. Rather than sleep during my preflight check, Coy was talkative. "Did you buy this plane military surplus? The last base I was stationed in had these planes painted in aerial camouflage. The army calls them C-16s and uses them for aerial surveillance and artillery spotting. Army pilots love them, but now drones are replacing most army manned flights."

"I inherited it from the original owner as payment for an investigation job. Can't sleep?"

"No. I am too wired at finally getting my cousin back. If you don't mind telling, I'd like to hear how you came by an airplane as payment."

"Why?"

"I'm just wondering what else about you I don't know yet."

So, I told Coy in the early days of QQ I took on an unnecessarily complicated waste of my time private eye case. The client insisted we meet over dinner at his home with his wife present. He kept insisting something was wrong in his life and wanted me to find out what and a remedy. He was sure he'd been cursed. But wouldn't do what his wife and I both wanted and get a complete physical examination. Before I completed my final report my client died when his heart exploded, it was a preventable heart attack not a curse.

When I approached the dead man's wife for my fee, she said all monies were tied up in probate and could be for years with past wives vying for money. Then she suggested I take her husband's plane as payment. As his executor she could do that and hated her husband's taste in aircraft. She preferred piloting twin engines planes. She said she needed an extra engine if one failed.

At that time, the Cessna 208 was worth more than twice my bill, and then some. Her husband kept it in her name for tax purposes. The aircraft came with prepaid maintenance and indoor parking, for ten years. My client had gotten a great deal on a long-term contract. "Coy, what else do you want to know about me?"

"Between social work school and the Probation Department, when did you learn to fly small planes?"

"During high school I was an Air Explorer Scout. We logged hours flying small planes with our Scoutmasters for our future license. Then you know I was a Peace Corps volunteer for two years right after high school, right?"

"Doing what? I should have expected you'd been a boy scout. Weren't all social workers?"

"Crop-dusting was part of an agricultural program I was promoting in Africa. We were always short of pilots. I already knew how to fly by the seat of my pants from scouting. By the time I came home I had enough documented flight time to get my private pilot's license one two three."

"You've lived an interesting life before I joined it."

"I can say the same for you. But I have a strict rule, no talking on takeoff and landings, got it?"

With finger to lips zipping closed, Coy uttered, "Mumm," then shook his head up and down.

***

The control tower was expecting us as per the flight plan, I'd filed from home. Directed in without cross winds we had one of my famous smooth as glass landings. I completed the paperwork formalities on the ground quicker here than at my chatty home field. Then I left orders to gas up the Cessna and have it ready for takeoff in an hour.

The waiting Uber had us across the Ambassador Bridge in record time. After Coy's signature was witnessed on the missing persons form we were told to wait outside the office while copies were made. We were no sooner getting comfortable in front of the building, then Darrell-Wayne with Cox on one side and Dewberry on the other came out of the building's side entrance. They greeted us formally and handed over copies of necessary documents to clear U.S. Boarder Control.

"Hey, guys! Job well done. Why does Darrell-Wayne look so droopy?"

"Eh! We had to shoot him with a tranquilizer dart. He dynamically didn't want to leave the Innuits. By the way, they weren't exactly happy to see him go. But with international assassins and the Canadian government on his tail you folks better get out of town while you can. Good luck, we'll be in touch."

With that said we walked over to our waiting Uber. Darrell-Wayne looked to be somnambulating but gave the slightest sleep laced acknowledgment to Coy. Me he ignored as if I wasn't there. We packed Darrell-Wayne in the back seat, Coy on one side me on the other.

I said, "Driver, back to our pickup point as fast as is legal. Please."

Coy gave me a side glance and then said, "Driver, to be on the safe side, let us know if we are followed after we clear U.S. Immigration."

Then it hit me. "What is that gawd awful smell?"

Coy pointed down at already sleeping Darrell-Wayne. I'm a detective, I'm supposed to notice these things. It was then I saw he was wearing an outfit made from small animal furs, stitched together by hand with the fur on the inside of the garments. The repugnant smell he gave off was forty percent stinky fish, thirty-five percent something warm blooded too long dead, and twenty-five percent heavy dollar store artificial rose scented cloying perfume.

Right after the border check, the driver staring in the rearview mirror said, "We got a tail. It's a good one, I can't shake him."

"Are you armed?"

"This is Detroit, what do you think?" After saying that, the driver produced a heavy frame revolver Dirty Harry might have liked and put the big weapon on the seat next to him.

"If you can't lose the tail prepare for shooting." The driver stomped on his accelerator and wildly maneuvered in and out of medium dense traffic. The big silver colored Town-car handled better than I'd expect from an American vehicle. Checking through the back window I saw we were pursued by a new model Swedish high-performance automobile. Rather than take expressway then highway to airport, the way we came. The driver exited the expressway into an industrial area of winding streets and alleyways. Just when I thought we'd ditched the pursuit car it was right back on our bumper.

Our driver said, "They must be local. Their driver knows these alleys as good as me. Watch out he's coming along side us."

I pulled both my forty calibers from shoulder holsters and elbowed open the left rear passenger's door twelve inches. As the chase car came along side, I fired rounds from both weapons into its right front tire sidewall while keeping the door propped open on my shoulder. Between my pistols' reports and an exploding tire, I hardly got my car door shut as the chase car sunk hard to the pavement then swerved at us. Our driver was on the ball and veered just out of range of the careening big Swedish car experiencing sudden loss of inflation at high speed. Coy had his nine-millimeter service weapon in his fist at the ready, to back me up. Darrell-Wayne slept deeply through the noise and rough swerving bouncing ride.

Sparks flew as the big Swedish car scrapped its right side along a brick alley wall before stopping a fraction of an inch short of a line of overflowing metal garbage dumpsters filled with industrial scrap. I watched with interest as our driver made rights and lefts racing down twisting alleys. Then apparently, he decided we were no longer being chased. He slowed and pulled over to the curb, and like it just dawned on him said, "I'm calling the police."

"You have a uniformed police officer in this car with you. How many cops do you need?"

"You people are not from around here. Those guys acted local."

"Then I'd suggest while the bad guys are replacing their tire with a donut spare, we get the hell out of here before they come limping back after us. Isn't that what you'd expect around here?"

"Sounds right."

"Then, driver, I imagine you have a choice, lose a whole day's wages repeating I don't know. To too many local cops of different ranks. Or finish what you started and get us to the airport quick, pocket a generous tip, and get on with the rest of your workday. It's your choice because you don't know anything and don't want to know. *Do you? This is Detroit.*" With that said I reloaded and holstered my guns. The driver didn't need much time to settle on what was in his best interest and had us back on the highway moving fast toward the airport.

Actions speak louder than words. While Coy loaded Darrell-Wayne into the back of the Cessna, I gave our driver three $100 bills plus the agreed amount fee for the ride. Then I went and paid for the aircraft's fuel, its fees, and had us airborne faster than I expected.

***

I circled our home field three times checking the ground for assassins before landing. I'd phoned my friend Willis right after takeoff and told him we had Darrell-Wayne and how and why we needed an armed escort home. He was waiting with a couple of his men as I taxied the plane up to its hanger. They were in two unmarked cars. I'd asked for one. There were no bad guys in sight.

"Willis, I didn't expect you to personally meet us. You must have better things to do."

"Get in the damn car Oliver OK." When I got into Willis' car he said, "I'm taking you home. The train looks like asking for trouble."

"Trouble?"

"It smells like you've already had your slice of Detroit trouble today."

"Yeah?"

"You smell of gunpowder." With that said he had us heading back to my place. Coy and Darrell-Wayne in back, me in the right front passenger seat. Periodically, the other unmarked police car passed us on the road scouting ahead, then it would fall back and followed as we passed through intersections.

When we approached the turnoff to the train station I said, "Don't you think I've put you out enough, today?"

"No. I don't. I know you; you wouldn't have called if it was nothing."

"You've got my number. I just hate being a pest."

"I've got no love lost for Boston, but as an American citizen I won't let foreigners' level our historic monuments. You, sure your house is safe enough for the teenager."

"I recently upgraded security to use it as a model for clients, even put in a safe room in an existing cave below the house. How about I do something similar at your place as a thank you for all your help?"

"That's okay, what's new besides a safe room?"

"I've got every inch of my place surrounded by highest quality lowlight cameras activated by motion detectors. I got the equipment wholesale. It's state of the art. Sure you don't want?"

"No, that's all right. At the moment I only want that kid safe. I've already received reward money from this caper from you, a promotion in rank, and a fancy new job with the District Attorney."

"Okay then, do you have any news?"

"Coy's general got those nerve gas shells back after a shootout up in Boston. The bastards were going to wait until first responders from the surrounding area arrived and then blowup nerve gas from four different wind directions. Can you imagine the devastation? But the Feds are still trying to unravel the source of the plot and details. They think it's some rich foreign guy with a grudge against Boston. My guess is they don't know anything yet."

"It's good news those shells are back, thanks a lot for that."

"Oh, you'll like this, the General had those shells' teste fired. They were all duds the biologicals were too old."

"That's one of the many things I like about you, Willis, you're objective and never take matters personally. I used to be just like you until I lost my mind in a pizzeria shootout in my early twenties."

"It is personal. I just don't show how I feel when unknown persons are trying to kill a kid whose life, I had a hand in rescuing. I'm invested in keeping your family alive."

"I'm touched, you care."

"Oliver OK, *I have to*, I know you'd do the same for me and mine."

"Thank you, Willis Washington. I'm choked up with emotion and I would kiss you except my future husband is in the back seat and could get the wrong idea."

"Yeah, okay. Oliver, that and a Metro card will get you a ride on the city's subway."

***

The first order of business once we were securely locked in my house was to scrub Darrell-Wayne's stink away in the shower. Then let him soak in calming lavender scented bath while his indigenous clothing was sealed in multilayers of heavy plastic and stored in the back of the garage. My next role should have been to go to the kitchen and prepare a late lunch. But I dilly dallied on the off chance Coy needed an extra hand dressing his cousin. I'd noticed Darrell-Wayne viewing Coy's police uniform with unease.

Sure, enough dressing the kid turned into a battle of wills and much more than a one-man job. Darrell-Wayne squirmed, kicked, hit, bit, and continuously shrieked loudly at high pitch. Finally, we hit a stalemate with the three of us sitting on the floor looking defiant at each other. Darrell-Wayne wearing nothing more than one sock and undershirt.

Having had enough, I got up and marched to the kitchen, to quickly return with a cylinder-shaped box of dark-chocolate ice cream, and a spoon. While Darrell-Wayne got busy spooning the frozen confection while I held the box. Coy got him into his new-old freshly washed clothes. Then Coy picked him up from the bathroom floor and the two disappeared into the boy's new-old bedroom replica, formally my guestroom.

Dutifully I went to the kitchen and put together a lite lunch. A repass I imagined an eighteen-year-old who looked twelve and acted much younger would want to eat after a chocolate ice cream starter course. In the end it was a simple menu of fridge contents displayed with a smidgen of creativity. Even an autistic teen whose been living on whale blubber has to have a post bath inclination toward soup and sandwich lunch. Or so I hoped.

As the leftovers' meal on the fly finished coming together Coy and Darrell-Wayne entered the kitchen, dressed in his familiar clothes from his old home. He sat down looking ready to eat. When he wasn't freaking out, he was a good-looking, if spooky young man to be. Overall, Coy looked relieved his cousin was with us safe and sound. Or at least relieved he was dressed.

I'd put together an assortment of meat and cheese sandwiches and fresh tomato soup. It wasn't much but was filling. Darrell-Wayne only became animated when I presented him with a bowl of more chocolate ice cream, covered in dark chocolate sauce, with dark chocolate sprinkles on top. Yes, I'd remembered Darrell-Wayne had a thing for chocolate on chocolate on chocolate. After lunch, the cousins took a long nap together in Darrell-Wayne's recreated bedroom.

I went to work in my home office and was making good headway clearing up an overdue paperwork backlog on a pending court case. Then the motion detector camera at the front gate pinged and a screen clicked on showing an extra-large black SUV drive up and park. Then the other gate's camera pinged, and a second SUV with dark windows was at that gate. Realizing who might be calling, I flipped a coin to decide whether to telephone my lawyer, or not.

I gave MT an urgent call. She's my lesbian lawyer who prefers to be called Mack Truck. MT is the best I can muster during the Me-Too Movement against misogynist language. I gave her a brief account of recent events. At the same time SUV visitors at the gates incessantly pushed both doorbell buttons.

MT said, "Patch me through to the main front gate, record the conversation and only speak if I tell you." That's why I pay her a high fee. When she takes charge there is never talk back.

She spoke to my suburb visitors from her city office through the all-weather outdoor audio speakers. "What's your business here?"

"We're FBI and have a warrant to take Darrell-Wayne Goff into protective custody. Is he inside this house?"

"Show the security camera each of your identification papers and forementioned warrant."

"Who are you?"

"I'm Darrell-Wayne's lawyer."

"I'm agent in charge Jameer Nacho and if you don't open this gate, I *will* have heavy equipment bought here and break it down."

"Keep your pants on, Agent Nachos. I am recording this conversation as is the property owner whose costly security system you just threatened to damage."

"Cut the bullshit lady and open the damn gate. This is an official FBI matter."

"The youth mentioned in your warrant has witnessed horrific trauma and needs therapeutic rest. He is currently napping with his cousin an armed local police officer."

"We have a threat warning from Canada. He is in danger and one police officer is not adequate protection."

"Can you really trust what the Canadians say? Remember they burned down our White House in 1812. If your employer is the federal government, I wouldn't be too quick to forget that agent Corn Chip Dip."

"It was the English who burned down our White House because we tried to annex Canada. That was a long time ago, we don't want Canada anymore, too much ice and snow."

"You must have had a good breakfast to be ready to debate history with a lawyer."

"It was a misunderstanding, and we got a National Anthem and a new White House out of it, and the Canadians forgave us with a promise not counter invade us anymore."

"Wasn't that lovely."

"For your information lady my name is Nachos not Corn Chip Dip, *show some respect.*"

"How do you plan to assure us you won't further traumatize Darrell-Wayne's delicate mental state after all he's been through?"

"It has been reported to us, *officially,* international assassins want to kill the teen. The FBI is not in favor of such an action and has the capacity to assure his safety and mental health while fending off physical threats on his life. Now open these gates or I'll knock them down."

I could tell MT's threat tolerance had been reached when she said, "Oliver, allow agent Nachos and only him into your house and video his every move. If Darrell-

Wayne doesn't want to go with him, I'll have a court injunction hand delivered to his boss at FBI headquarters and he will go on his merry way empty handed. Did you understand everything I said Mr. Jameer Nachos?"

He had, and when he entered my house wanted to speak with my lawyer face to face. When I showed him how he'd spoken with her virtually, he seemed even more pissed off.

When I produced a video camera and turned it on Nachos took his anger down a notch and treated me with a minimal degree of IRS tax paying homeowner courtesy. To stall for MT to explore options. I made a show for agent Nachos to see the rest of my state-of-the-art home electronic security system that was also recording his every invasive move.

Impressed with the advancements in home security he said, "I suppose you also have a safe room in this house?"

"I do, except it's secret and separate from the house. It's underground in a cave but can only be entered from inside this dwelling. Pretty neat, right? Sorry, I can't show it to you."

"Why didn't you stash the teen there and tell me he wasn't here?"

"I was expecting the FBI to come calling sooner or later. Canada tends to be forgiving about our imperialist grab for their country but conscientious about citizens' personal safety."

"You didn't answer my question."

"You'd eventually find out. That's what you do and lying to the FBI is a crime. I wanted to get a good look at you, because I'm not convinced you can do a better job protecting Darrell-Wayne than I can. That's why my lawyer is virtually with, us during our recorded conversation."

"Let me ease your mind, fella, there are a lot more of us than just you, and we have safe houses everywhere, not just one safe room. Not to worry, we won't charge you beyond your annual taxes for fantastic protection."

"I wonder why I don't feel reassured."

"Think about this, if you don't cooperate, we'll put you in jail, while we do what we do best, protection. By our standards *you* are small potatoes and protecting the boy is our priority right now. Understand?"

Just then MT zoomed back in and said through the speaker system, "The judge says if the child goes willingly today, we'll settle this in court on another day soon. If he fights you, the judge says he will stay with his cousin for now. I can have an injunction saying that they're in your hand within minutes if he refuses to go. Oliver, you may let Agent Nachos see Darrell-Wayne."

My man and his cousin were curled together sleeping soundly on top of the covers in Darrell-Wayne's new bed in his old bedroom facsimile. Nachos took a moment to look around the boy's room. Then he went over and gently separated the two sleeping figures, and lifted Darrell-Wayne into his arms and carried him out of the room. I saw the teen's eyes open wide and register what was happening. He was on the edge of a meltdown, then saw me. I smiled and waved at him, and Darrell-Wayne reclosed his eyes and went back to sleep. The FBI man gave off a good gentle vibe with the teen, like he had experienced handling volatile children. Nachos cologne smelled light and fruity, maybe Darrell-Wayne was ready for a snack. I waved goodbye as they left my house and drove off in a convoy of big black SUVs.

***

I was just about ready to go wake Coy for his three to eleven shifts when he walked into the office and said, "Where is Darrell-Wayne?"

"He willingly left with the FBI."

"Why didn't you stop them?"

"They were ten people with guns and a warrant, and I and MT couldn't get an injunction if he left willingly."

"You should have *woken* me."

"You haven't slept more than a few hours in the last forty-eight. I didn't need backup with MT on the phone the whole time. She and I did what we could, but your cousin didn't fight going."

"How long will they hold him?"

"They said not long. But it's open-ended because of the idea of a thermo-baric event in Boston on everyone's mind. The local police there have killed or captured low-level creeps involved. Your friend the general, using military intelligence operatives has the nerve gas shells back and killed or captured higher ups in the chain of bad guys to a point. As soon as Homeland's terrorism joint task force has identified and eliminated or captured the masterminds behind trying to kill your cousin and Boston, Darrell-Wayne comes home."

"That doesn't sound like soon."

"I'm just saying what the FBI had on their warrant."

"Sounds bureaucratic."

"The FBI agent in charge thinks only a week or less to wrap it up. I don't know, in my experience the big fish are harder to catch than the little ones. But hey, I'm not much of a fisherman."

"I wonder, is he safer with the FBI than the Inuit. Ugh, no, I don't think my cousin is safer in government hands than he'd be with us?"

"The FBI seems to think otherwise, they told me there are many of them and few of us. Plus, they work twenty-four-seven, and have a wide array of safe houses."

"Do you agree with them?"

"No. Personally, I'd feel better if we had him here. I don't like the arrangement but couldn't stop them without going to jail."

"Damn, just think about it, all this because I ran out of gasoline, and you needed a blow job."

"Speaking of which, as a protective future measure, what do you say we replace our current vehicles with all electric cars?"

"Don't try to be funny. I'm in a serious mood."

"Who me? I'm deadly serious. The future is electric wheels."

"Are you going to be neutered as part of your electric car plan? If you are, I don't approve."

"*I like it* when you are so assertive. After work tonight I can show you how much."

"Promises, promises. That reminds me, we've been so busy lately I forgot to mention something."

"What?"

In the police station changing room getting ready for his shift, without intending to Coy overheard gossip. Two older police officers were chatting while putting on their uniforms to go out on patrol. It seems one of their wives had fallen and broken her neck while equestrian jumping, or playing polo, he couldn't remember. Anyway, a professor at the university recently implanted electrodes on either side of her spinal cord break. Though still at an experimental stage, she now shows limited ability to move her lower extremities. According to that cop, his wife is making up for the sex they missed during her full paralysis.

"Oliver, I thought you might want to pass that information on to Ameli."

"Why? She didn't break her neck. But I'm seriously considering firing her along with that neck."

"For what reason?"

"Hiring Chucho after I said not to. I'm still the owner CEO of QQ."

"Don't fire her, yell at her, what she needs is discipline. That's what we did in the army, make her run laps, and do pushups. You might be surprised, what you'll find out after she shapes up."

"You know what? I like your common-sense approach to solving my problems. You have my permission to do that whenever the spirit moves you and I'm being erratic. Although, I'm not so sure your methods work with people in wheelchairs. You know running laps and doing pushups may require more than she can manage."

"Thank you and fuck you."

"Tell me again why this prattle has relevance to a university professor with electrodes and my receptionist."

"The why you ask? Well, maybe her handicapped support group isn't keeping up with the latest advancements in electricity. Or your new employee Chucho's spaghetti limp dick doesn't drive him nuts like it would me."

"I'm touched you care about QQ's staff before joining my rag tag team."

"It's you I care about, doofus. It looks like you have a major aversion to acting as boss."

"The army really taught you to be a disciplinarian, didn't they?"

"Yes. The army said I had potential for a career, and then they changed everything around to downsize."

"Did you get a name and phone number for this university guy?"

"I did."

"Then I'll talk to him first, rather than get Chucho's hopes up for disappointment."

"Coming right up my leigh. Let me see I know it's here somewhere."

"Uh. What confetti are you fidgeting with?"

"I have pockets full of these little scraps of paper people scribbled on for me not to forget something. Before I met you, I would have called them trick slips."

"I remember trick slips."

"Those I threw away as soon as I received them, these are not from tricks."

"Why throw away the numbers who cared enough to want a repeat tryst?"

"As I have demonstrated for you, I am a connoisseur cocksucker. After Eddie, precious few cocks or their attached owners were worthy of a second go round. I was looking for Mr. Right. Now I'm stuck on you and no other need apply. I've always been a one man's man. I just needed to find my man, and that would be you."

"I'm flattered. Now where's that professor's trick slip?"

"Ah, flattery makes you uncomfortable. Oh, here you go, Professor Gabriel Graboski, MD, PhD. He's a neurologist, whatever that is, and has a doctorate in electrical-medical-bioengineering. He works at the university, and I overheard has a private practice for the disabled obscenely rich."

Chapter 9.

A week came and went and then after a court hearing the FBI started bringing Darrell-Wayne to my house for semi-regular visits. But supposedly on one of Coy's rotating days off which also changed without warning. Seldom were we given more than a day's advance notice of a visit. Consequently, it was hard to make elaborate future fun plans before he arrived. The visits lasted six hours, no more or less, except when they were canceled at the last minute leaving us with an overabundance of dark chocolate ice cream.

After dropping off the teen, federal agents stayed just outside the perimeter of my house, on guard. It looked like a regent, or at least the hoy ploy was visiting. Then just when we were into having fun Darrell-Wayne was whisked away without a word when he'd be back to finish whatever we had been doing. A lot of cookies got burned because of that.

Coming to us Darrell-Wayne appeared out of it, probably stupefied from association with his stiff FBI minders. But he was lively with us and never wanted to leave when it was time. The FBI supervisors swore they weren't giving him drugs. What we could see was weight he'd gained with the Inuit was melting away fast, and he didn't look happy with his new caretakers.

The whole situation felt unnatural, and I didn't appreciate the minuscule shifting information as to when the teen would be returned permanently. To add to my consternation, every few visits the FBI would cancel at the last moment, without explanation giving a namby-pan-by weak apology. I sensed unspoken anger directed at me by Coy for the FBI's unacceptable rude behavior followed by insincere feeble apologies.

Part of our FBI problem was our developing relationship while working different hours. Coy's restrained anger at me noticeably changed how we gave up small secret bits of information to each other as relationship building gifts. We slowed the exchange, became cautious, then stopped sharing as our frustrations with the FBI intruding on us seemed to peak.

The problem finally came out when Coy said, "Lately you look like you are walking on eggshells around me and that's making me tiptoe around you. What's going on with us?"

"I think you're mad at me for letting Darrell-Wayne go without a fight."

"I'm not. There was nothing you could do with a 10:1 ratio. Maybe you are mad at you for what *you* haven't done so far. Anything else on your mind?"

"No."

"Want to spar a few rounds to clear the air?"

"Not really. I like putting my hands on your body, but not with violence."

"Oliver, I'd like to know what you are thinking when you shut down like you've been doing lately. With what's going on out there, we don't have time for misunderstandings between us. Do you hear me?"

Then the alarm started. It was a day the FBI canceled their visit just a few minutes earlier, and as usual without explanation. With the ear-piercing alarm blaring up and down the chromatic scale with robust high to low shrieking pitches. We ran to my home office at full speed. Coy punched numbers into our everyday handgun safe, during Darrell-Wayne's visits gun safety was a priority. I scrutinized the security screens for an intruder.

"Stop. This won't be a job for sidearms. I'll get us better weapons from the saferoom. While I do that, check online for Kamikaze drones." I rushed to open the saferoom bomb proof door then the locked armory inside. I pulled out two Remington 1100 twelve-gage shotguns and grabbed two boxes of high brass, steel shot shells.

Back in my home office I tossed Coy a shotgun and box of shells. "Load up, did you find our birds?"

"Yes. The five smaller ones are #46s, Swiss made for Hiromoto. They each have a thirty calibers mini-machine gun with fifty rounds of ammunition, and an explosive shrapnel payload equivalent to a stick of dynamite."

"Those little devils."

"They get attention after emptying their machine gun by crashing into a target and blowing themselves up. According to the World Wide Web, that big drone hovering over there is unarmed and for reconnaissance only. It directs those little Kamikazes but can be replaced by direct base command if knocked out."

My shotgun loaded I brought a straight back chair to below each high casement window. One corner, and the opposite side of the room were then covered. I cranked the windows all the way open. Without a word Coy climbed on a chair as I had the other, and we poked shotguns through the open windows. I said, "Lead your target by a gun barrel width, like shooting traps. They seem to be looking for something to shoot at, let's take them down looking."

We both found a target in range and fired. Coy's blew apart in midair. When I hit mine, it dipped, wobbled, then rapidly flew straight up into electric power lines, and burst into a fireball raining sparks. The home office went dark, and all the electronics shut down with a whoosh followed by palpable silence. Then I heard my propane whole house electric generator in the saferoom kick on and then there was light again.

Both our shotguns had extended magazines, so they took five shot shells instead of the usual three. By the time I was reloading a third time, all the kamikazes had exploded, and only the big reconnaissance drone was still hovering air born just out of shotgun range. Then Coy hit it twice with his sidearm. Its rotor-blade detached, slicing sideways down the hillside. The body full of no doubt expensive electronic gear crashed landed onto my driveway with a muffled thump spilling circuit boards and optical scanners hither and yon.

After making sure all the visitors from the unfriendly skies were fully dispatched to drone heaven. I telephoned Owen at our local police antiterrorism unit and suggested he and his people might like a look at expensive hardware that once flew and now littered the grounds around my house. He asked if I could give his people two hours before telling the FBI, who would come at once and scoop everything up and whisk it away. I said take three and grabbed Coy and we headed for a quick shower and possibly *rub and tug* to celebrate our win over lethal flying robots.

***

Four hours later I explained to Jameer Nachos I hadn't phoned him earlier about our drone attack because he never informed us of reasons for canceling Darrell-Wayne' visits, or even meant it, saying sorry. He was royally pissed at me, a lowly private investigator not respecting his betters. Owen's people hadn't only taken photographs they'd made plaster impressions and hadn't cleaned up after themselves. I could see Jameer was trying to think of something to save face or arrest and charge me with offending the FBI's high and mighty prominence in the law enforcement world. But he'd already spoken to my lawyer MT and was not man enough to face her again, and a sincere sorry didn't seem to be in his vocabulary.

"Bureau policy is you don't need to know every little thing about our operation."

"Then I don't think the Bureau needs to be contacted every time I'm under terrorist attack when my local police have a perfectly good antiterrorist unit ready to help quid-pro-quo. *Comprendo. key-mo-savy?*"

"I'm not arresting you at the moment only because it would take time from protecting the kid, and that's my primary mission. But you are skating on thin ice with me. I see jail for you in your future."

"On what charges?"

"I can always come up with something. We're always looking."

"Do you want my lawyer's number. Just so you know, she is feared in high places."

"Yeah, yeah. Just between us, Darrell-Wayne woke up with the sniffles today and the medical committee decided it better he not travel. Consideration of your health was a factor in the decision."

"An elected committee concerned with my health. I don't know what to say."

"No election, appointed by the bureaucracy."

"Oh, so how are his sniffles doing?"

"It's a common cold. He'll be fine soon so say auguries that indicate safe travel."

"You people are too much. If you'd given Coy or me advanced notice, we wouldn't have been home for a drone attack today. Oh, while I'm going off about *unsafe* travel for my health, what are you going to do about your glaring security leak that put Darrell-Wayne and the rest of us in danger today? Are special prognostications required?"

"How about I move your notification level up one notch and we send you a coded message an hour before we leave for visit?"

"At this point anything you did would be appreciated. Just between us, I'd still find your leak and plug it as a matter of concern for my safety. But hey what do I know? I don't understand bureaucracies or go fishing that much."

***

It was supposed to be Coy's day off. We'd gotten a coded FBI alert the night before, Darrell-Wayne would be visiting the next day, as usual exact time left blank. We were looking forward to the visit with fun plans we knew the teen would like. Lately he'd been missing scheduled visits for purported legitimate reasons.

Eagerly waiting for the FBI's indeterminate early or late arrival, Coy and I were sitting at the kitchen counter with mugs of coffee, chatting. Then the phone rang, one of Coy's undercover investigations had blown up. He was ordered to rush to the police station to observe, through a one-way glass, the questioning of his main suspect, in custody for a different crime. With mixed emotions Coy left the house giving me a perfunctory kiss going out the door.

I was just heading back to my coffee when I noticed a glint from the foothill opposite the back of my house. It was a brief sparkle; one I'd never seen there before. Grabbing a pair of high-power binoculars, I scanned the hillside. Then I telephoned the special agent in charge Jameer Nachos on his cellphone. "Hey, is that your sniper nest behind my house?"

"Hell no. When did you see it?"

"Just now."

"I'll divert Darrell-Wayne back to the safe house and get a chopper in the air. Don't go outside or talk to anyone."

Ten minutes later I heard the unmistakable sound of a helicopter chopping air overhead. It was combing back and forth over my back foothills. Then two of the usual three cars that bring Darrell-Wayne to visit, honked to enter the side gate. I buzzed open that gate and two oversize black sports utility vehicles drove in. I rushed upstairs to see if Darrell-Wayne had arrived despite being diverted. I still had trouble trusting my government to keep its word, broken promises went back centuries. Three FBI agents were standing guard as a third dressed in Darrell-Wayne's blue ball cap and Levi jacket exited the second SUV.

After a skipped heartbeat, all hell broke loose. The Darrell-Wayne look a like's head exploded in a geyser of blood and bone fragments sending the ballcap flying back a distance. Off in the distance I heard a muffled rifle's report and noticed the FBI agents had pull their weapons while scurrying for cover. After a scant second, I heard bursts of heavy machine gun fire mixed in with helicopter sounds. It was coming from the direction behind my house where the sound of the rifle shot originated.

I rushed back downstairs and into the house to the kitchen wall of windows, I grabbed up my binoculars. Scanning the hill, I found the sniper and her spotter dressed in ghillie suits. They looked dead lying lifeless in dark pools of what must have been their blood. Then the larger of two helicopters reared up over the hills and circled twice. Both choppers landed, and crews disembarked, took photos, then carried off the dead sniper, her spotter, and their equipment. Then left as deftly as they arrived. With the whirly birds gone the hills became deathly quiet.

My cellphone chimed; it was agent in charge Nachos sounding upset. "Oliver, you alright?"

"I guess. One of yours is down and left quite a bloody mess in my driveway. Should I call the local police and report it?"

"No. I told you, don't talk to anyone, let me manage this. She was a good agent."

"You should be sensitive replacing Darrell-Wayne's cap and jacket. They were his favorites from before his Inuit adventure. As you may have noticed, he goes ballistic when his belongings are touched."

"What about you? You don't sound like yourself."

"I just saw a young person gunned down a few feet in front of me. What do you expect, I wasn't prepared to see that."

"Yeah, I lost a good agent today. She volunteered to be the decoy. I should have said no. Yours should be such a simple case and it seems like one thing after another with you."

"Treat Darrell-Wayne gently. He's seen too much death in his young life."

"For God's sake don't tell me how to do my job. In fact, for that, I'm suspending all his visits until we find the leak that led to this."

"I trusted you. Jameer, you told me everything was under your control. I'm contacting the Attorney General over the death and mayhem you brought to my front door today."

"The Attorney General will only make my job more difficult. In fact, don't talk to anyone about anything without clearing it with me first. Understood? Otherwise, I'm taking you into custody as a material witness."

"Fuck you!" To show my displeasure and unprofessionalism of the moment I broke the phone connection with prejudice. I'm trained not to show emotion, and always to be completely objective in search of solutions. I wasn't feeling my training just then. What I felt was numb and walked to my home office like an automaton. I'd just witnessed a Darrell-Wayne lookalike's violent death mere feet in front of my face.

What I witnessed was too personal. Locked doors deep inside my psyche suddenly flew open flooding me with fears I never expected I'd have. Maybe because I wasn't prepared to see it, or because the victim was dressed exactly like Darrell-Wayne. It could have been Coy or me felled by the sniper. My knees buckled and I wanted to roll into a fetal ball, but I didn't, social workers are trained to fight no matter the odds.

Without forethought or any thought for that matter, I unlocked my personal gun safe, removed my old Probation Department issue six-shot revolver, loaded it, and pocketed an extra handful of .357 magnum hollow point Kevlar piercing bullets. I hadn't touched the weapon in decades, other than keep it oiled. My unconscious mind must have been at work, normally I carry modern semiautomatic sidearms with large capacity magazines. The old weapon from an earlier simple time functioned as a security blanket to sooth my scrambled psyche. It had saved my life in that pizzeria shootout years ago, then never saw service again, and now some part of me wanted it back protecting me.

Like a tennis player self-coaching during a match, I said out loud to myself, "What are you doing?" Stunned at the sound of my voice I said, "This situation does not call for a gun, any gun, especially an old six shooter. Are you sucking your thumb because you saw something you didn't want to see? Grow up, okay, don't regress to age four?"

That thought got no traction in my upset over stimulated brain. Without premeditation, I mechanically tucked my old service revolver's six-inch long gun barrel into the waistband of my slacks. I don't know why handling the old weapon felt comforting like slipping into an old pair of perfectly broken in slippers.

My full consciousness rushed back when the desk telephone buzzed, "Queer Queries. This is Oliver, how my I help you?"

"I'll be pulling up in less than five minutes, have the front gate open. Lately my van stalls out when it's supposed to idle."

"Ameli, this is not a good time for a visit."

"I'm not visiting, I have important papers for you to sign along with checks made out by the accountant to keep your business running, and my rent paid. *Open the damn gate before I get there. Okay!*"

"I'm mad at you."

"Get over yourself you have a business to run."

One reason I have my own business is an aversion to taking orders. I checked all the security monitors, nothing was moving. So, I pushed the button to open the front gate for Ameli's van and hit a second button for it to close automatically once she passed through. I walked upstairs to the front of the house leaving the front door below open behind me. Just then Ameli drove up, her van engine coughing. She nodded a greeting while hydraulically lowering her chair to the ground. Then she lowered Chucho in his wheelchair. I felt something was off, even ominous, or I might be losing my mind from before. I walked; they took the wheelchair ramp downstairs into the house in silence.

We'd no sooner entered the living room than the security screens flipped on and beeped. Out of the corner of my eye I watched a car pull up to my now closed front gate. Two men got out of the car and left a driver behind the wheel. Without a word to my new arrivals, I ran back upstairs to the driveway. Seeing me suddenly show up, they waved for me to come over.

Feeling myself again, with both my receptionists safe and secure inside the house, I walked close to Ameli's van, as if I were heading toward the men outside the gate. When at the last second, I took evasive action by ducking down, the men I'd never seen before pulled out automatics with silencers attached and fired large caliber handguns at me . Their bullets pierced the back of the van causing ping sounds that snapped me back alert.

I duckwalked back to the stairs, then ran down into the house and said, "Anyone hit? You, okay?" When I got looks that said, *What are you crazy*? I said, "Go to the safe room, lock yourself in, now!"

Ameli glanced at the security screen and saw bullet holes in the back of her van. Then with her hand on her holstered pistol said, "I see what you mean about this wasn't a good time to visit. Oh shit, look at the screen, that guy is climbing over your gate."

I ran back outside, up the stair. One of the intruders had climbed to the top of the stone column that supports one half the heavy metal sliding electronic gate. Seeing me, he stopped climbing over to the other side, drew his gun, and fired three shots in my direction.

I didn't think about it, my old double action revolver was in my hand, hammer cocked, from years ago training my finger squeezed the trigger, and a bullet caught the intruder in the middle of the chest.

The man froze a second, then fell backward, off the flagstone column and onto the top of the car he'd arrived in. He landed with a loud bang, concaving the car's roof. The other guy, now with a pistol in each hand, let loose a barrage of bullets in my direction. He was a little late coming to his friend's aid. I sidestepped seeking cover behind Ameli's van again. When he stopped shooting, I crept around to the front of the van.

Our eyes met, his were cold dead fisheyes. He was quickly reloading ammunition into his gun's magazines. Finished, he slammed the ammo-clips into the gun butts, slid the bolts back to cock the hammers, and raised his guns to shoot at me some more. I shot first and hit him between his dead eyes. I ducked down and moved, then a quick peek showed that second man had also fallen backward. It's hard on you to stop a .357 bullet with your head. So, now he was draped over the right side of the car hood. His dead fisheyes were wide open staring at the clear blue sky, an automatic dangling from each fist. The third guy behind the wheel hadn't moved. He sat scrunched down behind the car's steering wheel, not moving a hair. He looked young. I crouched down again and duckwalked back to get Ameli's van full length between us.

I turned and ran down the stairs about to go into the house, but Ameli was in the doorway, her pistol in hand. She said, "I called 911. Give me your noisy gun." My brain fog stupor had returned. I didn't hand it over right away, so, she grabbed it out of my hand, then rolled back inside. I stood there immobilized, staring like a mannequin with a thumb up his kazoo, I was barely cognizant of what had just happened. *Had I just killed two guys who were shooting at me? Who were they? What was that about?* In a daze I wandered back upstairs to the driveway to see what I'd done.

What happened next was fast, in a blur, no doubt due to my surging adrenaline or other hormones, or some other excuse. Who knows, I don't, I was in a fog. The driver of the shooters' car got the engine started, put it in gear, and then must have realized he couldn't see to move the vehicle. A dead body on the roof was draining blood onto the windshield while another corpse draped artfully across the hood further blocked the driver's visibility.

Just then a police car pulled up, siren blaring, emergency lights flashing. Two uniformed officers jumped out of their patrol car, saw dead bodies and blood, and drew their weapons. The interloper exited his vehicle, a gun in hand. The cops shouted something unintelligible from where I was crouching. Then there was an exchange of gunfire. I don't know who shot first but lying on the ground looking very dead was the bad guy's driver who looked like a kid Darrell-Wayne's age. It was stairstep symmetry, one dead man draped on the roof, one laying on the car's hood, and junior lying dead on the ground next to the vehicle. It wasn't staged, it was a real death tableau, with two discombobulated police officers showing mixed emotions flashing across their faces. I could guess what they were thinking, I was on the same channel.

The younger cop's face drained white in acknowledgment of what just happened, while the older cop spoke to his radio. The younger officer mustered himself and walked over to the downed youth, who they'd shot multiple times, and checked him to see if he was alive. At least that's how I interpreted what I saw. The dead boy didn't respond to being checked. Then two more patrol cars suddenly arrived, sirens screaming and lights flashing.

Staring dumbly, the next thing I registered was a sergeant standing at my front gate demanding I open it. That brought me back into semi-focus as my brain fog lifted a little. Without knowing why, I mumbled, "Do you have a warrant?" I guess some training dies faster than others.

"I don't need one. These three dead bodies serve that purpose. Open the damn gate or we'll dismantle it.

"Well, don't be like that, it's an expensive gate."

She just glared at me.

"All right then, let me accommodate you." Fumbling in the bushes I found and pushed the hidden outside button to slide the gate back.

"What happened here?"

"Duh, I give. What?"

"Is this your house?"

"Yes."

"Can you see those three dead bodies outside your gate?"

"Yes. But you said it, they are not on my property, and weren't there earlier. Anyway, I don't know them, and it looks like I will never have that opportunity."

"I'm taking you to the police station for lack of cooperation. I don't need this shit today. Is anyone in your house?"

"What is your name, sergeant? You have black tape stuck over your badge number."

Turning to her officers she said, "Would somebody please cuff this retard?" Turning back to me she said, "I'm patrol sergeant Jackson of the local police. At the expense of redundancy, let me repeat myself, *IS ANYONE IN YOUR HOUSE?*"

"You don't have to shout. Yes, two of my employees. We are all fine, and you are bullying me. I'm a taxpayer who doesn't appreciate being bullied."

"Is this your van?"

"No."

The sergeant walked to the front of Ameli's van then stopped short. She was standing over the pool of FBI blood and gore, a blue ball cap with bullet hole front to back. "Where's the body for this one?"

I shook my head no, and honestly said, "I don't know."

"Four dead bodies in one day will not improve this property's value, mister. You trying to set a record or what?"

"No comment."

"Better speak up and cooperate buster, or I'll let my baton demonstrate bullying in action."

"Actually … so far today's count is six dead. One was an FBI agent, two were snipers, but I was ordered not to speak about them under penalty of law. Your threat has put me in an untenable position. I'm in trouble if I speak and you threaten me with physical violence if I don't. I need a nap, or at least my lawyer present."

"Who gave you an order not to cooperate with me?"

"Special Agent Jameer Nachos of the FBI. Just so you know, he doesn't like to be yelled at and tells me that all the time. I don't like it much either." Hanging my head and shutting up, I took out my wallet and handed her Jameer's business card. Then it occurred to me why Ameli had taken my gun. All the cops drew their weapons when I reached for my wallet. They were trigger happy by association with three shot dead outside my front gate. The sergeant standing so close to me is what saved me from being plugged full of holes.

"Nachos, I like nachos with a cold beer and a thick extra spicy dip on the side. How'd you come by this card?"

"He gave it to me."

"Is this his only telephone number? It looks like a main switchboard."

"Turn the card over. The handwritten number on the back is his personal cell phone."

"Won't you need this number, after I beat you bloody to demonstrate bullying?"

"I have both his numbers on speed dial. Oh, and my lawyer is on her way. She knows a thing or two about police brutality. Just a word to the wise sergeant."

"Speed dial the handwritten number and hand me your cellphone."

With clarity, I realized in a flash, by following the Sergeant's orders I wasn't just saving myself wasted time repeatedly answering the same questions at the police station, but most likely my private detective's license to boot. "Here you go Sergeant Jackson." I handed her my cellphone with a bow and obsequious hand gesture. She made a face showing displeasure at my dramatics.

"Hello. This is Sergeant Melissa Jackson local P.D. Who am I speaking with? ... Agent Nacho, I know this is Oliver Kulgu's cellphone ... He just handed it to me ... Let's cut the crap, agent, did you or didn't you tell Mr. Kulgu not to talk with the local police about a homicide on his property? ... by whose authority? ... Listen, buddy, we have three bloody corpses outside his front gate ... I don't know who they are yet ... hold on, ... just wait a God damn second will yah, ... I'll check on that for you because *I am a professional.*" With that said, the sergeant handed my phone back with a look I suspect *was serious* gastric distress. Possibly her heartburn was caused by too spicy corn chip dip, *or* realizing I wasn't as developmentally delayed as she first concluded.

"Hello, Jameer. It's me. Is Darrell-Wayne all right ... did he get a new hat and jacket?" With that said Melissa was back with her hand out for my phone. I complied, not wanting to be bashed with her baton in the other hand.

"The driver's name is Andrew Boynton III, the other two bare a slight family resemblance but are without identification ... no, I never heard the name Boynton ... a family ... international what ... assassins ... shit ... you're welcome to it ... then how long will it take your people to get over here? ... tell you what I'll leave two men to guard the crime scene till your people show up ... you are most welcome to this case ... my cops' and my written report can be gotten from Captain Vega ... Goodbye and good luck with this shitstorm." Turning to me she said, "Go inside your house and wait for the FBI. Oh, and don't talk to anyone." She winked when she said it and handed me my cellphone.

Walking back down the stairs to the house and Ameli and Chucho I felt my brain click back into full function. I tried to fill in the missing half of a phone conversation I'd just overheard. For the moment it appeared I wouldn't be held responsible for the two men I'd killed. For my conscience it was a case of self-defense, although not everyone might see it that way. Equal parts of relief and indignation stirred around in my restored brain and gut. Then reality set in, I had to protect Coy and Darrell-Wayne from who knew how many more of these shooters before I could formally take responsibility for what I'd just done.

When I got to the front door, it was slightly ajar. Pushing it open I found two wheelchair jockeys parked, ears alert eavesdropping on the other side of the door. "Okay, you two couldn't find the safe room, fine. Go to my home office." I led the way down the short hall, plopped behind my antique black-walnut desk, and gave the two an expectant look. When nothing came forth, I told Ameli, "I'm still angry with you."

" What did I do?"

I gave her a disbelieving stare.

"What I saw was self-protective any way you slice it. I'll swear to it in court. I don't think they can hang you for defending us and your home against criminals."

"That's mighty Christian of you Ameli to come to that conclusion as my judge and jury."

"Oh, here is your gun back. I never saw you use this one at the firing range. It's much heavier and louder than your Glocks, and Sigs. Why are you mad at me?"

"I told Chucho I'm considering firing you for hiring him after I told you not to."

"Whatever you do, don't call me *a dragon lady*, or I'll sue you for discrimination."

"I never called you that! It would be racist. But since you always bring it up when we have these disputes, I think you want me to."

"No. I don't. Chucho did he say he was going to fire me for hiring you?"

"He said *thinking* about it. I didn't say anything because it was still at the thinking stage, and between you two. I'm not stupid, I know it means to be out of a job one way or another. What's to talk about?"

"Well then, I quit. But why do I have to?"

"I already said, you hired Chucho after I said not to."

"For your information I hired him for me not you. I pay him to help me keep up with your work, that's true. But only when my own detective work interferes with keeping my office duties up to five-star quality. He works for me not you. I pay him from my private investigator work."

"How long did you plan to subcontract?"

"Look, I had two cases, solved them both and now don't need Chucho's help until I get more work. You know how this business goes. Sorry Chucho."

"Ameli, where did you pick up the tail that shot at me and holes in your van?"

"We were talking, I wasn't paying close attention."

"Think! Where?"

"I first saw them parked at the end of your street. They weren't a tail, more like on a stakeout."

"If you are still working for me, I need you to go on the dark web."

"Then move your but from behind your desk, what am I looking for?" I got up and moved my desk chair out of her way and took a seat on the sofa, as her chair whirred behind my desktop computer. "You overheard the Sergeant's conversation, try Boynton family."

"So, Chucho have you given any thought to my job offer?"

"I did but wanted to see if you and Ameli worked out your differences. I'm not a home wrecker but can start right away if you still want me."

"Does your aunt have a gun?"

"What does that have to do with me working for you?"

"Six people died from guns around this house, so far today. I can't be responsible twenty-four seven for protecting my workers."

"Give me a gun."

"Don't know you well enough. Have you had firearms safety training?"

"No. I don't know if my aunt has a gun. But she definitely knows how to use one."

"How's that?"

"In her younger days she was a guerrilla fighter in Central America. She fought on our side against your fascist President Ronald Reagan's side in our civil wars."

"Reagan's undeclared war in Central America and against the U.S. Congress doesn't get taught in school up here in North America."

"Do you at least teach Reagan's blunders in the Lebanese civil war. Oh, hope you don't mind my speaking about what's taught back home and around the world since you don't teach it here."

"Whatever. Ask your aunt if she has access to a firearm. I may have a job for her."

"She could use a steady job. How about she cleans your house and office for a fair-trade price and less than you pay now?"

Ameli lit up and ejaculated. "Holy shit!"

"What?"

"You won't like this. Boynton is the name of a family of assassins based in Belarus formerly from Ireland. The Belarus president uses them to eliminate dissenters in his country. They also work freelance hit jobs outside Belarus. Look here is a picture of three generations of the family, there are forty-two family members and more associates. No birth control for them. Any look familiar? Hint, hint, front gate."

"Damn! What a big family. I bet they're Roman Catholic and can hold a grudge."

We heard shouting from inside the house, *"Honey I'm home. What's Ameli's van doing in front* with shiny new air holes in its backside." Coy continued to talk to himself loud enough for us to hear. "I had to park up the street, there are officious looking men power washing our driveway and the street in front of the house. You never mentioned exterior work for today."

I shouted back, *"We're in the office."*

Coy came in and gave me a kiss, looked around, and said, "I see Ameli has finally taken over. Good for her. Have you retired to cook and care for me full time in the manner to which I wish to get accustomed?"

"Come look at this photo on the computer. Anyone look familiar?"

"Huh, isn't that the guy the Canadians snagged at their border. The one who wanted to kill Darrell-Wayne in the artic."

"These two were killed by the FBI earlier today, out back, after they killed an agent dressed like Darrell-Wayne, right in our freshly power washed driveway. These three met their end outside our front gate a little while ago. And that is why the power-washing you mentioned is taking place to cause you inconvenient parking."

"How many you shoot?"

"These two. The local cops exchanged fire with that one and then he got dead. It was a two: one ratio both times going in different directions."

"Damn! Is that why Sergeant Jackson has the mad out on you?"

"I could tell she suspects me of something but knows better than mess with the FBI's Nachos, without cold beer. What'd she say?"

"Nothing. She just threw me an evil eye when I was pointed out to her. Normally she doesn't know I exist. She's the best training sergeant but a real ball buster."

"Sorry I screwed that up for you."

"That's okay, I got you. What should *we* do about this over large family of killers?"

"Get Darrell-Wayne back from the FBI. Set up our own twenty-four-seven-armed security and wait for the other thirty-six Boynton and God knows how many associates to come calling."

"Sounds like a tall order. Want the U.S. Military to help?"

"On what grounds? You aren't suggesting starting a war with Belarus, are you?"

"No. I'd have to find out where it is first."

"In my experience, sometimes smaller is better. No FBI leaks for instance."

"If I didn't know you better, I'd think you were anti-FBI."

"I'll talk to Jameer after he gets over losing an agent due to *leaks*, I've been warning him since that drone attack."

"That was less than memorable and should have been prevented by them in the first place."

"Be nice, in a pinch we could still use the FBI for back up, as a last chance option."

"Fine! What's for dinner? Oh, did you tell Chucho about the university professor?"

"I didn't have a chance. My day has been disrupted by shootings. Why don't you?"

"You know more about it."

Chucho perked up at the sound of his name. "What professor? What?"

"Assistant Professor Gabriel Graboski, M.D. neurologist, Ph.D. bioengineer, the guys got a whole alphabet soup of letters after his name."

"I don't impress so easily stuck in a wheelchair. What's he want with me?"

"It is my hope you don't mind I spoke to him about your accident. As a result, he wants to speak with you. That is if you're interested in being one of his test subjects in a clinical trial."

"Let me guess, you told him I'm depressed over my dead dick. Thanks, Oliver."

"He just got new funding for his ongoing research study. So far, he's only had female test subjects and wants male participants also."

"Why is that do you suppose?"

"You could ask the good doctor yourself. I have his number if you want."

"How about tell me what you know. Then I'll decide."

"What you said before about your cock wasn't that far off the point. Apparently, many females don't know when they are lubricating, or so they say. At the same time, it would not conform with university rules for the good doctor, his doctoral fellows, or university graduate students to place a finger or other probe inside to find out."

Ameli, feeling left out of the conversation after quitting then keeping her job said, "It comes from how we are socialized for MEN's use. Most of us are taught that part of our anatomy must be avoided at all costs except for biological necessities, cleanliness, or to pleasure males."

Looking frustrated Chucho said, "What's this got to do with me? "

"Depending on your degree of modesty, being a test subject may be more than you want to show to strangers regularly."

" I know what modesty means. What are you trying to say?"

"It sounds like his research, subjects are naked on and off an exam table, the doctor and his team remain clothed."

"Ugh, oh, to see if I can do the male version of female lubrication. Well, I can't. So, this conversation was just a big waste of my time."

"Now we have that out of the way. "

"What if I told you before my accident, I used to pose for life drawing classes and knew how to control my physical outcropping for the sake of art?"

"Then my assumption was incorrect, and I'd have egg on my face. Did you really pose nude for artists?"

"No. But how come you haven't told me what you know about the experiments before worrying about my modesty? Is something fishy going on? "

"Chucho. You didn't tell Ameli I offered you a fulltime job, one you needed, to protect her feelings."

"I explained that."

"You did. Explained being willing to forego for Ameli's and my sake a job you wanted. I think that was generous of you."

"I didn't do it to be generous. It was the right thing to do."

"Exactly, especially since you don't know me."

"What's this to do with a university doing experiments on my nude body?"

"In return for your kindness, I didn't want to get your hopes up for something that might be embarrassing with iffy results."

"Get to the point, how does this Graboski guy plan to see if my package can rise to life again?"

I explained Dr. Gabriel Graboski was trying a new angle for repairing injured spinal cords. The extensive pretesting to get into the research study, some quite invasive, was to predict success. Phase one temporarily attached electrodes on either side of the spinal cord break and other necessary areas. A weak electric current was then pulsed back and forth over the damaged area for increasing lengths of time to stimulate new growth.

If or when a physical and neurological response of new growth is detected, phase two is triggered. It involves surgically implanting small electrodes and nerve grafts in and around the new growth site area using phase one results as a map. After healing the implants are electrically activated with increased higher voltage for three to four weeks at each increased level. Naturally, with rest breaks between sessions as needed. With positive results, the next phase is triggered.

In phase three a battery mechanism with an on off button is implanted near the groin area and connected by radio waves to implanted electrodes and graphs on either side of the spinal disruption. Also, at that time a tiny monitoring unit is implanted that sends a signal every time the button is pushed.

If the study participant continues to have measurable positive response for six months, they are referred to neurosurgery for human and porcine large-nerve-graphs and aftercare work with physical and occupational therapists. As I said the program just received new funding and is looking to expand with a few new test subjects with potential. I explained most participants drop out between phase one and two, so aren't counted as subjects until phase three for results.

To anticipate Chucho's next question, I explained the implants' battery life expectancy was ten years. When it appeared he wanted more information, I took a breath and elaborated as far as I knew to go. Analytical computer models predicted thirty percent of test subjects will regain some level of measurable improvement possibly including limited mobility, neurological sensations, feasibly even both. Thirty percent are expected to show slight barely measurable improvement, twenty percent will receive no benefit, and twenty percent are predicted to quit or die before the experiment is concluded.

"Graboski said it's a rigorous program with a high dropout rate. That's all I know. This is his number if you are interested. Toss it if you're not."

"I'm not huge down there, but not small either. Why would you think I'd be embarrassed to show what nature gave me?"

"Fair question, I guess. Between guys who like to streak football games and concerts and the cloistered ones who don't even *show their faces* to the public, most humans I know revere a modicum of modesty, admittedly some of us more than others. That's what I was thinking. It wasn't personal about you how could it be? I still don't know you."

Ameli sensing a fight not involving her *Dragon Lady*, or just feeling left out said, "Women giving birth are allowed absolutely no modesty at all. And if you gay guys ever notice, most naked statues are of women showing no modesty for male stimulation or is that called titillation. Oh, maybe that's because men can't tell when we are lubricating without sticking something inside us."

Coy looked over at Chucho, probably read his level of discomfort as embarrassment, and said, "You don't have to decide right away, take time to think on it before and after you chat with the doctor. Just ignore Ameli when she gets like this."

"Thanks, Coy, I appreciate good advice."

"If it were me, I'd want to talk with test subjects about their experiences to find out what's to be expected, and if it's worth the results."

Clearly, Coy's remarks to Chucho were intended to relax him. It worked, throwing me a sly smile, Chucho said, "Is the professor good looking?"

Caught off guard I mumbled, "He's not my type … Coy is." Regaining composure I said, "He's kind of frumpy actually, if that's your type in tweeds, he's your man."

Coy snickered to me, "I'll bet the doctoral fellows and graduate students will be to Chucho's taste." Catching a potential faux pa, turning to Chucho, Coy said, "Ugh, whatever your taste is, no offense intended."

"Touche." I had to acknowledge Coy rescuing me from yet another case of my foot in mouth disease, an ongoing problem of late.

"If you're at all curious, you can ask to meet his team. He didn't seem homophobic when I mentioned my husband told me about the research."

"Everything you said sounds hopeful. I'll phone Dr. Graboski and tell him I was about ready to kill myself over my lifeless dick and memories of yesterdays' fun and games when it would rise for any occasion."

"If it were me, I wouldn't mention that."

"Why not, it's true?"

"That information might be interpreted as counter his hypothesis."

Once again Coy jumped into the conversation to save me from awkward over explaining and said, "Just remember Chucho, expectations breed disappointment."

"Hell, if he can make it stand even halfway at attention, I'll sing 'Yankee Doodle' waving an American flag, on Route 52, during rush hour, naked, to celebrate."

"See, that's exactly what I was worried about. It takes a high degree of coordination to sing and wave a flag in rhythm, naked, during rush hour, with all that rubber necking and car horns honking."

"I'm very coordinated and would love to perform for an eager audience. Although, I never did before. However, with all this talk I'm in the mood to get nude with heavy traffic watching."

"*Right* and getting your hopes up for a thirty percent chance at *a partial recovery* isn't the best odds for a betting man who loves traffic congestion during flag waving while singing."

"Or woman! See how sexist you are?"

Chucho shrugged his shoulders at Ameli's comment directed to me and said, "I've got nothing to bet, so, nothing to lose, right, non-gender *guys*?"

Coy had been watching Chucho go from elation to down in the dumps and now trying for a mellow middle mood. Speaking to me while watching Chucho's reaction, Coy said, "Oliver, that must be what the routinely circumcised think coming of age."

"What?"

"Anything is better than nothing."

"What do you mean?"

"If harmed is all they've ever known Then that's their normal."

"Or they know what they got and want to chop the other guy to conform to them."

"That's it!" Chucho perked up and said, "Coy, your comment just now made me realize why the professor would want *me* for his research. I'm young, healthy, my accident wasn't that long ago, and my dick is natural not circumcised. See that Oliver … it's not just about my junk not working. I think I'll start eating spaghetti again, I used to love it with meatballs."

I'd had a rougher than usual day facing and then dealing death and said, "If it's all the same to you fine gentlemen and lady, this talk of circumcision makes me uncomfortable."

"Why is that? We are all getting to know each other." Chucho said this with a high degree of enthusiasm.

To support Chucho's mood stabilization Coy said, "The sexism Ameli mentioned for one. Personally, I think it's the act that causes misogyny. Only boys allowed, but not most boys, which permanently divides males from females and males from each other, permanantly."

"New friend do you mind explaining that for me?" It appeared Chucho was forming a friendship with Coy.

"Simple, it sets up a male hierarchy over women. Ironic really, those with less than the other fellows elevate themselves to be superior to women. "

"Huh?"

"Yeah, as if mother and son relations weren't tenuous enough. Right?"

"I don't know, maybe it goes deeper than that. To compensate for loss of bodily integrity, the less than tell stories, like their diminished status makes them enhanced. So, they want all males to look like them since they believe they're superior."

"Isn't that what I said?"

Ameli appeared to have had enough of Coy and Chucho's banter back and forth and said, "I hope to never understand men's obsession with their penises dominating womanhood. Too much ado about such petty little things is gross to me. What's for dinner? After the shootings we've just witnessed, a nice dinner, *on you, boss* is expected. Let's see, I'd like …"

"Mine is not little, *I already said that. It's bigger than average.*" With that explanation Chucho went into a passable representation of teenage girl or drag queen's flustered pout.

"Boss, for the extra work I've done for you today, I'd like a T-bone steak, medium rare, with all the trimmings. I seldom see steak on the pittance you pay."

"Given the day I've had being shot at, somebody should buy *me* a steak dinner."

"All right, stop all your moaning and groaning I'll spring for steaks for everyone." Coy said this knowing I couldn't object to his paying after agreeing to our new financial arrangement and he was flushed with cash after selling his dojo and hot to spend some.

As it turned out nobody was enthusiastic about leaving the safety of the house to eat in a nice restaurant. It was understandable, given the number of deaths right outside the front door. Then as luck would have it, we found four ribeye steaks buried in the freezer and jerry-rigged the rest of the meal with what was on hand and called it trimmings. We semi-thawed the steaks outside outback on the patio grill, dark, crusty flavorful, well done on the outside and rare in the middle. Nobody complained, they were still tender and delicious.

Not wanting to increase the day's body count, and I didn't feel up to playing armed guard escorting to and from our guests' far afield homes. I invited Ameli and Chucho to sleep over. Ameli took the guest room and Chucho bunked in Darrell-Wayne's bedroom. Coy and I snuggled ignoring the fact that we had visitors sleeping in the house.

Chapter 10.

After an early breakfast I handed the two still drowsy sleepover guests a roll of duct tape and suggested they cover Ameli's van's bullet holes to keep the rain out and local traffic police at bay. They complied yawning with nary a complaint.

First, I phoned MT and told her after sleeping on it and discussing with Coy, we want Darrell-Wayne back for his protection. She asked if I was sure. Then at her suggestion, I telephoned FBI Agent Jameer Nacho and told him we were taking possession of Darrell-Wayne. First, he said, "No." Then after a beat to consider his previous encounters with MT said, "Why?"

I said, "Because the FBI relocation security program is dangerous with leaks in it. I've warned you before, yesterday they caused people to die on my doorstep." I expected Nacho to get on his high horse and have one of his all too familiar and most inappropriate for a butch straight man his age, hissy fits. Instead, he calmly offered to take Coy and me into the same witness protection program they supplied Darrell-Wayne.

After I stopped laughing, he heard me the third time I explained I couldn't run my business from protective custody or Coy keep his job as a police officer from a different location. Consequently, I respectfully declined his generous offer with guffaws at the idea we both change our identities and physical locations to be killed due to an FBI leak. Then calm as you please, Jameer said if I wanted to risk my family's life and limb without FBI protection, he would take my request to his supervisor. Then he would put our names on his special Christmas shopping list for people with unrealizable requests for Santa.

For once he was right. There was no chance in hell the FBI was letting me protect Coy's cousin when they couldn't and just lost one of their own proving it. I didn't defend my position or point out the flaws in his big, bloated agency with *serious* security flaws. I didn't mention the fact that their court ordered legal grounds to hold Darrell-Wayne had expired. Immediately after speaking with Jameer, I telephoned MT back, she already had drawn up legal writs to get the youth back in our primary care, for his safety. I suggested the bureau should play a secondary role, supporting us with back up since the FBI wanted to play a role. She said sure, why not.

Later than usual for a late breakfast, Coy seemed nervous. He was all dressed up, spit shined, in his new court witness suit. The night before he mentioned an early court appearance for his first arrest leading to a trial where he was expected to testify. His worry was he'd forget something pertinent and be ridiculed by the defense attorney on the witness stand as an incompetent fool.

To distract his apprehension, I asked Coy to escort Ameli and Chucho to my downtown office and make sure they were secure before going on to the court appearance. He threw me a look to let me know he knew distraction when he saw it. One of the things I love about the man is he gets me and doesn't let me get away with anything.

As he was going out the door, I asked Chucho for his aunt's phone number. He said, "You're not her type."

"Good for her."

"No really, she hates gringos. But if you must find out for yourself, give me your phone. I'll put it on your contact list. She will do a good job as your housekeeper."

"Thank you for your concern and wanting to take care of everybody. "

"Then ..."

Chucho couldn't know, I wasn't interested in replacing my three days a week transgender male to female housekeeper. She'd been with me for years before her transition. Carmen, formally Carmine, did excellent work at a fair price, and looked out for me when I wasn't eating.

At my downtown office I used the same minority owned cleaning service from the start of QQ. Like my part-time housekeeper they went above and beyond what I paid them for. They watered and nurtured our office plants, brought fresh cut flowers every Monday, removed them on Fridays, and Ameli had the hots for one of their workers with a limp.

Shortly after a brief telephone call Esmeralda Nascence, Chucho's aunt, met me at a coffeeshop she suggested near her home in New Jersey. She wasn't tall, had a strong handshake, and made direct unblinking, challenging eye contact. She wasn't young but how old I couldn't tell and knew better than inquire. I judged the way she carried herself and her body language she'd survived mortal combat. As a parole officer I'd met people like her who'd given their experience of war a permanent home in their head.

Somehow, I sensed she'd taken human life without regret or apology, unlike me. And she hadn't let the ghosts she carried with her rest in peace. I knew the look on her face too well from my years as a parole officer with unrepentant non-sociopath killers. With all that said, there was something likable and trustworthy about her. Despite her challenging toughness. Crazy to say, I imagined she'd taken human life for a cause she believed in, and then was disappointed with the result. No, she was not the usual house and garden psychopathic killer, like the ones I'd known on parole.

I got right to that point and asked, "Are you interested in a job that could be dangerous protecting an autistic boy your nephew's age?"

She cast her eyes up to a distant horizon point outside the coffee shop's big front window. Then after a full silent minute considering said, "I've heard about that young man's troubles from my nephew. Before we get to that, just so you understand, we didn't know what we were taking to Boston. I found out after we did the job."

"Your nephew told me, I believe you."

"To be straight with you, I know nothing about autism."

"Me too."

"I really do need a fulltime job. We will be evicted soon if I don't find some money. I'll give your job a try if the boy cooperates. Just so you know, I don't like to be bossed around."

Not sure how to take her last statement and establish *I was the boss*. I gave her a couple of hypothetical scenarios for protecting an autistic teenager from known international assassins. At the end of the interview, she appeared exactly what I needed to rest easy Darrell-Wayne would be in as safe hands possible if Coy or I weren't present. She impressed me she was a fighter and knew her way around weapons but wasn't gun crazy.

We agreed on what I considered a fair wage. Later I came to realize she was worth much more. And *she disliked me from the start*. Still in the coffee shop, I telephoned MT to include Esmeralda in the immigration work visa package leading to a green card she started for Chucho. In addition, I requested Esmeralda get issued a bodyguard conceal carry permits once her green card came through. Without thinking it through, as we got up to leave, I suggested Esmeralda demonstrate on me a basic bodyguard protective stance. My plan was to feign a lunge in one direction then reverse course when she responded with a fake Judo move. The plan was a mistake. In a short breath she had me flat on the floor with a knife, I didn't know she had at my throat.

She let me up off the floor, dusted me off, and said, "You're too slow and telegraphed your intention wasn't real. That's why you're not dead. Where I come from, we don't play around, it's kill first talk about it later. Understand, I broke a rule to take your job, I hate male gringos like you, but need work, badly."

I wasn't 100% sure I'd hired the right person to protect Darrell-Wayne. But did it without wasting days on background checks, interminable interviews, checking references, and expensive fingerprint background investigations. I guessed time would tell if we all lived long enough to know. I gave her an advance to pay rent. Then later called it a sign on bonus.

***

After compressed, and yet still long-drawn-out legal formalities, Darrell-Wayne was returned to his cousin's supervision without pomp but with well-armed circumstances. A casual observer would have thought we'd had a mafia death in the family from the number of heavily armed FBI agents wearing dark glasses and dressed in black funeral garb in and around my house. *Except* one guy stood out. For some reason I noticed immediately he did not wear well shined black leather shoes, like the others. He wore high-end high-top sneaker knockoffs. Normally I'm not into feet with or without shoes. But for some reason he grabbed my attention.

Also noteworthy, my friend Willis had posted plain clothed cops, half-hidden, with long guns, across the road and in greenery outside the front of my property. I suppose they were ostensibly there to protect the FBI agents from somebody else's snipers. I later discovered Willis had been told by the sergeant about my previous sniper incident and the FBI's refusal to believe they were vulnerable even after losing an agent.

Just before the date and time of transfer was revealed, a confidential informant told Willis through George Reynolds, one of Nacho's FBI agents that day, might be a plant, not an agent at all. I told Nacho what I'd learned from the police. He dismissed it as a rumor designed to belittle the FBI at a time when Rabble in Congress were trying to defund and downsize the FBI. Apparently, the problem's origin was a lost election that had stupidly been declared a victory by those not able to tell the difference and fear the Black Lives Matter movement's effect on interpretation of American history.

I didn't mention to Coy the rumor of a fake agent because he was about at the end of his tether with constant obstacles to keep his cousin safe. I did inform Esmeralda to expect trouble and we both surrounded Darrell-Wayne as he stepped down from the oversize sports utility vehicle. Coy was standing back to scope a wider field of protection, if needed. I was happy when I saw a glimmer in Darrell-Wayne's eyes as he remembered me.

The assassin wearing cheap-sneakers pulled out a weapon just as Darrell-Wayne's feet hit the ground. Then the shooting started, Darrell-Wayne and Esmeralda seemed to meld together running to the stairs down to the house. As they ran past Coy, he had his gun out. My man and I covered his cousin and new nanny's backs with a converging barrage of fire. We took shots at the sidestepping sneaker guy as FBI agents scattered in all directions pulling their weapons. It was one of Willis Washington's men who hit the hitman first, but he didn't go down easy. Both Coy and I scored hits too. My security cameras recorded the whole event for posterity. The assassin was wearing body armor, several of us shot him with little more effect than bruising. Until another cop with a rifle connected with a head shot, then it was finally over.

At the sound of all the live fire a getaway car sped up containing, I guess backup shooters. Four car doors flew open, and shooters dispersed running into the FBI agent chaos. The late arrivers moved like a well-choreographed attack squad opening-up with submachinegun bursts, randomly, using new fully automatic short-barrel-weapons. They were clearly looking for and not finding a particular target. The scene reminded me of a coop of chickens in chaos with a hungry fox looking for a particularly plump chicken for his dinner.

The local cops hiding in unlikely places returned fire as FBI agents scrambled until they finally joined in the fire fight. When the shooting abruptly stopped, five hitmen were dead. Two were later identified as Boynton clan associates, three were locals who wanted to be gangsters. The guy dressed as an FBI agent but not shod like one was a Boynton clan member. Six FBI agents were injured, two seriously, and the outside of my garage would need extensive cosmetic bullet hole plugging puddy and spent brass casing collecting.

Then ambulances with police car escorts arrived, the air was still thick with gun smoke and Coy and I were out of ammo. So, we went downstairs into the house to check on Darrell-Wayne, Esmeralda, and get more bullets just in case any other surprise visitors arrived. Our absence allowed room for the local police and FBI to introduce each other and divvy up the crime scene. In the meantime, Emergency Medical Technicians separated the live from dead, then tended to the living.

The last thing any of them needed was Coy and me confusing the mess they were trying to sort between who fired first, and by what authority. Then, who shot who exactly, and how many times. I guess the why, how, and seniority rankings would be settled with interviews, followed by pouring over lengthy written firsthand reports since the perps would not cooperate being dead and all. It was a colossal intramural task. I did not envy them, their incident and after-incident fatality reports. Even though my house's security cameras take high-resolution motion-activated video that could substantiate written words about a confused gun fight.

Inside my vertical house, after a big sigh of relief I went to the kitchen freezer like an automaton. Then I served up bowls of dark-chocolate premium ice cream, covered in dark-chocolate sauce, decorated with dark- chocolate sprinkles on top of spritzed whipped cream from a can. The mental relief washed over me as I handed a spoon and bowl to Darrell-Wayne, Coy, Esmeralda, and none for me.

My endocrine system had had too much stimulation for one day. So, I had a glass of ice water, and vicariously enjoyed watching the others blissfully spoon-feed themselves dark chocolate to smooth over the latest murder attempt. Watching people, I cared about self-soothing, made words unnecessary to get my heart rate back down to normal speed and rhythm.

Darrell-Wayne used his opening Christmas and birthday gifts face to show his appreciation to be home with people who knew his love of dark chocolate and provided it. Right there I resolved, we'd gone through a lot to get Darrell-Wayne back and were not about to let him out of our collective sight again. I'd stake my private investigator license on it.

***

We moved Esmeralda and Chucho from a cramped studio apartment in Newark, New Jersey to a neighbor's two-bedroom rental house one-quarter mile up the road from my upside-down house. But ever since the bad planning incident at the coffee shop, I sensed Esmeralda had something against me. Or maybe she didn't like having me as the boss even when I handed her a regular paycheck.

To manage recent events more efficiently, Queer Queries bought a new passenger van with hydraulic wheelchair lift for Ameli to supervise as part of her expanded role with the firm. The bullet proof glass and armor plates would have been extra with any brand we bought.

I knew an excellent fey auto mechanic, Clarence Rose. He'd hired QQ a few years back when he was being harassed by a homophobic landlord. It was the kind of job QQ was created for. After I had a friendly chat with the offending Mr. Landlord where he fell-down and bruised himself bloody. The man came up with the idea to change Clarence's business arrangement to rent to own. The new arrangement was agreed to by all parties involved, and QQ had another satisfied customer's recommendation.

Clarence is a bit girly for a middle-aged big strapping hairy man, but a true sweetheart to work with. QQ insisted on paying him for bodywork and a new paint job on Ameli's old Kia van, along with much neglected engine maintenance. At no extra cost to QQ he got Kia to make good on lapsed manufacture upgrades. I lent the restored Korean van to Esmeralda and Chucho to replace their unreliable junkier car on its last legs. I could see Esmeralda hated Clarence at first sight. He just ignored her while showing Chucho the finer points of his wheelchair lift improvements.

Having a magnetic QQ removable logo on both vans made them and their maintenance, business tax deductions, and with the logos removed, they were perfect for undercover work. Or so said my part-time-accountant. Without a business plan to follow I'd gone from a successful one-man private eye firm to heading a shaky four-person operation, intending to make it five persons when Coy was ready to quit the police and join in. I often pondered whether it was madness to go from one to five without a plan, or frankly exciting, if I could stave off bankruptcy.

The landscape around my house had suffered badly from too many cops, FBI, and hitmen's' trampling feet, live-fire projectiles, and red-hot spent cartridge casings assaulting the horticulture and environs. Then just when I was about to call a light in the loafers' landscape architect QQ knew. I discovered Esmeralda had gardening skills and Darrell-Wayne liked to dig in dirt.

It didn't take long for the two working together to have my greenery restored better than before. After that, for good measure they created a vegetable garden down the slope behind the house, and a potted herb garden on the kitchen outdoor stairs. Esmeralda appropriated discarded ten-gallon soy sauce buckets from Chinese takeout restaurants and used them as oversize herb pots. Esmeralda vigorously stabbed drainage holes in the pot bottoms, and Darrell-Wayne painted the buckets in bright primary color with autistic designs. I was learning to stand back and let others express their creativity. It wasn't easy for the sole operator of a recently expanded small business control freak, who knew how to use muscle when appropriate. Then again nobody said any of it would be easy.

One of the flagstone posts for the front-gate was wobbly after a hefty hitman climbed up it then pushed off kicking it hard during his death throes. That image would be with me for years. Having the post fixed nagged at me every time I had to finagle that gate open or closed. I knew I needed to call the lavender lady contractor but was morphing into a penny pincher. Then, I returned from work one evening to find the gate blocked with neon-orange rubber pilons.

After grumpily entering the side-gate. Storming into the house, Esmeralda addressed my foul mood in the kitchen before I could say a word. She grimly informed me Darrell-Wayne had dug a deep hole around the wobbly stone gate post, on his own, without asking her permission.

Seeing the hole, she called the home center to deliver rebar and a new product she'd seen on a television home improvement show. She taught Darrell-Wayne to use the new material by briskly squishing two bags of chemicals together and then released the resulting foam into the deep hole he dug reinforced with rebar. Once the foam set, they covered the area with dirt and planted ground cover over it.

In addressing my unarticulated bad mood, Esmeralda explained I had to wait forty-eight hours to use the main entrance. She suggested I should leave my bad attitude outside that gate, and under no circumstance bring it into the house she had just dusted, vacuumed, and made oatmeal cookies.

I saw something new in Darrell-Wayne's eyes as he listened to Esmeralda harangue me like a wife not a nanny. Subtle, but yes … it was there … cause and effect … Darrell-Wayne showed pride in what he'd done. He'd demonstrated initiative and gotten praised from Esmeralda, an unexpected result, and then I was put in my place for not showing appreciation. I could have missed it from being annoyed not able to use the gate I wanted. Esmeralda dressed me down severely for being a grouch, and autism watched feeling pride. I was on a new journey and not the band leader of the ensemble. My inner social worker approved, and for once so did my private detective persona.

***

It was Sunday after our big afternoon meal. I was preoccupied with a case with more twists and turns than an earthworm's maze. So, I wasn't paying close attention when Esmeralda with a flourish presented us with an old beat-up hand crank ice cream maker. She'd found it at a flea market on her day off and considered it a treasure. Then I watched with interest how Darrell-Wayne liked to hand crank homemade ice cream and willingly shared the fruits of his labor with the rest of us. He was showing pride again. I didn't have to be told his behavior was not typically autistic. Somehow, I had become too uptight tense for my own or anyone else's good. It could be argued my recent behavior did not reflect well on a graduate school education in social work.

I had to work on me being so trigger happy jittery to help Darrell-Wayne continue to blossom. It recently became obvious Darrell-Wayne was spending less time locked in his shell and more gardening, doing masonry, or his latest favorite, ice cream making. He'd relaxed his stiff irritated face to show a sweet young person behind his anger mask. Whether it was from all the violence he'd witnessed or from adapting to life as an Inuit in the arctic, or having a new mother substitute, we'd probably never know. What I did know was, I had become altogether too rigid over safety, finance, and growing a staff I hadn't intended.

As home repairs and landscaping tasks ran their course, Esmeralda replaced them with making Central American style Aboriginal handicrafts. Once again, she'd found another way for Darrell-Wayne to turn introspection outward into colorful wristbands, lanyards, and bolo ties. At first, they gave the craft work to Coy, me, friends, delivery people, even the neighbors.

I'd ignored those living close by for years; my house is hiding under a garage, work can be dangerous, I come, go, and sleep at odd private eye hours. As far as I'm concerned, the less neighbors know the better off we all are. I don't remember which busy body neighbor suggested the handicrafts were good enough to sell on the internet. Which illustrated my point about avoiding neighbors' minding my business.

Soon the internet became a big enough business Darrell-Wayne had to learn the banking system. It was necessary for his buying supplies and storing his mounting profits. With coaching from Esmeralda, Darrell-Wayne learned the social conventions of banking without expressing rage when everything didn't go exactly as he intended. Who among us enjoys waiting in long lines at the bank to give over our money? Darrell-Wayne finally reached his limit for abuse at the hands of the finance system. He abruptly quit making and selling arts and crafts. Suddenly, for him videos, audiobooks, and drawings were all about dolphins.

To keep everyone in my house safe, we made security rigid but simple. For example, I insisted none of us return using the same route we left by. In that spirit as much as possible, I also worked from home to give Esmeralda a break to have her own life. Often if I had to be away from home on a job, Coy juggled his schedule to help her have free time. In return, when we both *had* to be away, Esmeralda stayed over in our guest room with a Kalashnikov for company. But she knew, because I told her, I had per diem workers ready, willing, and able to protect Darrel-Wayne, one phone call away, if she needed help.

Purchases for household goods were made online, delivered outside the front gate, and inspected out there before COD payment was made. When Darrell-Wayne needed to go for an outside appointment like the dentist or such. We went in two cars and always picked up a police escort on the way going and another coming back. The local PD knew our story and I was a reliable source of side hustle for many of them. We practiced the idiom one hand washes the other within the limits the law allowed.

As normal domestic routines fell into place, Coy, or I, or together made sleepy Darrell-Wayne's breakfast most mornings. During the week, the teen and Esmeralda prepared their own lunch. When possible Coy, I, and Darrell-Wayne wash and chop vegetables to cook for dinner. I worried complacency breeds inattention, so I called a family meeting to keep us on our toes. After his high school graduation Darrell-Wayne's parents applied for him to attend the Activity Center for Developmentally Challenged, ACDC. Its day program serviced a wide spectrum of individuals with disabilities; mental, physical, and both.

His parent's estate was large enough to pay for him to attend the prestigious ACDC day care program long into the future. After reading their brochure, Esmeralda pointed out she had already taught the young man safe practices for activities of daily living. For instance, he now knew not to put a knife in the toaster to remove stuck toast. She taught him electric shock could be fatal, by giving him an unpleasant mild dose.

On her own Esmeralda searched for alternatives to ACDC and discovered Darrell-Wayne might function at a high enough level for the university's impaired students' program if he brought a helper. Her research found the university programs were much more advanced than the basic life skills at ACDC. With her as shepherdess and with the university's tutoring help it was possible to bring Darrell-Wayne up to his full potential if he was of a mind to complete the work.

If successful at the university, Darrell-Wayne could either earn a certificate leading to a job as supervisor in sheltered workshops or continue on to earn an impaired student general undergraduate degree with a special education major. With that he'd get work as a classroom helper, or it was even possible to earn full certification as a special-ed teacher, with additional classes.

Esmeralda said she was willing to take on the extra work of guiding Darrel-Wayne through the university bureaucracy, if her nephew Chucho, could be included. Up to that point neither Chucho nor Darrell-Wayne wanted more than very limited interaction with the other. They were like two strange dogs sniffing each other and the chemistry or karma wasn't right to be friends or fight.

We found out later that Chucho had not shared with his aunt what he'd learned from Dr. Graboski about research for paraplegics. He told us he didn't want to get his aunt's hope up and disappoint her as usual, they had a fragile relationship. She blamed him for his accident. When I asked him why he was protecting her from disappointment. He said she thought both their lives had been as losers. Consequently, he was thinking of giving Dr. Graboski a try to prove his aunt wrong. But not telling her until he had positive results.

Surprised at the prospect of a university education for both our teenagers and to buy time to digest it, I asked, "Does everyone have what the university requires to get in?"

Esmeralda proudly said, "Chucho and I both have our GEDs."

"GED."

"Yes. It stands for Good Enough Diploma. It's a substitute for a high school diploma. We'll have to find some kind of exception for Darrell-Wayne, I'm a mender, I find solutions. It shouldn't be too hard to get an exception given how his life is constantly under attack." Then she and Darrell-Wayne exchanged a high five followed by a conspiratorial smile. I'd never seen him smile so much before Esmeralda joined our security team.

Coy, who was not Esmeralda's biggest fan, looked ready to attack, so I said, "Darrell-Wayne graduated high school's special education program. He earned a real high school diploma. The university is required to accept it, otherwise what was the point?"

I'd only been looking to keep us alert for safety's sake. Now I was confronted with Darrell-Wayne and the others going to college several days a week. I can be dense sometimes, but the tone Esmeralda spoke to me in and faces she sometimes made were negative and getting harder for me to disregard.

Normally it was my style to address negativity straight ahead. But my original assessment was she'd only be with us a brief time, only until the danger to Darrell-Wayne was eliminated. Jameer Nacho had repeatedly assured me the danger would soon be history. With so much else going on, I choose to ignore an obvious problem rather than find a replacement for her. Taking short cuts seldom worked for me.

Given our deteriorating rocky relationship, I didn't see any reason to tell Esmeralda GED stands for General Educational Development, not a second-class high school diploma. Although, I suppose that's how it functioned for most dropouts. Later that day Coy and I discussed the pros and cons of Darrell-Wayne going to college with international hit men out to kill him. Keeping him home all the time was not healthy at his age. He needed a purpose and socialization to continue to bloom. ACDC could supply a positive if restricted social setting, but the university sounded much more rewarding.

I wondered out loud how we could pay tuition for them given recent increases in my operating costs while rapidly depleting my reserve funds. Then it dawned on Coy, his cousin would be eligible for crime victims' fund money to pay his university tuition and even give a stipend to his helper Esmeralda. That got me thinking, if Chucho was accepted as a bioengineering study subject, he should be entitled to university compensation for his time and trouble. It certainly wouldn't hurt to have MT inquire with her ass kicking boots on.

When Coy and I were alone, he was unusually quiet, as if his electric power were reduced in a brownout or his dimmer switch was turned way down. He wasn't talking, so I asked, "What's bothering you?"

"Can you imagine, Darrell-Wayne with a college degree and I don't have one. You even have a masters. I'm feeling grossly uneducated."

"If you think you'd like to make the police a career you'll need a law degree to advance up the chain of command, eventually. Want me to explore getting a family discount group rate at the university? They must have something like that."

"NOT YET! Too much change has happened to me too quickly. But you're right I like being a cop and could see it as a career. It has the same kind of structure I liked about the military. Although lately I'm also thinking of following my hero, you, with a degree in social work. I'd be good at it except I was never a good student."

"Our priority right now is keeping Darrell-Wayne safe. After that I'll support you whatever you want."

***

The electronic security at my house was monitored and regularly upgraded to state of art by the university's electrical engineering school. It was one of the ways my business worked with the university engineering curriculum. Along with my house as a model. I had use of an office building in the city, a factory out here in the burbs, and a big rural farm, all were working models of the latest high end electronic security systems money could buy.

If some board of directors was planning to invest millions of dollars in the latest greatest state-of-the-art security, they wanted more than charts and graphs to shuffle with color photographs. It was actual detailed elaborate working model demonstrations that usually closed our most expensive collaborative QQ-university deals. At one point early on the university had come to the realization QQ's limited partnership with them was bringing in bucks big enough to subsidize specialized projects that couldn't be funded in the usual way.

It was the student security crew at the university that gave me a heads up an attack was coming. They noticed from outside perimeter sensors at my house someone was trying to block GPS five miles around the property. The first time it happened they thought it was a glitch in their software but nevertheless went on alert. Second time, the university kids brought a professor in on what they found, and he had them send up a drone and reverse tracked the interference. They found the address of a house trying to block the Global Positioning System to my home for five miles around it.

I didn't wait and passed along the jammer's address to Jameer Nacho. He was still technically held responsible for Darrell-Wayne's safety. The bureaucrats just love complicated. Willis was unavailable and lately showed a little attitude. I knew I'd been putting a strain of overuse on our friendship since Darrell-Wayne came into my life with Coy. On the other hand, our long friendship had a history of ups and downs stemming from his moods and how busy we were individually and life's other pressures.

The bad guys' house was put under surveillance by a doubtful Nacho. Then after two days, a joint FBI, ATF, and the State Police raided it. Twelve heavily armed bad people were preparing for an unfriendly visit to my home. They had maps, our schedules, and assigned positions during the attack. Caught by surprise, preparing explosives, they were captured without a shot fired. Three of the arrested twelve were associates of the Boynton family of assassins. That family was really getting under my skin.

Since the United States of America gives GPS free to the whole world from our select orbiting satellites, few relevant laws are on the books to cover interfering with the free service. Consequently, the FBI was going to release those captured without Interpol outstanding arrest warrants. Which meant those wanting to eliminate Darrell-Wayne without warrants were scheduled to be released, after a mandatory forty-eight-hour hold. Coy leaped into action and telephoned his old boss General Ivan Navarro.

The good general phoned his contact at Department of Homeland Security, and they labeled the warrant-less prisoners domestic terrorist for messing with the GPS and had them transferred to Guantanamo Bay, Cuba. Using unusual methods of interrogation, DHS discovered after blocking GPS access to my house, a diversion would be created outside the front followed by blowing a hole in my back patio concrete block wall large enough for the assassins to enter. Then their plan was to kill everyone in the house and then blow it to shards with C-4 explosives they were putting detonators in when law enforcement arrived. They planned to escape before any emergency services could find my place without GPS and get the front electronic gate open with no garage, house, or controls still standing after the blast.

It baffled me how in any way Darrell-Wayne, the now studious dolphin specialist, could be responsible for the level of danger he faced. With that thought in the front of my brain I was as calm as I ever am when facing life and death situations. I imagined graphs in my head, to distract me from ruminating on the unknowable to no conclusion.

A graph made from my earliest days serving in the peace corps would show a gradual steady raising line. At college with my roommate, his suicide, graduate school, the graph would take a sharp dip and again rise smoothly. Then my head graph dropped precipitously when I worked at the probation department. Next, with QQ's success and meeting Coy, a bump up followed by steady uninterrupted increase as the graph line rose above the chart in my head.

But since international hits went active on Coy's cousin my internal head graph line has zigzagged down worse than a Wall Street Bear Market in trouble. I suppose international assassins intruding on one's more or less hum drum life would cause any graph to crash.

My mental graph allowed me to imagine a level of control, even though I knew better, and accepted we might die in gunfire having Darrell-Wayne in our family. And we might never know why. The teen came as part of a package deal, in my experience nothing in life worth having is easy or comes free of problems.

Coy a police officer and me a private investigator could die in a gun fight just trying to earn our daily bread while working. Darrell-Wayne was family and that meant protecting him was an expectable dimension of the loving relationship we were building outside of work. When I met Coy, I didn't expect much more than a short-lived slap and tickle or a rub and tug with suction adventure. I know I'm almost old enough to be his father, too close in that direction for my overdeveloped sense of decorum. I should act my age, except I love feeling a couple of decades younger around Coy.

What was crazy in that department, I never thought I deserved to have the depth of what I was sharing with Coy. Now we're traveled well beyond a short-lived affair. Yet I was still flying without expectations, parachute, or net, and that has worked to keep my agist apprehensions in check. These days my introspections run to, if one or both of us are killed protecting Darrell-Wayne, it's what we chose with our eyes open, so be it. I've already gotten more than I believed worthy to experience and am grateful for it.

Chapter 11.

We expected Darrell-Wayne to fight giving up his carefree independent study of dolphins for strict classroom regimentation. Once again, he surprised us. The Impaired Student Center housed the special education programs in one of the oldest buildings on campus. It was a squat three story beige stucco rectangle with dark-green hip style metal roof, and lighter-green windows and doors trim.

It has four wheelchair ramps, extra wide glass doors, jumbo size elevators, and raised Braille symbols larger than the Arabic numbers to aid navigation. The Impaired Student Center Lounge is in the basement containing a snack bar, game room, dim lit quiet space, and study salon complete with computers that speak.

The ground floor of the building has classrooms, a small auditorium, formal and informal meeting room, everywhere is wheelchair accessible. On the second floor beyond the waiting area were individual counseling offices, and a small first-aid-medical treatment area. The lobby directory indicated the third floor was administrative and access was by appointment only.

Darrell-Wayne's first order of business at the university was to meet his navigator, Ms. Carrol Chow. She greeted us in the ground floor lobby, gave us her business card, passed around the day's itinerary, and led us to the second floor. With her help we then met Darrell-Wayne's academic coach Ms. Gloria Thompson, and Ms. Chow left to help other students.

Ms. Thompson's small office was near the busy second floor waiting area. She was a well-dressed dark-skinned woman with short-cropped hair, of average height and weight. Her thick eyeglass frames were a bright ivory-color, and she wore understated gold jewelry accents. There was a large Jamaican flag pinned to her neat office wall and she had a strong British accent to match the flag.

After shaking our hands all around, Ms. Thompson suggested her office was too small for five people and Coy and I might have better things to occupy our time in larger spaces. Leaving the office, I asked Esmeralda to give me a call when they wanted transportation home. Coy and I left to get on with the day's toil.

***

That evening I took Coy, Darrell-Wayne, and Esmeralda to my favorite diner for dinner. Chucho had to spend the night in the University Hospital awaiting further all day invasive neurological tests starting 5:30 the next morning. Then that would be followed the next day with test result consultations and possible retesting, if necessary, lunch, and an interview session with the full team of researchers at 4:30 PM.

At dinner, Esmeralda asked Darrell-Wayne if the classrooms at the university and their stringent rules reminded him of his years of special education classes in public school. In answer, a look of happiness wiped over his face. He didn't need words to express being back on well-known turf.

To fill the silence I said, "Which Mama substitute do you like best? You had three today." I was expecting him to say Esmeralda since he knew her longer and they'd had fun escapades.

"Not best, three are better than one. They all should get married like you and Coy want to do."

Coy and I exchanged a loaded look and Esmeralda got busy looking uncomfortable fiddling with the menu fold out specials. I wondered, do we have a homophobe in our midst or did the remark hit too close to home for her. As far as I knew she never married or had children due to the ongoing civil war in her country.

In response to my staring she said, "With these selections you get soup, salad, and dessert, over here it's either soup or salad, no dessert, and these only come with coleslaw and French fries. What if I want it different?"

"Order what you want. If they can't be flexible, we'll negotiate."

***

To matriculate at the university for credit, with only a GED, Esmeralda and Chucho had to pass remedial exams in English, math, critical thinking, and social awareness. If they failed any topic, make up classes were required for no credit, at full tuition. They were encouraged to repeat the remedial classes until passed.

Chucho was game and easily passed all the remedial requirements. But Esmeralda refused to take the exams. Esmeralda was not shy loudly expressing her opinion up and down the university's impaired student program.

Coy, and I offered to help if it was wanted in any way allowed. It was interesting to me how Esmeralda could be so adamant against the university's requirements for her and at the same time supportive of Darrell-Wayne and Chucho attending their university's classes. It didn't make sense other than she'd manipulated them to let her assist Darrell-Wayne without the required effort to get certification. Or she believed she couldn't pass, and her ego wouldn't let the younger ones best her.

The university's Bioengineering Spinal Cord Paralysis clinical trials project accepted Chucho Nascence as a test subject. MT got him a fifty percent tuition reduction for classes at full credit, and some engineering independent study credit for taking part in bioengineering research and writing about his experience.

Everyone except Chucho was surprised when he progressed to phase two of the clinical trials. He had started experiencing pain in places he'd not since the accident. The fellows and students were mapping where his nerve response failed by sticking him with pins or needles connected to electricity. It was like a light switch was turned on in an area Chucho usually felt nothing, and then suddenly sharp discomfort from the sharp pins pushed into his flesh looking for live nerves endings to surgically connect and run more electricity through to grow.

As I had foretold. Once he was accepted into the clinical study everyone in the room, male, female, young, and old focused their eyes on Chucho's nakedness. Call it human nature or unfiltered curiosity, his exposed private parts drew the most intense scrutiny especially when the professor's emphasis drifted to be elsewhere on his body. But he said it was his atrophied extremities below the crotch that made him feel most self-conscious and vulnerable, not his limp dick.

Perversely missing the loss of his crotch's visual attention, and to help counter the physical pain they were now regularly inflicting with jolts of electricity, Chucho played a joke on his tormentors. He popped popcorn. When food was scarce, where Esmeralda and Chucho came from, they ate a handful or two of popcorn and called it the meal of the day. Consequently, the smell of popping corn reminded him and his aunt of hunger's hollow times. Despite that, just before his next grand rounds clinical session. Chucho pushed back his foreskin and placed two plump kernels of fluffy popped corn behind his dickhead's rim and then pushed its convertible top back up to cover the maize.

He watched with glee as first those males he suspected of being gay, noticed. Then younger straights of both genders noticed what the gays stared at, and finally all but the professor was eyeballing Chucho's deformed looking dick. The bewildered class knew it hadn't looked like that the day before. Befitting his position, Dr. Gabriel Graboski finally saw where his fellows and graduate students' attention had gotten stuck, away from his carefully crafted lecture. He said, "Mr. Nascence would you be so kind to retract your foreskin?" All present crowded around closer to Chucho prone on the clinical exam table.

When Chucho complied with the professor's request, two kernels of pudgy popped corn came into view sitting just where he'd put them. They were none the worse for wear. Startled, the researchers didn't know what to think, penis popcorn was not on the syllabus. Seeing their confused faces Chucho said, "Oh look, there's my lunch. I wondered where it got to." The seminar room erupted in laughter when Chucho made a show of munching his hidden popcorn, even though food is not allowed in the lab.

The work of phase two progressed to surge more electrical current through newly identified and mapped damaged nerve pathways and bypasses. It was supposed to stimulate, often painfully, new growth. By the end of phase two Chucho had regained limited feeling and movement in his lower extremities and was working hard to rebuild atrophied muscles through regular rigorous exercise with a physical trainer. Nevertheless, his cock hadn't been paying attention to the other good news.

Chucho asked for and got a private consultation with the esteemed professor, and said he was thinking of quitting the research study since it wasn't working the way he'd hoped. Up to that point Dr. Graboski and his students had been more than pleased with Chucho's progress, after an initial prognosis of no benefit. So, the professor scolded Chucho for not being honest with him about a hidden agenda during preliminary screenings.

Chucho had guessed if his intention was known he'd been disqualified from participating in the program. Then out of genuine kindness, and seeing positive results, the good medical doctor gave Chucho an injection of testosterone. That injection caused an immediate erection, with minimal manual motivation, but without erotic sensation, or any feeling.

Outside class, regular hormone injections became routine from Dr. Graboski and put lead in Chucho's pencil, which he liked to proudly display to clinical trial fellows and graduate students. Nevertheless, working together none of them could find a pathway to promote feeling to accompany his erection. He could masturbate to ejaculation. But without any feeling, Chucho said it felt like he was watching someone else masturbate. A clear memory of sex before the accident blocked him even enjoying seeing his release pulsing out and from between his fingers at orgasm.

Nobody was listening to Chucho complain about his disappointment from the lack of results he was experiencing. He'd accomplished a lot, but not what he wanted. The professor didn't want to talk to Chucho about colluding in violation of the experiment's guidelines. He compartmentalized the hormone injections as something separate from the experiment's hypothesis. Chucho's dead dick hit a no feeling plateau and Dr. Graboski had no new ideas to resurrect it back to a sensual life. So, Chucho quit the research study.

In general, he'd found the bioengineers a cold, distant lot, whose study intentions ignored his very human suffering. As a lab rat for neurology, he found them to have even less empathy than the engineers. He might as well have been a cadaver for the little they seemed to care about him beyond what they were trying surgically. Chucho became clinically depressed feeling damned if he did and damned if didn't cooperate with them. He saw no hope for rehabilitation on the horizon, and without hope saw no reason to live.

Ameli was getting small, short, private eye jobs only one or two at a time. The problem was they didn't bring in enough money to pay her share of the rent or even keep our lights on. Let alone put food on her table at home. With doubts I started giving her cases beyond those I didn't want, and with good sense QQ should turn down. Giving her more trouble than they were worth cases was bad PI business practice, but good social work because the clients and Ameli often benefited.

With Ameli kept busier it meant we were increasingly depending on Chucho to keep the office functioning at our high professional standards, and me earning to pay three. Except, lately Chucho was looking totally depressed which wasn't a good look for our now busy office reception desk. Just when we needed to depend on him most to coordinate our fieldwork the office was pooping out by degrees.

Deciding to face the situation I went to the office after dropping off Darrell-Wayne and Esmeralda at college. At least for the moment that part of our lives seemed to be going as planned. They both looked forward to a fun challenging day at school with the FBI shadowing them at a short distance.

The first thing Chucho said as I walked through the door was, "Hello, boss. When can I have a gun?"

"For what reason do you need one?"

"Esmeralda has guns now. Thanks to you. I want one too."

"Is someone bothering you? I can fix that if someone is."

"How come she gets guns, and I don't?"

"Her job is to guard Darrell-Wayne while people are trying to kill him. Your job is to greet clients, answer the phone, fill out forms, do filing, keep Ameli and I efficient, look friendly, and handsome." Then I told him why I dropped by the office. It was to discuss the various pros and cons of medications available to treat depression. I guess once a social worker always a social worker. Chucho adamantly claimed not to be depressed. But he looked like he was, and so I ticked off his symptoms of depression as I saw them. After losing a haggling match with me, he agreed to see a therapist friend of mine, as a compromise, but refused to take antidepressants.

***

One week later, on the way to a client's housing security assessment, I stopped by the office to leave a stack of finished final reports for filing. An ambulance was just pulling away from the fire plug in front of the hardware store as I parked around back. Upstairs my office waiting room was a mess, furniture pushed back out of the way, discarded used purple colored rubber gloves scattered on floor, with paper wrappers of different types, plus colorful hypodermic needle caps. The discards were littered here and there, everywhere, and Ameli's face looked ashen-green. She looked in shock.

"What happened?"

"Chucho tried to kill himself."

"How?"

"The EMS people who just left say he took street pills laced with fentanyl. I know it was not an accident. He's no junky."

"Talk to me, what happened here."

"I stopped by to coordinate our schedules. He and I had agreed to meet later in the day, but at the last minute earlier worked out better for me."

"And?"

"When I rolled in it looked like Chucho was having a seizure. Then I saw pills scattered on the floor. I squirted Narcan up his nose, I always carry it just in case. You never know out and about on a private dick job. Then I called 911."

"Narcan was quick thinking on your part. You, okay?"

"I'll be okay. I wasn't expecting what I found. When my heart slows down, I'll clean up this mess. Give me a minute boss."

"That's not a full answer to my question. How *are you* doing?"

"This very second, I feel like a disgusting lowly insensitive creature unworthy to be scraped off the bottom of my shoe."

"Wow. That's harsh, and graphic."

"I should have seen how miserable Chucho was before he tried this. All wrapped up being the world's greatest wheelchair detective is no excuse to ignore a friend."

"I'll save the lecture on being too hard on yourself till later. Right now, go to my office and lay down. I'll clean this up and then go to the hospital and see Chucho."

"Thank you, boss. What I need right this second is a lie down. Tell him I'll visit as soon as I can forgive myself."

"One reason I dropped by today was he hadn't called the therapist I suggested last week. I should have followed up sooner. There's enough guilt here to go around."

***

I lied to the hospital security guarding his floor and said Chucho Nascence was my nephew. Then I signed their clipboard with more information than should be needed but was nevertheless required, checked my ID against what I wrote, they photocopied it. After a long wait, a nurse arrived and unlocked the intimidating entrance to the public hospital's psych ward. After letting me pass, she relocked the way behind us. Then she walked with me to a holding room.

The ward was deathly quiet, not expected Bedlam. I noticed through open hallway doors, most rooms had four or six beds holding stupefied looking, probably over medicated adult patients. It appeared rooms were assigned by gender. Before I could ask how he was doing, the nurse volunteered Chucho might still be hostile. Their protocol was to let all the drugs in his system clear with a saline-sucrose drip before his psych observation began in earnest and then psychotropic medications were usually administered to get the patient out. Once medicated to docile Chucho's restraints would be removed, he'd be moved to a dormitory, and *I'd* have to observe regular visiting hours.

When we arrived at his room the nurse stuck just her head in and said, "How are you doing so far?" When she wasn't acknowledged, said, "Okay Mr. Grumpy-puss you have a visitor. Your uncle is here," with that said she turned on her heels and disappeared back the way we'd come.

I'd never seen Chucho look more miserable. He was contained in a small single room in an oversize hospital bed tied in four-point restraints. "Mind if I have a seat?" Without waiting, I sat in the chair crammed in next to his bed.

"I do mind if you came here to fire me from my job."

"That's an unusual greeting. People usually just say hello."

"I'm good at that job. Give me another chance, don't fire me, and yes you may sit."

"Don't put ideas in my head. Firing you is not why I came."

"Oh, okay, but I don't need a lecture on just saying no to drugs. What happened was an accident. I'm accident prone."

"If you want to continue to hold both sides of the conversation I could wait in the hall until you are ready to talk to me."

"Oliver, will you please untie me?"

"Is that a clipboard hanging from the foot of your bed? Ah ha, this is your hospital chart, let's see if your visitors are allowed to untie you."

"Don't be a ball buster boss, just do it, untie me."

"Hmm ... it says here, you are on a forty-eight hour hold and red flagged on suicide watch. Wonder why that is do you suppose?"

"I don't remember."

"Someone wrote here in your chart you tried to run away. Huh, I guess that's why you are in restraints. Hmm, but how is that possible I wonder, your metallic midnight-blue motorized wheelchair is still back at the office."

"Look in the corner ... there, see? The hospital has outdated manual wheels."

"I can't imagine how it would feel to expect to be dead, and wakeup to find a big fiasco."

"You aren't my uncle why'd you say you were? And if you aren't going to fire or lecture me, what do you want?"

"I wanted your opinion whether to hire a replacement or know if you planned to stay among the living. It's so Ameli and I can get on with our work. We need someone dependable to hold down the office when we're in the field, remember?"

"I said it was an accident."

"Clearly, nobody believes that."

Chucho had come to believe any future life worth living ended with his motorcycle accident. Bottled up self-pity spewed out of him like an unanticipated rainstorm. Cool as I could I pointed out it was not a good look for an attractive young gay man to be bawling like a baby. He didn't want to hear that or have his pity party depreciated.

I knew I'd hit my target when he flipped his middle finger and hurled profanities. He threw expletives I had not heard directed my way since I worked for parole. When he ran down calling me names, his face crumpled up and tears were streaming down his face again. The poison that led him to end his life was draining out. I got up, took his hand in mine, and somehow ended up sitting on the side of his bed with one arm holding his sobbing shoulders and the other a box of hospital supplied tissues.

When his tears ran out, he tensed under my fingers. I sensed an awkward moment had arrived, broke physical contact, mopped tears from his face, and then scooted back to the bedside chair still holding the box of tissues. An uncomfortable heavy silence descended and then my mouth was saying words unconnected to conscious thought. "I don't know you very long or well, but just so you know I am glad you are still alive and considering continuing to work, for me."

"I didn't expect to wake up. And instead of being dead I've made everything worse for myself. Only I could do that."

"Like I said, I'm glad you're still here with us and I'm probably not the only one."

"Right. On top of everything else, now I have a load of guilt for what I almost did to my aunt, Ameli, Coy, Darrell-Wayne, and you, boss. Oliver, a stern lecture would have gone down a lot easier than you being nice to me ... is this visit over?"

"If you want to get full value from my visit, you need believable answers to a couple of questions."

"What am I supposed to say?"

"The truth usually works for me."

"Then they'll keep me locked up forever."

"No. They won't. It's your one chance to get out of here." I briefed Chucho on what to expect during his forty-eight-hour-hold for observation and psychiatric evaluation. The most important thing was, he had to convince every hospital employee he spoke to *he was not a future danger to himself or others*. To make staff believe *that* he had to *believe it himself*. That meant he had to believe his life was worth living and sell it. The staff were trained to spot lying.

When he adamantly bemoaned, he couldn't convince anyone he wasn't a danger to himself after what he'd done. I suggested, then months in a psych hospital on a judge's involuntary commitment might help him find faith and belief.

"What am I supposed to say?"

"Didn't I just say, the truth."

Then he told me about his suicidal ideation plan and preparation that led up to it. He needed to talk about it, and so I listened. After a while I felt us connect heart to heart, it was the first time since I met him. He spoke as if laying his soul open. Old and new festering wounds from the homophobia in his culture, the Church he was raised in, and then his own internal homophobia magnifying the outside indoctrination.

When Chucho stopped talking to catch a breath I said, "Details of recent events might be most helpful."

"What details."

"The aftereffects of the motorcycle accident, your feeling life as a university lab rat. Lay out a cause and effect that makes it easy for them to give you what you want."

"I see what you mean."

When he finally ran down, after telling his life's recent events. I searched my mind for counterproductive flaws in his story and found none. Yet, I wasn't ready to leave. With nothing coming to my mind, I said, "Your aunt really hated the late President Nixon's burglary hobby, didn't she?"

"Did she tell you about the Vietnam War?"

"No. Why?"

"If you really want to see her full-on anti-Nixon, mention how the Paris peace talks almost ended the war to all party's satisfaction."

"Wait, that's not right, the North Vietnamese kicked the U.S. out of South Vietnam."

"Just as the peace talks were wrapping up Nixon told the South Vietnamese to drag them out for is purposes. The North Vietnamese had been negotiating in good faith and even agreed to accept a divided country like Korea."

"Where did I hear that before? I know I never learned it in school."

"The North felt suckered and betrayed when they found the South was cow towing to Nixon. So, the North Vietnamese brought their regular army south and kicked the puppet-master invaders out of South Vietnam and unified the country they had just agreed to divide."

Once restarted Chucho talked and talked incessantly again. It was clear he had a great deal of heavy emotional baggage to unload, but in chunks. I listened to how Ameli's young adult support *got tired* of listening to his bellyaching about life's unfairness. Most group participants had adapted to their handicaps years before he had an accident to join them.

The gist of Chucho's new soliloquy came back to being disappointed to still be alive *and now, what that meant to him in the larger scheme of things.* "Oh, and just by the way I left my aunt a suicide note. It won't be pretty when she reads it."

That thought thread led to Chucho rapid talking again, "Nothing ever worked out for me." Before this round of self-pity got thick again, he stopped himself. Then across his face, like a flood light turned on bright showing clarity he said, "I wonder if my being alive means it just isn't my time to die. That makes some kind of crazy sense."

Not wanting to dilute his thought I said, "That thinking might get you out of here in forty-eight hours. You know Buddhist believe with consciousness everything is possible."

"Are you a Buddhist?"

"No. When I was in social work school *Mindfulness* was the in-vogue flavor in psychology. It draws heavily from Buddhism."

"You mean psychology isn't just one set of rules like mathematics?"

"If your adventures in academia lead you to philosophy, or economics, or many other fields you'll find they all come in different flavors."

"Okay … just saying … if it's meant to be for me to still be here, and like you said I have to convince shrinks I'm not crazy enough to lock up forever. "

"Why?"

"Because you insist. "

"Sometimes how results are measured or what separates one from another, and there are variables from originalist orthodoxy to more general eclectic interpretations."

"For instance?"

"In his early writings Sigmund Freud, considered the father of psychology, was homophobic. But late in his career in a letter to the mother of a homosexual Freud was not homophobic at all."

"Let's see if I have this right, you want me to use Freud's ambiguity to convince hospital staff I'm not dangerous to myself or them. Uh, shouldn't I try to understand where this gobbledygook voodoo comes from before getting it switched around?"

Jokingly, I suggested my social work license could be imperil if I invented cliff notes for him to understand psychology. Not getting the joke, he didn't laugh. So, I explained Dr. Sigmund Freud, a neurologist medical doctor developed a vocabulary to discuss normal and abnormal mental processes and it became known as Freudian psychology and from that he developed *Psychoanalysis* to treat deep seated emotional problems. After Freud and his disciples, the *Objects Relations* psychology sought to deemphasize sex. Winnicott and others settled for *good enough mothering* and often asked, "How does that make you feel." The *Psychodynamic* flavor usually asked about first memories as a starting point, and future indicator of quality of life, and to set up a therapeutic alliance from there. They were followed by Eric Erickson's six stages of development, and three-leg stool of meaningful work, caring family, and fun recreation to have a contented old age and good death. Then Karl-Heinz Kohut's most empathetic self-psychology was the new flavor. Next came cognitive behavioral therapy, and we just spoke of mindfulness.

"Chucho did I just give you a thumbnail version of psychology with more flavorful information than you could possibly use or want to know?"

"Not if they are color coded for an easy way to know one from another?"

"These days most practitioners are eclectic not orthodox. They mix flavors."

"Why does everything have to be so hard?"

"Go on the offensive, talk about what you know, and ask them about their psychological preferences. Show them you're mildly interested in their field. That gives you some control of the situation. You like to talk, snow them, but ever so lightly."

"You give me too much credit. How will I know who's who? Tell me how to know the important ones from the others."

"Every staff person you come in contact with here will matter. They expect to be asked to write or at least testify about your mental health and possible risk to self and others."

"Everyone?"

"That includes the person who mops the floor. It's called a team approach. So, be nice, respectful, and always courteous, to *everyone*. Talk but not too much to all who will listen. Don't give them reasons to commit you involuntarily. That's how you control your destiny in the short term."

"Damn it, why does everything have to be so hard *all the time*?" Chucho leaned his head back on his pillow, closed his eyes, his face muscles relaxed, and soon he was taking deep breaths showing he'd fallen asleep.

I'd accomplished what I came for. How it shook out now was partially on him. I'd be around for support however it ended.

I left the way I'd come in, picking up a nurse escort as I approached the intimidating locked exit. When asked, she informed me, Chucho wouldn't even be in attendance for his forty-eight hours hold hearing. The attending physician and resident doctors would facilitate hold cases, rapidly, one after the other. However, if they decided on involuntary commitment, those cases would be formally adjudicated at proceedings open to outside interested parties and I and his lawyer could attend.

***

Just as I pulled alongside the fire hydrant, where I usually pick up, or drop off Darrell-Wayne and Esmeralda. They left the university building where they were waiting and headed in my direction. I was late from staying at the hospital with Chucho longer than intended. Call it instinct or paranoia, I spotted someone dressed like a student but older looking. He was suddenly moving with purpose in Darrell-Wayne's direction.

The situation didn't feel right. I jumped out of my car, pistol in hand. As the interloper headed to intercept Coy's cousin I saw a glint from his knife blade. He held the weapon low beside his leg, like an experienced knife fighter. My running changed to sprinting at maximum speed as he approached them. I pulled back my automatic's hammer, cocked and ready to fire while racing, but didn't see a clean shot without risking innocence by standers.

Esmeralda saw me running gun in hand. Her facial expression changed from curious to on guard warry. Then they were all bunched too close together for me to get any shot. Just as I tried to separate Darrell-Wayne from the knifer, Esmeralda tossed the intruder into the air. When he landed, she was on the assailant like white on rice and then, he was dead. His knife stuck between ribs directly into his no longer beating heart. We'd decompress later, without a word I rushed Darrell-Wayne and Esmeralda to my car, and we sped home. It all happened so fast nobody had seemed to notice.

Chapter 12.

The hospital telephoned. Chucho was being discharged and they needed a signature from a responsible adult to see he attended follow up visits. They also required someone to clear his bill of extras above and beyond what Medicaid paid, like television, telephone, and computer use. His aunt refused to sign for him because he'd attempted suicide and the hospital couldn't guarantee her, he wouldn't again.

I agreed to take responsibility and signed and paid Chucho out of the hospital. They assured me, he complied with taking medications on schedule, and met and agreed to weekly sessions with a psychotherapist. The hospital had done everything by the book, but stubborn Esmeralda, his only blood relative in this country was holding up his release. What I knew was the longer someone is in hospital the greater the chance of catching a hard to cure illness that could kill them.

I telephoned Ameli and we picked Chucho up in the new QQ van. It still had that new van smell. For some reason Ameli seemed to have a bug up her ass, and I wasn't in the mood to play psychoanalyst just then. When we arrived at the hospital, I was surprised by the tension between the two wheelchair jockeys, it was palpable. Not at all the kiss, kiss, hug, hug, I anticipated.

Before I could neutralize the developing friction Ameli said, "I brought your wheelchair and office personal stuff, so we can take you directly to your home. Do you need any prescriptions filled on the way?"

"There is no reason I can't work half a day today. Let's go straight to the office, and I'll catch up filing. It will be therapeutic for me. Just so you know, I can't go home, my aunt kicked me out. Tonight, I'm sleeping in a homeless shelter the hospital social worker arranged." I was so happy to see Chucho looking healthy, I'd forgotten the hospital discharge clerk had mentioned he was homeless, thanks to his aunt.

Ameli's icy cold shoulder made it no secret she wanted to shed Chucho, quickly. If I didn't intervene it was going to get locked horns ugly, so I said, "Good idea Chucho. We are overdue for a staff meeting at the office. Any objections?" I followed my question with a stern look at Amelia who was driving. She gripped the steering wheel hard, tensed her shoulders, made a sour face, but kept quiet.

Once back at the office, I let my two workers unload their motorized chairs themselves and went on ahead to make coffee, light the lights, and open windows. A quick perusal of my current voice mail netted no emergencies. When my workers got upstairs, I directed them to coffee and then the conference room.

I took my usual seat at the head of the old fashioned, long, knurled-oak table and said, "Ameli, Chucho, this is a place of business. If you two can't be pleasant with each other, find jobs somewhere else. Our clients don't need to deal with your discontent on top of their troubles. Clients come here for help not your grumpy faces. To be blunt either clear the air or both pack up your belongings and good luck to you in a future somewhere else."

"Oliver, how can I be pleasant at work never knowing when or where I'll find Chucho's dead body from his own hand for me to clean up ."

I could see from Chucho's facial expression he wanted to shut down and crawl away. On the other hand, his eyes showed he knew it was a do or die moment, and said, "What I did was stupid. Oliver helped me realize it wasn't my time to die. I promise not to put either of you or myself through that again. I'll make up for the damage I caused by being the best employee humanly possible."

Ameli clearly wasn't taking him at his word and said, "The support group says you are not completely honest with us. I think that's true too."

"It's true. There are things about me and my aunt it is better for you *not* to know."

I wasn't expecting where the conversation went, and said, "Your aunt seems to dislike me more and more all the time and I bend over backwards trying to be friendly and generous."

"Now that she read my suicide note I'm on the outs with her too. She knows how to hold a grudge, forever."

"Chucho, I haven't knowingly done anything to offend her."

"She's like that with me now. In your case she always hated gringos and with no way to reciprocate your generosity it makes her hate being your dependent,too."

"That doesn't make sense she earns what she gets protecting Darrell-Wayne."

"She feels she is disrespecting herself for taking what we need and can never repay back. We were raised to be proud and always self-sufficient."

"Why does she hate gringos and live in a country half full of them? She could live anywhere in the world she wanted."

"Esmeralda was indoctrinated and sent here when young. It was long before I was born. She was supposed to assassinate President Ronald Regan because he interfered as an imperialist in our civil war. The leaders thought she would be killed doing her assignment. There was never a plan to bring her home, or alternative if someone else got in the way."

"Is this for real?"

"Just when she was ready to pull the trigger some nutcase named Hinkley beat her to the shot. He botched it, and she never got another chance, or ticket home. She can't forgive herself for the failure. Even today, if she went home, they'd kill her for not doing her duty."

I couldn't tell for sure if Ameli was buying his story when she said, "Are you an assassin too?"

"No."

"What is your story, Chucho? What are you doing here?"

"I don't like having my private business in the street, but if it means keeping this job, I'll tell you. A local gang with connections tried to recruit me when I grew underarm hair. When I said no the last time, they planned to slaughter me to make a big show of my dying slowly in front of everybody. They were going to make an example of me to demonstrate their power in our neighborhood."

"Why not join the gang?"

"If I had joined, they expected me to kill a much older person for initiation. I couldn't do that, I like old people, and so ran away. My aunt didn't want to take me up here. But she did, rather than know I'd been killed back home, and she could have prevented it. She's my father's oldest sister, they aren't friendly. The whole family says she's hard to get along with."

"And that's why you expect to sleep at the men's shelter?"

"She's a hard person. Nothing ever pleases her, and sometimes I do stupid stuff without thinking."

"Do those gangs reach up this far?"

"Yes, some do. We did odd jobs for Pachuco-88 to keep other gangs from killing us. I was never a member of any gang. I wanted to be a lover not a killer. Now I'm just an all-around loser."

"Are you and your aunt so different? You said she is a killer, and you are not, and yet you keep pestering me for a gun. That doesn't compute."

"Esmeralda doesn't have a problem killing people like Regan mixed up in our civil war. And here am I not even capable of killing myself. That's funny don't you think? I want a gun to protect myself from others who want to do me harm, and all the rest of you carry guns. I feel left out and even more inadequate."

"Hate me or not, your aunt is doing a great job protecting Darrell-Wayne, that's what I pay her for. You, my young friend, haven't figured out a reason why you need a lethal weapon. However, you are more than adequate keeping this office running smoothly."

Not used to compliments, blushing slightly and to control the narrative Chucho changed the subject. He suggested I ask his aunt about U.S. presidents since Eisenhower and watch her shovel dirt on their graves. He suggested she and I might find common ground to lighten the mood between us criticizing bad U.S. Presidents.

When I asked his favorite president, he said Obama. Although he knew a lot more about our greedy presidents elected to serve only the rich and powerful at the expense of every other citizen.

He also despised President Bush selected by the Supreme Court to be the president because his brother was governor of Florida with a vote hanky-panky scam. Bush received many less votes than his opponent but won in the elitist supreme court. Chucho thought it was unique to America that losers got to be declared victors, and real winners were the losers.

I didn't apologize for any of our mad scoundrel dry-drunk or drunk-drunk presidents because our history is full of them. Who in their right mind would want such a thankless job, except some narcissistic greedy bastard.

We may be done with all that wrangling anyway. The American people seem to be in a mood for a ruthless authoritarian dictator for a change. This time they appear to want to keep the divide between hate tribes and others for the benefit of extremely rich few. Lately inclusiveness for everyone seems not to include everybody. Having lost the thread of what we had been talking about, I asked Chucho what he knew about presidents Roosevelts. He said they were long gone before he was born.

I explained Teddy Roosevelt was a rough and tumble kind of man's man who few remember beyond his bluster, killing Aboriginals, wild animals, and changing his political parties from Republican to Bull Moose. He was an egotistical showoff history remembers as an amusing Americana meat-eating-naturalist character.

On the other hand, his wheelchair bound Cousin Franklyn is loved to this day for acknowledging the forgotten destitute, old, and crippled have needs to eat and shelter. Franklyn's programs eliminated the need for the poor to sell pencils on street corners in order to eat.

Both cousins had a war to manage. Teddy Roosevelt had a small war, while Cousin Franklyn took on World War II. Teddy looked after the well to do. Franklyn improved the lot of the impoverished sick, widows, and destitute orphan children, despite formidable opposition.

Ameli was not active in the conversation, which wasn't like her. She looked withdrawn so I said to her, "Sooner or later, we must stop talking about presidents and clear the air in this office. And sooner is always better than later in my estimation. Look, I've already opened all the windows."

"You want to pick on me boss, fine. Let's throw down, right now. Workers have rights!"

"What's your problem?"

"Chucho is my best excuse to quit this lousy job. I could work full time as a private eye."

"Don't let me stand in your way. Give us a Nancy Regan and just *DO IT*."

"Just a minute there fellow. I owe you money and probably can't pay it back working out there on my own, *yet*."

"Well then I know an alternative … you two shake hands and let bygones be bygones and we super glue Humpy Dumpty back together as best we can."

"I can't do that. Chucho is a coward while his aunt kills people for politics."

"I've never seen you so judgmental. I wouldn't take you to the gun range if I didn't think you capable of killing to defend yourself and innocents."

"Oliver, you have no idea how hard it is in the country of my birth to be born disabled. So, suicide is never an acceptable excuse for any reason, ever! What it is, is a gutless copout I can't tolerate."

"Don't hold back, what do you really think."

"In homogeneous societies all the people have common ancestry. They are expected to be sympathetic and accommodating by blood from birth to death. In the U.S. we are the opposite."

"Okay fine, our diversity is *our* greatest strength, and for you a symptom of weakness. How do you explain the homogeneous Japanese cultural acceptance of suicide?"

"There is an exception to every rule. For me suicide is a sign of weakness, I'm Chinese American not Japanese. There was never an American president who kill themself. They let others."

"That we know of. Our history is revisionist according to Texas textbook publishers."

"Why do you always pick on Republicans?"

"Democrats had a few crummy presidents too. Ameli, life goes on, get over yourself. Chucho promised to accept help to stay among the living, and we should be in his life to hold him to what he promised. It's the right thing to do."

"I can't."

"Why not?"

"I just can't."

"Cut the bullshit, either we run this business in an open, friendly, welcoming way or close it back to a one-man operation."

"It was the disabled, Hitler experimented exterminating first, and he got the idea from the United States of America's Supreme Court's racist writings to support racial purity by eliminating the handicapped."

Looking uncomfortable, by degrees, watching the back and forth between Ameli and me. It appeared as if Chucho was watching a tennis match turning his head one direction than the other. The expression on his face looked like he bet all his money on the losing player. Chucho finally said, "I'd better leave. No don't move I'll call a cab and send for the wheelchair once I have a place." With that said he reached around behind his motorized chair and retrieved his crutches from their vinyl carry sleeve. Then he stood, and stiffly walked toward the open conference room door.

Never having seen him walk that well, Ameli and I watched open mouthed in silence for a second. Then without pre-thought I stood and said, "We aren't done here." Turning to Ameli I said, "If you can't shake Chucho's hand and forgive and forget you're both fired, right here right now no tears. Go collect your personal belongings, I'm done coddling you both."

A hush filled the room, the type of quiet after the last gunshot rings out. It was heavy with anticipation of what's next. The quietude pause was broken when Ameli shakily stood and hobbled over to Chucho standing-still leaning heavily on the conference room door frame. He looked deflated hanging on crutches tucked under his armpits to keep vertical.

Ameli slowly moved with effort and awkwardly said, "If you try suicide again, I swear to my God, I will shoot you dead," and she thrust her hand straight out for a shake.

Chucho took her hand in both of his. "Thank you. You won't be sorry for giving me another chance."

In that tender moment, my feelings were mixed, leave the room and let them sort it out, or assert myself again. "As the owner and operator of this place I demand a group hug."

***

That night we had a late dinner and lingered over the last of the wine. It was Mary Renault's best South African retsina wine. No one was in a mood to talk. Coy was working odd hour shifts, either he didn't want to talk about, or more likely he was ordered not to share outside the job. Nevertheless, as much as possible, we tried to have an evening meal together as a budding new family under threat. After washing up the dinner things while Coy was helping Darrell-Wayne with a shower, I pondered how much of my day's events to share. In hindsight it seemed mundane even after my posturing and threats. It was an office meeting, boring, about office etiquette, doubly boring.

Before my man's new undercover, hush hush assignment we had gotten into a routine of happily telling each other how our day went. Lately, Darrell-Wayne only wanted to talk about Dolphins to my mate and my distraction. So, I doubted Coy would be interested in my day's office soap opera. In truth I didn't feel much like rehashing. It was beginning to feel like what was going on outside normal expectable activities, lately, were getting to be too much mix in with everything else, or I was getting too old for the adventuresome life I was living.

Finally, with Darrell-Wayne tucked into bed wearing his earbuds listening to a recording of baby porpoises singing. Coy came out to the kitchen, grabbed me from behind, nuzzled my neck and said, "I had an uneventful day I can't talk about, and I'm talked out about big mammals that look and behave like giant fish. And how was your day my dear?"

"I had an overdue staff meeting doubt you'd find it interesting."

"I miss back in the day sharing our mundane work lives. Lately it feels as if we are drifting apart unless it's about Darrell-Wayne's safety. When do we get back to just plain us, a new couple starting out as husbands?"

In response to what he said, I'd planned to give a quick abridged version of events, not reliving the whole meeting. I guess I was more troubled by the event than my rational mind wanted to admit, and I repeated every boring issue that came up despite not wanting to.

Then I noticed it was Esmeralda's obsession with U.S. Presidents that grabbed

Coy's interest most. So, I said half joking, "You seem obsessed by her obsession. Am I wrong?"

"No. It's true, I have my own preoccupation which I'd not shared with you in detail since it makes you uncomfortable."

"What might that be, if I may be so bold as to ask?"

"Routine circumcision."

"Oh, that again. Boring."

"See you don't really want to know everything about me, warts and all."

So, my inner social worker said, "If we aren't careful this could turn into an all-nighter just talking about your obsession with routine cut cock. We haven't talked the night away since we first got together."

"I can handle redo, can you?"

Then it sank in, *I saw the depth of his fascination or preoccupation with chopped meat*, Coy's face took on a guilty patina like he'd just been caught scrutinizing something he shouldn't and quickly said, "All right, forget it, looks like you have judgement problems with my obsessive-compulsive fixation."

"No judgement, it has been a while since we really talked anyway. Tomorrow I can work from home, which means naps for me if needed. How will you manage?"

"Cops often function on little sleep. Oliver, we're still a new couple. You need to know what comes with me."

"All right then, I'm all ears."

"Do you ever get super curious about things?"

"Sometimes, I'm a private investigator, built on a social work chassis who was a Peace Corps volunteer right after high school, and I never want to stop learning how things work."

"In that context could you give a for instance?"

"When I became a teenager all the boy's talked about was making girls bleed by having sex with them. I had a real problem with the idea of getting pleasure giving a female pain. I liked girls to dance with and kiss but didn't want to hurt them. So, I had sex with boys, and nobody got hurt doing it, and I like it. Then I grew up and found out girls wanted the same thing boys wanted only with feelings, without pregnancy."

With a mischievous grin Coy said, "Then if you prefer males, why does something I think about all the time make you uncomfortable?"

"It sets up an unnatural dichotomy of haves and have nots. Docs' code of ethetics says NEVER perform surgery on infants except in emergencies."

"I noticed *you are always* a little quick on the trigger."

"Working with cutthroat felons at parole it was called survival device, shoot first, and I had a reputation to uphold. How can they call something they vow never to do routine?"

"I know I'm a police officer. If what is done to baby boys and called routine were done to infant girls, it would be a serious felony in every country of the world. The

United States is the only developed country worldwide that allows infant boys to be permanently altered for life without criminal consequences."

"So, as I said the matter is beyond what I can do anything about it's a profitable crime."

"I guess that means you don't want to hear all about me."

"Not true, I want our marriage to be a once in a lifetime commitment. That makes it special and honors the spirit of the institution. That's what matters to me."

"Okay then. What do you want to know about *me* you don't already that isn't about routine circumcision?"

"What religion were you raised in?"

"Presbyterian. you already know that."

The question in my mind was why I was blocking Coy from telling me what he wanted to. I'd need to do some self-analysis soon, but right then said, "Mm hmm, that's interesting, I noticed when we showered your cousin, he'd been circumcised, and I intimately know you're a natural. Does your family practice more than one religion?"

"Are you teasing me?"

"I don't want you to feel you can't tell me any and everything."

"Oliver, it's a long story. I don't think you want to know."

"I thought Presbyterians were similar to Lutherans, my lapsed faith."

"We're all protestants. I refuse to nitpick who is more Calvinist, or why I dislike Anglicans."

"Hmm, I'm still confused, Saint Paul, one of Jesus's apostles wrote that Christians needn't be circumcised unless they were like him, Jewish first. Was Darrell-Wayne Jewish, Muslim, or Mormon before becoming Presbyterian?"

"Still sounds like you are teasing me. Or do you want into my mind's deepest recesses to get at my most taboo obsessive-compulsive subject. You know the one I've been trying to tell you about."

"I'm not teasing, you asked what I want to talk about all night. I want to know everything about the man I intend to marry. And at your request I've explained why before tonight I find the topic superfluous."

"Disclaimer then, once my demon gets out, he doesn't go back in quietly. You still want to know about my inner self when I'm too hungry, angry, lonely, or tired?"

"Yup, now you've whetted my appetite, I want more."

"This has become more than *why* Darrell-Wayne's dick was shortened and is now my obsession."

"Tell me."

"This will take a while. Fasten your seat belt."

"I take full responsibility for whatever I unknowingly stumbled into. You now have my full attention, disclose whatever you want. Just nudge me in the ribs if I start to snore."

"With that level of interest, I better give you the whole megillah and see if you really do want to marry me or just need sleep."

Coy went on to say from birth Darrell-Wayne developed normally. Hitting developmental markers within normal time frames, walking, talking, feeding himself, even using the toilet ahead of schedule. Then at age four for no reason he started to regress, unlearning basic activities of daily living he knew. It was troubling to watch. After testing by professionals, the specialists diagnosed him with moderate autism.

His parents took him to see experts, far and wide, desperately hoping for a miracle or at least a magic elixir to slow regression before he needed infant care. One charlatan toward the end of a long line of quacks assured the Goff family Darrell-Wayne would become transexual since most transexuals were autistic unless he slept with powerful very expensive magnets. Desperate, digging into that diagnosis, the family discovered there wasn't research to definitively come to that conclusion.

Exhausted, financially strapped, knowing time was about to run out, they found a quack who promised the pain from routine circumcision would shock Darrell-Wayne back on to his normal developmental track and have future benefits as well. At that point they would have tried almost anything. It was greatly disappointing when the surgical procedure had the opposite effect.

What happened was the cutting was done in the doctor's office. As the anesthesia wore off the pain increased to excruciating and lasted for weeks. Recuperation at home for Darrell-Wayne included severe embarrassment at his privates constantly scrutinized by professionals, family, and strangers. Meanwhile, his autism symptom regression continued rather than stopped or reversed as promised. He withdrew deeper inside himself, his outbursts became more frequent, louder, and then violent.

Bathing him turned into an extreme psychotic event that accelerated and regularly turned into out-of-his-control manic violence. Remembering back, it was like when Darrell-Wayne returned from the Inuit, a real horror show. Initially the family primary care physician prescribed antipsychotic drugs not tested on children to get a little peace at bedtime. They worked with bizarre side effects.

Eddie finally asked his parents to let him take charge of daily washing his little brother, to have a modicum of normalcy before going to bed. The brother's nightly dual allowed the parents to get sleep without being assaulted first. Once Eddie got a handle on the situation, he convinced his parents to stop Darrell-Wayne's use of prescription drugs. As he suspected the side effects made behavior worse than what little benefit.

When Eddie was just eighteen, Coy turned sixteen in 2016, and their close friendship changed, unexpectedly. It happened after a day at the public swimming pool while dressing. Both had hit puberty early but internalized homophobia or the incest taboo kept them from talking about mutual feelings. But that day at the pool, with their hands touching each other accidentally, accidentally at first, they just couldn't tamp down unspoken feelings any longer. A stolen kiss spontaneously burst forth into full-fledged burning desire that required wordless warm friction to quench.

***

Darrell-Wayne, born in 2004, was six years younger than his brother Eddie and didn't hit puberty until age seventeen. Both Eddie and Coy, exploring their sexuality, wondered why it took little brother six or four years longer than either of them to come of age. Trying to satisfy his curiosity, Eddie came across an article on late bloomers in the public library. The article mentioned empirical evidence that circumcised boys start puberty later and lose interest in sex earlier than their natural counterparts. Reading the footnotes, Eddie discovered scientific research on the subject was restricted due to patents.

Since their family had been duped by a medical doctor and received the opposite of what was promised, routine circumcision became a taboo subject in conversation for family members. Nevertheless, Eddie constantly overheard his parents fight, in private, over Darrell-Wayne's unnecessary suffering at the hands of an expensive swindler who performed sloppy surgery in his back office.

To escape the constant family drama Eddie joined the Army and after basic training was shipped overseas. Before leaving he asked Coy to look after his younger brother while he was away. He also left his pro and con research on dick-cutting with his cousin to hold until he returned. Eddie wanted to become a journalist after military service and expose the fraud of routine circumcision. Then Eddie was killed in war.

To find out more information about what routine circumcision was supposed to accomplish as opposed to what was promised and didn't deliver, Coy asked probing questions of any adult who would listen. All answers fell into one of two baskets. Either the respondents acted guilty, ashamed, or angry at the question. Or there was a lack of interest in the question and the idea of an answer was dismissed with a hand wave showing no interest, "Don't know, don't want to know, it doesn't affect me." Coy wondered how one simple question could garner such different responses.

To increase his knowledge while exploring what was fast becoming a forbidden subject to explore. Coy discovered most of the information at the library and online was bogus propaganda . Who could prove infant penis surgery prevented bedwetting or thumb sucking when the conditions didn't exist in the first place.

Not getting straight answers, from professionals. Young Coy decided he had discovered a classified top-secret government narrative everyone he talked to was afraid to discuss. Which was thrilling on one hand. On the other it seemed dangerous given the strong emotions fifty percent of respondents had. His original adolescent quest was to expose a lie told by his aunt and uncle that caused hurt and made his cousin's condition worse.

The more he dug the bigger the problem he uncovered, that nobody wanted to talk about. Soon it was a lot more than just his family having been scammed. After receiving anonymous threats for asking embarrassing questions, Coy got serious about doing his martial arts training for self-protection.

In general, the international respondents were not interested in pursuing the subject beyond it didn't make sense in their country to perform unnecessary surgery on healthy infants for no known benefit and possible complications . When Coy pushed harder, he got empathy for infant boy *victims* without bodily integrity and sense of full autonomy, and distain for those who profited. Which opened another front in Coy's battle with the U.S. establishment."

Where was the impeccable hard data to settle the argument one way or the other? Why was the procedure taught in international medical schools for life and death medical emergencies only? To confuse that, in the U.S. it had been officially downgraded to cosmetic elective surgery that prevented nothing. Coy decided it wasn't saboteurs and spies he'd stumbled into but rather cults wanting to limit normal male sexual activity and duration. If it was some kind of social control nobody admitted to that.

On fire to expose con artists ripping off the gullible wishing to improve their baby's prospects for a better life, Coy found and then was guided by an online group of anti-circumcisers. In searching, he was astonished to discover the routine procedure in the U.S. was still touted to prevent every form of cancer, heart disease, diabetes, kidney disease, indigestions, athletes' foot, and cure or prevent mental illness. Even after the American Medical Association proclaimed its only use was cosmetics, medical students were encouraged to push the procedure's magical cures for future illness on new mothers. Coy thought, *Damn, they say it does everything snake oil can and much more, without snakes or oil. If only the claims could be proved. But who puts cosmetics on penises using surgery.*

Venting his frustrations when called upon in high school sophomore civics class, he was supposed to praise the glories of his country's winning every war it fought, which he knew wasn't true. Instead, Coy unloaded his frustrations trying to understand the duality in thinking in answers to his simple question about routine circumcision. "What's it supposed to accomplish?" His old, wizened teacher, Mr. Wannamaker, assured the class natural and circumcised boys could both make babies, fertility was not governed by length or girth, and a condom should always be used. The girls all laughed, and some of the boys wanted to know how sex related to winning every war the U.S. fought.

When asked for evidence, teacher Wannamaker said, "Everybody knows natural boys are more incline to breed more often that's why they have to be cut. However, this is a topic for geography not civics so let's move on with glorious American wars not anyway related to imperialistic intent."

Mr. Wannamaker held Coy after class and as promised answered further questions in a way any high school student could understand. "Mr. Goff, when I was a youth, I read all of Charles Dickens and Rudyard Kipling writings and was appalled how the poor of their days were exploited for the benefit of the aristocracy. What seems stuck in your craw is history seems to be repeating itself by manipulating the gullible against their best interest. You are in an unwinnable fight where neither Dickens nor Kipling could prevail. Your writing is not even close to theirs. Quit while you are behind young man or get your behind in a sling."

"Who was Rudyard Kipling?"

"Ah, the textbook monopoly must have revised history again and dropped Kipling for fear of being called racist, which they are, and he wasn't."

"Why call Kipling a racist if he wasn't?"

"He coined the phrase 'white man's burden,' because he wanted his bosses in England to improve the lot in life for Indians in India he worked with, instead of just exploiting them. Coy if you don't lighten up people will call you names too, just like well-intended Kipling."

"Are you trying to change the subject? … Oh, okay if you say you're not, what is your opinion about the routine circumcision of infant males."

"Your topic is too sensitive. We don't want those physically reduced to feel bad."

"Coy, are you on some kind of vendetta because you discovered you have less dick than your peers?"

"No. I have all the parts I started life with. What I'm trying to understand is why routine circumcision is done, for what purpose, and why the topic gets under people's skin if it's a good thing."

"Maybe you are jealous you didn't get that attention."

"Funny you said that, I asked my family doctor about me getting circumcised. I was curious why he wouldn't talk about it. He checked me out, then said I was healthy, and it was a totally unnecessary procedure for me to have a happy sex life. That was as far as he would go talking about circumcision with me. "

"Keep in mind, he must defend his profession's financial interests, and at the same time protect you from unnecessary medical profiteering. "

"In civics you taught us about ethics in government. Do all professions have conflicts with ethical practice like the medical profession?"

"I think so, but because medical doctors deal in life and death they get a little more leeway to steal than the rest of society ."

"That helps me cut through some of the confusion of this topic. Ha, ha that's a pun, right?"

"Spare me. Speaking of confusion, one complication for those who start life with surgery on their tiny privates is fictions to explain their deficit to others."

"I've run into that in the gym shower room."

"For some of your classmates, truth and fiction becomes blurred below the belt to compensate loss and answers that don't add up."

***

"Coy you are yawning a lot."

"You're right, how about I finish this litany tomorrow at breakfast?"

"Sounds like a plan. I know a way to send you off to dreamland with a smile on your face."

"I'm up for that."

***

"What's that racket?"

"Jackhammers. It looks like the utility company is digging up the street out front."

"What! Can't be, I pay extra for them to give me a heads-up warning before they dig." My feet kicked out of bed and hit the floor moving. I slipped into a pair of silk boxer shorts and marched over to the periscope-screen for a look. At the same time, I hit speed dial for twenty-four-hour customer service at the electric company. The computer's voice answered on the third ring ...

"Coy, guess what?" That truck, air compressor trailer, six men all wearing the utility company's logo, are not their employees. What do you suppose?"

"Not good!"

"The utility company's central office knows nothing about street work being done at this address. What's your best guess?" After I asked the question I started coffee, then buttered English muffins to broil.

"Hmm, could it be they're digging a tunnel to invade us with an underground assault. Of course, I'm just guessing."

"See, we think alike, that's good. How about you grab a box of flash-bang concussion grenades along with those left-over fireworks from last Fourth of July. They're in the safe room closet. I'll call my friend Willis to send the calvary?"

"Flash-bangs aren't lethal."

"Neither are fireworks, let's try a different approach with these fake utility yahoos. How about we don't kill them for a change of karma."

"Killing is faster and surer."

"True, but for a change let's let Willis' guys spill blood if it is necessary."

"Yeah, okay, but still ... I want to grab a couple of assault rifles since it looks like they are trying to invade. This could get personal for me."

"Good man, a few boxes of those outdated rifle cartridges might spice up the party with lots of noise and reduced punch."

After a brief, all business conversation, Willis had SWAT and regular PD on the way coming to us from two directions. They were coming with lights and sirens off.

When Coy returned pushing the rolling snack cart he'd borrowed from under the kitchen counter, it mostly contained items to make a lot of noise with low lethality. Darrell-Wayne slept like a log through the jackhammers. We shut his bedroom door to see how he did replacing pneumatic hammer with flashbangs and fireworks. Since staying with the Inuit our teen seemed able to sleep through raucous anything.

In most action oriented high anxiety situations Coy and I didn't talk. We'd already started finishing each other's sentences months ago during placid times. So, we just lobbed concussion grenades over my security fence and most went into the hole being dug or under their rented dirt digging equipment.

Having their handywork disturbed, the phony workers showed displeasure by shooting at us with rather lethal looking large caliber long and short guns. Naturally, we interpreted being shot at as an attack and returned fire with past due date ammunition. We went for quantity rather than quality since the local police were about to arrive. Who were we to spoil the bad guys' fun when about to be fighting on three fronts. On the other hand, as a deterrent, it's much less paperwork for the cops on the scene to process live bodies than dead ones, it requires less forms to be filled out and a lower level of sign-off-approval.

When SWAT arrived from one end of the street and regular emergency services police led by Sargent Melissa Jackson from the other. The bad guys threw their hands in the air to surrender. I met with the local gendarme leaders once the perps were wearing handcuffs seated in the back of police vehicles. I gave them the name and number of the executive at the electric company operations headquarters who claimed the perps were spurious.

Once the early morning visitors left, I served my spouse to be, toasted English muffins, with a fried egg and quicky-hollandaise sauce on top, a side of bacon, and refilled our coffee mugs. Then sitting down to eat I said, "We've got a couple of hours before Darrell-Wayne gets hungry enough to leave his bed. Want an early morning luxury snooze?"

"Sounds like a plan."

<h1 style="text-align:center">Chapter 13.</h1>

"How about I finish what I started last night. I'll feel better if you know what you're getting by marrying me. Also, I hate to leave a story half finished."

"Sure, if that's what you want. I can't imagine where such an autocratic idea of cutting-off baby boy genital flesh came from."

"Okay, Oliver, I'll tell you what I know about the origin."

"Oh goody, a breakfast story."

"Are you mocking me?"

"I love you. My ageism made it hard to say at first, now looking you in the eye and saying it makes me happy. You know me I wouldn't mock an enemy. Punch him in the nose, maybe."

"Okay then, the original source was easy to find, here let me show you on this paper napkin."

Then Coy drew the Mandarin character *jia* (first tone). By itself it means family. The pictograph is of a pig under a roof. It dates the time in history when the Chinese went from nomads to farmers. It is carbon datable provable that character has been used continuously in written communications for 25,000 years.

Ancient Chinese farmers discovered to have productive livestock most roosters had to be turned into capons, bulls into steers, and except for a few breeding males, all other male farm animals were neutered to make more efficient, peaceful, fat livestock.

"Wait, Coy, are you now talking about castration? I thought routine circumcision was your objection."

"Be patient, Oliver. You asked where genital cutting started. 25,000 years ago, seemed like a good place to begin."

"You're right, I did ask And I'm impressed your Chinese character calligraphy has progressed to *jia*. Please continue,"

"Like I said before it's a long story."

Coy went on to describe the ancient Australian aboriginals coming of age ritual for adolescent boys. It involved the teens being brutally beaten, and then circumcised. Each year the elders marked certain boys they didn't want to reproduce for physical or mental reasons. During the circumcision, the marked boys had their urethra slit down to the base of their penis so their ejaculate couldn't enter a vagina.

"Gross! Were the youths told of the life-long limitation before initiation?"

"Doubt it, they'd all run away. But there is no way to know. The Aboriginals didn't write their history down. It is passed from one generation to the next by word of mouth."

"Huh, I guess they wouldn't want to document damage to a teenager's ability to procreate for political or superstitious reasons."

"No. I suspect oral tradition leaves out inconvenient details."

"Does that count as a twofer, both circumcision with castration? I've lost track from where your soliloquy started last night."

"Hold your horses, Oliver. All will be revealed in time."

"Stallions or geldings?"

"You only think you're funny. For that remark you get a smile not belly laughs, my good man."

"Oh dear, I rack up another deficit rating. I hope it won't negatively affect QQ's overall customer approval ranking. Please hurry and continue with your story before I'm sent to the poorhouse."

"According to Darwin, yes, I too read as a teenager. Darwin wrote, when the cavemen around ancient Persia formed into tribes, they castrated captured enemy warriors and sold them as slaves. Happy now?"

"How could that knowledge make me happy? Oh wait, let me ask the geldings they have firsthand knowledge."

Coy went on to clarify, slavers had a business problem. Sixty percent of the castrated worriers died of postsurgical infection before they could be sold. Then an enterprising slave trader discovered if he circumcised instead of castrating the captured warriors, he realized a higher yield of salable slaves. Initially the living postsurgical castrated, and the circumcised was the same, *impotence*. Consequently, at that time, around ancient Persia, and Egypt circumcising slaves became an identifier and fashionable for marking slaves. At first it looked like a win win for slave traders with sixty percent more slaves to sell.

The captured big strong worrier slaves were most often used to guard harems, and over some years it was discovered slaves' postsurgical impotence was not a permanent condition for either castrated or circumcised. What caused the big social upheaval was the circumcised slaves, after recovery, left genetic inheritance in horny fertile harem ladies. Raising children that did not resemble the harem owner met with his extreme disdain leading to torture and a cruel death.

There were other practical reasons for circumcision to fall out of fashion for designating slaves. Enterprising slaves bought their freedom. Also, it became popular in Persia and Egypt, to copy the Roman and Greek slave owners and bequest freedom onto household slaves at the owner's death.

It was during this time of social change that freed ancients started the Jewish religion. They had been circumcised Egyptian slaves and so made circumcision a ritual part of their new religion. Going against the anti-circumcision vogue of the day got the new religion noticed as old fashioned and newfangled simultaneously in revolutionary times.

According to founding rabbis' writings, the stated purpose of circumcising young male converts to the new religion was to diminish sexual expression except for reproduction. In addition, to keep their randy youth away from the very popular fertility cults that used orgasms as part of their religious ritual. Besides desensitizing sexual response, the surgery was supposed to assert power and control by identification.

An often-cited example of the confusion about circumcision in ancient Egypt is the story of Moses. When fished out of the Nile River by the Pharos's daughter, infant Moses had a natural penis. In that Egyptian household there were freed circumcised slaves and natural domestic slaves working together performing everyday tasks. In the five books of the Jewish Torah, Old Testament of the Christian Bible, and the Quran, Moses had a running dispute with God over keeping his foreskin. Then later refusing to circumcise his sons. Moses' ongoing dispute with God was over penis fashion and status of that day, ran throughout the holy books where he is mentioned. In the scriptures of the three modern religions Moses gets to keep his foreskin.

"Wait what? Are you saying Moses led his people to the promised land, went through all the trials and tribulations to get them there and then wasn't allowed entrance because God wanted part of his penis? That seems unfair to me. What a mean god."

"Ever read the Book of Job?"

"I have and that's why I find the Buddhists kinder, gentler, and doesn't require sacrifice of living body parts. They don't eat any kind of meat."

"Some obscure Buddhist sect might conceivably have a secret practice nobody knows about."

"Or you might be projecting that to foster your obsession."

"Ah ha, you might be right."

"I hate to bring this up but, Coy, you are against dick cutting in an all-consuming way. Do you think such an obsession is healthy? There's nothing you can do about it, and as you say it's been going on a long time, not that I recommend it."

"You say you wanted to know me, warts, and all. Healthy or not I'm giving you an easy way to bail on me for sharing what I've wrestled with since Darrell-Wayne was circumcised to cure his autism."

"That was a long time ago."

"Yeah, I know, sometimes it even seems like forever. Ready to escape marrying me before it's too late?"

"No. So far, you've not scared me off, yet. It's only I've never met anyone with such a well-organized detailed fixation. To use your words, 'A subject nobody wants to talk or know about.'"

"Pheew! What a relief there's still hope for a big church wedding."

"I have to wonder though, if your preoccupation with dick has anything to do with your self-designated title of connoisseur cock sucker."

"When did I mention that?"

"You said it with pride when we first met negotiating a price for a tank of gasoline."

"Did that scandalize you?"

"Well, yes. Truth be told, it both attracted and repelled me at the same time."

"How so?"

"You caught my interest at first sight. But I had serious puritanical reservations at how forward you were."

"Part of my coming out as gay was to stop lying and *start* being honest with myself. Initially, my curiosity about cock and then routine cock cutting was *to expose medical quackery for the sake of profit only.* Then searching for more information, I found life-long harm caused to innocent babies, physically, emotionally, and developmentally within the same family over baseless lies about nonexistent protections."

"What do you mean?"

"It's not unusual to have unresolved conflict between father and son or between brothers when some are intact and others reduced, within the same family fighting both sides of a lie."

"You know what, I never gave any of this a thought. I just accepted it as status quo, the way it was without knowing why. Now that we are discussing the unkindest cut, I can see how it divides men one from another in spoken or unspoken conflict. Now I can even imagine wars fought over who is a real man."

"You were paying attention. I bet you've even heard about the Muslim conversion by blood."

"Do you think this subject shaped your development?"

"No. I think I developed into an expert cock sucker independent of what eventually became my fixation with injustice below the belt. But check yourself out, to make my point people won't talk about it, you haven't said the words routine circumcision is what we are talking about."

"You're right, now you've really got my attention. Tell me more of your story if you don't mind."

"Watching Darrell-Wayne' family's drama, before and after being ripped off is when I got started on my quest, to understand autism and what was being done about it. I had so little to go on, nobody wants to talk about it or dick in any way shape or form."

"Now all these years later maybe you can purge your obsessive compulsion. None of us can really do anything to change the way the world is. But you can free your thinking *to things you can change.*"

"Yeah but, if I can help one boy trying to make sense of why he's less than the other fellows, maybe it was worth having an obsession."

"If that's what you want, then I'm all in for you."

"For real?"

"Yes, I accept you warts and all. I just don't get why it is so important for you to fight battles you can't win, after you learn they are unwinnable. Why bother?"

To justify his obsession, Coy spoke of an incident before he reached puberty. His cousin Eddie got a crazy idea to take Darrell-Wayne to the beach. The boy had never been. Their parents were against the idea. Eddie knew it could turn into an autistic acting out disaster, which was why he wanted Coy to come along in case it went south.

As it turned out the day trip to the beach was a big success. The ocean awed and soothed the autistic preteen rather than over stimulate him. Darrell-Wayne had never become so animated and yet unafraid out in the world. Being outdoors in the sunshine, having almost no clothes on, and among strangers of all shapes, and ages, brought the nine-year-old Darrell-Wayne temporarily out of his usual brittle autistic shell.

At the end of a fun day, the three were showering together on the beach open to the sky dressing area. They were dutifully trying to get the beach sand off swimsuits and out of their body crevasses. Although younger, Coy was the same six feet tall as Eddie. After they started showering it became obvious Darrell-Wayne noticed his brother Eddie had pubic hair and Coy hadn't yet. He kept looking back and forth between them curiously.

Then Coy witnessed Darrell-Wayne take an intense look down at himself. He was comparing himself with Coy, and Eddie. His eyes flitted between his crotch, his brother with pubic hair, Coy's without and back to himself. As he looked his facial expression grew stormy. He was trying and failing to understand why he looked so different than the older boys with him.

As they dressed the nine-year-old who had been so filled with joy and wonder at the ocean, regressed back into an armored hard shell. There was a look of betrayal in his eyes. Coy doubted it was only about pubic hair or not. Eddie and Coy looked the same, other than crotch hair. Darrell-Wayne discovered he was missing more than pubic hair, without the words necessary to understand.

Seeing his young cousin confused, trying to make sense of why he looked different, made Coy wonder about all the other routinely circumcised boys' coming to the realization something permanent had been done to change them, without their consent.

"I guess it was wake up time."

"Imagine what stories they were told or had to make up to justify being less than equal in the eyes of their contemporaries."

"Fortunately, that is not your problem, Coy."

"But they faced a lifetime to wonder what they were missing, why, and who was responsible. If their quest dug deep, they'd find out their mothers signed the consent to make them less than their peers for cosmetics reasons.

"Coy, you've made it clear *with over kill* how you feel about routine circumcision. Do you feel the same about religious ritual penis reduction?"

"No, not at all. There it has a religious purpose. The recipient's loss is also their mark of acceptance by family, congregation, and traditional identification."

"Despite Moses fighting with God about it?"

"In modern times if a boy has a problem with what was done to him in the name of religion, he can talk to his father, grandfather, uncles, brothers, or cousins to understand his modification. It doesn't have to be a big mystery nobody understands or can explain. Or be linked to snake oil scams."

"So, your obsession with routine circumcision began before you reached puberty. See, I said the word."

"That's right. I started fooling around with other boys when my orgasms started waking me up from deep sleep. They cleared up many abstract mysteries I wondered about. Suddenly strange adult behavior had a context, even if they still seemed silly."

"I suspect most the rest of us were not as penis preoccupied as you. I wasn't, except for orgasms."

"Yeah, you're right, after I decided to become the world's greatest cock sucker, I took detailed notes. I discovered most guys my age didn't share my passion about differences between natural and cut cock or subsequent orgasms. Nevertheless, I still asked a lot of questions of the boys I played with, but few had realistic answers. It was good I knew martial arts for some of the adverse reactions I got. Naturally all that stimulated my curiosity into the full-fledged fascination it has become."

"Should I ask, or is it obvious?"

"Sex is more than just dick. The brain is the biggest sex organ, followed by glands, nervous system, and then finally tactile warm friction."

"You didn't mention dick, which is better?"

"Natural gets bigger, better outcomes. But everyone I blew got a climax they said they liked, a lot. You know I'm good at what I do."

"But?"

"But for me the differences were noteworthy. If a guy was having a great time I shared it, if it was ho hum, it brought to mind what it could have been."

"Coy, I'm not trying to change the subject but if you don't mind me being a bit finicky what you just said sounds a lot like the final in Plato's *Republic.*"

" *The Republic.*"

"If shadows are all an individual has ever known, then shadows *are* his reality. I wonder what modern research says about that in regard to your obsession?"

"Sorry Oliver, profiteers won't allow unbiased scientific research to interfere with a nine billion dollar a year routine circumcision industry with a constant renewable revenue."

"Infants don't get to voice how they are mishandled."

"Are you showing revolutionary colors for baby boys to have a high-quality life, or just being contrary?"

"You're getting close. I always maintain that every person should have a hobby. But for me social engineering doesn't qualify."

"Don't tell me you're suggesting stopping routine circumcision is my hobby, and not my vocation. Oliver, what did you know about all this before I started talking?"

"I knew the ancient Greeks considered sex between men superior to sex with women but occasionally performed the drudgery with their wives to produce children to work alongside the household slaves. By necessity the ancient Romans were bisexual, their military campaigns often lasted ten years at a shot. The legions spent more time sleeping with the men they fought beside than their wives back home."

" Huh, I wonder when sex became such a bug-a-boo."

"After the Roman Empire fell people just enjoyed sex however, with who or whatever, and where-ever they felt an urge, hopefully with a willing partner. Then the sex police came along with the medicalization of sex in the mid-1800s." I could see Coy took my comment as oppositional to what he was revealing about himself. That was not my intention.

"But my empirical evidence is accurate. I know strong versus weak orgasm are the result of many factors like diet and exercise, not only from damaged sexual equipment. I'm correct about this, don't argue with me."

"Let's not fight. I don't share your fire or knowledge, but I feel privileged you want to share your inner self with me. I'm trying and maybe failing to maintain a neutral nonjudgmental position about something different than my experience. I know this can't be easy telling me."

"Do you still love me ?"

"I do. I'm just not sure being stuck in ancient times is good for anyone, especially the man I love more than myself."

"Oh, okay, if that's an issue. Let me give you my modern findings for medically doing harm while pledging to do no harm for profit, at the same time claiming bogus future benefits from doing routine hurtful damage all the while being publicly forced to admit the permanent impairment is only cosmetic surgery for the sake of aesthetics."

"Don't hold back, tell me what you really think happened to Darrell-Wayne."

Coy grew reenergized at my comment and shared more of his passion. After the revolutionary war colonists got busy governing their new independent country. The system they used was called federalist *winner take all.* It replaced regal aristocracy, while some citizens' wish for a loose confederation of strong states with a weak central governance, and others mourned the loss of a king.

When the U.S. Congress decided on a medical system for their new country, they chose between the three most popular of that day:

[1] Naturopaths used elements found in nature to heal.

[2] Homeopaths which just had enormous success eliminating cowpox using their new discovery of immunization.

[3] Allopathy cut hair, shaved beards, and trimmed mustaches as a main source of income. Other sideline business included amputation of broken arms, legs, bleeding the sick, washing bodies alive or not, and preparing the dead for home wakes and funerals.

Like Naturopathy, Allopathy was an apprenticeship trade usually passed down from father to sons. Allopathy was the only one of the three systems to use invasive techniques such as bleeding the sick, trimming hair, and limb amputation. In its winner take all form of government, the U.S. Congress chose allopathy to be the country's official health care system. Consequently, naturopathy, chiropractic, homeopathy, and osteopathy were all made illegal in the United States of America for over a century. However, most of these crimes were not prosecuted except for political gain.

The American illegal medical systems were contrary to the rest of the world where different healing methods coexisted to complement each other in curing the sick. The U.S. Congress did require Allopathy to standardize their training like Homeopathy with universities. Consequently, the barber college augmented apprenticeships, and the price of a haircut and shave increased with a result of a better trained barber.

Two pressing medical problems in the 1800s were mental asylums overflowing with untreatable patients, and a syphilis epidemic coast to coast, north to south. Allopathy quickly found bleeding during haircuts, or otherwise didn't cure what ailed the country. So, they brought out their amputation knives and saws and a massive public health campaign paid for by federal tax dollars promised to circumcise the problem away. When it didn't cure anything, the allopath's and federal government couldn't admit they didn't know what they were doing in the face of an epidemic.

Relevant, but ignored in conjunction with decreasing new insane asylum intakes was an increased high rate of suicide after otherwise healthy adult males healed from coerced penis surgery. Although some suggested suicide was an acceptable pretreatment for mental illness, it never caught on in the literature. Nevertheless, hard to control, bad for business rumors had started to link sexually transmitted diseases specifically syphilis and mental hospital residency. But by then much more revenue could be generated by shaving a penis down to size than giving a haircut and facial shave.

A loose collection of barbershops eventually organized to become the American Medical Association in 1840. Sulfur drugs and then antibiotics eventually controlled syphilis and other STDs and thus most insanity of that day. The U.S. military adopted a sometimes-routine forced circumcision of recruits, if local command was inclined and wanted to take time away from training soldiers to fight, many commandants were not so inclined. No data was collected to compare which were allowed to remain natural and numbers otherwise.

In the meantime, the military high command squabbled over whether to have penises be natural, or otherwise. At the same time, to be safe, noncommissioned officers encouraged their troops to use mercuric acid based Pro-Kits immediately after visiting a prostitute. The kits were *mostly* effective preventing STD infection if squirted into the urethra and rubbed on the outer skin, no matter the status of their penis. Pro-Kits were developed during WWI to prevent STD infection .

Eventually, public health experts demanded urban and rural localities close cheap brothels to address the syphilis epidemic. As much as very young and old clients hated to see their favorite sex workers go out of business, their closures ended the national syphilis insanity epidemic. Nevertheless, circumcision advocates falsely claimed victory for public health work done by new pharmaceuticals, zoning boards, and the police.

In line with President Nixon's tax-payer-funded war on cancer because his sister died from the disease, members of the medical profession decided to cure breast-cancer before it could get started by snipping out infant mammary glands. They would not only become famous for curing breast cancer, rich doing nonstop surgeries, and rich again by cornering the baby-milk business. However, the idea was not particularly popular with heterosexual males and lesbians. Nixon had to squash his brilliant idea.

One U.S. research study intended to encourage infant mammary snipping found unintended results. Its goal was to compare female and male infants in preparation for the end of breast feeding and ad profitable pharmaceuticals to infant store-bought formulas to claim it made babies healthier and profits stronger. Trying to find a baseline, the study unintentionally discovered American male babies *were cranky, off their feed*, and *hard to manage* as compared to easily manageable, docile, female infants with mammary glands. The hypothesis was after surgery female infants would be as miserable as their male counter parts and prove that was a good unifying factor to encourage the surgery.

However, when the study was replicated in England, they found female and male infants present and were managed exactly the same. The only difference found between U.S. and English babies was American male babies were often routinely circumcised shortly after birth and the British like all Europeans don't circumcise except in emergencies.

As a result of comparing studies and not finding *any* benefit from unnecessary infant surgery, the Pentagon changed its policy of sometimes forced circumcision of unwilling recruits. Then a group of circumcised high-ranking officers convinced their command generals with political clout to quietly change the policy back.

Embarrassed that routine circumcision could not prove any value, medical lobbyist convinced southern-white bigots that circumcised Afro American males were less likely to rape white women and thus allowed to live longer without being lynched. The lobbyist sold the idea as an improvement over the status quo in race relations. Naturally the routine circumcision industry jumped on the case and claimed what was good for Blacks should also be accorded whites to discourage discrimination.

While at the same time, not to lose all creditability with peers the world over, United States Medicine establishment had to officially acknowledge there was no known benefit to circumcising other than aesthetic if the look was liked at the expense of sexual performance. As a result, the term *uncircumcised* was removed from medical nomenclature and replaced with the word *natural.* Nevertheless, the unnecessary practice was encouraged for medical students to con patients to score points with their professors' bank accounts.

Today, after extensive research in pursuit of profits, female circumcision also known as FGM, or female genital mutilation is illegal in every country of the world. Male genital mutilation or MGM is illegal in all developed and developing countries the world over, except the U.S. where profits matter more than infant well-being and lifelong unencumbered potential for a full human experience.

Worldwide most people don't understand why the U.S. a rich country needs to keep its poor physically, mentally, spiritually, and sexually diminished. Those in power here quietly say, what the world doesn't understand is the cash value of human exploitation.

"Coy, I'd wager you've been called antisemitic for bring up questions that make many folks uncomfortable."

"You have no idea. But *you do know* I'm not anti-anyone. Since I became a cop, I've had to get used to being called names."

"One of the many things I love about you is how you care about people. Yet, I can imagine your curiosity gets you mixed up in other people's belief systems, or what information they don't want to know lurking in other people's underwear."

"Yeah, so? Right is right. As a police officer I'm pledged to fight for what's right."

"Messing with superstitions can be dangerous. The history of religion is covered with blood."

"Oliver, you know I enjoy a good fight, whether I win or not. I train for them every day. What are you trying to say that I'm missing?"

"Things are usually not what they seem."

"What I'm talking about is unacceptable manipulation of exhausted women, dulled by drugs and the extreme exertion of giving birth. Then being coerced into signing a consent card to have their new baby boy bleed from the groin to please the student doctor or nurse."

"I don't think that is your main issue."

"Yes, it is. When a woman realizes she was hoodwinked by a medical professional, it's too late to undo the damage and embarrassing to tell her son ten or twelve years later she didn't know better. Exactly like my aunt and uncle with Darrell-Wayne."

"Think about it, your obsession is to challenge a belief that something has value that doesn't. Or put a different way, one opinion versus another."

"Then you don't get what I mean. It is so wrong to hurt new babies at the beginning of their life with unnecessary suffering and make them less than equal to their fellows in the process over their entire life."

"Coy, reality check, there is little you or anyone can do when *the medical organizations* are in bed with politicians primarily for the sake of making profits for campaign donations in return for legislative favor."

"Well, that's stark."

'Come on, everyone knows politicians lie and medical doctors seldom tell their patients everything they know."

"Huh, well that boils the cow down to the size of a bouillon cube, doesn't it? But wait a second, some victims no doubt rationalize being exploited as an advantage over their neighbors who were in fact less gullible. That pits one against the other and women's equality suffers from divided males. So, there!"

"Let it go, Coy, it isn't your fight to fight. Especially if as, you say, victims celebrate being duped believing it makes them superior. You are in a no-win situation."

"Let's see if I understand. You think I'm crazy for wanting life to be equal for all American boy babies like the boys in the rest of the world?"

"I didn't say that exactly. If you were crazy, I suspect I'd have noticed before today. I'm trained to look for symptoms."

"Then what?"

"My social work education makes me think there is a lot more going on with your circumcision fixation than unifying U.S. masculinity birth to old age."

"Yeah, like what? I need some new insights."

"Me, the private detective, wonders if the damage to Darrell-Wayne is worth the energy outlay you've put into trying to solve the mystery behind his victimization. As a do-gooder and regular recipient of your excellent cock sucking skills, I understand your wish that all receivers of your first-class ministrations attain the full rights and privileges with which they were born."

"And as my lover man the but is?"

"As an out gay man I have to wonder if routine circumcision was not a diversion to postpone coming out of the closet. In other words, you fought the status quo that would never accept you as queer, by showing them to be the corrupt ones."

Emotion sounding in his voice, Coy said, "You really do get all of me, don't you? No one has ever put it all together like that. You're probably right, I just need time to think on it to agree with you."

"Points for my team?"

"Yes. I took on a just cause and fought hard. According to you the battle is unwinnable. I still love to suck dick and refuse to feel guilty about it no matter what anyone thinks."

"I love you, Officer Goff. Is there anything else you want to get off your chest?"

"Wasn't what I said enough?"

"Yet, I sense we're not done."

"Yeah, okay, got me. My question is why, *would* you want to love me after I exposed my secret of deep compulsive obsession with other guys' cocks. For a long time now, my life has been about the struggle to right wrongs I spoke about. Many would say my preoccupation a perversion."

"I'm gay, I find cocks much more interesting than, say … deficient dead American presidents that Esmeralda and Chucho obsess over."

"I haven't had an interest in any dead presidents since eighth grade. You'd have a better chance to convert me to some cult."

"Actually, for me, you are fine the way you are."

"Really?"

"Pro and antiabortion, death penalty pros and cons, or carnivores and vegetarians hook up all the time. They learn how to disagree without being disagreeable by treading ever so lightly through each other's mine fields. Because they love each other and that matters more."

"You really know how to make me feel better after I spilled my guts and feel vulnerable."

"Before I show you my less than perfect inner self and belief that all of us are crazy to greater or lesser extends. My house cleaner is taking off for a month or two. Her parents need full-time care. Consequently, my plan is routine household chores will be done, by us, before Darrell-Wayne wants breakfast. You on board being a co-domestic for a month or two?"

"What's that sound?"

"Feel that? Damn, the whole house seems to be oscillating."

"What the hell is that?"

Rushing to the kitchen wall of windows we saw swarms of extra-large bees cocooning the garage above and house below. On closer examination they were those giant South American killer bees. They are bred to slay by suffocation while stinging their prey into immobilization before death throes start. Then as their final act, the dying bees form a mold using themselves to make the sarcophagus around the slaughtered victim.

"Coy, go grab Darrell-Wayne and seal yourselves in the saferoom. Close the ventilation louvers and cover them in duct tape."

"What about you?"

"I'll be all right. Go, go now."

"I'd rather stay here and help you."

"I won't need help if I know you and your cousin are safe. Now get out of here."

"No! I won't leave you to face the bees alone."

"Come on lover man what's the point of having a safe room if it isn't ever used. Now get your cousin into safety. I don't have time for arguing right now." Begrudgingly Coy left the kitchen and I telephoned the private number at the University drone lab.

After a very brief jittery conversation the lab dispatched three fire starter drones to my place. In the twelve minutes it took them to arrive I ran down to the basement. I brought up four logs of the greenest of unseasoned firewood from the cord we'd just had delivered and stacked them at the patio door.

The Firestarter drones are used to initiate control-burns in forest-fire prone areas. They are extremely accurate pinpointing where they drop their tiny napalm bomblets. Linking my computer's camera to the university drone lab computer through cyberspace they could see what we were up against. A plan was formulated while bees tried to attack the drones. Apparently, the down draft from the drones' rotors disturbed the big bees' navigation system and caused them to get agitated and lust for plastic.

I had just six minutes of fire cover to make it out to the patio propane gas grill and get back inside unstung. With all six burners turned on high I dropped the green (unseasoned) firewood on the grill and dashed back inside the bee quivering house. At first the door wouldn't close because the door frame kept moving. Then tenacity paid off. As the smoke rose and engulfed the outside of my home, drone fighting angry bees quit, and left for cleaner air. It is hoped they returned to where they came from with prejudice toward their handlers.

I started breakfast to give the less disturbed bees a chance for an orderly exit. Then went down the hall and retrieved Coy and Darrell-Wayne. We had a normal sort of breakfast evenwith bees. Coy kept staring at me like I had just performed a magic trick, and Darrell-Wayne knew something was up with us, but not what. I on the other hand was preoccupied that somebody or somebodies would go to such lengths to kill Darrell-Wayne. Jeez, what fight could we be facing next?

Once Darrell-Wayne was at the university studying, Coy was off doing hush hush police work, I returned home to vacuum up dead giant bee corpses lying on the ground all around the house and overflowing the garage roof-gutters. After hosing down the patio fire remnants a preliminary examination indicated a new propane grill was now in order. It made more sense to replace rather than try to clean the old one, now soot black gummed-up in sticky tree sap. My superego required close inspection of the morning's attack until I came up with a better defense strategy for the future.

***

I threw together a quick one pot nutritious evening meal with an elaborate store-bought dessert, and plenty of South African Mary Renault Festival King Wine. Darrell-Wayne skipped dessert, usually his favorite part of any meal. Believe it or not he was looking forward to starting his homework. Oceanography's infectious academic bug had bitten the teen.

Pouring the last of the wine into our glasses I said, "Coy, tonight you get a choice. We can talk about the bee attack this morning and what I did about it, or it's my turn to reveal inner obsessive-compulsive thinking. Your choice, but you can't have both tonight, I'm half pooped."

"I'm still feeling exposed from showing you so much of how my inner self works, last night. Mr. Right, did I turn you off saying too much?"

"No. In fact, after last night, I proclaim we will be together for the long haul. Although, I never had a long-haul relationship before. Like it or not, you get to be my first."

"Well, far be it from me to deny you the experience I want with you."

"Absolutely. So, where do I start, with the killer-bees?"

"Do you think it's unhealthy for Darrell-Wayne to be so distracted by Dolphins and Porpoises at his age?"

"I don't know. When Esmeralda joined us, she got your cousin engaged in landscaping, gardening, handicrafts, and going to the university. Along with keeping him safe. An interest in Dolphins seems to be something he initiated on his own with his own follow through. Yet he and she two remain as close as ever."

"You've been paying attention."

"I think it is age appropriate for Darrell-Wayne to develop his own passions."

Chapter 14.

We didn't strongly object to Darrell-Wayne's obsession with big fish like large mammals because deep water was a pleasant distraction from Kamikaze drones and giant killer bees' intent on slaughtering him. I for one didn't object to my not getting back to exposing inner quirks in true confession style like Coy had.

After the bee attack our life settled back down to our usual full routine. Then one morning we were running late, and nothing would work right. For expediency's sake some regular safety precautions might have been ignored in a hurry, like having a police car escort start out with us.

Coy, Darrell-Wayne, and Esmeralda were riding together in Coy's regular size American made passenger sedan. Chucho, I back tracked and picked up on the way in Ameli's restored van. Then I raced to catch up with Coy and then served as follow vehicle. The plan was, get gas for the van, then at that point acquire a police lead car escort, and drop off passengers at the university.

The police would go back on patrol, and Coy would proceed on to the police precinct and paperwork. Chucho and I'd go on to the office and have a quiet day wrapping up my own cases making telephone inquiries while Chucho answered phone calls and did filing. Whether Ameli would be in was a question without an answer that day.

Coy had recently purchased, at auction, very cheap, a five-year old, grayish-green muddy looking by design decommissioned unmarked American made police car. In a previous life it did service in undercover surveillance work. Before that it was a brightly colored confiscated auto by the DEA in a big buy and bust drug sting. The undercover car looked like a well dented Rent-a-Wreck by the time Coy bought it. But the engine was souped-up, and the other end was loaded with sophisticated electronic gear creating an amazing audiophile sound system in the trunk.

Suddenly Coy wasn't in counter terrorism any longer. He'd been spotted as a suspected cop. His new undercover assignment was to get illegal handguns off the street by setting up bogus buy busts. The sophisticated audiophile sound system in Coy's current car was not for your average underage white boy's taste but did draw illegal gun buyers like ants to honey, and my concern for his safety.

Our only deviance from the usual three day a week plan to get Darrell-Wayne and Esmeralda to and from the university, was to gas-up at the new Fifty-Two Pickup and pick up the police escort there. Ameli's old-refurbished gas guzzler van was already showing empty on the gasoline indicator gage accompanied by multi-colored blinking idiot lights to assure attention was paid. Like I said we were having a bad day.

Before we got to the old Fifty-Two Pickup spot, Coy telephoned Chucho and me to listen to the lead car's singing. They were doing the round *"Row, Row Your Boat."* It was the first time I heard Darrell-Wayne and Esmeralda singing together. They weren't bad if you don't mind children's rounds. While listening to the Boat go Merrily Down the Stream my periphery vision caught an orange ROADWORK sign on the shoulder of the road, then another diamond shaped sign LEFT LANE CLOSED, MERGE RIGHT sign popped up.

A flagman appeared and slowed me down with hand signals. He was wearing a blue hard hat and dayglo orange vest. He took half my attention away from the singing from the cellphone. The flagger waved us onto a dirt detour off the black top Route 52. Something about that guy didn't look like an average highway worker, but without my paying full attention wasn't sure what, and mindlessly followed the detour.

All at once several things coalesced, the phone connection abruptly broke off, the road got too bumpy, and we were driving alone off Route 52. Suddenly a pickup truck with a camper-cap appeared out of nowhere. He passed me then Coy and started slowing down. All of a sudden, a large silver-gray SUV was on my rear bumper. Where did he come from? Clearly, a four vehicles traffic jam on a detour off busy Route 52 didn't make any more sense than no other traffic off the route. We'd been caught in a trap. What to do about it?

Up ahead of Coy I noticed the pickup swerve sharply, he took a sharp left to drive completely off the rough rutted dirt road we were on. Then Coy did the exact same maneuver, I guess *monkey see monkey do.* The SUV was driving too fast pushing up against my back bumper protector. He couldn't see anything up ahead other than me in a tall wide van.

I accelerated a short distance beyond where the others had swerved off the road then hit the brakes hard. The chase car had no choice other than to slam my rear end, hard. Foot off brake, I used the hit's extra momentum to spin the steering wheel fast to the left. With me out of the way the SUV was propelled fast forward into what those ahead wanted to avoid.

Back on planet earth, the van fishtailed into a full on 360 skids. Then rotating sideways, the van made donuts in the dirt. I managed to wrestle control back just before slamming sideways into Coy's stopped rent-a-wreck looking car blasting children's music. Up ahead of Coy the pickup had stopped 100 yards or so in front of him. Miraculously, QQ's van stopped a few feet from the side of Coy's car. I had Chucho slide-back the van's side door for Coy and his passengers to scurry into the heavier steel reinforced van.

When Ameli's van was refurbished, I'd had eighth inch armor-plates welded where possible, and the windows replaced with bullet proof glass. What drew my attention away from offloading passengers was a concussion. I felt it before seeing the SUV levitate a good three feet straight up followed by a loud explosion. When it landed hard, another explosion burst into an all-consuming car fire.

My guess was the SUV hit two IEDs. Coy and I didn't even know that's what we were avoiding. But the pickup truck knew, and the SUV should have. I'm no expert, but in my limited knowledge of traditional landmines, they would have flipped that big car over front to back due to its high center of gravity and front engine weight. I also think those IEDs had a lot more umph than a traditional landmine and that caused the levitation. In any case the trap we were in now got my full attention. I had no doubt those explosions were intended for Darrell-Wayne and the rest of us.

Up ahead three passengers from the pickup truck driver's compartment exited the vehicle holding handguns. At the same time the back door of its camper-cap opened to reveal a mounted heavy machine gun with three men manning it. I supposed that was their backup plan. But for me it was round two, clearly, we'd won round one.

Adrenalin pumping full on, I ran around to the back of the van, unlocked the welded to the frame steel box and extracted a shoulder fire heat seeker. How I came by the Javelin missile prototypes is a story for another day and one with less hormones. I no sooner had the shoulder missile launched than the machinegun barked a few test rounds in our direction, missing us by not very much. But giving the Javelin fresh heat to seek.

My small missile made a direct hit finding the heat from the now rapidly firing big gun. The force of impact was about the same size as a medium mortar shell. As always bigger would have been better, but the mother of invention says you use what you have. The truck, camper, machine gun, and gunners in back went the way of the SUV, in an unexpected fire ball, but there was no levitation. Rather, it blew apart, deconstructing chunks of metal and flesh in most directions.

One of the men from the front of the pickup witnessed his compatriots' demise and ran for the woods. Esmeralda was right after him. She'd grabbed an assault rifle when I opened the van's steel gun safe. A quick glance inside our van showed she'd put earphones playing loud music on both Darrell-Wayne and Chucho. She had them holding each other, sitting on the van floor. Second hand, it sounded like they were listening to Amazon Forest Indigenous music turned to high volume.

Coy was engaged in a furious handgun fight with two men from the front of the pickup. My man needed my help, so, I dropped the bad guy closest to me. He caught my first slug in the forehead and the next two in the chest. The surprised look on his face was from he'd just turned to shoot me. Silly man, he thought I was an easy kill.

Rethinking what I'd just done, when both Coy and the other bad guy were reloading. I ran up and introduced the toe of my right shoe to the villain's inner right wrist just as he was attempting to slide a full ammo clip into the butt of his automatic.

His weapon looked like a H&K .45 caliber semiautomatic; it flew skyward out of his hand, went air born, and landed a good distance away.

Simultaneously, the perp grabbed his right wrist with his left fist hand ejaculating the sound of pain, loudly. The look on his face and flared tonsils indicated he'd not experienced a broken wrist before. I can attest all those nerves bundled there hurt a lot, along with a long recuperation, and longer physical therapy to regain mostly full use, except on rainy days. I never said my time working as a parole officer was without physical conflict. My recommendation to our latest assailant should have been to avoid contact with steel toed shoes during gun fights. But I wasn't feeling talkative. The constant parade of strangers was starting to piss me off.

Begrudgingly, my next order of business should be to cuff the bastard. But when he wouldn't roll over as I requested, politely, I introduced my left foot, with prejudice, to where his legs connected to his torso. My steel toed shoes will go just about anywhere, even on rainy days when my wrist hurts. With a hard second kick the perp complied with my request. Well, actually he did more than I'd asked and curled into a fetal position mumbling to himself in a foreign language.

Hands cuffed behind his back I said, "What's your name, stranger?"

He vigorously shook his head side to side. I assumed that meant he wasn't in a mood for a nonviolent conversation. Actually, I wasn't either. So right off we had something to agree on. In case his broken wrist and assaulted gonads by footwear had made him shy. I repeated myself, something I seldom like to do. Then I recalled in social work school they taught us to never assume anything, because it makes an ASS out of U and ME. So, as my breathing returned to normal, I pondered my dilemma, use my fists, or reintroduce shoes to lubricate the interrogation.

At that point Coy had walked up, his nine-millimeter Barretta freshly reloaded in his right hand. Looking at my cuffed perp he said, "Let's put this bastard out of his misery, you ready to die asshole?" With that said, Coy bent at the waist and gave the perp a hard righthanded slap across the face. It left a hand imprint on the perp's pale milky white right cheek.

Then we heard the crack of a rifle shot coming from the woods. Shortly thereafter Esmeralda walked out of the dense trees and toward us, a huntress' satisfied look on her face. Taking pity on the cuffed guy I said, "It's still possible to have a painless conversation and you get to live a little longer, otherwise it will get very unpleasant for you. Your choice of course. I'll give you a moment to weigh your options."

Our uninvited guest was not feeling talkative when Esmeralda walked up and said, "Who's this?" Her facial expression looked like a cat who just captured a mouse.

Coy said, "He won't tell us. Maybe he'd rather talk to you."

Without further ado she pulled the guy up by his hair and went through his pants pockets. Then she handed me loose change, the ignition fob for the pickup, a Belgian passport, European credit cards, and local Antwerp, Belgian identifications for discount groceries, fitness center, and gas station. Of most interest to me was a folded eight and half by eleven computer printout of Darrell-Wayne Goff, his date of birth, height, weight, and a four-year-old black and white photo. He also had a roll of U.S. currency amounting to $1,163. I dropped the loose change on the ground and took everything else.

Using the name on the passport whose photo resembled the perp on a better day, I said, "Johannes Ballew, let's pretend you understand English. I want my friend Esmeralda here to tell you what to expect, if you don't answer questions truthfully. Esmeralda please be as graphic as necessary for our guest's motivation."

Without so much as a howdy do, she was behind his back and pulled out two of his fingernails, one from each hand. The stranger screamed in pain each time. Then Esmeralda said, "Mr. Ballew, you just felt me give two of your fingers a nail treatment, now, I'll do the same to your other eight fingers and if you like, ten toes. Or I could reserve my nail salon technique for other customers, if you'd rather talk about it, a lot."

He grunted. It wasn't bluster. We had a genuine tough guy on our hands.

Esmeralda said, "I won't stop at nail salon treatment for a big fella like you."

Johannes Ballew shook his head no. His face indicated he was evaluating whether Esmeralda would do what she said.

"Seriously, you want all your nails yanked out, and digits removed joint by joint till you have nothing left to wipe your ass with but broken wrist bones?" Esmeralda turned to Coy and me and said, "He wants to scream opera until his lungs give out. Ready boys for the opening aria."

Studying Ballew's face, Coy spoke up, "You gave him a chance. It was his choice not to practice high notes."

I was curious if she'd really torture the man, and how I'd stop her if she went too far.

Esmeralda said, "Okay, let's get started. Take a deep breath, you are going to need it."

Speaking English with a strong Flemish accent the visitor said, "Just kill me. Get it over with. I'm dead already, and no rat."

"No, we can't do that, yet. You must earn that."

"Bitch!"

"Bitch? I've shown you nothing but respect up to now. Okay if you want to be rude, you need to look the part. How about your ears and nose come off in thin slices. I'm a woman from a poor country, I slice red meat very thinly. "

"Don't waste your time lady I'm stronger than you."

"Oh, okay, no vanity, let's see about that. How about I start slicing your nipples?"

"FUCK YOU, BITCH!"

Grabbing his shirt in her fist, Esmeralda sliced straight down, and buttons flew off their buttonholes. Then she yanked the garment over his head saying, "I never understood why men need such small nipples. Bigger makes better earrings. After

I cut yours off, I'll give them a purpose for the first time. Get as comfortable as you can cuffed like that, we could be here awhile with you screaming in anguish between slices."

Johann's facial thinking seemed to have reached a conclusion. "And if I answer your questions?"

Coy gruffly said, "Either we turn you over to authorities or if you're grossly disfigured by the time you talk, we'll give you a quick death for finally cooperating. Or if you piss us off and make this harder than it has to be, expect hours of suffering and total loss of pride begging to die, and eventually nature will get around to a slow lingering end to you. Your choice."

I chimed in to illuminate, "Understand, we haven't heard what you have to say just yet, stranger. So, make it good, and believable or pay dearly."

"Like how?"

"There are other parts of your anatomy she can turn into art and crafts projects. She is quite imaginative."

To emphasize her impending impetus for crafts, Esmeralda broke the first joint of Johannes's first finger left hand. The snap was louder than I expected followed instantly by his hollering in pain. After the loud low-pitched outcry, he whimpered and then took a moment to catch his breath.

Esmeralda said, "These bones make nice wrist bands strung altogether," and she took hold of his second finger's first joint same hand.

Johannes Ballew got chatty after ordering us, curt military style, to stop breaking his bones. He said, "I'll tell you because my colleagues on today's mission failed and any who survived could only expect death from our employer."

"Nobody pays for failure."

"I know I'm dead already. I'll talk to you in exchange for a quick painless death, but not at hands of that lady torturer."

"It's his cousin, he'll do you quick for the truth. We want details."

Johannes explained, any person in the know with a paid-up subscription could find and decode changing encryptions on the gyrating international job-board maintained to employ assassins. It was financed for by hitwomen and men through a stiff annual subscription fee. The board was usually hiding in plain sight, located on the dark internet for highly qualify death dealers who warrant a high fee.

When I looked dubious, Johannes rushed on to say he only took work there when money at home was short and the Belgian hit business were slow.

Ballew monitored all aspects of any hit job he'd take, down to the last second. In addition, local jobs allowed him to help-out his aging mother by crocheting big special orders for her specialty crochet shop but were drying up. Which meant he's had to accept work for group hits and go further afield than even today's disaster of disorganization .

The Boynton brothers' organization offered the most and best paid work on the dark web. Since they were part of the government of Belarus, they had official cover for their outside murder for hire racket. Over time the Boynton brothers and associates were cornering the freelance hired killer market with high volume, guaranteed almost risk-free work. Eventually, Johannes had no choice but to work for them to support his mother's shop."

"What do you know about today's attempt."

"The guy Darrel-Wayne Goff was giving the Boynton group a bad reputation in the hit business. Golf was proving to be an exception in their category of easy risk-free kill at a discount price. He refused to die. They were losing too many assassins trying to fulfill a contract. So, they posted a large reward in crypto currency for a successful kill.

Today's hit on Darrell-Wayne was a ten-man subcontracted bounty hunter job. Normally, it would not be the kind of work Johannes would consider, except the rent on the crochet shop was overdue and this job paid $100,000, each man after the confirmed kill, plus the big bonus when the crypto paid out.

One of the Boynton family immediate associates was the subcontractor, and it was his plan that didn't work. All the other hit men were strangers to each other and from different countries.

"How exactly does one sign up for a job like this?"

Once Johannes Ballew began talking, information we didn't know gushed out of him. He went on to say he didn't know who paid the Boynton Brothers to kill Darrell-Wayne or why, or the need for ten men, an elaborate road work ploy, special vehicles, and explosives. At first it seemed to him a simple hit on a goofy looking teenager. After his failed try, he understood why Boynton and associates were losing face and a lot of assassins attempting to kill the teen.

Then as if he'd just completed a hard test Mr. Ballew straightened up and said, "That's all I know and now I'd like a bullet to the back of the head. Don't dilly dally, please be quick about it."

"Wait. After hearing your tale, you don't strike me as an arrogant son of a bitch. How could any of the ten think you could just waltz into this country and kill a teenager without resistance?"

"What! Are you kidding? The whole world knows of the corruption and rot of democracy in the United States of America. You have regular mass shootings wherever a few of you gather. Your country is rotting from the inside out."

"It's a dichotomy."

"I learned in school the U.S. was once a great nation. It even came to Europe's aid against fascists in the last century, twice. They taught us that was the last of your greatness. Ever since then you keep losing the wars you start ."

"Yeah, well that's not how we tell it."

"What we in Europe can't understand is why you kill your children in school and mothers shopping in grocery stores to feed those kids."

"Maybe I was wrong about you being arrogant."

"My crew *was not arrogant.* We were instructed what's one more or less dead teenager when the U.S. slaughters them by the *thousands every year. We were told you'd never notice if we hit one.*"

"For your information stranger, not everyone in America approves of mass shootings. It's just some of our politicians sold their souls to the gun lobby."

"I don't believe what you say. "

Feeling left out Coy jumped into the conversation and said, "Yeah well, we find you strange. Just so you know, most of us don't approve of mass shootings for any age group or you."

"Are you saying a minority controls the majority, what a silly notion. Unless it's like some say, these days you are settling alternative facts with bullets, rather than ballots and science. Ah, no, that makes too much sense for over here."

"The thought you want to keep in mind is ten of you came here to kill one teen and three of us adults stopped you. I'd say you had a math problem."

"You're right, I about to die salute you three, and one was even a woman."

"Mr. Hollier Than Though, don't go and get all sexists on us at your end."

"What I told you won't make any difference, because I don't give a shit."

I could see Esmeralda had had enough babble from our guest. She gave me a look I clearly misunderstood, and I shrugged my shoulders to show I didn't understand. She interpreted my shrug as an okay to act.

In one smooth fluid motion she wrapped her right elbow crotch around sexist Johannes' head, twisted hard in one direction while forcing his shoulder in opposition to the twist. Mr. Ballew's neck snapped, with a loud sharp crack. It happened before I realized what was done. Johannes shuddered violently head to toe, twitched, then went still while draped hanging from Esmeralda's elbow.

Like I said before, I was having *a bad day.*

Greatly troubled, Coy stared at Esmeralda, and then me. A disturbed questioning look on his face. His body language and empty hand gestures showed he didn't have words to express what he wanted to say in that instant. He seldom went into verbal overload.

Meanwhile, stimulated by what just happened, my brain was thinking, *I've got to improve my communications skills. Ballew should have been arrested not killed. Interrogated by federal agents and sent to prison.* Unconnected to my brain my mouth said, "We don't have cellphone reception out here. I tried calling for help before, but there was no reception. Anyway, we don't know for sure if this is the end of today's varmints, or only an appetizer. More and more assassins keep coming at us and being more sophisticated."

Finally finding his voice and words Coy said, "I'm a police officer. Ballew should have been brought in to face justice, *alive.* How can I write *this* up in a report and explain what just happened? I mean so Esmeralda isn't accused of murder?"

Looking contrite Esmeralda said, "It was self-defense." Then showing her usual alpha wolf demeanor said, "Whose handcuffs are these?"

I raised my hand, and she tossed me the cuffs she'd opened without a key. The eye contacts she and Coy were making looked like a war was about to break out.

Coming to her aid, when what I wanted was to scold her, I said, "Coy, you're a cousin first. Today we all kept your cousin alive for another day, so far. Let's not waste the whole day trying to explain what we don't understand to officials who won't believe us anyway."

"The alternative is?"

"Stick to the original plan, take your cousin to college, and go to work. We are the only witnesses still alive, other than us there is no one to tell the tale."

"But ballistics will show I shot that bad guy with my service weapon."

"Get back on Route Fifty-two, call for a police escort from Fifty-Two Pickup to the university, as usual. I'll follow you to Route fifty-two then double back. Chucho and I will clean up slugs and brass-casings from this mess as best we can and then sweep over tire tracks."

"Then what?"

"Hopefully Chucho and I will have a quiet day at the office from which an anonymous tip about this location and dead bodies on the ground will be reported for a police response. I think I have exit interviews and new case intakes all afternoon into the evening."

"Shouldn't we write this up in case it doesn't go away like you imagine?"

"Okay, then I'd suggest we each write up an incident report while it's fresh. Then compare them in case it comes back at us. The common theme is there was no cellphone or radio reception out here to call for help. That was no doubt by design. Then if it becomes necessary to say more, we were too traumatized to report what we didn't see or forgot through a haze of gun smoke, afterwards."

"Who would believe that?"

"It's what just happened. *You must* believe it to get others too."

Chucho and I followed Coy, Darrell-Wayne, and Esmeralda up to the highway. No big surprise, the road work signs, and highway workers were gone, no work had been done. After seeing Coy's car safely merge with traffic, we went back to the burned-out hulks and two men lying dead where we left them on the ground.

Since the new state law forbids merchants giving customers plastic bags with purchases, all our cars had a small supply of shopping bags, on the off chance we were struck by an uncontrollable urge to shop. I handed an empty bag to Chucho and said, "I was shooting .40 calibers, and Coy 9 millimeters. If in doubt put all spent shell casings and bullet fragments in this bag. I'll go look for spent projectiles farther afield."

My job proved easy. Only one of the dead men on the ground had been shot by Coy and me. My bullets and Coy's went through and through. Following the trajectory, they ended up smashed or melted in on the burned-out pickup truck. I went into the woods and found the guy Esmeralda wasted and dug her steel jacketed slug out of a tree some distance behind him. When I got back Chucho had collected all the ejected shell casings and discarded guns the bad guys came with. I locked everything away in the van's steel gun safe.

Next, I grabbed a broom from the back of the van and swept over all visible tire tracks. Then driving back to the highway, I made a point of riding over our tracks or Coy's going in the other direction. Once on Route Fifty-Two, it was a short drive to the old Fifty-Two Pickup spot and a gasoline fill up.

With all post shootout chores completed I told myself to relax and tried to make small talk with Chucho. "I want to thank you for keeping Darrell-Wayne calm through all the excitement back there. His having a meltdown when all hell was busting lose would have made a bad situation much worse."

"Do you think that Belgium guy was right, the U.S. shouldn't go around the world telling everybody how wonderful democracy is, when it seems finished here?"

"Like how? What do you mean?""That January sixth insurrection at the national capital. The Republicans say it was no big deal just some enthusiastic tourist."

"Investigations are ongoing."

"But maybe he was right, the majority no longer rule or want democracy."

"What are you saying?"

"The election deniers say a majority vote win in an election does not mark the winner. "

"The Belgian guy didn't say that, exactly. Do you want to listen to some music?"

"Not really. What he said was majority rule no longer exist in the U.S.A. "

"How about we leave politics to politicians or diplomats."

"But that's why I think I should have a gun."

"Oh, really? How do you suppose I missed *that*?"

"I don't know."

"Give me an example of our democracy requiring you to have a handgun?"

"Sooner or later the Republicans are going to kill social security and Medicare and the people will revolt and I'll need a gun to protect myself."

"Ah ha, but Chucho, Bush didn't succeed in privatizing Social Security for the rich to plunder. In fact, he wasted his whole second term trying and failing. Why do you care you're not social security eligible yet?"

" I need a gun, to stand up for democracy?"

" Democracy is a messy process, but all sides must participate. Lately one side only wants to obfuscate and take power for the sake of power."

"I know all that I watch the news that isn't propaganda pollution. In the Central American Triangle, we have lying, cheating, crooks, too. That style seems to have caught on here."

"Maybe we are not too far gone yet."

"Be careful, when Chile privatized their Social Security only the bankers benefited while old people returned to eating pet food or starving."

"That news never got mentioned here."

"We watch such things closely in the Spanish speaking world. Obviously, in the U.S. people don't care whether they have Medicare or social security because canned cat food is cheap and not disgusting like down south."

"Huh, I wonder if your college courses are warping your brain. You know too much critical thinking may not be all that healthy."

"I think that Belgium guy was right. I didn't have a gun, today I should have, to protect Darrell-Wayne."

"You were protected."

Chucho's demeanor showed he wanted to disagree with me. Finally getting hot enough under the collar he loudly said, "*It is about change*. It's good guys versus bad guys and I need a gun to do my part for the good guys."

So, as calmly as possible while driving in heavy traffic said, "I respectfully disagree. The old hierarchy has been replaced by women, nonwhites, and the others. Uneducated Caucasians have slid into *minority status,* and they are not pleased."

Chucho dug in on wanting to have a gun and said, "The psychiatrists at the hospital all say I'M NOT CRAZY, only sad. So, I should have a gun."

Unpersuaded, I said, "I agree you aren't crazy. "

"You are not a psychiatrist, they count more."

"You don't have to be a psychiatrist to see that everyone doesn't need a gun."

"I just knew you would make this about my suicide attempt."

"If so, that was unintentional."

"See what I mean?"

"Crazy is usually synonymous with disorganization. "

"I don't understand your double talk."

"Did I somehow get ahead of you?"

"Okay then, explain so many guns around this country and I don't have one."

In their favor American gun owners point to historical precedent for the second amendment to the U.S. Constitution allowing everyday citizens, women, man, or infant, to own guns to protect them from their government. Nobody in the 1770s expected the ragtag colonists to beat their most formal British colonizers and well-equipped and trained German mercenaries. With the monarchy and its oppression expelled from the new country, the common people wanted to keep handy their means to rebel if the King's men returned or the new government turned out as bad as the last.

The founding fathers wanted a democracy as closely modeled after ancient Greeks as possible. In ancient Athens only property owners were allowed to speak and vote in government. A 1776 compromise had to be struck to avoid continued revolution by landless armed, the rich and powerful called rabble. The results were *all* adult white males, property owners or not, were allowed to vote, and to keep their guns.

However, open conflict between having a loose confederacy of strong states or a powerful central government ruling subordinate states was postponed until the Civil War that ended in 1865. In 1865 Black males were also allowed to keep guns, but voting, like today, was only regionally allowed.

"Then how come you won't let me have a gun? I'm an adult mixed-race male and I don't own property."

"Chucho, I know we've been over this. Again, what do you need the responsibility and headache of a gun for?"

"Talk radio says another civil war is coming soon. I want to be ready. I'm Latinx not white or Black and hated by both, as well as being gay, and handicapped. That's four good reasons."

"Talk is cheap, especially on radio stations forecasting space invader invasions imminent any minute. You must do better than that to convince me."

"Today, if one of the bad men had tried to hurt Darrell-Wayne or me, we were defenseless. With a gun I could have protected both of us. Defending against assassins seems to be common for us these days. Think how bad you will feel if I'm killed when I could have lived with a gun."

"Coy, your aunt, and I protected you. More guns don't make it safer they make for more shooting. That means less safe because more people get hurt." I sensed we had hit yet another impasse.

As I pulled the van into the parking lot behind my office, I could see Chucho was simmering up to a boil, stewing, he believed he needed a gun. I guess it was understandable, he'd just witnessed irrational violence and clearly thought his feeling traumatized would be assuaged from future senseless bloodshed having a gun. So, I changed the subject to give myself a second to consider what was best all-around and said, "Someone is parked in my designated van parking place."

"That's a rental car license plate. Maybe it's a new to town hardware store customer."

"They have clearly marked customer parking spaces on both sides of the building. The sign back here *says* employees only, and that space has the QQ logo on it."

"What does that have to do with me having a gun? You say you are proud of me for getting out of my chair and finding a way to use crutches. Why can't I have a gun as a reward for all the hard work it took to get vertical and move on two feet with sticks instead of four wheels taking it lazy?"

"Now who is changing the subject?"

"Me, I guess. A gun would make me, and everyone around me, safe. Do you understand, I'd like to feel safe with all that's going on?"

"This is a conversation I've been putting off, *and now is* neither the time nor place for it. We will have it another day."

"No."

"All right, if you insist on pushing me, you're boss."

"YES! I do."

"My lawyer MT is working on immigration documentation for you. Part of your package for a work permit will now include a concealed carry handgun permit. But understand when it comes through, I may still not be ready to teach you to shoot."

"Why not?"

"I'll be blunt, you tried to kill yourself in my office. How am I supposed to explain if I teach you to use a gun and you use it on yourself?"

"I won't. How can I prove it? My words used to be worth something. Oh, I know, how about I take a lie detector test promising not to shoot, or otherwise harm myself and have it notarized by the Pope."

"Honestly, you don't know the Pope that well. At least not from attending church on Sundays. Your aunt says you are a godless atheist fag, and the church would fall in on itself if you ever went."

"That wasn't true today. I was praying hard during the shooting and cars exploding. My aunt doesn't always mean it when she says hurtful things."

"We all prayed a lot today. Especially when I ran out of bullets while others were reloading."

"If I work for you, it's important you trust me to make the right decisions, not just about handling money and face to face with your clients. But in your line of work, and with assassins jumping out at Darrell-Wayne constantly, I should have a gun to protect him, your money, and myself."

"Do you think he knew he was in danger today?"

"No. He got upset we were going to the university a different way, and then again when we changed from Coy's car to the van."

"Why do you suppose?"

"He's all about things staying the same. If I just move a piece of furniture at your house, he gets upset. Autistic people don't like change, and that's another reason why I need a gun to protect them."

"Convince me I can trust you not to use a gun to kill yourself or innocent people and then we'll see."

"The psychiatrist who signed my discharge papers from the hospital told me those who attempt suicide once almost never try again. He said it was a sign from heaven, it wasn't my time yet. He said if I did try again, he'd personally kick my ass. I could tell he was serious. The dude wears a size fifteen shoe, they're big."

"Two against one is that fair?"

"Come on! I'm doing everything but beg. You know begging is not acceptable in my culture at least between men."

"Okay, there are two parts to my gun safety rules, you disassemble and reassemble the weapon in two minutes or less blind folded, and you hit eight out of ten bulls' eyes, shooting from different distances and positions using the gun range's variety of paper targets. You up for all that?"

"Yes. But not today, can I have a gun to hold until I practice for the test?"

"Why?"

"As a sign you aren't bullshitting me or won't change your mind and make me beg. Don't look skeptical, trust is two-way."

"My .40 caliber is out of ammo. See no bullets. It's empty. You could hold it as a paper weight until another time."

"How about your backup gun?"

"You know it's a good thing I like you. All right … since you insist … but handle it carefully it deals death just like its big brother."

"Honest, I will."

"You are responsible for every bullet you fire, wherever it goes, and destruction it does. Trust me it's a heavy responsibility to hold someone's death in your hand." I said all that as I reached down, pulled up my cuff, and drew the five shot S&W .38 Special revolver from its ankle holster and handed it over butt first.

The awed look on Chucho's face as the gun changed hands eased my concern. It was worth the risk I took after all his endless talking. He had to arrive at the exchange he most coveted, now he could keep it.

"I promise not to use this gun until I meet all your gun safety requirements. It's only a symbol of trust between men. You won't be sorry."

"My young friend, you get credit for convincing me to do something I'd worried I would be sorry for. *Do not tell Ameli,* until I do."

"I promise."

"Now, make me proud, not legally liable."

"That sounds like a typical social worker."

"What? I don't know any social workers who carry pistols. Oh, except at the Department of Parole."

"Since my accident I've met many hospitals' social workers. That's how you all sound, kind but stubborn. Ameli warned me what to expect."

"Honey, if I'm anything it ain't typical. You saw that gun fight back off Route 52 today. Did that look like high quality social work, or what?"

"Before I met you, I thought social workers worked only in hospitals."

"No, it's a female lead profession, so we work almost everywhere, like nurses."

"Like where for instance?"

"Hospice, schools, nursing homes, prisons, abused children, handicap service, mental health clinics, addiction services, courts, the military, and I probably left some out by accident."

"But why?"

"Accountability."

"You say what?"

"It's about money, Ph.Ds. and MDs are expensive and not overly plentiful. The master's degree is the terminal degree for most social workers."

"But how can they know about so many difference fields of work?"

"They get specialized training, and we live in a time that requires continuing education. You learned most of what you do on the job at QQ. Speaking of which, you ready to go inside and get to work?"

"Yes, boss, I'm ready."

"Then tuck that .38 special in your pocket before you shoot one of us?" To distract myself from my own chatter, I did a last-minute check before locking the van in a spot other than my designated clearly identified van parking space. *Some people are so inconsiderate they park just anywhere.*

As we headed toward the back door of the hardware store Chucho said, "After all the excitement today I'm taking the backfire exit stairs to spend nervous energy. Also, I don't get enough exercise."

I waved him on his way to the fire exit tower and went through the hardware store back entrance directly to the elevator. For no reason, a strange feeling of foreboding washed over me as the elevator approached my floor. It must have been a delayed reaction to ten unexpected dead people early in the day and feeling naked without a loaded weapon. As I stepped out of the elevator, I could tell from Ameli's face something was seriously amiss.

In a reassuring voice I said, "What's up, Ameli?"

"Four very large, rude galoots are in your office trying to break into your locked filing cabinets."

I suppose from hearing talking, four extra-large professional football linemen size pug ugly looking types lumbered out of my inner office to crowd the waiting area. All were vertically well over six feet, the slimmest might have weight in slightly over 300 pounds, none wore a fat bulge around his middle.

"Hello, gentlemen, how may I be of service?"

"We are looking for Darrell-Wayne Goff. Where is he?"

"Not here. Who might you be?"

"Don't get cute FAGGOT! Produce him or wish you did after you pick up your teeth from the floor."

The way he said faggot was not the campy collegial way my hair cutter does. Rather, it showed his great distaste for bundles of German sticks, bassoons, and gay people like me. As I was formulating a smart retort to the uncouth homophobe, he closed the distance between us. Then in a blurred flash he hit me hard, fist to gut. His short hard bellybutton punch pushed-in my solar plexus. My lungs evacuated air with a sudden whoosh and forgot for a minute how to reinflate. The next thing I knew, lying flat on the floor looking up at the ceiling was this level of immobility hasn't happened since I played soccer in high school. Frantically occupied figuring how to get my breathing started, I might have blacked out for a second.

The man who hit me must have grabbed my Sig Sauer .40 caliber as I went down. Because the next thing I knew he was standing over me, pointing my gun in my face. I saw him cock the hammer as he said, "First I'm going to shoot out your kneecaps, then elbows, and you'll tell me where to find Darrell-Wayne Golf before it gets really painful. An old guy like you wants to protect his heart while its beating. Because I wouldn't want it to stop by accident before you tell me what I want to know, then you can go to hell."

At that moment, I was the only one in the room who knew my gun was empty. Then I heard Chucho on his crutches out in the fire escape tower. The sudden realization of what was happening got my breathing back on automatic and in a hurry. I struggled to my feet as Chucho entered the office. He knew my Sig Sauer was empty, and in a flash had my S&W backup in both his hands, like a cup and saucer. Most revolvers don't have trigger safety locks, that one didn't.

The brute standing in front of me, swung my gun to point it at the young man on crutches.

Chucho didn't think, wasn't trained, reacted on instinct. He fired left to right like he was dealing cards. His first shot got the big man holding my .40 caliber in the eye, he went over like a struck giant bowling pin. The other three thugs grabbed their guns as Chucho took out the two closest to him, their guns in hand. Gun fire snapped Ameli fully conscious, and she gave the fourth man a full load of buckshot to the body as he ran toward her for cover. She was about to give him a second blast when he went down in a heap a mere millimeter from her wheelchair.

I regained CEO composure and said, "Any QQ employees hit?" Both shook their heads, "No," clearly too shook up to speak. Their faces were a mix of trauma, wonder, and something I couldn't read.

Just then Howie the manager from the hardware store on the ground floor, and Jake his old-wrinkled salesperson burst into my outer office with twelve gage pump shotguns at the ready. Howie said, "Oliver, you throw a party and not invite us?"

"Sorry about the noise. It was a surprise party for me, with ill intent. Honest, these are not dissatisfied customers cluttering up my floor. But thank you for the neighborly interest."

Looking at the four dead. Howie went over and kicked each one making sure all life was gone, and then flatly said, "You don't need us. Everything is under control up here. Keep up the good work we don't like riffraff like this hanging around the store. It's bad for business."

Jake nudged his boss in the ribs and said, "See ya later, Oliver, okay, we have customers waiting."

The hardware men were leaving when the dentist from the floor below me arrived wearing a surgical mask. He held a small caliber, chrome plated, pearl handled automatic in his plastic gloved hand.

Deadpan, Howie said, "You're too slow, doc, the party's over." Then the elevator doors closed, and the three left as quickly as they'd arrived. Having good neighbors respond quickly to my emergency helped me get my equilibrium back into control as I surveyed the carnage.

Now looking ashen gray, bewildered, Ameli said, "I just called 911. They'll be here in two minutes, give or take."

Chucho's face still showed mixed reactions, mostly revulsion at what he'd just done, running to, *beware getting what you ask for.* So, I said, "Since I have a license to carry that thing, and you don't yet, hand it back." He gingerly passed me my backup revolver as if it were too hot to handle. It did feel a little warm to the touch.

Stuck staring at dead bodies, blood seeping into the industrial carpet, Ameli looked like she'd just witnessed a trainwreck, Chucho's face kept showing strong contradictory emotions. To bring him back out of himself I said, "Chucho, focus, thanks to you we are still breathing, and it was these men's due date to expire. They intended to kill Darrell-Wayne. Your aunt too."

"I didn't prepare for this."

"We all die sooner or later, for these four guys it was today. If not by your hand those neighbors who just rushed in here would have accommodated without a second thought."

Chucho hobbled over and gave me a thank you hug.

I had just slipped the 38 back into its ankle holster when the first uniformed police arrived. They were a little rough with us, seeing carnage all over the office. The blood-soaked wall-to-wall carpet would have to be replaced. Then detectives I knew arrived, took off our handcuffs, and were willing to accept written statements in lieu of processing us at the precinct which minimized some of the unpleasantness.

Chapter 15.

The number of attempts on Darrell-Wayne's life seemed to be occurring faster with greater numbers of rabid gunsels. How could an eighteen-year-old autistic teen offend anyone in proportion to the animus sent to destroy him?

I touched base with everyone I knew to contact, asked them for information and to spread the word. And nobody knew more than I. That was *not* reassuring for getting out in front of this case. It made me question my competence as a detective, and QQ's many connections as an investigations agency. Big money had to be changing hands behind the scenes because we kept killing whoever they sent after Darrell-Wayne, and they just kept coming,

Jameer Nacho's renewed his nagging offer of the FBI's leaky, now supposedly leak plugged, witness protection program. I hate to admit it, but it was looking more attractive as danger increased. Except, the dichotomy was the more danger we faced the harder it was to trust anyone outside our immediate little family group. Since nothing came from my seeking information, I started carrying extra loaded ammo clips. We wouldn't go down without a fight, even as the odds seemed to be stacking against us.

As I keep telling myself, I'm not a superstitious nut. On the other hand, over the years I've evolved a little ritual to clear the air after it was unavoidable for me to shoot someone dead. For me by myself, it was contemplation with a candle, incense stick, and then reflection on a short Native-American poem about transitioning from this life to the next. The verse wished the dead joyful reunion with ancestors in the abundant happy hunting grounds. Then I usually played a recording of Giovanni Battista Pergolesi or Domenico Scarlatti's *Salve Regina*. Thus, sending positive energy to help my dead adapt to a new, and it is hoped, better dimension. The ritual worked for me, and maybe the deceased. To date I've not been haunted by ghosts, not even stray nightmares.

I scheduled a family style back yard Sunday barbecue to mark Chucho and Ameli's first kills. In addition, I added Coy, Esmeralda, and mine to send good wishes to the afterlife for all the death we dealt since my last ritual, alone before meeting Coy.

The bakery was firm they couldn't or wouldn't put that many miniature tombstones on a cake the size I'd ordered. The compromise we settled for was they'd write in white icing, RIP, on a black iced double chocolate chiffon cake. Then had the nerve to charge me extra for the black cake icing saying they couldn't use it for any other purpose. I just don't know what funerals have become, and how one supreme court ruling made hetero bakers so uppity.

Before eating barbecue grilled steak, we had a group send off for our fourteen dead in one day, and the others before. Coy agreed with me it would help Ameli and Chucho who were still shook up at what they'd done.

No one objected to my lighting fourteen candles, incense sticks, and then reading a poem. That was followed by sounds of somber music to finish the ceremony and send the spirits on their way to a better place, just in case they were still hanging around.

Before meeting me, when the mood struck him, *and geography was convenient,* Coy stopped by random churches of various denominations and lit candles, if they had any, for his cousin Eddie and lives they'd taken in war zones. Then later his aunt and uncle were added. Lately too many nameless assassins have gotten in front of both our blazing guns.

I was afraid Esmeralda would laugh, she usually seemed amused by North American gringo rituals, like hot dog or pie eating contests or public wringing of hands over this or that latest publicly exposed bigotry. The recorded music I played might also have been out of her music taste range. The *Salve Regina* I chose was a soprano and mezzo-soprano pondering, in Latin the mother of God. Roman Catholics do love to contemplate the virgin mother of Jesus.

As it turned out Esmeralda didn't laugh and was respectful during and after the poem I read. She also seemed to be listening closely to Pergolesi's music. In fact, I noticed a change in Esmeralda's attitude afterward, while helping set up the meal. Her mindset modification felt like a slight shift in direction toward me, Coy, and her nephew, or I could have been wishing it.

While grilling the steaks I slathered on my homemade secret sauce. I'm a stickler to grill exactly to each person's doneness request. I asked Esmeralda, who was putting out the salads and warm garlic bread, "Do you think my sendoff for the dead too over the top?"

"That's the first time I saw you as more than just a surface kind of queer guy."

"I was looking for a little deeper answer to my question. Enlighten this shallow gay guy further please."

"You, your boyfriend, and even silly Chucho are not as wimpy soft maricon as I first thought."

"Huh, you decided that after *how many* gun fights with Coy and me, on your side."

"Who was counting?"

"Interesting, my husband to be and I give better than we get when bullets were flying. That's why we are all still walking around. We never once let you down, Esmeralda."

"True, but I never thought you were deep enough to respect the death you caused ... until today's ceremony."

"And Chucho?"

"The truth is, I thought it impossible for Chucho to kill anyone, let alone three. He became such a gentle wimpy whoosh after his motorcycle accident; macho men would have gotten tougher not weaker in a wheelchair. I hate to say it, but you and your boyfriend have been good for Chucho's manhood. Now, let's see how he handles being a killer. Who knows he may even someday come out as gay to me."

Not sure where the conversation was going and if I wanted to go wherever *that* was, I said, "What did you think of the music?"

"I like Pergolesi's *Stabat Matter* better but it's twice as long. So, I see why you chose his *Salve Regina*. It's a barbecue not a baroque music festival."

"Ah ha. You are a connoisseur of early music."

"Oliver, to send your dead back to their mothers was a nice touch. I didn't expect that depth of spirit coming from you or Coy."

"I'm glad you noticed. You probably also noticed we've been killing way too many people these days. Once in a while when it's unavoidable, okay, but our body count is way too high. It offends my sense of propriety and scares the bejesus out of me towards the safety for Darrell-Wayne."

Clearly not comfortable where the conversation went, Esmeralda changed directions and said, "Pergolesi was a mama's boy who died at only age twenty-six."

"In 1736."

"Based on his music I'll bet he went straight back to his mother's arms after death. As far as killing goes, numbers don't count when done without malice for a good reason."

"That describes recent events."

"All your dead, that I know about, were to protect Darrell-Wayne, that's self-defense. Self-defense doesn't count as an intentional kill."

"Thank you for that. In the heat of a shootout, I sometimes forget. In that spirit, let me apologize, I fear I sold you short on sensitivity Esmeralda."

"That's all right, Giovani Pergolesi goes to show maricons are good for more than hair styling, makeup, and dress making."

"Gunfights?"

"In your case."

"Just so you know, if you weren't taking such good care of Darrell-Wayne I might take offense at your overt homophobia."

"What kind of name is Mack Truck for a woman?"

"It's my lawyer MT's preferred dyke name."

"She asked me for a date. I'm thinking of accepting. What's her real name?"

"Her law license says she is aka Maryann Thompson. But a word to the wise, don't call her Maryann, she doesn't punch like a girl."

"My kind of woman."

"Thank you for helping us bury our dead. Here's your steak, bloody rare, just as you asked."

To personalize his untimely murder, I'd laid in two cases of Belgium beer for the barbecue in honor of our short-lived acquaintance with Johann Ballew. Normally, I prefer dark beers like stouts and porters with plenty of body and strong flavor. I'm not a frilly kind of lite-beer fag, no offense intended. But the smooth light-yellow brew from Brussels had loads of taste and went down without complaint.

Everyone present was over eighteen and knocked back several brews in true wake style, regularly toasting the dead. Finally, sated from big thick well- aged barbecue steaks and beers, we five sat around the backyard fire pit lost in thought, digesting.

More to myself than the others I said, "The assassination attempts are coming faster with more gunners. Can we do anything to stop this that we haven't tried already?"

Darrell-Wayne looking a little stoned said, "Ask that question on the internet ."

Esmeralda gave Darrell-Wayne a reassuring look and said, "He's been studying probability theory in a regular class at the university. His teacher says he understands it better than her nonspecial education pupils."

I could see from Ameli and Chucho's faces they weren't as surprised as Coy and I by Darrell-Wayne's constructive contribution to the conversation.

Watching all of us, one beer short of three sheets to the wind, Ameli said, "Darrell-Wayne, I can help you handle the dark web if you want. I live there when no one is looking."

"Ameli, really, with all the different things you are into, where do you find the time?"

"Don't worry, Coy, if help is needed Chucho will pitch in. Right, Chucho?" Looking pleasantly hammered on beer, he nodded a wobbly head yes.

To draw fire away from Coy I said, "WAIT, Wait, Darrell-Wayne what are you going to ask on the internet?"

"I'll say *don't let them kill me please.*"

"That means everyone will see your face. Are you ready for that?"

"How do I know?"

"Okay, where on the internet are you going to go ?"

"Everywhere! I'll ask the whole world to stop it."

"Hmm, I don't know if that will work."

"Yeah, too much information can be worse than not enough."

"First, I could say I'm sorry if I made a mistake or did something wrong, then ask for help making it all better."

"How do you decide who is for real?"

"We'll know."

Esmeralda could see Darrell-Wayne getting flustered from my questions and said, "With MT's promised Green Card I get a U.S. passport. I don't mind a foreign trip to assassinate assassins. I've traveled to kill before I'm trained to send evil to heaven."

Coy looked skeptical at her foreign travel idea, and his cousin's idea . Despite his cynical look he said, "Esmeralda, what makes you so sure you can find international assassins who warrant heaven?"

"That's easy, true hell is here on earth, during draughts, wildfires, hurricanes, earthquakes, tornadoes, floods, volcanos, and all manner of suffering from not enough to eat, clean water to drink, sickness and disease."

With heaven and hell on the table, it felt like the right time to redirect the banter. "Wow, okay, I'll take your word for that. But let's not get ahead of ourselves, for the moment we must stay vigilant with constant dangers facing Darrell-Wayne. So, with that purpose does anyone object to my giving Chucho a gun?"

"No, Oliver, not since he shot those men dead in your office. Otherwise, we wouldn't have you here today for barbecue and beer. I volunteer to teach him to shoot." Coy said this slurring his words ever so slightly.

"Fine. As long as you use my gun safety rules."

***

That night in bed Coy and I rehashed the day, especially Darrell-Wayne using the internet to seek help from nameless strangers, righteous and bogus. We know how to pace ourselves with alcohol, even quite excellent Belgian beer. But we hadn't that day, it was a special bury our dead event. Nevertheless, we were mindful of not mixing alcohol with gunpowder. Consequently, our semi-sober consensus was, it was unprofessional and potentially dangerous to do what Darrell-Wayne suggested on the internet . Except we'd tried everything else we knew to try and to no avail.

The next day, sober Monday, Coy and I took Chucho to our favorite, and the police department's preferred gun dealer, Iron Works. With our tacit approval Chucho chose a Belgian made Browning 380 semiautomatic handgun. The weapon was small enough not to weigh him down but packed a lethal punch at the range he'd need to use it. As a favor to Coy a police officer and my repeat business, with a wink and a nod the dealer threw in at no charge a concealed carry holster with Velcro straps that wouldn't interfere with the use of crutches.

***

The next chance Coy and I had to spend time alone together, was a week after the barbecue. Then for no reason other than to break patterns, and feeling protective, we accompanied Esmeralda, MT, and Darrell-Wayne downtown to noon Sunday Mass. The church building did not fall down on itself when we two lapsed protestant old boys entered and awkwardly followed parishioners, crossing themselves, standing, kneeling, occasionally sitting, and repeating the movements. After mass the women took Darrell-Wayne horseback riding.

Coy and I took a stroll to a nearby park, found a shaded bench. He took my hand and said, "I spilled my guts to you about being stuck fighting against routine circumcision. I thought you'd reciprocate with something equally personal. Now that you haven't, I feel like I showed you mine, but you won't reciprocate."

"Then I better give in return. Is right now fast enough?"

Making a show of looking astonished with jazz hands, Coy said, "I'm all ears. What's your big secret obsession?"

"Don't be such a nervous nelly."

"I can be nelly if I want, it's Sunday and I'm not wearing a police uniform."

"Consider this, other cops don't treat Sunday nelly queens with any more respect than on Monday."

"Is that what you intend to talk about? I was in the Army I know about homophobia in the ranks. I already know lesbians and gays don't ever get a day off from *persecution*. If you are planning on rehashing old news don't bother."

"Your fixation with routine circumcisions resides at the intersection of pseudo-fake-science, politics, and individual belief systems real and imagined. What's stuck in my craw lives at the same intersection."

I went on to explain growing up if one of us kids got the sniffles mom handed out vitamin C tablets at the breakfast table to all of us. Then we either didn't get sick or not as sick as the neighbors and classmates. My mom was not a believer in vitamins, except C, during cold and flu season. Instead, she was a big advocate in our family doctor and pharmacist and kept them in business with rows of prescription pill bottles with all our names on them except my dad. My dad, who never missed a days' work in his life religiously took a multivitamin with minerals every day, was a careful eater, and swore he was healthier than a horse.

As a parole officer I noticed most of my parolees were either underweight or overweight and even the ones who worked out caught every infectious bug going around. However, there were always a few who had the vitality of good health energy. They were tough in a fight. When I surveyed all my clients about their personal lives, the healthy parolees took vitamins daily, didn't smoke, and were careful what they ate, the others often had self-destructive habits poverty and discrimination encourages.

I've already mentioned there was a high turnover rate at parole, but we did have a few old-time workers on the job. The young bucks used to joke the old timers weren't suited for any other kind of work. The thing I noticed was older workers looked healthy and never used up all their sick days by end of year's expiration. Parole was the kind of job if you took a day off, you got three or more extra days work waiting when you returned. I queried asked the old timers their secret and discovered the only thing the crusty old curmudgeons had in common was taking vitamins and doing daily exercise.

At my next routine annual physical, I asked my family doctor what he thought of me taking vitamins at my age. I was in my twenties then. He went off on me like I'd insulted his family name for seven past generations. The man was sure vitamin and mineral supplements were a complete and total scam to separate suckers like me from my money. He assured me the medical profession viewed vitamin pills as total hokum. After his tirade of an office visit, I stopped in a health food store on the way home. I discovered all multivitamins are not priced the same and there is more for true believers of vitamins than just alphabet letters. That started me on a quest not unlike your own to find answers to questions without answers or approved research.

"I'm not seeing a connection so far."

From the start of government regulated American Medical practice the pharmaceutical industry has spent billions of dollars to lobby to make vitamins illegal so then *they* could profit off them. Big pharma was almost successful more than once linking vitamins with all the illegal medical system bullshit you spoke of for profit only. Then the people who believe in the benefits of vitamin mineral supplements voted in new representation to protect their freedom to buy what they wanted without government interference.

Apparently, it is *not* in the best interest of medical doctors and pharmacists to have actual scientific research showing benefits or not of vitamins on health. Same as was your case with routine circumcision."

"It's not the same. For over a century in this country, until the weight of well documented scientific research from other developed countries forced the American Medical Establishment to replace the word *uncircumcised with natural* on standardized physical exam forms. To me, our obsessions are not similar?"

"Pseudoscience is in bed with the absolute authority of all powerful governments. The people's natural belief system is kept ignorant or confused. That's why both *are* the same not similar."

"Hmm, that's what you say. Convince me yours equals mine. I think mine is longer, fatter, and lasts longer."

"Doctors and pharmacists make their money treating the sick. Routine circumcision was supposed to treat phantom future sickness before they occurred."

"That's right, except it didn't cure autism, oppositional behavior, bedwetting, thumb sucking, or anything."

"What got my curiosity going was, how come there is no unbiased research to prove vitamins were all hooey like my doctor said. If it's all hogwash, how come vitamins earn billions of dollars every year? Do the people in power think we are so gullible as to pay for fraud continuously?"

"Yeah, sounds the same as the routine circumcision industry making billions of dollars selling something with no proven benefit, year in year out. Oliver, you do realize we are on opposite sides of our argument, right?"

"Yes."

"Was fraud what triggered you?"

"No. I was thumbing through a book of photographs of early Christopher Street Liberation Day Marches. They were taken to commemorate the 1969 Stonewall Rebellion. I noticed how demands on placards changed over time. Except one had a direct connection from earliest time to the present. In the first march women held up signs that said, 'Our Bodies, Our Selves.' In the last march in the book women had placards that read, 'Get your laws off my body.' In between the signs were about bodily integrity, autonomy, and women's legal rights to control their own bodies. That's what came to my mind when you were speaking. The multivitamin I take every morning professionals would deny me, without proof, solely for their profit. That denies me my right to autonomy."

"Ah ha, I see how you tied it all together, very interesting."

"People will believe what *they* choose, while authorities promote propaganda instead of producing scientific facts."

"They cater to the gullible and think the rest of us are stupid."

"Exactly. Some folks will believe any lie their government tells; 'My country right or wrong occupying Vietnam.' Others need to invent fantastical conspiracy alternate realities to swallow governmental doom and gloom propaganda. Many of us are going to do what we believe in our hearts, that makes sense, and we'll take the consequences."

"But why?"

"Common sense. By now I think it is human nature for many Americans to harbor healthy skepticism having been lied to by government's leaders so often. Most of us can tell when we are being hoodwinked for the benefit of rich and powerful. And if we can't, shame on us."

"Agreed. You believe multivitamins make you healthy."

"I didn't say that exactly. But close enough."

"Then what did you say?"

"If a person believes taking a daily vitamin pill makes them healthier, then it does, and if they don't it doesn't. It's what a person believes."

"I'm sorry, I lost track again, why are arguments for taking vitamins and against routine circumcision the same."

"My mother said during the Vietnam war the U.S. was divided fifty-fifty, *My country right or wrong,* versus *Peace now.* She said we were on the brink of a civil war here over a civil war over there. Think about it, the whole nation has access to the same media and comes up with opposite conclusions they're willing to spill blood over."

"So, you take a pill every day?"

"Sometimes more than one during cold and flu season. I take vitamin C and I get my annual flu shot plus my multi vitamin."

"What if it's all hype like your doctor says?"

"I just explained, it doesn't matter whether it is a placebo effect or not. I believe vitamins are the source of my good health, real or imagined the result is the same. That is based on personal experience, not hear say rumor or propaganda."

"Well to be honest I was hoping for something more personal, like what I told you. A topic that intrudes on your thoughts when you don't want it to. You know my talking about dick can be off-putting even embarrassing for a lot of people during polite conversation."

"If I bring up vitamins at a party, they are either dismissed out of hand, or completely accepted without discussion. So, maybe you're right."

"I know I'm right, about what I'm right about. Always."

"Hmm. Okay, without getting gross, what I'm about to tell you resides at the intersection of self-awareness, internalized homophobia, and unintentionally hurting others. It's one of those things that pops up when I'm too hungry, angry, lonely, or tired, and can't shake off easily."

I mentioned I'd previously told Coy I came out my freshman year of high school, and my dad had taught each of his kids how to stand up to bullies' years before. Being out gave me a different vantage point to assess my fellow students. Instead of hiding, I held my head up and handled the consequences. I was surprised by the positive reaction from many classmates, especially guys on sports teams I played on, and even a few teachers were supportive. The bullies had learned in middle school to avoid my fists and kicking feet.

At first when I witnessed a classmate being bullied, it occurred to me I was privileged not to endure public humiliation. Then I decided to share my privilege and started stepping in between the bully and his victim. Remember, I had been a boy scout. When it was more than one tyrant, I was pleasantly surprised to find I had unexpected allies, usually other jocks who knew me.

Reflecting on what I was doing, my gaydar indicated many of the worst homophobes with the loudest hateful angry voices would eventually turn out to be faggots. It was troubling and started me on an information quest to discover the damage closet cases caused themselves and others. Unlike different minority groups, *most* lesbians and gay males can let the majority assume they are heterosexual. It is too easy for most closet queens to pass, and then later the consequences are harmful to them and others close by.

Exploring this idea, I discovered many hate crimes committed against LGBTQ+ people were committed by homosexuals pretending to be straight. I know it is unpopular to say that, but statistically the data shows a better than average chance a queer basher bashing queers will eventually accept being queer, if they don't commit suicide first. My quandary was, refusing to accept the victimizer as victim, even though it was society and professions that caused the self-hate that led the basher to bash.

Ever bigger lies becoming less convincing are required from young closet queens growing into adulthood trying to pretend to be other than who they were born to be. Sooner or later the lies must be revealed by truth, and the liar and those close to him or her suffer disgrace worse than being gay would have been in the first place.

"And the loop goes round and round in your head, and there is nothing you can do about it. Am I right, Oliver?"

"Perceptive as usual. What's maddening there is nothing anyone can do about the set-up trap to be socially acceptable and lovable in a flawed society where all are not equal."

"That is heavy, deep, and too sad. As brooding obsessions go, … you now qualify."

"There is a traditional gospel hymn that captures my preoccupation perfectly."

"What's it called?"

"*I told Jesus*. It's on Roberta Flack's *First Take* album on Atlantic records. In the first stanza she sings 'I told Jesus it would be all right to change my name,' and he replies, 'The world will turn away from you if you change your name.' Then the words and music tell reasons not to try to change your identity."

"I know a song from that album. It's the 'Ballad of All the Sad Young Men.' It was a gay bar anthem way back in the 1950s, or so I was told."

"Right. Most people only listen to 'First Time Ever I Saw Your Face.' It was one of her biggest hits. Check out 'I Told Jesus' when you get a chance."

"I don't know anything about gospel music."

"Doesn't matter, check out *I Told Jesus*. It really captures my conflict offering empathy for all the closet queens causing queer bashing misery to self and others."

Chapter 16.

Instead of posting the assassin's print-out sheet marking him a target, as Darrell-Wayne had suggested. Ameli and Chucho produced a three-minute video of him politely asking for information from the public. It showed our eighteen-year-old, looking twelve, dressed in a new extra baggy baby-blue plain front hoody sweatshirt and pants. He spoke clearly of being under threat of death, not knowing why, and appealing to anyone with information to help him understand the reason. He described those after him as unknown to him .

Closing with his usual flat affect, he said, "I'm Darrell-Wayne Goff, just one young dude asking the world to help me fight against criminal intention to deny me my next birthday, please help me stay alive."

Coy and I assured each other little could come from Darrell-Wayne's heartfelt public appeal. We live in a world where big strong adult males knock each other down or worse, and pleading was worse than surrender. If my professional connections beating the bushes couldn't get results, what chance did a boyish video have?

On her own, Ameli set up *Darrell's Next Birthday Alive,* a website to give information or donate money. It had an encrypted inner portal no hacker could break into. Once inside the secure portal, visitors' identity instantly evaporated after leaving a bank verified donation. Any sign of those leaving information or money vanished, irretrievably, into dummy sites around the globe. Only information the *visitor wanted* known could be highlighted and left.

To leave her Scorpio mark, *a record of shame* was posted in large-font flashing in dayglo magenta letters on a flat-black background just outside the website's portal entrance. It named the hackers who tried to break Ameli's encryption, along with their photo, age, home address, political affiliation, work, home, and cell telephone numbers.

Only Ameli could have devised such an efficient yet simple means to face down meanspirited villains, troublemakers, and lay abouts, to publicly embarrass them. The harder the hacker tried to get back at her the more vehemently she repelled them with new insidious viruses she invented with true malice. Ameli could be venomous without half trying. Plumbing the depth of her anger was beyond my social work skill set.

Once the website started producing results, Ameli suggested rather than give me information in irregular dribs and drabs, as it came in. It would save time to collect new information, not burning fires, into a twice-a-week summary report. That worked well for both our busy schedules and allowed Darrell-Wayne to learn new abilities, editing, compiling, and collating from his brainchild. Chucho helped when asked. Previously they seldom made a distinction between mundane and crucial. It was a steep learning curve for both, they had been coddled too over protected.

The first week's consolidated responses had snippets from recorded live videos along with typed summaries explaining them from the respondents. It was surprising the number of real people who left helpful suggestions on Darrell-Wayne's website out of their goodness wanting him to have another birthday, alive.

The biggest surprise to me was how many respondents chose not to use Ameli's encryption tools or in any other way to hide their identities . None of us expected the public to be so magnanimous.

We discovered a pattern through our hair-splitting analysis. Several genuine human respondents, yes, we had to rule out robot responses from real human disgruntled domestic staff and the entire yacht crew of Grand Potentate Giles Gluckeridge III. They filled our inbox with disgruntled replies. Apparently, the Grand Potentate was a tyrant employer who regularly cheated his workers out of their wages after putting them in perilous work situations for his amusement.

One cellphone video captivated all our attention. It was from a two-year-old European Leaders' Conference. At first glance it seemed to be a silly slapstick skit. The video clip started just as the conference participants stopped for lunch. They looked bored and eager to feed and schmooze. Those older white male adults acted like small children just released for elementary school recess rather than the leaders of mostly large countries.

Although, unlike the others U.S. President Reginald Di Rump who had no business being there seemed to be enjoying his first meeting out of country this term. Those in the know knew it was being away from close media scrutiny after having just been caught *again* enriching himself and his family at taxpayers' expense. Most recently he was caught with his hand in the IRS cookie jar, after his supreme court ordered him to stop pilfering.

Di Rump compensated the country for his blatant thievery by eliminating all federal government contributions to Head Start and other early childhood programs. He announced it was a cost cutting measure, although the amount saved was much less than he'd stolen. But only a small minority of democrats in Congress demanded he payback the full amount *and* restore very young children's education.

When taking food out of the mouths of small children to repay his graft wasn't enough to satisfy the courts. By executive order he cut all public-school programs for older needy students including extracurriculars like, sports, band, chorus, drama, and whole school janitorial service. The president announced in leu of physical education the students would sweep, sling mops, scrub toilets, collect and carry out their school's trash. He was sure the older students would be grateful for an opportunity to clean up after themselves.

Still not close to paying back his original theft, the man's voracious greed reemerged with more force than the previous times since being selected president. Thus, he devised a new master scheme to pocket more public funds than before while claiming to be repaying his earlier graft. Consequently, by presidential order Di Rump eliminated all social programs that involved the words people or persons. The result sent social services back to before the day of the buggy whip when America was truly great by his estimation.

Di Rump's handlers and cabinet staff wished to get a break from constantly running interference as he decimated programs for the growing number of hungry, homeless, pregnant women, the dying and the profoundly handicapped, he helped to create. Since his party controlled the Congress, they rubber stamped all executive cost cutting that enriched them and their donors. One little problem they kept deferring until later was the economy tanking since the grand old party was purloining so much of it, there wasn't enough left over to run the government.

Presidential handlers were surprised to have their hands so full with the President in the company of other world leaders. Everyone knew Di Rump wasn't well educated or hardly socialized, but were nevertheless alarmed when he acted curious, abroad. It was a new wrinkle on his shriveled tiny dick. He was never curious at home. It was almost as shocking as if he tried to read a book, something he vowed he'd never do. He was convinced reading was the cause of brain cancer.

What sent the President off his usual self-absorption was, just before leaving uninvited for the European conference, his Supreme Court ruled unanimously against him. It was the first time ever after they had promised never to do that.

It was the very same court *that had* selected him president for a second term over the people's large majority vote for the rightful winner of the election. Suddenly remembering they had lifelong appointments, the court unanimously disapproved his abolishing presidential term limits and choosing each of his children's, grandchildren's, great grandchildren, and great great-grandchildren to succeed him after his death.

Finally, the nine Supreme Court Justices understood they had made a big mistake selecting Di Rump president, twice, after rightwing armed militias burned down their homes and blew up the Supreme Court Building. Conservative Republicans posted rewards on the Internet for the justices' heads on spikes. Also, namby-pamby leftwing Democrats placed wanted posters in post offices offering generous incentives for the nine justices alive to stand trial before a citizens' tribunal.

Unfortunately, for the presidential staff and cabinet, the President could not understand he didn't have absolute power over everything. It was part of his flawed belief system. His wild mood swings were demonstrative of his being on a short leash while being hunted by large segments the American population with lethal intent.

He was often quoted as saying, "When they don't like me, they need to drink bleach to be cured, and then will love me a lot."

His mindless staff hoped he would be more constrained out of the country diversionary trip, at least there would be less bullets flying in the presidential general direction. The video of the president's manic mood swings could have been hysterically funny slapstick if it were not so sad to see a major world leader act like a misbehaving toddler.

Then more detailed and longer lunchbreak cellphone videos arrived at the website. They were shot from different angles and showed a more complete picture of what happened with a moody reselected President of the United States. He was clearly in revolt against rules on his out of home country tour.

He was being advised to develop an agenda for his last designated term in office, his legacy. To complicate the matter, the man who wished to be the first U.S. King was trying to cope with his agoraphobia, while forced to travel for his safety with armed Constitutionalist after him in every state and territory of the Union.

Our president tried to use the same international travel gimmick that worked for him previously. But this time his generals wouldn't let him start another seemingly unintentional war to distract him from his agoraphobia.

What worked so well for Presidents Regan and Bushes I and II just wasn't working for President Di Rump no matter how hard he tried to launch ICBMs. Those pesky generals took his nuclear football away and wouldn't give it back. He'd meant to fire them and replace them with mannequins, and then got distracted.

Highlighted video clips showed President Di Rump brutishly push aside Giles Gluckeridge III, the Most-High Ruler of Della Monrocko, a small wealthy nation situated in the picturesque European side of the Mediterranean Sea. Fury is often the response from small rich nations' leaders who generally don't appreciate being knocked on their royal ass in public by brutish American Presidents. Recorded by cellphone for all the world to see, except in the United States.

Giles looked for a means to viciously vent his wrath for being manhandled in front of national peers from larger in stature and topography European countries. It was a double insult because included in that day's lunch were Della Monrocko's most cherished patriotic national dishes. Twenty different Della Monrocko shrimp delicacies would be on the buffet table, five were fizzing flambe luscious sweet and savory prawn desserts.

That morning word had been delicately disseminated to all invited delegations, and gate crasher Di Rump. The supply of bacon wrapped caviar stuffed shrimp was limited. It was highly recommended by the conference organizer that members share, in the spirit of international peace. Attendees were asked to take only a small portion of the delicacy so everyone could enjoy its uniqueness together.

Otherwise, it was warned, chaos could prevail with first come first served, till the dish was depleted. The high salt content and advanced age of most white male delegates, and smattering of older lesbians for feistiness, was the other reason for moderation. Nobody seemed much interested in the health warning as the attendees lined up ready to sprint to the stuffed shrimp end of the buffet table.

There was grumbling in line among conference attendees. The conscientious was if the conference were held in any other leader's country there would be enough of everything for everyone. It was well known among attendees, Gluckeridge III was a cheapskate, and Della Monrocko's national dish was expensive to produce in labor and materials. Nevertheless, a generous potentate would have supplied the conference with enough or not put the dish on the buffet table.

What happened next was, both the American President and Della Monrocko Sovereign were rushing at the buffet table to be first when the collision occurred. His Holy Highness Gluckeridge III was elbowed off balance then forcefully shoved aside in a sprint and then he fell to the floor, on his royal butt. Many of the other delegates formed a circle to look down on Giles with disgruntled faces, that he let the blow hard American buffoon beat him in a foot race, be knocked to the ground, and denied the invited delegates a tasty delicacy.

Meanwhile the President of the United States didn't stop to offer a hand up or an apology to the man he pushed aside. Rather he heaped two extra-large dinner plates, he'd purloined from the White House, and filled them to overflowing with stuffed shrimp. A notable portion of delicately stuffed and wrapped shrimp fell to the floor which the President trampled underfoot while shoveling prawns to plate, hand over fist heaping plates high. Thus, all the other conference attendees were denied the patriotic delicacy and signature dish of Della Monrocko. It was commonly known to also be its esteemed Monarch's favorite because he said so often in public.

Mission completed, all stuffed shrimp at hand, the U.S. president sat alone in a corner stuffing his mouth with both greasy hands and glaring viciously at any who dared come near. Caviar stuffing dripping out of both corners of his mouth made him look ghoulish. Bystanders doubted Di Rump tasted what he swiftly scooped into his mouth and gulped down his throat barely avoiding a witnessed upchuck calamity.

The kind-hearted worried the leader of the free world might choke himself to death swilling stuffed crustaceans too fast. While the more diplomatic saw an isolationist like George W. Bush's uncouth behavior parlayed to new heights of ugly American rude behavior demonstrating contempt for the rest of the world. The faint of heart feared the U.S. President would invade their country like President Regan did to cover his embarrassments by invading Grenada. They were all proven wrong. Di Rump made a second trip to the buffet table and filled his oversize plates to overflowing again this time with whatever food was leftover. His motto, "Healthy appetite healthy supreme leader."

The fourteen other Della Monrocko shrimp main courses were delicious and plentiful along with many tasty side dishes to distract from the expensive seafood's limited quantity. There was enough other food to leave all the attendees well satisfied, other than missing the signature dish.

However, for some reason the five flambe shrimp desserts did not curry favor with the conference goers and for the most part just smoldered untouched. Nevertheless, since that was all that was finally left, on his third trip to the buffet table President Di Rump stuffed his pockets with on fire shrimp. The President prided himself on always being ready for a snack attack, and a pocket full of sweet, flavored flaming shrimp was almost as good as his usual jellybeans, left at the white house in huge quantities by President Ronald Regan.

During the reign of the Soviet Union, Della Monrocko ingratiated itself with Soviet leaders by using exotic shrimp-based gifts, kow towing, and showing fear by quaking when appropriate. In return for the show U.S.S.R. threatened those bullies that were audacious enough to harass Della Monrocko and its stuffed shrimp industry. Nuclear missile saber rattling usually struck fear in bullies when all else failed.

The tribute in exchange for protection was delicious stuffed shrimp supplied to useful government leaders and their oligarchs. Thus, with friends like the Soviet Union, Della Monrocko didn't need a standing army or air force. However, they did have a mighty, if little, Navy to protect against shrimp pirates. With the Soviets gone, the very small extremely rich nation needed big tough friends to scare off bullies or after the leaders' conference, to kill a United States' President.

***

The second week's relevant respondents to Darrell-Wayne's web appeal also didn't try to hide their identities. In fact, they exposed themselves, and let it be known they were low level bureaucrats, not exactly in love with their Kremlin's new criminal bosses. For the most part this group sent audio recordings to substantiate their written messages.

They let it be known they expected to be killed for speaking out but had reached their fill of corruption and death seemed the only way out. The new Russia did not have whistleblower protection, or independent journalists, or any media that wasn't a mouthpiece for new mother Russia. Given all that, Coy and I were surprised at the ease of authenticating responses by those expecting to be killed for speaking opposition. We used the same generation of voice recognition software as their Russian masters. Both the U.S. and former U.S.S.R. bought the software from China which had become world masters in face and voice recognition software for enslaving their ordinary citizens.

The Prime Minister aka Russian President Vlad Mutein of New Russia, held both positions for life and beyond through his children and their children's children. He liked to compare himself to Peter the Great, the first Czar. Peter had appropriated a huge portion of Sweden to create Saint Petersburgh, Russia. The new Czar, as Vlad Mutein on occasion referred to himself, had big plans. He didn't want sainthood like Peter the Great, but he planned to expand Russia's territory by absorbing its neighbors. His expansion projects were grander than his long-ago predecessor Peter the Great, or even the late great Soviet Union.

Why take another chunk of Sweden when the whole country could be annexed easily, along with Finland, Norway, Denmark, and Iceland? In one fell swoop it would be an economy of effort with little resistance, accomplished in only a few days. Germany and France would have to wait to be invited to become members of New Russia, an invitation they wouldn't be able to refuse. Then the rest of Europe would follow like sheep or face serious consequences they couldn't even contemplate.

Some might have imagined a conflict, for cause, between Giles Gluckeridge III and Reginald Di Rump, might be right up Czar Mutein's trouble making ally. However, prime minister, president, new czar to be didn't see it so black and white.

Di Rump owed the Russian leader for his behind-the-scenes assistance, once again, to be selected President of the United States. Di Rump didn't have the wherewithal to completely control his base of white supremacists and Nazis to undo the American Constitutional Democracy, as he had promised them. Although, he tried to no avail. He even mentioned in his state of the union message that some constitutions die harder than others, and cursed the founding fathers.

However, Reginald knew the new czar had knowledge with photography of his sexual indiscretions with psychotic older homeless women, and the Russian wasn't afraid to use it against him. Consequently, the U.S. President idealized Vlad Mutein the Great for putting him in office, again, and promising to help get rid of the annoying U.S. Constitution, at the Russian's convenience of course. As was his trademark, Reginald would renege on paying his debt to Vlad. Gluckeridge III simply wanted help with bullies *again*. It should have been a small matter by Mutein's standards, since Giles always paid for his favors, and Di Rump never did.

Vlad was happy to help both without them knowing he played both sides of conflicts, when possible. Mutein didn't waste effort with modern revolutionary methods of persuasion. Instead, he used old tired and true Soviet style misinformation to dupe the stupid American people with false news, fanciful conspiracies designed for their short mental attention limits, and soul crushing self-hate in every conceivable form imaginable.

Mutein had been promised Alaska as payment for another successful presidential selection of Di Rump by the Supreme Court. So far, Di Rump had not returned Alaska to Mother Russia, or been able to dissolve the U.S. Constitution. It should have been easy to help Gluckeridge III against Di Rump except Vlad was working on a much bigger nefarious deal at the time.

Giles Gluckeridge III demanded and got his audience with Vlad Mutein. He bribed key oligarchs with his special pork stuffed shrimp. They were tasty, but not as expensive as butterflied bacon wrapped Russian beluga caviar filled shrimp.

At his meeting Gluckeridge III pleaded with Mutein the Great, for Russia to assassinate Di Rump. Because Della Monrocko didn't have a standing army to declare war against the slobbering swine U.S.A. President. After all it was the Soviet Union that had discouraged Giles' grandfather from forming an army. With an army he could have declare war on the stuff shrimp hoarder who knocked his royal highness on his hiney in front of everyone and be generously compensated after a brief unequal war of vindication with the United States of America.

Bemused. Czar Mutein said, "Don't take it so personally. We both know my dear friend and dupe Di Rump is a mental defective. But he idealizes me, like a lapdog, and soon I'll have Alaska back, for only one dollar. That is not such a bad deal for Russia to have a do over."

Gluckeridge III shouted in anger. "The capitol charges against Di Rump are buffet theft of bacon covered caviar stuffed shrimp, manhandling me, and knocking me to the floor in front of my peers, and being an embarrassment as a world leader. I'm a grand potentate and deserve respect even from uncivilized bovine like that uncouth Di Rump. I say off with his head then draw and quarter him for good measure."

Czar to be, Mutein, patted the disgruntled pudgy dictator on the head and forcefully explained it was not in Russia's best interest, at least for the moment, to decapitate Di Rump and start a war with the U.S. over a food fight. Vlad continued it was much more humiliating for the United States to leave Di Rump's head in place rather than remove it.

However, the Great Mutein thought the big buffoon Di Rump's time walking the earth might be limited, if not only because of his unhealthy diet, hefty bulging extra bellies, and unwillingness to pay his debts. To get Gluckeridge III out of his office and pick his pocket while having a little fun. Vlad offered Giles a means just short of presidential death to appease his bruised ego at Reginald's expense.

As it just so happened, Vlad Mutein, circuitously became aware of the availability of four American decommissioned nerve gas artillery shells, for sale on the black market at a very good price, for the right terrorist. Normally Vlad wouldn't be bothered by such small business. But nerve gas on the loose made everyone nervous, he liked that.

Also, he'd been promised Alaska for getting Di Rump the presidency again. *When was the handover?* That's what he wanted to know. He'd request a big ceremony with lowering the stars and stripes and raising the Russian flag overing Anchorage while a military band played Prokofiev's theme from "Love for Three Oranges."

Then Mutein was reminded Reginald had a reputation for never paying his debts. He announced to the world all debt givers liked to be swindled. Vlad saw an opportunity to shame Di Rump, get Alaska as promised, and send Gluckeridge on his merry way placated.

After a Russian snow job, Royal Potentate Giles Gluckeridge III jumped at the chance to pay for expired nerve gas as part of a revenge scheme for being publicly embarrassed. In a flash the new Czar mixed the nerve gas shells, vengeance, and the grand potentate's dislike of Boston, and Russia being cheated on the return of Alaska.

Gluckeridge III jumped at the chance to have Russia owe him a favor. Even if it was only Alaska.

A deal was quickly struck between monarch Giles Gluckeridge III and shortly to be Czar for life and beyond Mutein. Gluckeridge III would pay for the nerve gas shells and all other materials needed to cause Boston to be flattened in thermos-baric waves. Vlad would provide experienced operatives to make the memory of Boston a real nightmare for bumbling Di Rump to try to govern the rest of his terrified country.

Gluckeridge would get credit for destroying a historical city. It seems Giles had once visited Boston in his youth and found standing in long lines for sports amusements intolerably disrespectful for such a highborn about to be regal of Della Monrocko, such as himself. He found the very idea of naming a sporting team after smelly socks offensive.

The plan was, after Boston's demise Gluckeridge III would demand the U.S. pay Della Monrocko $10,000,000 tribute in gold. Or he would eliminate another historical American city. Furthermore, as art of the deal, President Di Rump would personally return Alaska to Russia and accept the one dollar given in exchange. At that time, he would also issue an international apology for his buffet bullying, stuff shrimp bogarting, and gross piggishness watched by the world's television cameras. The mouse *had* roared, and Boston and its first responders *were* scheduled to disappear into histories' rubble pile.

Being hustled out the door Giles said over his shoulder, "It would be so much easier to just kill that asshole Di Rump and save the fuss for something important."

With a hand gesture Vlad stopped his men bum rushing Gluckeridge III out the door, and pontificated, "When my operatives engineered Di Rump's Supreme Court selection to the presidency this time, they discovered few Americans still believe in their silly ineffectual three-part government. But the majority yearn for, no, demand, my style of authoritarianism to tell them what to do, think, when, and where. Too bad President Di Rump didn't have the gonads to give them what they wanted an insurrection against a constitution that favors the rich only."

"What's any of that to do with me?"

"Once I'm in charge over there, Di Rump will cease to exist on this planet as your favorite grumble. Be patient little man your dream of vengeance will come true soon, the American people yearn to replace their faux dictator with me, a real one."

Out of the blue, BBC international broadcast rogue U.S. nerve gas shells had been captured by federal agents in South Dakota where the governor claimed not to know they were stored in the basement of the governor's mansion. Caught red handed, the governor was forced to rationalize she was planning to extract the gas to eradicate covid-19 virus because she was an ardent antivaxxer.

Madam governor vehemently sought reasonable alternatives to any inoculation. The governor felt the gas, which she bought at an underground black-market auction, with discretionary slush funds was a bargain. It furthered her belief that poison gas was more therapeutic than having her citizens drink bleach. She found bleach had an unpleasant after taste, left a telltale smell on the breath, and some outrageous nuts even suggested were lethal.

Vlad Mutein missed the BBC announcement being distracted designing annexation plans for Russia's immediate neighbors first. He was surprised when his Royal Highness Giles Gluckeridge III came calling in a huff. Della Monrocko's fearless leader said, "I demand to know what happened to our plan to flatten Boston out of existence. What happened to sucking it into smithereens in a vacuum?"

Vlad was amused by the little man's temper tantrum. Rather than squash him like a bug, which was a thought. When the urge passed, he explained Alaska was mostly ice and snow and was full of undesirable poor people living off the public welfare tit. He didn't want them draining his resources.

His current interest was bigger-better-richer prey. Vlad had the Scandinavians in his gunsight. Why not? The new Czar to be told the portly potentate, "Cool your jets, boy. You'll get your vengeance just not a spectacular thermo-baric one. Since we no longer needed the nerve gas and you already paid for it, I sold those shells to the highest bidder. She lives in South Dakota, a deep freeze worse than Alaska. I doubled my profit, aren't you proud of me?"

Totally frustrated at not being taken seriously, Giles slammed his fist down and demanded, "Then I want all my deposit money back plus interest, and for you to never put Alaska in any future deals with me."

Both men stood and faced each other, toe to toe. Not very tall himself, Vlad was nevertheless an inch taller and a few years younger than the corpulent Giles. Czar to be Mutein said, "What's an old pipsqueak like you going to do if I don't?"

The two men lunged at each other, and blows flew. Though well past middle age, Giles nevertheless practiced jujitsu drills daily at morning rollcall to keep his employees in line. In his younger days Vlad had been well versed in hand-to-hand combat book theory and kept up his textbook skills by torturing opposition political candidates before putting them to death.

As they slammed together violently mixing it up, the two over the hill despots gave as good as they got battering each other, with ineffectual blows, throws, kicks, and head butts. As much as possible elbows and knees were not involved due to aging joint pain. Blustered more than bruised, lightly pummeled, greatly short of breath the two adversaries finally could do little more than stand and have a staring contest until Vlad said, "Tell you what, rectum face, I have an open active Platinum account with Boynton International Assassins and Associates. I'll gift you one hit as return payment for your pathetic greasy little deposit money. Is there anyone, except Di Rump you want dead in a hurry?

"Who queered my dream of flattening Boston?"

"Oh, ho hum."

"I'm more than greatly disappointed, I wanted that whole city and surrounding area dead. What one person could equal the loss of a whole historical American city?"

"Let me think. Their names right on the tip of my tongue."

"You know if it had happened, that would have put *me* in the history books. It could have been my most crowning achievement, think of it, more dead than Hitler, Stalin, Mao, or Pol Pot. Who stole my fame?"

"Oh, right, my intelligence agents say Darrell-Wayne Goff is responsible."

"Then I want him dead, grotesquely slowly dead. That's the payback I want for ruining all my fun."

"That should be no problem for such a simple ask. But of course, I'll need a transfer fee. It's just a legal formality."

"Then how's this going to work?"

"I'll give the Boynton family a heads up. Remember, you only get *one free hit*. Just mention for them to charge it to my account."

"Who are they?"

"Belarus's executioners. They guarantee full gratification and won't stop trying until the job is done to your satisfaction. They stake their reputation, and given the neighborhood they work in, their lives are on finishing what they start."

"Sounds good. How do I get in touch with them?"

"It's tricky. Since it's so important to you, I'll have it done for you. Give my people a week or so to set up an anonymous meeting. You know you can trust me."

"Can I trust you? You have a reputation like Di Rump's for defaulting on deals."

"Are you sure you really want this mastermind Darrell-Wayne Goff dead, if you can't trust me?"

"Of course, if I can't have Di Rump dead than he's the next best fatality."

"Just remember, there are no free do-overs. Any additional hits will cost you dearly and I get a double fee, going and coming, for all referrals to Boynton."

"Most assuredly, if Mr. Darrell-Wayne Goff messed up my Boston Spectacular, I want him dead preferably after a long, hard suffering."

"I'll have copies sent to you of what we know about the mastermind Goff. Then it's between you and the Boynton associates."

"But will everyone know it was me behind killing Goff?"

"Yes. For an extra fee, you can have publicity credit for killing Demon Darrell-Wayne Goff in retaliation for queering the Boston endeavor."

Their business completed, no debts owed, and for the moment everyone was satisfied.

***

The next morning while reviewing open case files from per diem operatives the desk phone jangled. "Queer Queries, how may I help you?"

"I've got good news and bad. What do you want first?"

"Willis, I'm fine, how are you? Sorry to be so long saying hi. Hi."

" What's your excuse?"

" Keeping Darrell-Wayne and the rest of my family of choice alive . Bad news first if you don't mind."

"The Arkansas Border Patrol snagged a rental-box-truck with twenty-five tactically dressed, heavily armed, neo-Nazi militia men in back. The reason they called me was the driver had a document with Darrell-Wayne's photo and particulars and your street address. The Canadians put out an international alert to save your boyfriend's cousin from terrorist. It prominently displayed my phone number as local coordinator. Nobody bothered to mention to me I'm a coordinator. Tell me, why am I always the last to learn these things?"

"You aren't the last. Didn't you just give me the news? Wait a minute, Arkansas doesn't have a border with Mexico or Canada."

"I thought your business plan included being acutely aware of current events."

"Well, mister, a coordinator usually does. As I just explained, keeping those close to me alive has narrowed my vision quite a bit."

"Then what you missed was most justices of the Supreme Court, not female, suddenly decided they are one hundred percent originalists. So now, they are refusing to take any cases involving women since women are not mentioned in the original constitution, and so have no rights. Their ability to vote was the first thing to be rescinded."

"WHAT! How can they do that?"

"By declaration. They removed all amendments protecting females. It appears there are no rights for women in the original constitution."

"You're being silly, right? Stop it."

"It's true. No more privacy, contraception, interracial relations, or any civil rights using the female gender as a determinant. Women's rights have been sent back to Bible times when they had less than none. My wife is on the warpath as are most non-Christian fundamentalist women."

"Willis, that's ludicrous, insane."

"No. Some women prefer being nothing more than a man's vassal and routinely beaten for the privilege. The police can no longer investigate domestic violence since women don't exist under law."

"The supreme court has become worse than the republicans who stacked it."

"I guess it's just as well the Equal Rights Amendment never got passed. It would be extinct now anyway."

" My God the court has undone centuries of their own precedents."

"When the court allowed a national ban on abortions, they left themselves open to all sorts of lawsuits and other recriminations from people of goodwill of all genders. In response, as expected, they took the cowards way out declaring females' noncitizens and so they and their supporters no longer have grounds to object to the judiciary."

"I don't want to believe this. I only took my eye off the ball for a second."

"Now the barren states had to set up border controls on their highways and byways since interstate buses, trains, and plains are not allowed to transport childbearing noncitizens under sixty across state lines."

"Barren?"

"Texas and its neighbors, except New Mexico, are called barren states because the women, children, and men who love them have left or are trying to flee. Those states are experiencing negative population growth, big time, which isn't good for business investment. On the other hand, real estate there is very cheap, and jobs are plentiful."

" I suppose the people are talking with their feet"

"To Illinois, the coastal states, Canada, Mexico, South and Central America, and Europe has made some attractive recruitment offers for gender equality and liberty for all."

"There is no hope beyond leaving the country I suppose."

"Illinois, and a couple of sanctuary cities scattered around here or there in the middle west and deep south. But they are overwhelmed with housing refugees. President Di Rump says it's states right issue and refuses to be involved."

"Jeez, you said there was good news."

"Sociologists have found *situational homosexuality* has increased 26,000 percent in the barren states. While in the sanctuary states and cities sympathetic gay men are helping with ejaculation drives for breeding."

"Wait, WHAT."

"The highest court of the land has created a situation where gay sperm is greatly valued where available. Countrywide due to the breeding imbalance, and gender flight, gay males have sociologically been moved up a notch in national accounting. Childbearing age women are trying to have male offspring for legal protection in their old age."

"Just wait one second there, bucko, why in the world would gay sperm be valued over good ole boy redneck spunk?"

"More than fifty percent of gay men graduate college and they all love their mothers."

"Everyone loves their mother."

"I'm told gay men are more mother inclined and generous to mom in old age."

"Did anyone think to declare a national emergency? This cannot end well."

"What could you possibly mean?"

"Those old white men who passed laws to control women's bodies will not be pleased to have their seed usurped by gay sperm. *Where available.* Not to mention five over the hill justices who wear long black dresses should know better than disrupt the natural order of things."

"Oliver OK, what makes you think anyone, but a few women care?"

"Willis, you have more sense than that. Anyway, there should be a campaign for the bigots to learn gay sperm does not guarantee gay babies. Lesbians and gay males are created by straight people. Jees, we don't want them taking away our right to vote too."

"Remember it's not the vote, it's who counts the votes. With womanhood under attack females have had to decide what matters most to them."

"Wow. This really doesn't feel good at all."

"Most straight men marry mother substitutes and those daughter in laws will fight mama to the death over power and control in the household and security in old age."

"Stop! Where in this mess is the neo-Nazi Militia caught in Arkansas? The one you mentioned earlier after Darrell-Wayne."

"Arkansas Border Control was going to turn them loose after forty-eight hours. So, I gave them the name and phone number of the guy at Homeland Security that's collecting Darrell-Wayne killer want-to-bees in Guantanamo Cuba."

"Every time I think that place can finally be closed, it gets filled up again. Thanks for the heads up and current events update. How are you and yours doing, otherwise?"

"We're fine, we live in a sanctuary city in a sanctuary state. Thanks for asking. By the way we have planned a birthday barbecue for Junior. You, Coy, and Darrell-Wayne are invited. Oops, there goes my other line. Call if you need anything. Got to go. Bye."

Chapter 17.

Darrell-Wayne needed new sneakers. He'd worn holes through the bottoms of his favorite pair, and others looked the worse for wear or unworn. But simple tasks, like buying shoes, were never easy for our little family. Part of the sneaker problem was he had three different sizes in his collection that he liked to wear. What I'm saying is, tracing his bare foot on paper was no easy matter, and after the results were seldom worth the hassle.

As it happened a shoe store popular with teens at the mall was having a sale. With a coupon, it was fifty percent off the second pair of brand name sneakers. For reasons I'll never understand Darrell-Wayne liked presenting coupons to store cashiers with his unique autistic aplomb. As if the coupon was more valuable than money.

To guarantee success on our shopping sortie, I also had, by luck, a buy one gets one free coupon for the new ice cream parlor. It just opened on the third tier of the mall and was desperate for foot traffic to find them. One sure way to get beyond autistic obstacles to shoe buying, was bribery by ice cream. Shopping went better than expected, and according to Darrell-Wayne the double dark chocolate-chunky ice cream was five stars excellent and worth the ordeal of shoe shopping. Ultimately, three different salespeople and the store manager were necessary to complete the sales to our finicky teenage shoe shopper.

However, through this mercantile event it suddenly appeared I needed eyeglasses. I kept seeing this same guy hovering near our vicinity. I knew he couldn't be in two places at once, yet he seemed to be. Another possibility was I was losing my mind, a distinct likelihood shoe shopping with Darrell-Wayne.

With so many recent assassinations attempts at my current level of heightened security, I regularly had to rule out early onset Alzheimer, Parkinson, or plain old house and garden paranoid disease. I use a self-applied mental status test I learned in social work school for self-reality checks. Based on my self-diagnostics I was fine except for seeing double, which wasn't fine at all.

The popup all over the place hallucination wasn't my type of stranger; the opposite was true. He was South Asian, maybe early thirties, going to seed around a potbellied middle. The gentleman was of average height, brown hair, eyes, medium brown skin tone, and dressed in nondescript blah brown clothes.

What made him stick out was the contrast between his unremarkable physical dull appearance and his God given extreme feminine mannerisms. At the expense of being graphic, his biped locomotion was more prancing than walking. Without putting it on, his hand gestures were over-the-top super stylized flamboyance. A drag queen would have to study hard to learn his over the top swish hand flailing. Transvestites resent being mimicked or mocked but this potbellied guy wasn't putting anyone-on. He was the real thing, straight from the Divine, but without flaming bright colors, feather boas, and sparkling sequins.

With a sincere apology to all the Philadelphia lawyers of the world, swish never turned me on. And this swish in question seemed to buzz around us like an annoying butterfly just out of shoo away reach. I was formulating a non-offensive way to scoot the annoyance away when I was distracted.

Darrell-Wayne noticed my shoe untied by pointing at it making facial gestures. I immediately squatted down to tie my shoe and Coy walked on ahead with our ward. Then I spied the swishy guy whoosh past me in a hurry to get directly behind Darrell-Wayne. I watched Miss Swish remove a small beige box from his side pocket and extract a hypodermic needle as he moved.

Before he could jab Darrell-Wayne with the hypo-needle, I shouted an alarm, sprang up, leaped forward, and tackled the swish, *hard to the ground* by his ankles. The flouncing attacker lay arm holding needle outstretched, face flattened to the dirty floor, and my knee pushing on the small of his back. I gave him a hard smack across the back of the head to neutralize wriggling energy.

Then I shimmied up his back, grabbed his hand holding the intravenous device and immobilized it with my fist. What I'd failed to notice earlier, being surprised seeing a weaponized hypo-needle, were the brass knuckles on the girly-man's other hand. Instinctively, he swung his free fist backwards, over his shoulder connecting with the top of my noggin. His blow opened a gash in my scalp. I dodged his next attempted blow. His strike wasn't feminine he'd been coached. Then a fog started to descend over my eyes while my blood poured into them.

Coy had heard my shouting, looked back, and now had the needle guy handcuffed with his hypo and knuckles safely confiscated. Wiping my eyes on my sleeve my brain-fog lifted and I was kissed on the mouth by my future husband. Then, unbelievable, there was the same guy, his double on the other side of the atrium. He swished in a hurry over to our side of the atrium using the pedestrian bridge. I saw him remove a case like the other's as he bustled on the move.

Son of a bitch, he wore the same clothes and God help us, same exact face as the man I'd just tackled and who currently wore Coy's handcuffs behind his back. Good heavens, this duplicate assailant also had a hypodermic and was poised to stick Darrell-Wayne who had moved on a few stores ahead, window shopping apparently oblivious to the commotion behind him.

For the life of me I couldn't find my voice, whether from overuse shouting or shock, nothing came out of my mouth but silent rasping air. Speechless, I raised and waved my arms wildly pointing. Two mall cops near Darrell-Wayne had just arrived alerted to the commotion. They saw me waving and where I pointed.

Darrel-Wayne turned at the last possible second, swung the shopping bags he carried, and the needle of death got stuck in his right hand-held shopping bag's shoe box. Just then the mall cops intervened, they assaulted *my guy's doppelganger* with their batons about his head and shoulders.

The identical twin had crumpled to the floor rolling into a ball covering his head with hands while the mall cops tried to figure out how to handcuff the guy. It looked like they seldom got to use their manacles. On the other hand, they'd obviously been practicing using their nightsticks in tandem. Bloodied, the body double now looked like a heap of discarded bloody rags. I mean really, who expects to find identical twin assassins at their local mall's third floor atrium during a big double coupon sales event?

The mall security supervisor arrived after the action was over. She looked flustered having missed all the activity. The perps were both handcuffed, one worse for wear than the other. So, she directed two additional uniformed mall cops, with their batons at the ready, to disperse the crowd that had formed to gawk at us. Then she announced, to no one in particular, she'd already called regular local PD about this disturbance, if the spectators knew what was good for them, they would disperse, and for everyone's information use of injection needles, brass knuckles, or any other weapon was strictly prohibited on mall property.

Moments later, of course she had to be the sergeant out on street patrol that day, Sergeant Mellissa Jackson appeared with three of her uniformed officers. They acknowledged Coy, took his statement, and confiscated needles and brass knuckles. Then Sergeant Jackson saw me and scowled. She promptly made a kiss-pucker face, pointed to then slapped her big butt. Now all business, she collected her team, our swishes, and departed as quickly as she arrived. I weakly waved goodbye to her, still voiceless. I don't know, possibly my middle finger was raised, it happens sometimes when I'm not all right with the world. Especially if I'd just been nonverbally invited to kiss someone's ass.

Up ahead of the mall commotion Darrell-Wayne was still in his own world window gazing, a new pair of sneakers in each shopping bag held triumphally, one in each hand. The look on his face was enthralled by fine window dressing while contentedly digesting double dark chocolate chunky ice cream.

***

My friend Willis called the next morning inquiring why I threw a finger at a police sergeant responding to a mall commotion. He said I was now prominently on Melissa Jackson's shit list. Without going into detail, I gave him an abridged version of my encounters with Sergeant Jackson. He sternly suggested I mend fences because she was a hero cop that could be an asset to me in a pinch. He went on to say he trusted her and lately I needed as many friends as I could find. Willis named Jackson's favorite brand of hooch and thought I should send her a bottle as a peace offering. Before I could find a perfect retort, with a smile in his voice Willis said, "Never mind I already sent a bottle with your name on it. You my friend are too slow, and need to show more respect for the local PD."

"Why'd you go and do that for?"

Then gleefully he said, "Call it the return of a favor, hee, hee."

"Which favor?"

With a smile back in his voice Willis said, "There's been so many, who's counting."

Willis then mentioned my doppelgangers Raynor and Rainer Ramanand only spoke a rare southeastern Hindi dialect, or so they first indicated. Since the local police do not have Hindi interpreters, the swishy men were sent to Washington D.C. where such translation service was available from the FBI without a need for cellphone service in between. It seemed the FBI was rather anxious to meet the twins on some other issues of mutual interest.

My friend thought I'd probably get an unpleasant follow up call from the Washington FBI Office wanting to take Darrell-Wayne back into protective custody. Because the local police lab was only able to identify the substance in the assassins' needles as a newer neurotoxin, most likely of South Asian origin. Subsequently, the needles also went to Washington D.C. for more sophisticated evaluation for origin, molecular breakdown, antidotes, and lethality.

***

With time, the illusion and nonthreat normalcy tried to fool our little family into complacency. After our adventure with hypodermic needles at the mall, I insisted we wear bulletproof vests and Kevlar long sleeves and pants whenever we left the house. Coy thought I was being paranoid from seeing double and refusing to get bifocals. Darrell-Wayne was opposed to any extra effort getting dressed, nothing new there. Both helped me stave off security complacency and Melissa Jackson sent a frilly lavender scented thank you card for the liter of liquor Washington sent her in my name.

During one of our quiet times together I pointed out to Coy, Darrell-Wayne was spending too much time plugged into his earphones. And not making enough effort to develop essential social skills with peers, autistic or otherwise. Coy groused my inner social worker should get more sleep. Nevertheless, during a parent teacher meeting Coy voiced my concern to his cousin's counselor. The university pedagogue strongly suggested we take Darrell-Wayne to the local aquarium and see for ourselves the results of the teen's independent studies in whistles, clicks, and claques. Which I had identified as a waste of his time.

I hadn't been to the public aquarium since an elementary school trip in fifth grade which now seemed a thousand years ago. The place basically looked and smelled the same after all that time, but the fish were different, they seemed much smaller. When I was ten years old, I had an unnerving staring contest with a huge Blue Fish through the wall of glass separating his wet world from my dry one. The fish seemed to know instinctively my family regularly *ate* blue fish and took offense.

Blue fish are local, our family friends that fish always gave us some of their overflow catch and in season it's the cheapest fish at the fish mongers. I like to eat the small to medium size blue fish we have for dinner. My mom said the big Blues were too fishy tasting to be good to eat. What can I say? We like our fish not to taste fishy. Mine was a strange family and the giant blue fish seemed to want to eat me. It kept showing me its teeth.

That fish staring at me in the aquarium that day seemed to be almost my size. He had very sharp looking teeth and I imagined an interest in knowing *if I tasted fishy*. That first and until today my last trip to the aquarium made me think about what I eat and how it triggered my interest in nourishing vegetables and fruit. That big blue fish saved many of his brethren that day from my fork and showed me without realizing it I've been paranoid since childhood.

Darrell-Wayne seemed to be having his own through the glass staring contest with a porpoise until an announcement proclaimed the aquatic show would start in fifteen minutes and we should go upstairs and claim our seats. Upstairs were two enormous pools facing outside bleachers with a walkway bridge over the pools. Darrell-Wayne found his way onto the walkway and leaned over the railing facing the larger pool. Then I watched him make clicks, claques, and whistles.

Before I could feel embarrassed, two dolphins surfaced in front of him to click, whistle, and claque back. Then suddenly there were a lot of dolphins whistling, clicking, and clacking at our teenager. Then from the smaller tank we heard a chorus of dolphins vocalizing. Seeing something amiss one of the large sea mammals' handlers rushed over to show us to our seats. Darrell-Wayne waved goodbye to his new friends, and they acknowledged him by jumping out of the water and into the air and doing tricks.

The show was what I'd expected, not great, but mildly entertaining if you'd been traumatized by a large blue fish at age ten. Unless you like watching dolphins do tricks in exchange for fish snacks while the local yokels clapped with glee like trained seals. At intermission when we were supposed to go to the gift shop and buy souvenirs, the dolphin handler supervisor found us and chatted with Darrell-Wayne. The chat ended with an offer of a part-time job for our teenager at the aquarium. Naturally our boy said yes, and my security nightmare grew exponentially the more I thought about trying to protect him from large crowds viewing giant aquatic mammals.

Jameer Nachos was having a mixed mood, he was happy I reached out to him when he'd been assigned to keep in contact with us. But not happy I involved him getting Darrell-Wayne from a handoff spot to the aquarium and being his security detail while working there parttime. None of his bosses had that in mind when he was told to make Darrell-Wayne's security his priority. But I had a court order and had learned to let Nachos' spleen vent between receiving information he didn't want to hear or act on. Like Coy said, my inner social worker seldom gets enough sleep.

Chapter 18.

Thanks to Darrell-Wayne's Internet discoveries the mystery of the *who* and *why* of his continued looming murder became known. The new question was what were we going to do about what we learned? I asked the same individuals who helped keep Darrell-Wayne alive so far. The conference room at my office over the dentist above the hardware store can hold eight comfortably. In a pinch, it would seat ten or twelve squished together or chairs behind chairs with the windows and door left open for ventilation. Physically in attendance at the brainstorming meet were Coy, Darrell-Wayne, Ameli, Esmeralda, Chucho, Willis, George Reynolds, and me. In virtual attendance via zoom computer screen were General Navarro, FBI Special Agent Nachos, and the windows and door remained closed for privacy. Otherwise, it would have been too cold for good idea germination and to open air for eavesdropping.

I started the meeting welcoming everyone, then cautioned them the proceedings were being recorded to protect the protectors present from future liability. Next, I gave a summary of what we had learned from the internet, mentioned in passing what we already knew and asked for suggestions for preventing future attempts on Darrell-Wayne's life using what we now knew.

The first to speak up was Esmeralda, who now possessed a new U.S. green card and passport. Her suggestion was, she go to Europe and eliminate Giles Gluckeridge III, and Bad-Vlad Mutein as recompense for bankrolling the eradication of Darrell-Wayne. Naturally Darrell-Wayne wanted to go along on the trip to explain to the two men in question, he was sorry if he did anything wrong.

I explained to Esmeralda none of us were allowed to travel internationally with weapons, and I didn't have a reliable means to get them once overseas. The general and Jameer both cleared their throats on Zoom but didn't speak. Esmeralda said she had trustworthy Catalan and Basque contacts in Spain for both weapons and additional gunners, as needed.

We could see negative body language on Zoom from the television monitor. The current topic of assassination was making the General and FBI man fidgety uncomfortable. Or maybe they thought their teams could do a more reputable job than the Catalonians and Basques. From my seat it looked like intramural rivalry among those not usually in the national leader assassination business.

To keep the meeting moving along, I said, " Any more expedient suggestions?"

George Reynolds, the narco-taskforce-leader said, "They wanted to flatten Boston, let's level Della Monrocko, fair is fair."

On the television monitor the General's face lit up with interest and then he quietly said, "Since we are being recorded, I won't divulge that my command could easily facilitate a Thermo-Baric disappearance of a small problematic island country … because it would be against international law, and so I wouldn't go on record to do that."

Showing disappointment Reynolds said, "But you'll agree right is right."

"As President Bill Clinton once said, 'Just because you can do something doesn't mean you should.' We ought to all learn from the leaders, not to get caught." Esmeralda said this in deadpan.

I'm not usually comfortable being an enforcer *but it was my meeting*, I'd called it. "We are here to stop a murder, not take revenge on the whole population of Della Monrocko. Plus, if we made it disappear *who* would supply the European stuffed shrimp market?"

Sneering Jameer Nacho said, "Of course you're right, big money could be made with us supplying the shrimp markets. Ha, ha, ha, good thing this meeting is being recorded so no one takes anything we say seriously."

Darrell-Wayne seemed to be following the obtuse shifts in conversation with annoyance and he finally said, "I like fried shrimp with lots of tartar sauce. Is anyone really going to get serious today? I have homework."

Coy came to my assist with his loud street cop voice and said, "Assassinating leaders of small countries or czarist want-to-be emperors, is a major undertaking and serious international crime. We are not interested in becoming criminals, only keeping my cousin alive."

Willis supporting a much lower ranked policeman said, "What do you recommend Officer Goff?"

"We need something simple and Thermo-Baric anything sounds too complicated from where I live. So does poisoning millions of innocent people who only want to eat shrimp and drink safe water."

"What then, patrolman?"

"I suggest we do whatever we do, simply, inconspicuously, and on the cheap. That would be ironic sweet revenge after all the money they've wasted going after Darrell-Wayne."

Looking down at the conference table, then speaking in a soft voice Darrell-Wayne said, "Coup."

"What?"

Putting his university education to good use Darrell-Wayne said, "Give them a coup. If there is fighting it will be them fighting themselves, no killing."

I could see from the faces around the table and on the television screen Darrell-Wayne had hit on something we could all get our brains on. Murmuring more to myself than the group I asked, "Anybody have an idea how to engineer a coup?"

Esmeralda said she'd read that a psychological war was heating up between Russia and Ukraine over Borsch. It seems borsch was invented in Ukraine centuries ago. Russians have always claimed they invented it by using slightly different ingredients, it's both countries national dish.

Belarus, which was on the verge of being annexed into the new and improved Soviet Union Empire, against the will of its people, also favored a borsch variant as a national dish. The difference between the three borsch was Belarusian variety had a few different ingredients than he Russian version, and so both were distinct from the Ukrainian original. No one in these three countries bothered to ask the Poles who also claimed Poland invented borsch and enjoys a slightly different version. It would be possible for a four-country summit to resolve the borsch problem if three of the four weren't fearing annexation by the new Russian Empire.

To capitalize on the squabble, Esmeralda suggested using free electronic media to start old Soviet style disinformation anti-borsch campaigns. She would fill social media with beet soup misinformation and rumor campaigns. She suggested it could be put out that Bad-Vlad is seriously allergic to beets *and* cabbage, some of the time. Consequently, forthwith the virulently hated and beloved new czar forbid any of his allergens be included in the Russian National borsch on the days he is allergic to them.

The reason for the proclamation was Vlad wanted to enjoy borsch with his people when all could eat the soup without an allergic reaction. This misinformation or disinformation sounded exactly like what the Russian people were used to hearing from their leader of many titles. Similar to how many Americans accepted chaos as normal from President Di Rump. The problem was it took several days cooking to make a decent borsch and from day to day the new emperor-czar couldn't predict his allergies. So, bland potato soup was offered as an alternative to deep red, rich, thick borsch, with a dollop of sour cream and sprig of fresh dillweed.

To manifest discontent, magnify the propaganda value, and deeply insult the Belarusian people, it would be reported the nameless strongman leader of Belarus, his most high and mighty majesty, aka Bootlicker, forbid borsch entirely within his country's borders in sympathy for all those allergic to beets. As a patriotic act, he would replace the national dish with dry chicken noodle soup, *from a box*. That disinformation would proclaim mere use of the word *borsch* in either Belarus or Russia warranted an automatic twelve-year hard labor prison sentence without possibility of parole, or death, depending on the whim of the day at that gulag.

General Navarro liked the plan, but wanted to add the phrase, "Vlad's borsch is tasteless watery Chinese congee, a rice soup faking it by using red food coloring. In truth or truth decay depending on preference, it is a Chinese Communist plot to destabilize Mother Russia's founding roots." The general volunteered to coordinate, "Vlad is anti-beets, cabbage, potato, and coarse brown bread campaign." He would have leaflets dropped from drones all over Russia and Belarus, just before mealtimes.

George Reynolds knew a subtle way to start anti-borsch rumors at the DEA's international division. He shared DEA women and men were strictly hot dog and hamburger muncher and didn't believe in soup of any color or nationality, but cartel spies watched their every move and reported to Russia.

That reminded Willis Washington he knew Interpol cops who'd love to give Moscow a dose of what they usually exported to the rest of the world. In response to quizzical looks, he knowingly said, "Think Brexit."

Since the people of Della Monrocko preferred cold gazpacho soup, and beets didn't grow well in their rocky soil they would be excluded from the borsch coup. Rather, separate, and distinct action would have to be taken against Giles Gluckeridge III the man who marked Darrell-Wayne for death. Giles' comeuppance needed to be equal to the crime, so said all those present, except the target himself.

In that spirit, with her own unique twist, Esmeralda offered to take a vacation to Spain and look up some old hand revolutionary fighters she knew from her younger days. Then they could vacation on Della Monrocko together. Enjoy bacon wrapped stuffed shrimp, and when opportunity presented itself the high potentate leader could be disappeared into white slavery in one of North Africa's many Mediterranean Sea coast countries, never to bother anyone again. Nobody was surprised when the local police, FBI, and Army representative nodded their heads NO to Esmeralda's plan.

For another time in the meeting, Darrell-Wayne showed off his university work and said, "No!" In opposition to Esmeralda. In his flat affect low key style said, "No more killing those who want to kill me. It's my new rule. The old rules don't work."

"What's the plan?"

The core of his new plan was to use dolphins and porpoises for both their benefit. Darrell-Wayne discovered his large sea mammal friends, in response to global warming, were looking to expand their diminishing wild fish and squid diet with commercial farm raised sea food. When he told his friends who live in the sea about attempts on his life, they took offense like any friend would. Then they brought up grudges of their own needing to be addressed to Della Monrocko. They insisted on helping keep Darrell-Wayne safe, while settling their old scores, and taste testing farm raised shrimp.

We all concurred, if all the Della Monrocko shrimp got eaten by big sea mammals the people would revolt. Then it wouldn't end well for their meanspirited exploiter of a leader. Esmeralda was gracious yielding her vacation project to larger mammals with their own revenge plan. Although not sure she'd call it a coup, she offered to help her charge and his watery friends any way she could.

With all in agreement on the plan, volunteers chose tasks. The misinformation and disinformation to confuse with multiple contradictory alternatives and occasionally *facts,* was taken by Ameli, and me. It looked like a fun job using President Di Rump's ghost-written play book for destroying established governments. Darrell-Wayne, and Chucho, designed the Internet campaign, flyers, and leaflets. General Navarro, and

Jameer Nachos took on distribution of fake news flyers to places they usually weren't allowed. Willis, Coy, and Reynolds took care to build local and national security screens to hide what we were up to from prying eyes interference. Darrell-Wayne would also be the liaison between his underwater friends and us.

Darrell-Wayne, and all but Esmeralda, were glad the new plan wouldn't directly involve anymore killings. I'd done too much of that in the name of self-defense since he came into my life. No doubt I'd atone for all those deaths in some future existence, and truth be known I lost track of my body count trying to keep Coy's cousin alive.

Since Darrell-Wayne was mounting a nonlethal campaign, Esmeralda proposed a new option. Giles Gluckeridge III could be scurried away, against his wishes of course, and detained in Spanish Morocco for an indeterminant term. The alternative was to let his irate citizenry lynch him. When asked how, she had revolutionary connections in North Africa as well. In the meantime, Della Monrocko could go through a bloodless economic restructuring without worrying their ruthless leader would return.

The general and FBI man objected to involving foreign governments. Exasperated, Esmeralda said, "If you want, I could simply dispatch Gluckeridge III, quietly no muss no fuss. If his people are squeamish about his being killed on their island, no problem it could be done in the Basque region of Spain. I have blood oath connections there."

Esmeralda is a treasure, helpful and flexible in so many ways. But with a sharp look, Darrell-Wayne put the kibosh on her latest plan to purify by bloodletting, once again demonstrating his new self assurance.

****

Darrell-Wayne's Della Monrocko coup worked as planned. Under cover of night the porpoises harassed their small navy boats, assaulting their wooden hulls from underneath. The violent nudging caused the boats to sharply bow up and stern down, then reverse, suddenly list sharply side to side, and finally shutter like a dog shaking off rainwater, up and down going side to side at the same time. For the sailors onboard the boat it felt like they were in the middle of a violent cyclone surrounded by calm moonlit seas.

When the porpoises thought they'd had enough fun they danced around the boats up out of the water on their tails, laughing at the agitated sailors. At first the sailors quaked in fear thinking it was the end of time. Then they caught on, they'd been made the butt of a joke by sea creatures longer than the boats. The Della Monrocko Navy did not appreciate being toyed with and chased the porpoises farther out to sea and away from their territory's fenced-in shrimp farm waters.

With the navy gone on a fool's errand, the big dolphins showed up and broke through the farm fencing and guzzled shrimp. They ate their fill having a wild destructive party as only huge dolphins can bash a place with resentment. No part of the shrimp farm was left unmolested.

In response to the farms' distress calls the Monrocko navy stopped the pursuit and headed back. Only to be enjoined in a battle on the high seas with just fed high-energy gigantic full-size dolphins with a grudge to settle. The small-scale navy was made up of old wooden hulled WWI vintage gun boats, bought on the cheap at a liquidation auction. Although equipped with modern electronics too big for their diminutive size, they were no match for adult dolphins on a mission.

Della Monrocko's armada was not equipped to have a contest with enormous dolphins who suddenly appeared to replace their smaller cousins, the more affable porpoises. The tiny flotilla lost the sea battle before a shot could be fired. Their boats were flipped over, and hulls smashed in the bright moonlight by pissed off large raucous sea mammals. Then those broken wooden hulls were battered into splinters because they could be. The sailors in the water on inflatable life rafts were left unharmed. To add to the total confusion, some sailors were given rides on dolphins back to shore while their compatriots swimming in the water cursed.

Meanwhile the porpoises raced back to Della Monrocko and finished what the dolphins started. They gorged on the abundant shrimp the dolphins left for them. Then they broke into the domestic fish farms that fed Della Monrocko residents and ate their fill and set the rest free.

Morosely, the next morning Della Monrocko radio told the story. Their livelihood, shrimp, were all gone, there would be no fish for dinner, and their navy lost in an unbelievable story about a sea battle. To add insult to injury, their sailors were demanding combat pay which was never included in the national budget.

Outraged, the citizens wanted to skin alive their self-proclaimed infallible potentate. Alas, like the shrimp, fish, and navy, he too was nowhere to be found. A change of address card was found at the royal palace post office signed by the great grand monarch himself. It read, "Forward only first-class mail, but absolutely no bills to: Giles Gluckeridge III general delivery, Melilla, Spanish Morocco, country code to follow."

Darrell-Wayne was well pleased with his new seafaring friends' handy work. The dolphins were happy an old score had been settled. Esmeralda claimed no part in the nautical escapade. She couldn't swim. When asked about the regent being in Morocco, she said nobody was killed. However, she expressed pride at her charge's ingenuity and its result.

At that point, given all that went before, I would have gladly bought underwater swamp land in La La land Florida in celebration. Coy on the other hand seemed to be operating in disbelief mode and who am I to interfere with belief systems. I'm no Pope.

***

Belarus had a hard and fast official policy to hold elections every once in a while, or thereabouts, but never too often, and not bother count the votes. Usually, the winner was announced long before the actual election was held, so people didn't need a vote count. The people considered their system new and progressive and called it American-style Democracy.

But the idea of boxed dry chicken soup was too extreme for these progressive folks and even caused the commoners to angrily revolt. As an unintentional consequence, a spontaneous actual election, something new for Belarus happened. Votes were cast, *counted* and for the first time ever their fearless nameless leader was not the only name on the ballot. In fact, his name did not appear anywhere until it was widely rumored, he fled to Russia with his dry box synthetic chicken soup franchise. Russia was the only country in the world that didn't have a shoot on sight order out for Bootlicker.

Bad-Vlad was able to read the sour mood of his impoverished, shivering cold, hungry people and before they could muster a revolution. He invaded Ukraine for claiming to be the originators of Borsch, which they were. Czar to be Mutein then falsely claimed Ukrainians committed blasphemy by putting rutabagas, *and turnips* in beloved Russian borsch, a cardinal sin warranting at least a death sentence.

The erroneous Russian propaganda worked until Bad-Vlad made a tactical error. He invaded Ukraine with an army not up to the task. It was the same stupid mistake most recently made by the Chinese when they invaded North Vietnam in 1979 and were promptly kicked out with tails between their legs. It had also been a humiliating lesson to learn for the French, Japanese, French again, and the Americans in 1975. What all invaders learned was the stupidity of invading either North or South Vietnam with young green conscripts to fight combat veterans. Veterans who had been fighting invaders continuously, in modern times since the 1930s. Vietnam had been expelling invaders for centuries and became expert at it.

Like bunglers before him, Bad-Vlad sent his ill-trained green eighteen-year-old conscripts by the 100,000s to fight against Ukrainians who had been preparing since the last time Russia annexed pieces of its territory. It was an old Russian tactic to send in overwhelming numbers of soldiers to be slaughtered until the enemy ran out of bullets or got tired of killing them and in either case quit the fight exasperated. Russia always declared it a victory no matter the actual outcome anyways.

The European Union (EU) was put off by the idea someone could rearrange geography over a particular soup ingredient or who wrote the original recipe first, and without interminable bureaucratic meetings. So, rather than muddy their troops' boots the EU sent Ukraine advanced weaponry to show their disapproval to Bad-Vlad Mutein redrawing national border lines at will, without consultation or paying a transfer fee.

With bigger, better, newer weapons, the Ukrainians took the offensive and somehow ended up with portions of what was formally known as Russia, oops.

Suddenly residents of the capture lands who spoke Ukrainian, claimed Ukrainian heritage and allegiance to the original borsch. These formally Russian folks demanded Ukrainian citizenship as compensation for having to replace now outdated maps and globes.

A condition of the peace settlement was all parties agreed they liked root vegetables, but not all root vegetables were welcome in national patriotic soups. At the end of the conflict released Russian prisoners of war refused to go home and demanded refugee status. Their claim was, they were better fed and kept warm in Ukraine and wanted to bring their families to have the same better life. At the time Ukraine needed workers to rebuild after the war, so most asylum seekers were granted resident permits.

The Russian economy went in the toilet due to losing the war they started. However, the economy didn't stop oligarchs from bellyaching for ever more greed to park in London and New York real estate, against it getting worse. To rattle their chains, Bad-Vlad cut the cost of rebuilding what was left of his over bloated ineffectual military by half as military punishment. He stuffed his own pockets with the other half.

As a result of losing the war Russia's border with Ukraine contracted by neighborly annexation to create a new smooth logical boundary line. After centuries of appropriating other countries territory, the undefeatable badly beaten Russian people were not happy to be known as losers on the world stage and give portions of their land to Ukraine.

The Kremlin claimed domestic change wasn't caused by the war. In fact, smoothing out the borders had been Moscow's idea. So, it was easier for the people to believe their government's lies than revolt. After all, in history Russia had stopped Napoleon and Hitler, how could a pipsqueak country like Ukraine defeat them, right? It was unthinkable, except the onetime Mother Russia had been thoroughly trounced by the Japanese in 1905. However, that chapter of history like the new Ukrainian one wouldn't be taught in Russian school, so street protestors didn't need to know about it on their way to prison for decades."

When the Russian people started demanding a little more winter heat from their fearless leader. He reassured them that everything would be back to normal again soon. Then unexpectedly where abouts of Bad-Vlad were unknown. A group of Chechens with a grudge found and boarded Bad-Vlad's multimillion dollar yacht hiding out between Malaysia and Singapore. The Chechens reported Vlad, his family, and guests were not found on the yacht. The yacht crew implied all were lost scuba diving for sponges. Defective air tanks were suspected, or so the yacht crew suggested.

It was reported in international media the new Free Russia had sent a delegation to Belarus to learn how to hold free and fair elections. It was something new and different for both countries, used to relying on disinformation and preplanned outcomes. Without a body or any confirmation, a state funeral could not be held for Vlad and family. There were many true believers who doubted Bad-Vlad's death and willing to wait his glorious return. But any who knew Chechens with a grudge understood the New Czar and his family most likely were not still walking around.

***

I was thinking of having a celebration party to declare success over state sponsored terror aimed at Darrell-Wayne's existence. As I was imagining a large, decorated cake with lots of national symbols on top, the news broke of a leadership void in Russia, Belarus, and Della Monrocko. Now that required more than a backyard barbecue. Ah but alas, where could I buy caviar stuffed bacon-wrapped butterfly shrimp? The only source had gone out of business.

About then Darrell-Wayne wandered into my home office, and I asked, "What do you think of a big party to celebrate your coup plan's success?"

In his inimitable way, he said, "Don't forget Boynton still wants me dead, and I don't understand why if I didn't do anything wrong."

He was right, I forgot the most troublesome part, the tip of the spear. They vowed not to stop until their contract was fulfilled as a matter of honor. After a moment's contemplation, I hit nothing but blanks and said, "Okay, Darrell-Wayne, what should we do about the Boynton bunch?"

He had no plan or idea either. Later, after dinner we gathered around the living room television to watch the BBC News explain Della Monrocko and Belarus formed new more enlightened democratic search for governments less harsh on their citizens. Their new humanitarian leaning spokespeople promised not to forget the common people in their countries, the way previous leaders had, and was still done in the United States.

Meanwhile Russia was being deconstructed from within by its citizens of different ethnic backgrounds. Whole regions were choosing to become part of neighboring EU NATO nations whose language they spoke, and ethnicity they could identify with, that had acceptable beet soup traditions. The news program ended with the United Nations (UN) giving Ukraine naming rights for *the* recipe to make authentic original Borsch. The UN declared beets are healthy good food. While in the much-emulated United States tradition of winner take all, every other form of Borsch was declared illegal by the UN.

After the news broadcast, we agreed to meet in two weeks to kick around ideas for eliminating the Boynton family and associates' threats to eliminate Darrell-Wayne. It was the last piece of the puzzle. But arriving at a workable plan didn't look promising. There was more we didn't know than we knew about that international organization, and all the faces in the room looked empty of ideas. I was still of a mind to have a celebration after downing three of four adversaries. However, my compatriots voted the idea down in favor of a party when all threats were gone.

Chapter 19.

It was supposed to be just a lucrative workday for me. I was collecting the balance in cash on a big deal high end security job. For the teenager living with us in our house it was to be just another day at aquarium. I had no sooner handed-off Darrell-Wayne to his large FBI security detail than my dashboard light blinked repeatedly and then stayed lit demanding gasoline. Ugh, my big European car became thirstier as the price of fuel increased.

I know it defied logic, but since adolescence I made it a point of honor to refuel at a quarter tank, back before benefit of dashboard idiot lights, or I could afford to fill the tank. However, now I could afford to fill the tank, and protesting by not adding fuel didn't lower the price or increase milage or accomplish anything but cause more headaches. Fifty-Two Pickup was the closest filling station, what's new, and on my way to hopefully a big payday.

No sooner than I had the gasoline nozzle gushing in my fuel tank than Melissa Jackson pulled up to the adjacent gasoline pump. I appreciated European automotive engineering, especially the fuel hatch always on the right side of the vehicle to protect the drivers' safety in case of running out of gas on a busy highway. American and most Japanese car manufacturers put the fuel hatch on the left, the better to be struck and killed while adding gasoline.

Sergeant Jackson was pumping gasoline into the left rear quadrant of her American made mid-priced-sized older car. Seeing me standing close by, she gave me a little half smile. I gave back a bashful wave, without my middle finger extended and said, "The thank you card you sent was a pleasant surprise. It reminded me of a time when people were kinder and gentler with each other. I'd like a do-over meeting you. I was clearly out of line, and out of my mind the day we first met." I finished my comment with a nod.

"You didn't have to send the booze, but *it was thoughtful of you.*"

"I wanted to apologize."

"Fine, let's clear the air, we got off on the wrong foot. My boss says you aren't such a bad guy after all."

Suddenly, a battered pickup truck sped up and abruptly stopped with brakes squealing. Engine revving, it was stopped at a right angle cutting off both our cars access to exit, and conversation. The driver rolled down his window, shouted something at Melissa Jackson, and I saw her go for her gun, so I grabbed mine on instinct. That moment seemed like molasses in March slow motion but must have happened in the blink of an eye.

Mister angry white pickup driver had to have his pistol unholstered in his lap when he drove in. He fired one shot at close range into Melissa's brain before her weapon was fully drawn. While he was turning his revolver on me, I got off three head shots. That was not how I planned to start what was to have been a good day.

I rushed over to Sergeant Jackson, she was beyond reviving, her nine-millimeter automatic in a death grip half in half out of its holster. The asshole shooter was very dead and would need massive, sculptured reconstruction for an open casket funeral. In death he clutched a nickel plated .357 magnum revolver as if it might run away.

The next thing that happened was a lot of commotion all around me. People shouting, rushing here and there like buzzing wasps. Then uniformed cops arrived, lights and sirens blaring. Low-level brass arrived after a long-anticipated pause and finally big police brass showed up with all the pomp worthy of their lofty gold star rank.

I had to give over my gun and repeat what happened several times before getting tired of hearing my own voice. Out of frustration I mentioned the whole event was most likely recorded on the station's security system. Which it was, and as a reward for that information I was given my gun back. It seems my .40 caliber had a detailed record back at the police station from previous self-defense incidents over the years. I'm sure giving it back was not proper police procedure, but I didn't want to start an argument, someone might get hurt. My intense emotions were running on too high octane. A highly decorated police officer was killed, I dispatched her attacker, and the press had arrived looking for a gory story.

After being shuffled around, the next thing I remembered was silently sitting across from convenience store manager Martha Matatus, cups of weak coffee between us. She looked sympathetic and said, "You ever been eighty-sixed from a gas station before?"

"No, and I don't want to start today. There's been enough blood shed already."

It felt like hours had passed at that point, but who knew, my sense of time was lost in an after incident blurred confusion. I was just beginning to get to know Melissa Jackson and like her when she was murdered a few feet in front of my face. Then without thought, operating on raw animal instinct I killed her killer. It was a terrible habit I seemed to be forming, *too much killing* equals *bad karma*. Suddenly feeling goose bumps I knew I was teetering on the edge of a deep dark depression hole. It felt like what I'd experienced before quitting the Parole Department.

Martha looked me up and down and said, "Oliver, maybe I won't eighty-six you. I know that look on your face. I've worn it myself and seen it plenty on my troops fighting in war zones."

"What look?"

"Did I ever tell you I'd had a short career in special forces where I saw combat?"

"No. Why did you leave to manage this place? Wait, hold on … we don't know each other well enough for that level of inquiry."

"My store my rules."

"That makes you the boss."

"Purple heart discharge. I regularly saw the face you're wearing on my soldiers after bad firefights. We even had a jingle about it."

"Please, I'm not in the mood for sing song."

"Your loss, the words without the music went, 'Every time I take another's life a piece of my soul goes with them. But tralalah, I'm still here and they are not ha, ha, ha,' then there were versus fit for the occasion. It has a catchy tune, sort of like *I've Been Working on the Railroad,* and ends like it started with a tralalah ha, ha, ha."

"You know that's macabre, right?"

"We weren't looking for a five-star music review. Look around at these cops' faces, it's obvious which have taken life. Its written all over their ugly mugs."

"OR! The difference is those who worked with and respected Sergeant Jackson and those oblivious of the personal nature of what just happened."

"Nah, they all lost one of their own today. All should show the same degree of grief. It hit close to home and got more personal for some."

"Please don't make up a jingle and sing about it."

Cops had the entrance to Martha's business blocked off. Customers who were present during the shooting had been questioned, documented, and sent on their way. The subsequent others to show up were told business was closed due to police activity, come back later. Ms. Matatus' face told of her corporate bosses not being happy at the loss of a day's revenue and possible repercussions for her.

When Martha got busy with an employee, I got bored and tuned in to overhear the big brass talking among themselves over by the donuts' display case. According to the brass, Melissa Jackson's ex-husband thought he still had exclusive conjugal rights. The man imagined she was seeing other men for sex. Watching her and me shyly chatting. Her stalking ex-spouse thought he saw his fantasy and lost his grip. The security cameras clearly showed he pointed his gun at me before I fired.

The big problem for the high up brass was Sergeant Melissa Jackson was *a real hero cop.* On Street patrol as a beat cop, she had rushed into a burning building. She even carried babies out of a house fire in her arms. Photojournalists captured her heroics for big frontpage news. Her death seemed too mundane for her bosses who could of, should of, done more for her after the larger than life she lived on the job. In hindsight, promotion to police sergeant seemed meagre. The police brass seemed mostly worried about how they looked after the tragedy.

I guess my brain fog had lifted because I'd finally had enough of their pussy footing around indecision and said, "Look, you guys are ruining Martha's business, and I'm already late for an important business transaction. How about you make

Melissa's memorial a major event worthy of a fallen hero? Make her memorable an all stops out demonstration of how the force showed its appreciation for her dedication. No mention of the creep that killed her, if you please, or my hand in it. Bring out the Police Bagpipe Band."

The brass dismissed my humble suggestion out of hand. Which made me suspect their squabbling was more political than police department face saving, and the Bagpipe Band had not been rehearsing regularly. Nevertheless, for my effort I got unfriendly looks that inferred disdain for private investigators in general and me in particular.

I can take a hint and shut up except just then my cellphone buzzed, "Queer Queries. How may I help you?"

"Is this Oliver Kulgu?"

"Depends, who wants to know and why?"

"Coy Goff suggested I speak with you about a sensitive personal matter."

"Speak." Glancing over at Martha I whispered, "It's a personal sensitive matter, do you sell baby powder?"

The cellphone voice said, "It's not something to be discussed on the phone. Where are you at present?"

"By popular demand the name was changed to *New Fifty-Two Pickup.*"

"Hold on let me consult my driver."

"No. You hold on, cowboy. Who says I have the time or inclination to meet with you right this minute or ever?" I guess my nerves showed they were frayed raw at the edges.

"I do."

"Listen, buster, I don't even know your name, or what this is about, plus I'm running late. Hint, hint, this is not a good time, call my receptionist for an appointment and I'll be happy to talk with you then."

"It'll be fast once I tell you."

"Then tell me."

"After I arrive."

"Good luck with that, at the moment local police command have me *otherwise occupied*, and as I said, I'm already late for an important meeting."

"My driver says we will be there in less than five minutes. I'll deal with the police. This won't take long."

"Whatever floats your boat fella. Just be aware, I've already killed one stranger today and I'm going to tell you in person to telephone my office for an appointment."

"I'll be right there. Bye."

The police big brass was still quibbling over the official statement to make for the press, if any. Their problem was a fallen hero Black female street cop, not killed in the line of duty. Oh, and by the by did they have any grounds to arrest me, or could they maybe find some to link me to her killing.

It was clear to my inner social worker these men had little experience doing public relations when emotions were running high. Ah, what to expect from a bunch of high brass old white men morning a tough Black female street cop.

They had no legitimate grounds to hold me on anything. What worried my inner social worker was many illegitimate occurrences are regarded as legitimate for the sake of making the PD look good. Fortunately, I paid my attorney MT to eat these sorts of good-for-nothing bureaucrats raw.

Right then, through the big plate glass front window, I witnessed a new top-of-the-line American made black stretch SUV pull up to the police car blocking the entrance to the New Fifty-Two Pickup. It appeared a brief altercation took place that the police lost. With their heads bowed in submission, the cops moved their patrol car back out of the way. They looked chastised.

The long, large sleek car glided to the front door of the convenience store. A chauffeur packing a submachine gun slung over his shoulder opened the back door. An expensively dressed older white man exited the vehicle. He moved like someone used to wielding authority and being kowtowed to. The stranger looked early seventies, was easily over six feet tall, thin, worked out, had salt and pepper hair expensively cut like a Washington bureaucrat.

Martha Matatus pushed a small plastic bottle of baby powder to my side of the table, and said half under her breath, "Now who could this big kahuna with a personal problem joining our after-death gas station soiree be?"

"Beats me."

"I know it's not the mayor or governor. This guy is donned higher up the fashion chain."

The impeccably dressed visitor entered the store, walked over to our table, flashed an ostrich-leather encased identification, and with a strong Irish lilt said, "I am Gavin O'Dwyer, first assistant attorney general of the United States of America. Which of you is O.K., Oliver Kulgu?"

I wanted to point to Martha for fun but raised my hand out of habit. Then with a flick of my wrist I indicated to Martha we wouldn't be needing the baby powder. I did it without thinking.

"The rest of you people may stay or go away, as you please. Detective Kulgu, come with me."

Martha and the police brass stood as we walked out of the store. None waved goodbye, or spoke a word, but their faces were the definition of intimidated. I guess some people cultivate menacing contact, most of us strive for the opposite result.

"What exactly is your interest in me or Queer Queries, Attorney General Gavin O'Dwyer, sir?"

"Let us speak in my car. I had it swept for bugs just before I left this morning." With that said, we walked to his luxury rock-star vehicle. His driver stood outside the car, looking threatening with a short barrel, large ammo capacity, high velocity H. K. submachine gun. Neither man looked particularly friendly.

As soon as we settled into the buttery soft burgundy leather seats facing each other, the car door was shut by the driver who then drove us onto the highway. Without baby talc for protection, it seemed only proper to ask, "Do I need my lawyer or accountant present for this confab?"

"No. That won't be necessary."

"Then what's going on?"

"Let me get right to the point. Through unofficial channels, the Attorney General's Office of the United States of America has discovered covert intelligence impacting our national defense."

"What has that got to do with me?"

"Indirectly, you are to blame for disrupting the status quo."

"WHAT! Wait, want to explain that so I understand."

"Due to the upheaval in Belarus, which you indirectly had a hand in orchestrating over the beet soup. The whole Boynton criminal organization along with half of Belarus' treasury is relocating to Ireland."

"Uhm. I hear Ireland is a beautiful peace-loving island with much better weather and politics than Belarus."

"It is the intention of your government to keep it that way."

"Good for us. What do you expect from me about that? Oh, and how do you know Coy Goff?"

"Coy headed my personal security detail in Iraq. On my first trip he saved my life, twice, I requested him on subsequent investigations. I make it a habit to keep track of people who do me good turns."

"Pardon my ignorance, sir, what was our Attorney General doing in Iraq?"

"For those junkets it was a top-secret joint mission with the pentagon. There had been claims of weapons of mass destruction."

"Ah so, you are a man who wears many hats. I know nothing about that, and on the other hand still don't know what I'm doing sitting here in this fine American made luxury car."

"Don't be a wise ass, it doesn't suit you, private detective. Just focus on what I'm telling you."

"Yes, sir. I'll try that then, sir. Because I can see, so far, you haven't noticed I'm having a *very bad day.*"

"Boynton and Associates' intention is to have offices in both Dublin and Belfast. That could result in north and south political repercussions. With the large amount of money, they stole from Belarus, it's conceivable old wounds could be opened that would destabilize the whole of Ireland. That bunch likes to stir-up trouble."

"I always wear green on St. Patrick's Day. If that isn't too glib to say."

"If they settled into only one Ireland, we'd let an Irish government handle it, with only a little help, if asked. As it stands Boynton's intention could be a big problem for international peace and order for both Irelands and the EU in different ways, and therefore peace on earth."

"Well now, we wouldn't want that. So, what exactly do you want Coy and me to accomplish for you?"

"You both have an interest in stopping the Boynton Group's murderous attempts on Darrell-Wayne Goff's life. Your government wants to help you with that."

"Sorry, Queer Queries business license doesn't allow for Washington DC's kind of help. We are strictly a small local business. Don't take it personal, I say the same thing to the neighborhood drug pusher."

"You are making this harder than necessary."

"Then I'll make it simple to understand. QQ doesn't take government or international work. Well, except our northern neighbor Canada, but only on rare occasion. Because they keep their hands clean."

"Organized crime in the whole of Ireland is for the most part run from Boston, Massachusetts U.S.A."

"No, no, Queer Queries definitely does not take organized crime related work. It requires a higher degree of death wish to benefits than interests me. We never did that and never will. If I'm not mistaken that's your work sir, and good luck to you with that."

"And we have reasons for keeping it that way, except in this unique special case. Let's just say, hypothetically, we needed your approval for expediency's sake."

"Huh. Now I'm wondering … maybe I do want my lawyer present after all."

"That would be counterproductive and slow us down. Let me get right to the point, the Irish mob in Boston will permanently eliminate the *Boynton* gang in Ireland and the rest of the world once a large sum of money changes hands. Don't worry about the money, U.S. taxpayers will cover that. The snag in the agreement is, the head of the Boston mob also wants a special sexual favor to seal the deal and immediately begin his eradications. The mob boss thinks by satisfying his sexual request he will be immune from our future prosecution."

"Pardon me, a suburban dullard, but somehow this conversation just took a strange murky turn."

"Indeed, agreed, it's not how we like to conduct high level negotiations. However, the Irish mob has the organization, manpower, and motivation between what we will pay and their appropriating most of what was left of the Belarusian treasury."

"Yup, sounds like a massive motivator for them and you, and I and QQ do not fit in it. Sorry to have wasted your time."

"As I said, we have high confidence the Irish underworld can eliminate the Boynton scourge, north and south branch and root, before the transplant can establish itself. It should make you happy not to be on constant look out for assassins."

"Sorry, like I said, I'm not your boy. Whatever you want from Coy, it's out of his league too and you can tell him I said that."

"Liam Murphy runs things in Ireland from Boston and has it on indisputable authority Coy Goff gives the best blow jobs in the whole world. Murphy requires one for our deal to go forward. I knew Coy long before you, so, I can attest firsthand he is a genius at cock sucking."

"Now you just hold on a second. You are talking about the man I love and intend to marry. He is not a street whore for public hire like a taxi, and I'm not his pimp."

"Yes, yes, I understand all that. But this is a national security matter. Sometimes our country asks us to make sacrifices above and beyond normal convention. The United States of America expects you to do your patriotic duty today."

"See that, just when I thought the day couldn't get any worse, you come along. I vote NO."

"Coy says he won't do his duty if it affects your relationship. Understand Detective Kulgu, this is a matter of great national importance for your country, both Irelands, EU, and the United Nations. You and Coy are being called upon to be international heroes, behind the scenes."

"Let me see if I have this right, you are asking permission, from me, for my future husband to give head to some strange Boston gangster?"

"I understand it's a big sacrifice to ask of you. But after only a few minutes of Coy's time the Boynton menace will become a distant memory. You and your family won't have to live with one eye out constantly looking for killers."

"Coy takes more than a few minutes, as you may remember. Anyway, he is an over twenty-one-year-old police officer and war veteran. He nor you need my permission for this cockamamie scheme."

"But alas he won't do it if you say it will negatively affect your love for him."

"For your information, Coy and I have never once discussed whether our marriage would be monogamous or otherwise. It feels tawdry for me to have this talk with *you* without Coy present."

"He refused all incentives, until he knew how you felt. That's why we didn't just have you extinguished."

"You do know this should be a private matter and our government should keep out of its citizens' bedrooms."

"Normally I'd agree with you. But think of this small aspect from the long hard negotiations as only a little wrinkle necessary to permanently eliminate the Boynton murder for hire gang."

"Bla-ze bla-ze."

"Sorry you feel that way. Right at this moment, your nation needs your help to resolve this important international matter. So, please don't let your countrymen, people of Ireland, and Europe down."

"I already said this is a matter between you and Coy, not me."

"Coy requires your go ahead. He thinks if he were present that would unduly influence both of you. I can't accept anything less than a yes."

"You and I are going around in circles."

"Then do what's best for God and country. Say yes, I'm ready to record it."

"Gavin O'Dwyer you can butter my toast any time. You really know how to slather it on thick. Now I suppose you want me to sign some document saying it's all right for my intended husband to give blow jobs at the behest of the Attorney General in Washington DC for national security. How do I know for sure he isn't being coerced?"

"He isn't. Without your go ahead he won't do it and refuses to be present in case of a negative reaction from you to this proposal. And you're right good cops don't approve being used by gangsters or anyone outside the police force."

"Simple, find a substitute and say he's Coy."

"If only that would work. The mob has seen a recent Coy photo.

"Ugh, I don't want to be involved in this mess. It is what I pay taxes for you to do."

"Coy is so in love with you and insecure about it, it's interfering with my ability to resolve this case for every one's benefit."

"Let's make this official, I say NO! Coy is not available to work for you."

"You don't understand, Mr. Murphy will not accept a substitute."

"Is that supposed to incentivize me?"

"You want incentive? Mr. Murphy believes he and Mr. Goff share a unique appreciation for an often-maligned common interest."

"I didn't want to mention this before for fear of hurting your feelings. But this talking has gone on way too long."

"Spit it out."

"No, is all I can say. A yes would open Coy and me to blackmail from you or our government."

"Oh, come on now, Murphy is adamant, no Coy no deal. Can you continue to take on the Boynton gang single handed forever?"

"I have a few friends, and I think I just said no to you. YES, I did say NO, not interested! What part of that didn't you understand?"

Gavin O'Dwyer made sure I saw his watch when he checked the time. I'd seen that number one European brand's most expensive time piece in the world, worn on the wrists of my clients who owned large office buildings. They liked to show off its solid gold case with diamond marked numerals, mentioning its six-figure cost when hiring my expertise to provide the most elaborate and expensive electronic security systems available for buildings they were constructing.

Attorney General O'Dwyer delicately tucked his wristwatch back under his hand made custom-fit shirt cuff and said, "This watch costs more than most people's primary and secondary residences. It could be yours for cooperating with your government to have world peace."

"It's a nice watch."

"Just so you know, my driver is licensed to kill."

I watched Gavin reach into the leather pocket of his car seat. Then he came up with a silver plated .45 caliber refurbished 1911 colt semiautomatic in his right hand.

He gazed wide eyed as I cocked back the hammer on my plain blue-black steel Sig Sauer. I held my finely engineered weapon in both hands for accurate shooting in a moving vehicle. I saw just the hint of surprise in his eyes. I'd outdrawn him and held an advantage over him, so I lowered the saucer, now held the gun only in my right hand. He had no way of knowing the police had returned my piece when they had nothing to hold me on.

When he blinked, I thrust my left hand forward grab his right wrist and gave it a sharp twist. Then calmly sat back with his shiny colt automatic in my left hand. It had fine-grain red- mahogany-wood pistol grips. After uncocking my gun and tucking it back in its holster, I slid back the slide on O'Dwyer's handgun. Personally, I always keep a round in the chambers of my automatics, one extra projectile if the opposition is counting. He didn't. Upon releasing the magazine, I found he didn't have *any* bullets; the ammo clip was empty.

"*What the fuck is wrong with you?* I could have shot you dead while you were holding an empty gun. *How could I explain that?*"

"But you didn't. You don't have to explain anything."

"What did you just bet your life on?"

"That the police didn't break protocol and give you back your gun, and you'd heard me. In the grand scheme of things one blow job between strangers should mean nothing compared to taking a human life or a loving relationship."

"You risked your life to change my no to a yes?"

"Did I?"

"You have to know I was breaking your balls for being an arrogant prick. Coy and I agreed early on when we were together it's monogamous. When we are not together it's nobody's business unless we want to share. I could tell he was playing with you. Your high-fluting manner put me off too."

"You were totally obnoxious from the start of this meeting."

"If I wasn't almost old enough to be Coy's father, I wouldn't have given him dispensations from my usual value system. In many situations, age doesn't matter."

"What are you trying to say?"

"You can tell Coy he has my blessing to visit Boston. I'm sure he knows that. I don't want details from either of you."

"That will make Mr. Liam Murphy happy."

"Dude, you'll never know how close you just came to a whole lot of .40 caliber slugs in the middle of your chest."

"You're no killer, Private Detective Kulgu. I did my research before meeting you."

"Tell that to the guy whose head I blew to pieces this morning."

"Self-defense doesn't count in my book."

"What am I then?"

"A latent social worker."

"Oh, okay, if that's how you see it. Sigmund Freud said a fee should be set slightly higher than can be afforded to motivate change. In that vein, I learned in social work school, if possible, a fee should be set at what can almost be afforded."

"Uh huh."

"Thus, I will base my latent social work fee on this new top of the line luxury vehicle with well-armed driver and you wearing a grossly expensive suit, shirt, and tie. Hmm, I think your showoff watch and this fancy .45 caliber should almost cover my laten fee."

"That was the price Mr. Murphy preset for your permission. He was the one who required your approval to borrow your betrothed, he's such a stickler and queer duck. Coy said the same thing you did." Removing the watch from his wrist and handing it to me the assistant attorney general said, "Enjoy this watch it's a good one," and he winked.

Scrutinizing the absurdly expensive time piece top and bottom, I said, "Coy needs a new watch. Personally, I prefer a digital timepiece, what's on your other wrist?"

About the Author

Peter Melillo was born in New Haven, Connecticut, moved to Tucson, Arizona, at age seven, then moved to New York City at age twenty-five. In 2013, JM Snyder Books published a collection of twelve of his gay war short stories: *For Man and Country*. In total, JM Snyder Books published sixteen short stories by Peter Melillo online as e-books. In 2018 Querelle Independent published *Fairy Swatter*, six short stories with murder as a side issue, *Improbable: Gay Male Love Stories*, and *Accidental Parents*. Peter can be reached at mabide8790@yahoo.com